Conspiracy

It wasn't till afternoon that Alvin realized something serious was wrong. A couple of months ago, Alvin had asked Clevy Sump, Goody Sump's husband, to teach them all how to make a simple one-valve suction pump. It was apart of Alvin's idea to teach folks that making is making, and everybody ought to know everything they can possibly learn. Alvin was teaching them hidden powers of Making, but they ought to be learning how to make with their hands as well. Secretly Alvin also hoped that when they saw how tricky and careful it was to make fine machinery like Clevy Sump did, they'd realize that what Alvin was teaching wasn't much harder if it was harder at all. And it was working well enough.

Except that today, after the noon bread and cheese, he went on out to the mill to find the men gathered around the wreckage of the pumps they'd been making. Every one of them was broke in pieces. And since the fittings were all metal, it must have have took some serious work to break it all up. "Who'd do a thing like this?" Alvin asked. "There's a lot of hate goes into something like *this*." And thinking of hate, it made Alvin wonder if maybe Calvin hadn't come back secretly after all.

"There's no mystery who done it," said Winter Godshadow. "I reckon we ain't got us a pump-making teacher no more."

"Yep," said Taleswapper. "This looks like a specially thorough way of telling us, 'Class dismissed.'"

TOR BOOKS BY ORSON SCOTT CARD

ORSON SCOTT CARD

THE
TALES OF
ALVIN MAKER
IV

TOR® fantasy

A TOM DOHERTY ASSOCIATES BOOK
NEW YORK

This is a work of fiction. All the characters and events portrayed in this book are either products of the author's imagination or are used fictitiously.

ALVIN JOURNEYMAN

A Tor Book
Published by Tom Doherty Associates, LLC
175 Fifth Avenue
New York, NY 10010

www.tor-forge.com

Tor® is a registered trademark of Tom Doherty Associates, LLC.

ISBN   978-0-7653-9359-3
Library of Congress Catalog Card Number: 95-22693

First Edition: September 1995
First International Mass Market Edition: February 1996
First Mass Market Edition: September 1996

Printed in the United States of America

P1

To Jason Lewis,
long-legged wanderer,
walker through woods,
dreamer of true dreams.

Acknowledgments

FOR THE PAST few years, at every book signing or speech I gave, I was asked one question more than any other: Will there be another Alvin Maker book? The answer was always, Yes, but I don't know when. My original outline for *The Tales of Alvin Maker* had long since been abandoned, and while I knew certain incidents that would happen in this book, I still did not know enough about what would happen to Alvin, Peggy, Taleswapper, Arthur Stuart, Measure, Calvin, Verily Cooper, and others to be able to start writing.

At last the logjam broke and the story came right, or as near right as I could get it. As I composed, I was constantly aware of those hundreds of readers who were waiting for *Alvin Journeyman*. It was encouraging to know that this book was much looked for; it was also frightening, because I knew that for some, at least, the expectations would be so high that any story I wrote would be bound to disappoint. To the disappointed I can only express my regret that the reality is never as good as the anticipation (cf. Christmas); and to all who hoped for this book, I give my thanks for your encouragement.

I thank the many readers on America Online who came to the Hatrack River Town Meeting and downloaded each chapter of the manuscript as I wrote it, responding with many helpful comments. These sharp-eyed readers caught inconsistencies and dangling threads—questions raised in earlier books that needed to be resolved. Newel Wright, Jane Brady, and Len Olen, in particular, won my undying gratitude: Jane, by preparing a chronology of the events in the previous books, Newel, by saving me from two ghastly continuity errors, and Len, by a thorough proofreading that caught several errors that all the editors and I had missed. Thanks also go to David Fox for an insightful reading of the first nine chapters at a key point in the composition of the book.

Quite without my planning it, a peculiar and delightful community has grown up within the Hatrack River Town Meeting on AOL; people began to arrive, not as themselves, but as characters living within Alvin's world, and set up in trade or farming in that fictional town. Thus Hatrack River has taken on a life of its own. The temptation was irresistible to include mention of as many of these characters as I could within this storyline; I only regret that I couldn't work them all into the plot. If you want to know more about the wonderful characters these good people have created, come visit us online (keyword: Hatrack).

The only active online character I made extensive use of in this book was one I devised myself as a fictional foil, whom Kathryn Kidd (town identity: GoodyTradr) and I (town identity: HoracGuest) referred to from time to time in a comical way as a notorious gossip: Vilate Franker. A couple of years after we invented her, along came a good friend, Melissa Wunderly, who volunteered to portray her in the online community; so it was Melissa who brought her to life, false teeth, hexes, and all. Vilate's "best friend," however, was mine, and Melissa is not to be blamed for Vilate's unpleasant behavior in this book. And I appreciate Kathryn Kidd's allowing me to use her character, Goody Trader, at a couple of key moments.

I must tip my hat to Graham Robb, whose excellent, well-written *Balzac: A Biography* (Norton, 1994) gave me not only respite from writing but also the foundation of a character I personally enjoy.

As with many previous novels, each chapter was read as it emerged from the printer or the fax machine by my wife, Kristine; my son Geoffrey; and my friend and sometime collaborator, Kathryn H. Kidd. Their responses have been of incalculable value.

My thanks also go to those who keep our office and household functioning when I'm (too rarely) in writer mode: Kathleen

Bellamy, who tends to the business, and Scott Allen, who keeps the computers and the house itself in running order. A tip of the hat also goes to Jason, Adam, and (on one occasion) Michael Lewis, for holes dug and holes filled; and to Emily, Kathryn, and Amanda Jensen for giving us those nights out.

If it weren't for Kristine, Geoffrey, Emily, Charlie Ben, and Zina Meg, I doubt that I would ever write at all: They make the work worth doing.

Contents

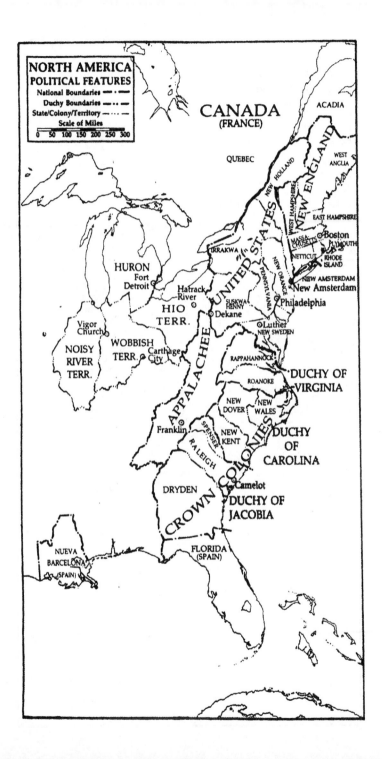

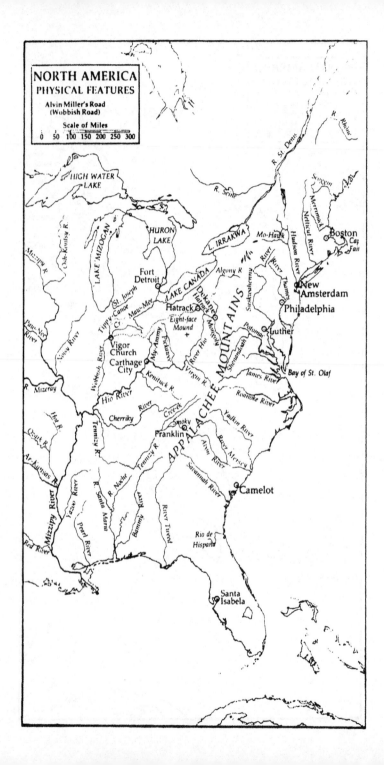

NORTH AMERICA
PHYSICAL FEATURES
Alvin Miller's Road
(Wobbish Road)

Scale of Miles

0 50 100 150 200 250 300

HIGH WATER LAKE

HURON LAKE

LAKE MIZOGAN

Och-Kentsy R.

Mizzipy R.

Pau-Net River

St. Joseph

Tippy-Canoe

Maw-Mee

Fort Detroit

LAKE CANADA

L. IRRAKWA

Mo-Hawk

Algony R.

Dekane

Hatrack

Eight-face Mound

Vigor Church

Carthage City

Noisy River

R. Mizeray

Hio River

Cherriky

Wobbish River

My-Ammon

Pickaway

Kentuck R.

Tennizy River

River

Creek

Franklin

Smoky

APPALACHEE MOUNTAINS

Virrin R.

River Hio

Mongelly

Shenandoah

Potomac

Luther

James River

Roanoke River

Yadkin River

Bay of St. Olaf

Suskwahenny

Hudson River

River Thames

Boston

Cap Fair

New Amsterdam

Philadelphia

R. St. Denis

R. Seine

Merrimak River

Neftitsit River

Saugus

A. R.

Rhine

Hot R.

Ozar R.

Ar-Kansas R.

Mizzipy River

Red River

Yazoo River

R. Noche

R. Santa Maria

Bammy

Pearl River

Tennizy R.

Alvin River

Savannah River

River Tweed

Rio de Hispania

Camelot

Santa Isabela

1

I Thought I Was Done

I THOUGHT I was done writing about Alvin Smith. People kept telling me I wasn't, but I knew why. It's because they'd all heard Taleswapper and the way he tells stories. When he's done, it's all tied up neat in a package and you pretty much know what things meant and why they happened. Not that he spells it all out, mind you. But you just have this feeling that it all makes sense.

Well I ain't Taleswapper, which some of you might already have guessed, seeing how we don't look much alike, and I don't plan on becoming Taleswapper anytime soon, or anything much like him, not cause I don't reckon him to be a fine fellow, worthy of folks emulating him, but mainly because I don't see things the way he sees them. Things don't all make sense to me. They just happen, and sometimes you can extract a bit of sense from some calamity and sometimes the happiest day is just pure nonsense. There's no predicting it and there's *sure* no making it happen. Worst messes I ever saw folks get into was when they was trying to make things go in a sensible way.

So I set down what I knew of the earliest beginnings of Alvin's life right up till he made him the golden plow as his journeyman project, and I told how he went back to Vigor and set to teaching folks how to be Makers and how things already wasn't right with his brother Calvin and I thought I was done, because anybody who cares was there from then on to see for themselves or you know somebody who was. I told you the truth of how Alvin came to kill a man, so as to put to rest all the vicious rumors told about it. I told you how he came to break the runaway slave laws and I told you how Peggy Larner's mama came to die and believe me, that was pretty much the end of the story as far as I could see it.

But the ending didn't make sense of it, I reckon, and folks have been pestering me more and more about the early days and didn't I know more I could tell? Well sure I know. And I got nothing against telling it. But I hope you don't think that when I'm done telling all I know it'll finally be clear to everybody what everything that's happened was all about, because I don't know myself. Truth is, the story ain't over yet, and I hope it never will be, so the most I can hope to do is set down the way it looks to this one fellow at this exact moment, and I can't even promise you that tomorrow I won't come to understand it much better than anything I'm writing now.

My knack ain't storytelling. Truth is, Taleswapper's knack ain't storytelling either, and he'd be the first to tell you that. He collects stories, all right, and the ones he gathers are important so you listen because the tale itself matters. But you know he don't do nothing much with his voice, and he don't roll his eyes and use them big gestures like the real orators use. His voice ain't strong enough to fill a good-size cabin, let alone a tent. No, the telling ain't his knack. He's a painter if anything, or maybe a woodcarver or a printer or whatever he can use to tell or show the story but he's no genius at any of them.

Fact is if you ask Taleswapper what his knack is, he'll tell you he don't have none. He ain't lying—nobody can ever lay that charge at Taleswapper's door. No, he just set his heart on one knack when he was a boy, and all his life that seemed to him the only knack worth having and since he never got it (he thinks) why then he must not have no knack at all. And don't pretend you don't know what knack it was he wanted, because he practically slaps you in the face with it whenever he talks for long. He wanted the knack of prophecy. That's why he's always been so powerful jealous of Peggy Larner, because she's a torch and from childhood on she saw all the possible futures of people's lives, and while that's not the same thing as knowing *the* future—the way things will actually happen instead of how they might happen—it's pretty close. Close enough that I think Taleswapper would have been happy for five minutes of being a torch. Probably would have grinned himself to death within a week if such a thing happened.

When Taleswapper says he's got no knack, though, I'll tell you, he's wrong. Like a lot of folks, he has a knack and doesn't even know it because that's the way knacks work—it just feels as natural as can be to the person who's got it, as easy as breathing, so you don't think *that* could possibly be your unusual power because heck, that's *easy.* You don't know it's a knack till other people around you get all astonished about it or upset or excited or whatever feelings your knack seems to provoke in folks. Then you go, "Boy howdy, other folks can't *do* this! I got me a knack!" and from then on there's no putting up with you till you finally settle down and get back to normal life and stop bragging about how you can do this fool thing that you used to never be excited about back when you still had sense.

Some folks never know they got them a knack, though, because nobody else ever notices it either, and Taleswapper's that way. I didn't notice it till I started trying to collect all my memories and everything anybody ever told me about Alvin Maker's life. Pictures of him working that hammer in the forge every chance he got in case we ever forgot that he had an honest trade, hard come by with his own sweat, and didn't just dance through life like a quadrille with Dame Fortune as his loving partner—as if we ever thought Dame Fortune did anything more than flirt with him, and likely as not if he ever got close to her he'd find out she had the pox anyway; Fortune has a way of being on the side of the Unmaker, when folks start relying on her to save them. But I'm getting off the subject, which I had to read back to the beginning of this paragraph to see what in hell I was talking about (and I can hear you prickle-hearted prudes saying, What's he doing putting down curses on paper, hasn't he no sense of decent language? to which I say, When I curse it don't harm nobody and it makes my language more colorful and heaven knows I can use the color, and I can assure you I've studied cussing from the best and I know how to make my language a whole *lot* more colorful than it is right now, but I already tone myself down so you don't have apoplexy reading my words. I wouldn't want to spend half my life just going to the funerals of people who had a stroke from reading my book, so instead of criticizing me for the nasty words that creep into my writing why don't you praise me for the really ugly stuff that I virtuously chose to leave out? It's all how you choose to look at it, I think, and if you have time to rail on about my language, then you don't have enough to do and I'll be glad to put you in touch with folks who need more hands to help with *productive* labor), so anyway I looked back to the beginning of this paragraph *again* to see what the hell I was talking about and my point is that when I gathered all these stories together, I noticed that Taleswapper seems to keep showing up in the oddest places at *exactly* the moment when something important was about to happen, so that he ended up being a witness or even a participant in a remarkable number of events.

Now, let me ask you plain, my friends. If a man seems to know, down in his bones, when something important's about to happen, and where, and enough in advance that he can get his body over there to be a witness of it before it even starts, now ain't that prophecy? I mean why was it William Blake

ever left England and came to America if it wasn't because he
knew that the world was about to be torn open to give birth to
a Maker again after all these generations? Just cause he didn't
know it out in the open didn't mean that he wasn't a prophet.
He thought he had to be a prophet with his mouth, but I say
he's a prophet in his bones. Which is why he just happened to
be wandering back to the town of Vigor Church, to Alvin's
father's mill, for no reason he was aware of, at exactly the day
and hour that Alvin's little brother Calvin Miller decided to
run off and go study trouble in faraway places. Taleswapper
had no idea what was going to happen, but folks, I tell you,
he was *there*, and anybody who tells you Taleswapper's got no
knack, including Taleswapper himself, is a blame fool. Of
course I mean that in the nicest possible way, as Horace Guester
would tell you.

So as I pick up my tale again that's the day I choose to start
with, mostly because I can tell you from experience that *nothing*
interesting happened during those long months when Alvin was
still trying to teach a bunch of plain folks how to be a Maker
like him instead of ... well, all in time. Let's just say that
while some of you are bound to criticize me for *not* telling all
of Alvin's lessons about Makering and every single boring
moment of every class he held trying to teach fish to hop, I
can promise you that leaving out those days from my tale is
an act of charity.

There's a lot of people and a lot of confusion in the story,
too, and I can't help that, because if I made it all clear and
simple that would be a lie. It was a mess and there was a lot
of different people involved and also, to tell you the truth,
there's a lot of things that happened that I didn't know about
then and still don't know much about now. I'd like to say that
I'm telling you all the important parts of the story, telling about
all the important people, but I know perfectly well that there
might be important parts that I just don't know about, and
important people that I didn't realize were important. There's
stuff that *nobody* knows, and stuff that them as knows ain't

telling, or them as knows don't know they know. And even as I try to explain things as I understand them I'm still going to leave things out without meaning to, or tell you things twice that you already know, or contradict something that you know to be a fact, and all I can say is, I ain't no Taleswapper, and if you want to know the deepest truth, get him to unseal that back two-thirds of his little book and read you what he's got in *there* and I bet, for all he claims to be no prophet, I bet you'll hear things as will curl your hair, or uncurl it, depending.

There's one mystery, though, that I plain don't know the answer to, even though everything depends on it. Maybe if I tell you enough you'll figure it out for yourself. But what I don't understand is why Calvin went the way he did. He was a sweet boy, they all say it. He and Alvin were close as boys can be, I mean they fought but there was never malice in it and Cally grew up knowing Al would die for him. So what was it made jealousy start to gnaw at Calvin's heart and turn him away from his own brother and want to undo all his work? I heard a lot of the tale I'm about to tell you from Cally's own mouth, but you can be sure he never sat down and explained to me or anybody why he changed. Oh, he told plenty of folks why he hated Alvin, but there's no ring of truth in what he says about that, since he always accuses his brother of doing whatever his audience hates the most. To Puritans he says he came to hate Alvin because he saw him trucking with the devil. To Kingsmen he says he hated Alvin because he saw how his brother went so far as to murder a man just to keep him from recovering his own property, a runaway slave baby named Arthur Stuart (and don't *that* set them Royalists' teeth on edge, to think of a half-Black boy having the same name as the King!). Calvin always has a tale that justifies himself in the eyes of strangers, but never a word of explanation does he ever have to those of us who know the truth about Alvin Maker.

I just know this: When I first set eyes on Calvin, in Vigor Church during that year when Alvin tried to teach Makering, that year before he left, I'll tell you, folks, Calvin was already gone. In his heart every word that Alvin said was like poison. If Alvin paid no attention to him, Calvin felt neglected and said so. Then if Alvin *did* pay attention to him, Calvin got surly and sullen and claimed Alvin wouldn't leave him alone. There was no pleasing him.

But to say he was "contrary" don't explain a thing. It's just a name for the way he was acting, not an answer to the question of why he acted that way. I have my own guesses, but they're just guesses and no more, not even what they call "educated guesses" because there's no such thing as education so good it makes one man's guess any better than another's. Either you know or you don't, and I don't know.

I don't know why people who got what they need to be happy don't just go ahead and be happy. I don't know why lonely people keep shoving away everybody as tries to befriend them. I don't know why people blame weak and harmless folks for their troubles while they leave their real enemy alone to get away with all his harm. And I sure don't know why I bother to go to the trouble to write all this down when I know you still won't be satisfied.

Let me tell you one little thing about Calvin. I saw him one day taking class with Alvin, and for once he was paying attention, real close attention, heeding every word that came from his brother's lips. And I thought: He's finally come around. He finally realized that if he really wants to be a seventh son of a seventh son, if he really wants to be a Maker, he has to learn from Alvin how it's done.

And then the class ended, and I sat there watching Calvin as everybody else went on out to get back to their chores, until only me and Calvin was left in the room, and Calvin actually talks to me—mostly he ignored me like I wasn't there—he talks to me and in a few seconds I realize what he's doing. He's imitating Alvin. Not Alvin's regular voice, but Alvin's schoolteachery voice. You all remember when he got that way—I remember he learned that flowery fancy talk when he was studying with Miss Larner, before she came out of disguise and he realized she was the same Peggy Guester who kept his birth caul and protected him through his growing-up years. The big five-dollar words she learned in Dekane or from them books she read. Alvin wanted to sound refined like her, or sometimes he wanted to, anyway, and so he'd learn them words and use them and talk so fine you'd have thought he learned English from an expert instead of just growing up with it like the rest of us. But he couldn't keep it up. He'd hear himself talking so high-toned and he'd just suddenly laugh or make some joke and then he'd go back to talking like folks. And there was Calvin talking that same high-toned way, only he didn't laugh. He just did all his imitating and when he was done, he looked at me and said, "Was that right?"

As if I'd know!

And I says back to him, "Calvin, *sounding* like an educated man don't make you educated," and he says back to me, "I'd rather be ignorant and sound educated than be educated and sound ignorant," and I said, "Why?" and he says to me, "Because if you sound educated then nobody ever tests you to find out, but if you sound ignorant they never stop."

Here's my point. Well, maybe it's not the point I started out to make, but I long since lost track of *that*. So here's the point I want to make *now*: I know more about what happened during Alvin's year of wandering than anybody else on God's green Earth. But I also am aware of how many questions I still can't answer. So I reckon I'm the one as knows but seems ignorant. Which kind are you?

If you already figure you know this story, for heaven's sake stop reading now and save yourself some trouble. And if you're going to criticize me for not finishing the whole thing and tying it up in a bow for you, why, do us both a favor and write your own damn book, only have the decency to call it a romance instead of a history, because history's got no bows on it, only frayed ends of ribbons and knots that can't be untied. It ain't a pretty package but then it's not your birthday that I know of, so I'm under no obligation to give you a gift.

2

Hypocrites

CALVIN WAS ABOUT fed up. Just this close to walking up to Alvin and . . . and something. Punching him in the nose, maybe, only he'd tried that afore and Alvin just caught him by the wrist and gripped him with those damn blacksmith muscles and he says, "Calvin, you know I could always throw you, do we have to do this now?" Alvin could always do everything better, or if he couldn't then it must not be worth doing. Folks all gathered around and listened to Alvin's babbling like it all made sense. Folks watched every move he made like he was a dancing bear. Only time they noticed Calvin was to ask him if he would kindly step aside so they could see Alvin a little better.

Step aside? Yep, I reckon I can step aside. I can step right out the door and out into the hot sun and right out onto the path going up the hill to the tree line. And what's to stop me from keeping right on? What's to stop me from walking on to the edge of the world and then jumping right off?

But Calvin didn't keep walking. He leaned against a big old maple and then hunkered down in the grass and looked out over Father's land. The house. The barn. The chicken coops. The pigpen. The millhouse.

Did the wheel ever turn in Father's mill anymore? The water passed useless through the chase, the wheel leaned forward but never moved, and so the stones inside were still, too. Might as well have left the huge millstone in the mountain, as to bring it down here to stand useless while big brother Alvin filled these poor people's minds with hopeless hopes. Alvin was grinding them up as surely as if he put their heads between the stones. Grinding them up, turning them to flour which Alvin himself would bake into bread and eat up for supper. He may have prenticed as a blacksmith all those years in Hatrack River, but here in Vigor Church he was a baker of brains.

Thinking of Alvin eating everybody's ground-up heads made Calvin feel nasty in a delicious kind of way. It made him laugh. He stretched his long thin legs out into the meadow grass and lay back against the trunk of the maple. A bug was scampering along the skin of his leg, up under his trousers, but he didn't bother to reach down and pull it out, or even to shake his leg to get it off. Instead, he got his doodlebug going, like a spare pair of eyes, like an extra set of fingers, looking for the tiny rapid flutter of the bug's useless stupid life and when he found it he gave it a little pinch, or really more like a squint, a tiny twitch of the muscles around his eyes, but that was all it took, just that little pinch and then the bug wasn't moving no more. Some days, little bug, it just don't pay to get up in the morning.

"That must be some funny story," said a voice.

Calvin fairly jumped out of his skin. How did somebody come on him unawares? Still, he didn't let himself show he'd been surprised. His heart might be beating fast inside his chest, but he still waited a minute before even turning around to look, and then he made sure to look about as uninterested as a fellow can look without being dead.

A bald fellow, old and in buckskins. Calvin knew him, of course. A far traveler and sometime visitor named Taleswapper. Another one who thought the world began with God and ended with Alvin. Calvin looked him up and down. The buckskins were about as old as the man. "Did you get them clothes off a ninety-year-old deer, or did your daddy and grandpa wear them all their lives to get them so worn out like that?"

"I've worn these clothes so long," said the old man, "that I sometimes send them on errands when I'm too busy to go, and nobody can tell the difference."

"I think I know you," said Calvin. "You're that old Taleswapper fellow."

"So I am," said the old man. "And you're Calvin, old Miller's youngest boy."

Calvin waited.

And here it came: "Alvin's little brother."

Calvin folded himself sitting down and then unfolded himself standing. He liked how tall he was. He liked looking down at the old man's bald head. "You know, old man, if we had another just like you, we could put your smooth pink heads together and you'd look like a baby's butt."

"Don't like being called Alvin's little brother, eh?" asked Taleswapper.

"You know where to go for your free meal," said Calvin. He started to walk away into the meadow. Having no destination in mind, of course, his walking pretty soon petered out, and he paused a moment, looking around, wishing there was something he wanted to do.

The old man was right behind him. Damn but the old boy was quiet! Calvin had to remember to keep a watch out for people. Alvin did it without thinking, dammit, and Calvin could do it too if he could just remember to remember.

"Heard you chuckling," said Taleswapper. "When I first walked up behind you."

"Well, then, I guess you ain't deaf yet."

"Saw you watching the millhouse and heard you chuckling and I thought, What does this boy see so funny in a mill whose wheel don't turn?"

Calvin turned to face him. "You were born in England, weren't you?"

"I was."

"And you lived in Philadelphia awhile, right? Met old Ben Franklin there, right?"

"What a memory you have."

"Then how come you talk like a frontiersman? You know and I know that it's supposed to be 'a mill whose wheel *doesn't* turn,' but here you are talking bad grammar as if you never went to school but I know you did. And how come you don't talk like other Englishmen?"

"Keen ear, keen eye," said Taleswapper. "A sharp one for details. Dull on the big picture, but sharp on details. I notice you talk worse than *you* know how, too."

Calvin ignored the insult. He wasn't going to let this old coot distract him with tricks. "I said how come you talk like a frontiersman?"

"Spend a lot of time on the frontier."

"I spend a lot of time in the chicken coop but that don't make me cluck."

Taleswapper grinned. "What do *you* think, boy?"

"I think you try to sound like the people you're telling your lies to, so they'll trust you, they'll think you're one of them. But you're not one of us, you're not one of anybody. You're a spy, stealing the hopes and dreams and wishes and memories and imaginings of everybody and leaving them nothing but lies in exchange."

Taleswapper seemed amused. "If I'm such a criminal, why ain't I rich?"

"Not a criminal," said Calvin.

"I'm relieved to be acquitted."

"Just a hypocrite."

Taleswapper's eyes narrowed.

"A hypocrite," Calvin said again. "Pretending to be what you're not. So other people will trust you, but they're trusting in a bunch of pretenses."

"That's an interesting idea, there, Calvin," said Taleswapper.

"Where do you draw the line between a humble man who knows his own weaknesses but tries to act out virtues he hasn't quite mastered yet, and a proud man who pretends to have those virtues without the slightest intention of acquiring them?"

"Listen to the frontiersman now," said Calvin scornfully. "I knew you could shed that folksy talk the minute you wanted to."

"Yes, I can do that," said Taleswapper. "Just as I can speak French to a Frenchman and Spanish to a Spaniard and four kinds of Red talk depending on which tribe I'm with. But you, Calvin, do you speak Scorn and Mockery to everyone? Or just to your betters?"

It took Calvin a moment to realize that he had been put down, hard and low. "I could kill you without using my hands," he said.

"Harder than you think," said Taleswapper. "Killing a man, that is. Why not ask your brother Alvin about it? He's done it the once, for just cause, whereas you think of killing a man because he tweaks your nose. And then you wonder why I call myself your better."

"You just want to put me down because I named you for what you are. Hypocrite. Like all the others."

"*All* the others?"

Calvin nodded grimly.

"*Everyone* is a hypocrite except Calvin Miller?"

"Calvin *Maker*," said Calvin. Even as he said it, he knew it was a mistake; he had never told anyone the name by which he thought of himself, and now he had blurted it out, a boast, a brag, a *demand*, to this most unsympathetic of listeners. This man who was most likely, of all men, to repeat Calvin's secret dream to others.

"Well, now it seems to be unanimous," said Taleswapper. "We're all pretending to be something that we're not."

"I *am* a Maker!" Calvin insisted, raising his voice, even though he knew he was making himself seem even weaker and more vulnerable. He just couldn't stop himself from talking to this slimy old man. "I've got all the knack for it that Alvin ever had, if anyone would bother to notice!"

"Made any millstones lately, without tools?" asked Taleswapper.

"I can make stones in a fence fit together like as if they growed that way out of the ground!"

"Healed any wounds?"

"I killed a bug crawling on my leg just a moment ago without so much as laying a hand on it."

"Interesting. I ask of healing and you answer with killing. Doesn't sound like a Maker to me."

"You said yourself that Alvin killed a man!"

"With his hands, not with his knack. A man who had just murdered an innocent woman who died to protect her son from captivity. The bug—was it going to harm you or anyone?"

"Yes, there you are, Alvin is always righteous and wonderful, while Calvin can't do nothing right! But Alvin hisself told me the story of how he caused a bunch of roaches to get theirselfs kilt when he was a boy and—"

"And you learned nothing from his story, except that you have the power to torment insects."

"*He* gets to do what he wants and then talks about how he's learned better now, but if *I* do the same things then I'm not worthy! I can't be taught any of his secrets because I'm not *ready* for them only I *am* ready for them, I'm just not ready to let Alvin decide *how* I'll use the knack I was born with. Who tells *him* what to do?"

"The inner light of virtue," said Taleswapper, "for lack of a clearer name."

"Well what about *my* inner light?"

"I imagine that your parents ask themselves this very question, and often."

"Why can't *I* be allowed to figure things out on my own like Alvin did?"

"But of course you *are* being allowed to do *exactly* that," said Taleswapper.

"No I'm not! He sits there trying to explain to those bone-headed no-knack followers of his how to get inside other things and learn what they are and how they're shaped inside and then ask them to take on new forms, as if that's a thing that folks can learn—"

"But they *do* learn it, don't they?"

"If you call an inch a year moving, then I guess you can call that learning," said Calvin. "But me, the one who actually understands everything he says, the one who could actually put it all to use, he won't even let me in the room. If I stay there he just tells stories and makes jokes and won't teach a *thing* until I leave, and why? I'm his best pupil, ain't I? I learn it all, I soak it in fast and I can use it on the instant, but he won't teach me! He calls them others 'apprentice Makers' but me he won't even take on for a single lesson, all because I don't bow down and worship whenever he starts talking about how a Maker can never use his power to destroy, but only to build, or he loses it, which is nonsense, since a man's knack is his knack and—"

"It seems to me," said Taleswapper, his voice sharp enough to cut through Calvin's raging, "that you are a singularly unteachable young man. You ask Alvin to teach you, and he tries to do it, but then you refuse to listen because *you* know what's nonsense and what matters, *you* know that a man doesn't have to make in order to be a Maker, *you* already know so much I'm surprised you still wait around here, wishing for Alvin to teach you things that you plainly have no desire to know."

"I want him to teach me how to get into the small of things!" cried Calvin. "I want him to teach me how to change people the way he changed Arthur Stuart so the Finders couldn't Find him anymore! I want him to teach me how to get inside bones and blood vessels, how to turn iron to gold! I want me a golden plow like his and he won't teach me *how*!"

"And it has never occurred to you," said Taleswapper, "that when he speaks of using the power of Making only to build things up, never to tear them down, he might be teaching you precisely the thing you are asking? Oh, Calvin, I'm so sorry to see that your mama did have one stupid child after all."

Calvin felt the rage explode inside himself, and before he knew what he was doing he knocked the old man down and straddled his hips, pounding on his frail old ribs and belly. It took many blows before he realized that the old man wasn't fighting back. Have I killed him? Calvin wondered. What will I do if he's dead? They'll have me for murder, then. They won't understand how he provoked me, begging for a beating. It's not like I planned to kill him.

Calvin put his fingers to Taleswapper's throat, feeling for a pulse. It was there, feeble, but it probably was always feeble, given how old the fellow was.

"Didn't quite kill me, eh?" whispered Taleswapper.

"Didn't feel like it," said Calvin.

"How many men will you have to beat up before everyone agrees that you're a Maker?"

Calvin wanted to hit him again. Didn't this old man learn anything?

"You know, if you hurt people enough, eventually they'll all call you whatever you want. Maker. King. Captain. Boss. Master. Holy One. Pick your title, you can beat people into calling you that. But you don't change yourself a bit. All you do is change the meanings of those words, so they all mean the same thing: Bully."

Calvin, hot with shame, got up and stood over him. He restrained himself from kicking the old man until his head was jelly. "You've got a knack for words," he said.

"True words in particular," said Taleswapper.

"Lies, from all I can see," said Calvin.

"A liar sees lies," said Taleswapper. "Even when they aren't there. Just as a hypocrite sees hypocrites whenever he runs across good people. Can't stand to think that anyone might *really* be what you only pretend to be."

"You did say one true thing," said Calvin. "About its making no sense me waiting around here for Alvin to teach me what he plainly means to keep secret. I should've realized that Alvin wasn't never going to teach me anything, because he's afraid if people see me doing all the things he can do, he won't be king of the hill anymore. I have to find it out on my own, just like he did."

"You have to find it out by learning the same things he did," said Taleswapper. "Alone or as his pupil, though, I don't think you're capable of learning those things."

"You're wrong," said Calvin. "I'll prove it to you."

"By learning to master your own will and use your power only to build things, only to help others?"

"By going out into the world and learning everything and coming back and showing Alvin who's got the real Maker's knack and who's just pretending."

Taleswapper propped himself up on one elbow. "But Calvin, your actions here today have made the answer to that question as plain as day."

Calvin wanted to kick him in his face. Silence that mouth. Break that shiny pate and watch the brains spill out into the meadow grass.

Instead he turned away and took a few steps toward the woods. He had a destination this time. East. Civilization. The cities, the lands where people lived together cheek by jowl. Among them there would be those who could teach him. Or, failing that, those he could experiment with until he learned all that Alvin knew, and more. Calvin was wrong to have stayed here so long. Foolish to have kept hoping that he'd ever get any love or help from Alvin. I worshipped him, that was my mistake, thought Calvin. It took this boneheaded old fool to show me the kind of contempt that people have for me. Always comparing me to Alvin, perfect Alvin, Alvin the Maker, Alvin the virtuous son.

Alvin the hypocrite. He does with his power just what I want to do—only he's so subtle about it that people don't even realize he's controlling them. Tell us what to do, Alvin! Teach us how to Make, Alvin! Does Alvin ever say, It's not your knack, you poor fool, I can't teach you how to do this any more than I can teach a fish to walk? No. He pretends to teach them, helps them get a few pathetic illusory successes so they stay with him, his obedient servants, his disciples.

Well, I'm not one of them. I'm my own man, smarter than he is, and more powerful, too, if I can just learn what I need to learn. After all, Alvin was only a seventh son for a couple of moments after he was born, until our oldest brother Vigor died. But I have been a seventh son my whole life, and still am one today. Before long I'm bound to surpass Alvin. I'm the real Maker. The real thing. Not a hypocrite. Not a pretender.

"When you see Alvin, tell him not to follow me. He won't see me again until I'm ready for him to square off against me, Maker against Maker."

"There can never be a battle of Maker against Maker," said Taleswapper.

"Oh?"

"Because if there's a battle," said Taleswapper, "it's because one of them, at least, is not a Maker at all, but rather its opposite."

Calvin laughed. "That old wives' tale? About some supposed Unmaker? Alvin tells the stories, but it's all a bunch of hogwash to make him look like more of a hero."

"I'm not surprised that you don't believe in the Unmaker," said Taleswapper. "The first lie the Unmaker always tells is that he doesn't exist. And his true servants always believe him, even as they carry out his work in the world."

"So I'm the Unmaker's servant?" asked Calvin.

"Of course," said Taleswapper. "I have the bruises on my body now to prove it."

"Those bruises prove you're a weak man with a big mouth."

"Alvin would have healed me and strengthened me," said Taleswapper. "That's what *Makers* do."

Calvin couldn't take any more of this. He kicked the man right in the face. He could feel Taleswapper's nose break under the ball of his foot; then the old man flopped back into the grass and lay there still. Calvin didn't even bother to check his pulse. If he was dead, so be it. The world would be a better place without his lies and rudeness.

Not until he was well into the woods, about five minutes

later, did the enormity of what he had done flow over him. Killed a man! I might have killed a man, and left him to die!

I should have healed him before I left. The way Alvin healed people. Then he would have *known* that I'm truly a Maker, because I healed him. How could I have missed such an opportunity to show what I can do?

At once he turned and raced back through the forest, dodging the roots, skittering down a bank he had so eagerly climbed only moments before. But when, panting, he emerged into the meadow, the old man wasn't there, though bits of blood still clung to the grass and pooled where his head had lain. Not dead, then. He got up and walked, so he can't be dead.

What a fool I was, thought Calvin. Of course I didn't kill him. I'm a Maker. Makers don't destroy things, they build them. Isn't that what Alvin always tells me? So if I'm a Maker, nothing I do can possibly be destructive.

For a moment he almost headed down the hill toward the millhouse. Let Taleswapper accuse him in front of everybody. Calvin would simply deny it, and let them work out how to deal with the problem. Of course they'd all believe Taleswapper. But Calvin only needed to say, "That's his knack, to make people believe his lies. Why else would you trust in this stranger instead of Alvin Miller's youngest boy, when you all know I don't go around beating people up?" It was a delicious scene to contemplate, with Father and Mother and Alvin all frozen into inaction.

But a better scene was this: Calvin free in the city. Calvin out of his brother's shadow.

Best of all, they couldn't even get up a group of men to follow him. For here in the town of Vigor Church, the adults were all bound by Tenskwa-Tawa's curse, so that any stranger they met, they had to tell him the story of how they slaughtered the innocent Reds at Tippy-Canoe. If they didn't tell the story, their hands and arms would become covered with dripping blood, mute testimony of their crime. Because of that they didn't venture out into the world where they might run into strangers. Alvin himself might come looking for him, but no one else except those who had been too young to take part in the massacre would be able to join with him. Oh, yes, their brother-in-law Armor, he wasn't under the curse. And maybe Measure wasn't really under the curse, because he took it on himself, even though he wasn't part of the battle. So maybe he could leave. But that still wouldn't be much of a search party.

And why would they bother to search for him anyway? Alvin thought Calvin was a nothing. Not worth teaching. So how could he be worth following?

My freedom was always just a few steps away, thought Calvin. All it took was my realizing that Alvin was *never* going to accept me as his true friend and brother. Taleswapper showed me that. I should thank him.

Hey, I already gave him all the thanks he deserved.

Calvin chuckled. Then he turned and headed back into the forest. He tried to move as silently as Alvin always did, moving through the forest—a trick Al had learned from the wild Reds back before they either gave up and got civilized or moved across the Mizzipy into the empty country of the west. But despite all his efforts, Calvin always ended up making noise and breaking branches.

For all I know, Calvin told himself, Alvin makes just as much noise, and simply uses his knack to make us *think* he's quiet. Because if everybody *thinks* you're silent, you *are* silent, right? Makes no difference at all.

Wouldn't it be just like that hypocrite Alvin to have us all thinking he's in such harmony with the greenwood when he's really just as clumsy as everyone else! At least I'm not ashamed to make an honest noise.

With that reassuring thought, Calvin plunged on into the underbrush, breaking off branches and disturbing fallen leaves with every step.

✠ 3 ✠

Watchers

WHILE CALVIN WAS a-setting out on his journey to wherever, trying not to think about Alvin with every step, there was someone else already on a journey, also wishing she could stop thinking about Alvin. That's about where the semblance ends, though. Because this was Peggy Larner, who knew Alvin better and loved Alvin more than any living soul. She was riding in a coach along a country road in Appalachee, and she was at least as unhappy as Calvin ever was. Difference was, she blamed her woes on nary a soul but her own self.

In the days after her mother was murdered, Peggy Larner figured that she would stay in Hatrack River for the rest of her life, helping her father tend his roadhouse. She was done with the great matters of the world. She had set her hand to meddling in them, and the result had been that she didn't tend to her own backyard and so she failed to see her mother's death looming. Preventable, easily, it was so dependent upon merest chance; a simple word of warning and her mother and father would have known the Slave Finders were coming back that night, and how many of them there were, and how armed, and through what door coming. But Peggy had been watching the great matters of the world, had been minding her foolish love for the young journeyman smith named Alvin who had learned to make a plow of living gold and then asked her to marry him and go with him through the world to do battle with the Unmaker, and all the while the Unmaker was destroying her own life through the back door, with a shotgun blast that shredded her mother's flesh and gave Peggy the most terrible of burdens to carry all her life. What kind of child does not watch out to save her own mother's life?

She could not marry Alvin. That would be like rewarding herself for her own selfishness. She would stay and help her father in his work.

And yet she couldn't do even that, not for long. When her father looked at her—or rather, when he wouldn't look at her—she felt his grief stab to her heart. He knew she could have prevented it. And thought it was his great effort not to reproach her with it, she didn't need to hear his words to know what was in his heart. No, nor did she need to use her knack to see his heart's desire, his bitter memories. She knew without looking, because she knew him deep, as children know parents.

There came a day, then, when she could bear it no longer. She had left home once before, as a girl, with a note left behind. This time she left with more courage, facing her father and telling him that she couldn't stay.

"Have I lost my daughter then, as well as my wife?"

"Your daughter you have as well as ever," said Peggy. "But the woman who could have prevented your wife's death, and failed to do it—that woman can't live here anymore."

"Have I said anything? Have I by word or deed—"

"It's your knack to make folks feel welcome under your roof, Father, and you've done your best with me. But there's no knack can take away the terrible burden charged to my soul. There's no love or kindness you can show toward me that will hide—from *me*—what you suffer at the very sight of me."

Father knew he couldn't deceive his daughter any longer, her being a torch and all. "I'll miss you with all my heart," he said.

"And I'll miss you, Father," she answered. With a kiss, with a brief embrace, she took her leave. Once again she rode in Whitley Physicker's carriage to Dekane. There she visited with a family that had done her much kindness, once upon a time.

She didn't stay long, though, and soon she took the coach down to Franklin, the capital of Appalachee. She knew no one there, but she soon would—no heart could remain closed to her, and she quickly found those people who hated the institution of slavery as much as she did. Her mother had died for taking a half-black boy into her home, into her family as her own son, even though by law he belonged to some white man down in Appalachee.

The boy, Arthur Stuart, was still free, living with Alvin in the town of Vigor Church. But the institution of slavery, which had killed both the boy's birth mother and his adoptive mother, that lived on, too. There was no hope of changing it in the King's lands to the south and east, but Appalachee was the nation that had won its freedom by the sacrifice of George Washington and under the leadership of Thomas Jefferson. It was a land of high ideals. Surely she could have some influence here, to root out the evil of slavery from this land. It was in Appalachee that Arthur Stuart had been conceived by a cruel master's rape of his helpless slave. It was in Appalachee, then, that Peggy would quietly but deftly maneuver to help those who hated slavery and hinder those who would perpetuate it.

She traveled in disguise, of course. Not that anyone here would know her, but she didn't like being called by the name of Peggy Guester, for that was also her mother's name. Instead she passed as Miss Larner, gifted teacher of French, Latin, and music, and in that guise she went about tutoring, here a few weeks, there a few weeks. It was master classes that she taught, teaching the schoolmasters in various towns and villages.

Though her public lessons were conscientiously taught, what

concerned her most was seeking out the heartfires of those who loathed slavery, or those who, not daring to admit their loathing, were at least uncomfortable and apologetic about the slaves they owned. The ones who were careful to be gentle, the ones who secretly allowed their slaves to learn to read and write and cipher. These good-hearted ones she dared to encourage. She called upon them and said words that might turn them toward the paths of life, however few and faint they were, in which they gained courage and spoke out against the evil of slavery.

In this way, she was still helping her father in his work. For hadn't old Horace Guester risked his life for many years, helping runaway slaves make it across the Hio and on north into French territory, where they would be no longer slaves, where Finders could not go? She could not live with her father, she could not remove any part of his burden of grief, but she could carry on his work, and might in the end make his work unnecessary, for it would have been accomplished, not a slave at a time, but all the slaves of Appalachee at once.

Would I then be worthy to return and face him? Would I be redeemed? Would Mother's death mean something then, instead of being the worthless result of my carelessness?

Here was the hardest part of her discipline: She refused to let any thought of Alvin Smith distract her. Once he had been the whole focus of her life, for she was present at his birth, peeled the birth caul from his face, and for years thereafter used the power of the dried-up caul to protect him against all the attacks of the Unmaker. Then, when he became a man and grew into his own powers enough that he could mostly protect himself, he was still the center of her heart, for she came to love the man he was becoming. She had come home to Hatrack River then, in disguise for the first time as Miss Larner, and there she gave him and Arthur Stuart the kind of book learning that they both hungered for. And all the time she was teaching him, she was hiding behind the hexes that hid her true face and name, hiding and watching him like a spy, like a hunter, like a lover who dared not be seen.

It was in that disguise that he fell in love with her, too. It was all a lie, a lie I told him, a lie I told myself.

So now she would not search for his bright heartfire, though she knew she could find it in an instant, no matter how far away he was. She had other work in her life. She had other things to achieve or to undo.

Here was the best part of her new life: Everyone who knew anything about slavery knew that it was wrong. The ignorant—children growing up in slave country, or people who had never kept slaves or seen them kept or even known a Black man or woman—they might fancy that there was nothing wrong with it. But those who knew, they all understood that it was evil.

Many of them, of course, simply told themselves lies or made excuses or flat-out embraced the evil with both arms—anything to keep their way of life, to keep their wealth and leisure, their prestige, their honor. But more were made miserable by the wealth that came from the labor and suffering of the blacks that had been stolen from their native land and brought against their will to this dark continent of America. It was these whose hearts Peggy reached for, especially the strong ones, the ones who might have the courage to make a difference.

And her labors were not in vain. When she left a place, people were talking—no, to be honest they were quarreling—over things that before had never been openly questioned. To be sure, there was suffering. Some of those whose courage she had helped awaken were tarred and feathered, or beaten, or their houses and barns burnt. But the excesses of the slavemasters served only to expose to others the necessity of taking action, of winning their freedom from a system that was destroying them all.

She was on this errand today. A hired carriage had come to fetch her to a town called Baker's Fork, and she was well on the way, already hot and tired and dusty, as summer travelers always were, when all of a sudden she felt curious to see what was up a certain road.

Now, Peggy wasn't one to be curious in any ordinary way. Having had, since childhood, the knack of knowing people's inmost secrets, she had learned young to shy away from simple curiosity. Well she knew that there were some things folks were better off not knowing. As a child she would have given much not to know what the children her age thought of her, the fear they had of her, the loathing because of her strangeness, because of the hushed way their parents talked of her. Oh, she would have been glad not to know the secrets of the men and women around her. Curiosity was its own punishment, when you were sure of finding the answer to your question.

So the very fact that she felt curious about, of all things, a rutted track in the low hills of northern Appalachee—that was the most curious thing of all. And so, instead of trying to follow the track, she looked inside her own heartfire to see what lay down that road. But every path she saw in which she called to the carriage driver and bade him turn around and follow the track, every one of those paths led to a blank, a place where what might happen there could not be known.

It was a strange thing for her, not to know at all what the outcome might be. Uncertainty she was used to, for there were many paths that the flow of time could follow. But not to have a glimmer, that was new indeed. New and—she had to admit— attractive.

She tried to warn herself off, to tell herself that if she couldn't see, it must be the Unmaker blocking her, there must be some terrible fate down that road.

But it didn't *feel* like the Unmaker. It felt right to follow the track. It felt *necessary*, though she tingled a bit with the danger of it. Is this how other people feel all the time? she wondered. Knowing nothing, the future all a blank, able to rely only on feelings like this? Is this tingling what George Washington felt just before he surrendered his army to the rebels of Appalachee and then turned himself over to the king he had betrayed?

Surely not, for old George was certain enough of the outcome. Maybe it's what Patrick Henry felt when he cried out, Give me liberty or give me death, having no notion which of the two, if either, he might win. To act without knowing . . .

"Turn around!" she called.

The driver didn't hear her over the clattering of the horses' hooves, the rattling and creaking of the carriage.

She thumped on the roof of the carriage with her umbrella. "Turn around!"

The driver pulled the horses to a stop. He slid open the tiny door that allowed words to pass between driver and passengers. "What, ma'am?"

"Turn around."

"I ain't took no wrong turn, ma'am."

"I know that. I want to follow that track we just passed."

"That just leads on up to Chapman Valley."

"Excellent. Then take me to Chapman Valley."

"But it's the school board in Baker's Fork what hired me to bring you."

"We're going to stop the night anyway. Why not Chapman Valley?"

"They got no inn."

"Nevertheless, either turn the carriage around or wait here while I *walk* up that track."

The door slid shut—perhaps more abruptly than necessary—and the carriage took a wide turn out into the meadow. It had been dry these past few days, so the turn went smoothly, and soon they were going up the track that had made her so curious.

The valley, when she saw it, was pretty, though there was nothing remarkable about its prettiness. Except for the rough woods at the crests of the surrounding hills, the whole valley was tamed, the trees all in the place where they were planted, the houses all built up to fit the ever-larger families that lived there. Perhaps the walls were more crisply painted, and perhaps a whiter white than other places—or perhaps that was just what happened to Peggy's perceptions, because she was looking especially sharp to see what had piqued her curiosity. Perhaps the orchard trees were older than usual, more gnarled, as if this place had been settled long ago, the earliest of the Appalachee settlements. But what of that? Everything in America was new-ish; there was bound to be someone in this town who still remembered its founding. Nothing west of the first range of mountains was any older than the lifespan of the oldest citizen.

As always, she was aware of the heartfires of the people dwelling here, like sparks of light that she could see even in the brightest part of noon, through all walls, behind all hills, in all attics or basements where they might be. They were the ordinary folk of any town, perhaps a bit more content than others, but not immune to the suffering of life, the petty resentments, the griefs and envies. Why had she come here?

They came to a house with no one home. She rapped on the roof of the carriage again. The horses were whoaed to a stop, and the little door opened. "Wait here," she said.

She had no idea why this house, the empty one, drew her curiosity. Perhaps it was the way it had obviously grown up around a tiny log cabin, growing first prosperous, then grand, and finally nothing more than large, as aesthetics gave way to the need for more room, more room. How, in such a large and well-tended place, could there be no one home?

Then she realized that she heard singing coming from the house. And laughter from the yard. Singing and laughter, and yet not a heartfire to be seen. There had never been such a strange thing in all her life. Was this a haint house? Did the restless dead dwell here, unable to let go of life? But who ever heard of a haint that laughed? Or sang such a cheery song?

And there, running around the house, was a boy not more than six, being chased by three older girls. Not one with a heartfire. But from the dirt on the boy's face and the rage in the eyes of the red-faced girls, these could not be the spirits of the dead.

"Hallo, there!" cried Peggy, waving.

The boy, startled, looked at her. That pause was his undoing, for the girls caught up to him and fell to pummeling him with much enthusiasm; his answer was to holler with equal vigor, cursing them roundly. Peggy didn't know them, but had little doubt that the boy, in the fashion of all boys, had done some miserable mischief which outraged the girls—his sisters? She also had little doubt that the girls, despite the inevitable protests of innocence, had no doubt provoked *him* before, but in subtle, verbal ways so that he could never point to a bruise and get his mother on his side. Such was the endless war between male and female children. Stranger or not, however, Peggy could not allow the violence of the girls to get out of hand, and it seemed they were not disposed to go lightly in their determined battering of the bellowing lad. They were pursuing the beating, not as a holiday, but as if it were their bread-and-butter labor, with an overseer who would examine their handiwork later and say, "I'd say the boy was well beaten. You get your day's pay, all right!"

"Let up now," she said, striding across the goat-cropped yard.

They ignored her until she was on them and had two of the girls by the collars. Even then, they kept swinging with their fists, not a few of the blows landing on Peggy herself, while the third girl took no pause. Peggy had no choice but to give the two girls she had hold of a stern push, sending them sprawling in the grass, while she dragged the third girl off the boy.

As she had feared, the boy hadn't done well under the girls' blows. His nose was bleeding, and he got up only slowly; when the girl Peggy was holding lunged at him, he scurried on all fours to evade her.

"Shame on you," said Peggy. "Whatever he did, it wasn't worth this!"

"He killed my squirrel!" cried the girl she held.

"But how can you have had a squirrel?" asked Peggy. "It would be cruel of *you* to pen one up."

"She was never penned," said the girl. "She was my friend. I fed her and these others saw it—she came to me and I kept her alive through the hard winter. He knew it! He was jealous that the squirrel came to me, and so he killed it."

"It was a squirrel!" the boy shouted—hoarsely and rather weakly, but it was clear he *meant* it to be a shout. "How should I know it was yours?"

"Then you shouldn't have killed any," said another of the girls. "Not till you were sure."

"Whatever he did to the squirrels," said Peggy, "even if he was malicious, it was wrong of you and unchristian to knock him down and hurt him so."

The boy looked at her now. "Are you the judge?" he asked.

"Judge? I think not!" said Peggy with a laugh.

"But you can't be the Maker, that one's a boy. I think you're a judge." The boy looked even more certain. "Aunt Becca said the judge was coming, and then the Maker, so you can't be the Maker because the judge ain't come yet, but you could be the judge because the judge comes first."

Peggy knew that other folks often took the words of children to be nonsense, if they didn't understand them immediately. But Peggy knew that the words of children were always related to their view of the world, and made their own sense if you only knew how to hear them. Someone had told them—Aunt Becca, it was—that a judge and a Maker were coming. There was only one Maker that Peggy knew of. Was Alvin coming here? What was this place, that the children knew of Makers, and had no heartfires?

"I thought your house was standing empty," said Peggy, "but I see that it is not."

For indeed there now stood a woman in the doorway, leaning against the jamb, watching them placidly as she slowly stirred a bowl with a wooden spoon.

"Mama!" cried the girl that Peggy still held. "She has me and won't let go!"

"It's true!" cried Peggy at once. "And I still won't let go, till I'm sure she won't murder the boy here!"

"He killed my squirrel, Mama!" cried the girl.

The woman said nothing, just stirred.

"Perhaps, children," said Peggy, "we should go talk to this lady in the doorway, instead of shouting like river rats."

"Mother doesn't like you," said one of the girls. "I can tell."

"That's a shame," said Peggy. "Because I like *her*."

"Do not," said the girl. "You don't know her, and if you did you *still* wouldn't like her because nobody does."

"What a terrible thing to say about your mother," said Peggy.

"I don't have to like her," said the girl. "I *love* her."

"Then take me to this woman that you love but don't like," said Peggy, "and let me reach my own conclusions about her."

As they approached the door, Peggy began to think that the girls might be right. The woman certainly didn't look welcoming. But for that matter, she didn't look hostile, either. Her face was empty of emotion. She just stirred the bowl.

"My name is Peggy Larner." The woman ignored her outstretched hand. "I'm sorry if I shouldn't have intervened, but as you can see the boy was taking some serious injury."

"Just my nose is bloody, is all," said the boy. But his limp suggested other less visible pains.

"Come inside," said the woman.

Peggy had no idea whether the woman was speaking just to the children, or was including her in the invitation. If it could be called an invitation, so blandly she spoke it, not looking up from the bowl she stirred. The woman turned away, disappearing inside the house. The children followed. So, finally, did Peggy.

No one stopped her or seemed to think her action strange. It was this that first made her wonder if perhaps she had fallen asleep in the carriage and this was some strange dream, in which unaccountable unnatural things happen which nevertheless excite no comment in the land of dreams, where there is no custom to be violated. Where I am now is not real. Outside waits the carriage and the team of four horses, not to mention the driver, as real and mundane a fellow as ever belched in the coachman's seat. But in here, I have stepped into a place beyond nature. There are no heartfires here.

The children disappeared, stomping somewhere through the wood-floored house, and at least one of them went up or down a flight of stairs; it had to be a child, there was so much vigor in the step. But there were no sounds that told Peggy where to go, or what purpose was being served by her coming here. Was there no order here? Nothing that her presence disrupted? Would no one but the children ever notice her at all?

She wanted to go back outside, return to the carriage, but now, as she turned around, she couldn't remember what door she had come through, or even which way was north. The windows were curtained, and whatever door she had come through, she couldn't see it now.

It was an odd place, for there was cloth everywhere, folded neatly and stacked on all the furniture, on the floors, on the stairs, as if someone had just bought enough to make a thousand dresses with and the tailors and seamstresses were yet to arrive. Then she realized that the piles were of one continuous cloth, flowing off the top of one stack into the bottom of the next. How could there be a cloth so long? Why would anyone make it, instead of cutting it and sending it out to get something made from it?

Why indeed. How foolish of her not to realize it at once. She knew this place. She hadn't visited it herself, but she had seen it through Alvin's heartfire, years ago.

He was still in Ta-Kumsaw's thrall in those days. The Red warrior took Alvin with him and brought him into his legend, so that those who now spoke of Alvin Smith the Finder-killer, or Alvin Smith and the golden plow, had once spoken of the same boy, little knowing it, when they spoke of the evil "Boy Renegado," the white boy who went with Ta-Kumsaw in all his travels in the last year before his defeat at Fort Detroit. It was in that guise that Alvin came here, and walked down this hall, yes, turning right here, yes, tracking the folded cloth into the oldest part of the house, the original cabin, into the slanting light that seems to have no source, as if it merely seeped in through the chinks between the logs. And here, if I open this door, I will find the woman with the loom. This is the place of weaving.

Aunt Becca. Of course she knew the name. Becca, the weaver who held the threads of all the lives in the White man's lands in North America.

The woman at the loom looked up. "I didn't want you here," she said softly.

"Nor did I plan to come," said Peggy. "The truth is, I had forgotten you. You slipped my mind."

"I'm supposed to slip your mind. I slip all minds."

"Except one or two?"

"My husband remembers me."

"Ta-Kumsaw? He isn't dead, then?"

Becca snorted. "My husband's name is Isaac."

That was Ta-Kumsaw's White name. "Don't quibble with me," said Peggy. "Something called me here. If it wasn't you, who was it?"

"My untalented sister. The one who breaks threads whenever she touches the loom."

Aunt Becca, the children had called the weaver. "Is your sister the mother of the children I met?"

"The murderous little boy who kills squirrels for sport? His brutal sisters? I think of them as the four horses of the apocalypse. The boy is war. The sisters are still sorting themselves out among the other forces of destruction."

"You speak metaphorically, I hope," said Peggy.

"I hope not," said Becca. "Metaphors have a way of holding the most truth in the least space."

"Why would your sister have brought me here? She didn't seem to know me at the door."

"You're the judge," said Becca. "I found a purple thread of justice in the loom, and it was you. I didn't want you here, but I knew that you'd come, because I knew my sister would have you here."

"Why? I'm no judge. I'm guilty myself."

"You see? Your judgment includes everyone. Even those who are invisible to you."

"Invisible?" But she knew before asking what it was that Becca meant.

"Your vision, your torching, as you quaintly call it—you see where people are in the many paths of their lives. But I am not on the path of time. Nor is my sister. We don't belong anywhere in your prophecies or in the memories of those who know us. Only in the present moment are we here."

"Yet I remember your first word long enough to make sense of the whole sentence," said Peggy.

"Ah," said Becca. "The judge insists on correctness of speech. Boundaries are not so clear, Margaret Larner. You remember perfectly now; but what will you remember in a week from now? What you forget of me, you'll forget so completely that you won't remember that you once knew it. Then my statement will be true, but you'll forget that I said it."

"I think not."

Becca smiled.

"Show me the thread," said Peggy.

"We don't do that."

"What harm can it do? I've already seen all the possible paths of my life."

"But you haven't seen which one you'll choose," said Becca.

"And you have?"

"At this moment, no," said Becca. "But in the moment that contains all moments, yes. I've seen the course of your life. That isn't why you came, though. Not to find out something as stupid as whether you'll marry the boy you've nurtured all these years. You will or you won't. What is that to me?"

"I don't know," said Peggy. "I wonder why you exist at all. You change nothing. You merely see. You weave, but the threads are out of your control. You are meaningless."

"So you say," said Becca.

"And yet you have a life, or had one. You loved Ta-Kum-saw—or Isaac, whatever name you use. So loving some boy, marrying him, that didn't always seem stupid to you."

"So you say," said Becca.

"Or do you include yourself in that? Do you call yourself stupid in having loved and married? You can't pretend to be inhuman when you loved and lost a man."

"Lost?" she asked. "I see him every day."

"He comes here? To Appalachee?"

Becca hooted. "I think not!"

"How many threads broke under your hand with that pass of the shuttlecock?" asked Peggy.

"Too many," said Becca. "And not enough."

"Did you break them? Or did they simply happen to break?"

"The thread grew thin. The life wore out. Or it was cut. It isn't the thread that cuts the life, it's the death that cuts the thread."

"So you keep a record, is that it? The weaving causes nothing, but simply records it all."

Becca smiled thinly. "Passive, useless creatures that we are, but we must weave."

Peggy didn't believe her, but there was no use in arguing. "Why did you bring me here?"

"I told you. I didn't."

"Why did *she* bring me here?"

"To judge."

"What is it that I'm supposed to judge?"

Becca passed the shuttlecock from her right hand to her left. The loom slammed forward, then dropped back. She passed the shuttlecock from her left hand to her right. Again, the frame slammed forward, weaving the threads tight.

This *is* a dream, thought Peggy. And not a very pleasant one. Why can't I ever wake up to escape from some foolish useless dream?

"Personally," said Becca, "I think you've already made your judgment. It's only my sister thinks that you deserve a second chance. She's very romantic. She thinks that you deserve some happiness. My own feeling is that human happiness is a very random thing, and bestows itself willy-nilly, and there's not much deserving about the matter."

"So it's myself that I'm supposed to judge?"

Becca laughed.

One of the girls stuck her head into the room. "Mother says it's nasty and uncompassionate when you laugh during the weaving," she said.

"Nanner nanner," said Becca.

The girl laughed lightly, and Becca did too.

"Mother mixed up something really vile for your supper. *With* dumplings."

"Vileness with dumplings," said Becca. "Do sup with me."

"Let the *judge* do that," said the girl. "She really *is* a bossy one. Telling *us* about right and wrong." With that the girl disappeared.

Becca clucked for a moment. "The children are so full of themselves. Still very impressed with the idea that they aren't part of the normal world. You must forgive them for being arrogant and cruel. They couldn't have hurt their brother much, because they haven't the strength to strike a blow that will really harm him."

"He bled," said Peggy. "He limped."

"But the squirrel died," said Becca.

"You keep no threads for squirrels."

"*I* keep no threads for them. But that doesn't mean their threads aren't woven."

"Oh, tell me flat out. Don't waste my time with mysteries."

"I haven't been," said Becca. "No mysteries. I've told you everything that's useful. Anything else I told you might affect your judgment, and so I won't do it. I let my sister have her way, bringing you here, but I'm certainly *not* going to bend your life any more than that. You can leave whenever you want—that's a choice, and a judgment, and I'll be content with it."

"Will *I*?"

"Come back in thirty years and tell me."

"Will I be—"

"If you're still alive then." Becca grinned. "Do you think I'm so clumsy as to let slip your real span of years? I don't even know it. I haven't cared enough to look."

Two girls came in with a plate and a bowl and a cup on a tray. They set it on a small table near the loom. The plate was covered with a strange-smelling food. Peggy recognized nothing about it. Nor was there anything that she might have called a dumpling.

"I don't like it when people watch me eat," said Becca.

But Peggy was feeling very angry now, with all the elusiveness of Becca's conversation, and so she did not leave as courtesy demanded.

"Stay, then," said Becca.

The girls began to feed her. Becca did nothing to seek out the food. She kept up the perfect rhythm of her weaving, just as she had done throughout their conversation. The girls deftly maneuvered spoon or fork or cup to find their Aunt Becca's mouth, and then with a quick slurp or bite or sip she had the food. Not a drop or crumb was spilled on the cloth.

It could not always be like this, thought Peggy. She married Ta-Kumsaw. She bore a daughter to him, the daughter that went west to weave a loom among the Reds beyond the Mizzipy. Surely those things were not done with the shuttlecock flying back and forth, the loom slamming down to tamp the threads. It was deception. Or else it involved things Peggy was not going to understand however she tried.

She turned and left the room. The hall ended in a narrow stair. Sitting on the top step was, she assumed, the boy—she could see only his bare feet and trouser legs. "How's the nose?" she asked.

"Still hurts," said the boy. He scootched forward and dropped down a couple of steps by bouncing on his bottom.

"But not too bad," she said. "Healing fast."

"They was only *girls*," he said scornfully.

"You didn't think such scorn of them when they were pounding on you," she said.

"But you didn't hear me callin' uncle, did you? You didn't hear no uncle from me."

"No," said Peggy. "No uncle from you."

"I got me an uncle, though. Big Red man. Ike."

"I know of him."

"He comes most every day."

Peggy wanted to demand information from him. How does Ta-Kumsaw get here? Doesn't he live west of the Mizzipy? Or is he dead, and comes only in the spirit?

"Comes through the west door," said the boy. "We don't use that one. Just him. It's the door to my cousin Wieza's cabin."

"Her father calls her Mana-Tawa, I think."

The boy hooted. "Just giving her a Red name don't mean he can hold on to her. She don't belong to him."

"Whom does she belong to?"

"To the loom," he said.

"And you?" asked Peggy. "Do you belong to the loom?"

He shook his head. But he looked sad.

Peggy said it as she realized it: "You want to, don't you."

"She ain't going to have no more daughters. She don't stop weaving for him anymore. So she can't go. She'll just be there forever."

"And nephews can't take her place?"

"Nieces can, but my sisters ain't worth pigslime, in my opinion, which happens to be correck."

"Correct," said Peggy. "There's a *t* on the end."

"Correckut," the boy said. "But what I think is they ought to spell the words the way folks say 'em, stead of making us say 'em the way they're spelt."

Peggy had to laugh. "You have a point. But you can't just start spelling words any which way. Because you don't say them the same as someone from, say, Boston, and so pretty soon you and he would be spelling things so differently that you couldn't read each other's letters or books."

"Don't want to read his damn old books," said the boy. "I don't even know no boys in Boston."

"Do you have a name?"

"Not for *you* to know," said the boy. "You think I'm stupid? You're so thick with hexes you think I'm going to give you power over my name?"

"The hexes are to hide me from others."

"What do you have to hide for? Ain't nobody looking for you."

The words struck her hard. Nobody looking for her. Well, there it was. Once she had hidden so she could return to her own house without her family knowing her. Whom was she hiding from now?

"Perhaps I'm hiding from myself. Perhaps I don't want to be what I'm supposed to be. Or perhaps I don't want to keep living the life I already started to live."

"Perhaps you don't know squat about it," he said.

"Perhaps."

"Oh, don't be so mysterious, you silly old lady."

Silly she might accept, but *old*? "I'm not that many years older than you."

"When people say *perhaps* it's cause they're lying. Either they don't believe the thing they're saying, or they *do* believe it only they don't want to admit they do."

"You're a very wise young man."

"And the *real* liars change the subject the minute the truth comes up."

Peggy regarded him steadily. "You were waiting for me, weren't you?"

"I knew what Aunt Becca would do. She don't tell nobody nothin'."

"And you're going to tell me?"

"Not me! That's trouble too deep for me to get into." He smiled. "But you did stop the three witches from making soup of me. So I got you thinking in the right direction, if you've got the brains to see it." With that he jumped up and she listened as his feet slapped up the stairs and he was gone.

The choice was for Peggy to be happy. Becca said that, or said that her sister said it—though it was hard to imagine that blank-faced woman caring a whit whether anybody was happy or not. And now the boy got her talking about why she was hiding behind hexes, and said that he had guided her. The choice she was being offered was obvious enough now. She had buried herself in her father's work of breaking the back of slavery, and had stopped looking out for Alvin. They wanted her to look back again. They wanted her to reach out for him.

She stormed back into the cabin. "I won't do it," she said. "Caring for that boy is what killed my mother."

"Excuse me but I think a shotgun is what did for her," said Becca.

"A shotgun I could have prevented."

"So you say," said Becca.

"Yes, I say so."

"Your mother's thread broke when she decided to pick up a shotgun and do some killing of her own rather than trust to Alvin. Her boy Arthur was safe. She didn't need to kill, but when she chose to do that, she chose to die. Do you think you could have changed her mind about that?"

"Don't expect me to accept easy answers."

"No, I expect you to make all the answers as hard as possible. But sometimes it's the easy answers that are true."

"So it's back to the old days? Watching Alvin? Am I supposed to fall in love with him? Marry him? Watch him die?"

"I don't much care either way. My sister thinks you'll be happier with him than without him, and he's dead either way, in the long run, but then aren't we all? Most women that aren't killed by having babies live to be widows. What of that?"

What *of* that? Just because she could foresee so many ways for Alvin to die didn't mean that she should avoid loving him. She knew that, rationally. But fear wasn't rational.

"You spend your whole life grieving for those that haven't died yet," said Becca. "What a waste of an interesting knack."

"Interesting?"

"You *could* have had the knack of making shoe leather supple. Just see how happy that would've made you."

Peggy tried to imagine herself as a cobbler and had to laugh. "I suppose that I'd rather know than not know, mostly."

"Exactly. Knowing hurts sometimes, especially when you can't do anything to change it."

But there was something furtive in her, the way she said that. "Can't do anything to change it my left eye!" said Peggy.

"Don't use curses you don't understand," said Becca.

"You *do* make changes. *You* don't think the loom is immutable, not one bit."

"It's dangerous to change. The consequences are unpredictable."

"You saw Ta-Kumsaw dead at Detroit. So you picked up Alvin's thread and you—"

"What do you know about the loom!" cried Becca. "What do you know about watching the threads flow under your hands and seeing all the grief and pain and suffering and thinking! It doesn't matter, they're God's cattle and he can herd them how he likes, only then you find the one you love more than life and God has him slaughtered by the treachery of the French and the hatred of the English and for *nothing*, his whole life meaningless and lost and nothing changed by it except a few legends and songs, and here I am, still loving him, a widow forever because he's gone! So yes, I found the one who could save him. I knew if they met, they'd love each other and save each other."

"But what you did caused the massacre at Tippy-Canoe," said Peggy. "The people of Vigor Church thought Alvin had been kidnapped and tortured to death, so they slaughtered Tenskwa-Tawa's people in vengeance. Now they have a curse on them, all because you—"

"Because Harrison took advantage of their rage. Do you think there wouldn't have been a massacre anyway?"

"But the blood wouldn't have been on the same hands, would it?"

Becca wept, and her tears fell onto the cloth.

"Shouldn't you dry those tears?" asked Peggy.

"If tears could mar this cloth, there'd be no cloth left."

"So you of all people know the cost of meddling with the course of others' lives."

"And you of all people know the cost of failing to meddle when the time was right." Becca raised her head and continued her work. "I saved him, and that was my goal. Those who died would have died anyway."

"Yet here I am because your sister wants me to look after Alvin."

"Here you are because we only see the threads and then half-guess as to what they mean and who they are. We know the young Maker's thread—there's no way to miss it in this cloth. Besides, I moved it once, I twined it with my Isaac's thread. Do you think I could lose track of it after that? I'll show you, if you promise not to look beyond the inch of cloth I show."

"I promise not to look. But I can't help what I chance to see."

"Chance to see this, then."

Peggy looked at the cloth, knowing that the sight of it was rarely given to those not of the loom. Alvin's thread was obvious, shimmering light, with all colors in it; but it was no thicker than any other, and it looked frail, easily snapped by careless handling. "You dared to move this one?"

"It returned of itself to its own place," said Becca. "I only borrowed it for a while. And he saved his brother Measure. Eight-face mound opened up for him. I tell you there are forces at work in his life far stronger than my power to move the threads."

"More powerful than me, too."

"You are one of the forces. Not all of them, not the greatest of them, but you are one. Look. See how the threads cross him. His brothers and sisters, I think. He is closely entwined with his family. And see how these threads are brightening, taking on more hues. He's teaching them to be Makers."

Peggy hadn't known that. "Isn't that dangerous?"

"He can't do his work alone," said Becca. "So he teaches others to help him in it. He's more successful at it than he knows."

"This one," said Peggy, pointing to the brightest of the other threads. It veered off widely, wandering through the cloth far from the rest of the family.

"His brother. Also a seventh son of a seventh son," said Becca. "Though the eighth, if you count the one who died."

"But the seventh of those alive when he was born," said Peggy. "Yes, there's power in him."

"Look," said Becca. "See how he was at the beginning. Every bit as bright as Alvin's. There was near as much in him then as in Alvin. And no more forces working against him than Alvin overcame. Fewer, really, because by the time he came into his own you and Alvin between you had the Unmaker at bay. At least, all the killing tricks. But the Unmaker found another way to undo the boy. Hate and envy. If you love Alvin, Peggy, find his younger brother's heartfire. Somehow he must be brought back before it's too late."

"Why? I don't know anything about Calvin, except his name and Alvin's hopes for him."

"Because the way the threads are going now, when his rejoins Alvin's, Alvin's comes to an end."

"He kills him?"

"How should I know? We learn what we can learn, but the threads say little except by their movement through the cloth. You will know. That's why she called you. Not just for your own happiness, but because . . . as she said, because I owe it to the Maker. I used him once to save my love. Didn't I owe you the same chance? That's what she said. But we knew that if I showed you this at first, before you chose, you would help him out of duty. For the grand cause, not for love of him."

"But I hadn't decided to watch him again."

"So you say," said Becca.

"You're very smug," said Peggy, "for a woman who has made such a botch of things herself."

"I inherited a botch," said Becca. "One day my mother, who crossed the ocean and brought us here, one day she took her hands from the loom and walked away. My sister and I came in with her supper and found her gone. We were both married, but I had borne a child for my husband, and in those days my sister had none. So I took the loom, and she went to her husband. And all the time, I was furious at my mother for going away like that. Fleeing her duty." Becca stroked the threads, gently, even gingerly. "Now I think I understand. The price of holding all these lives in our hands is that we scarcely have a life ourselves. My mother wasn't good at this, because her heart wasn't in it. Mine is, and if I made a mistake to save my husband's life, perhaps you can judge me more kindly knowing that I had already given up my life with my husband in order to fill my mother's place."

"I didn't mean to condemn you," said Peggy, abashed.

"Nor did I mean to justify myself to you," said Becca. "And yet you did condemn me, and I did justify myself. I hold my mother's thread here. I know where she is. But I'll never know, really, why she did what she did. Or what might have happened if she stayed." Becca looked up at Peggy. "I don't know much, but what I know, I know. Alvin must go out into the world. He must leave his family—let them learn Making on their own now, as he did. He must rejoin Calvin before the boy has been completely turned by the Unmaker. Otherwise, Calvin may be not only his death, but also the undoing of all the Maker's works."

"I have an easy answer," said Peggy. "I'll find Calvin and make sure he never comes home."

"You think you have the power to control a Maker's life?"

"Calvin is no Maker. How could he be? Think what Alvin had to do, to come into his own."

"Nevertheless, you never had the power to stand against Alvin, even when he was a child. And he was kind at heart. I think Calvin isn't governed by the same sense of decency."

"So I can't stand against him," said Peggy. "Nor can I send Alvin out on errands. He's not mine to command."

"Isn't he?" asked Becca.

Peggy buried her face in her hands. "I don't want him to love me. I don't want to love him. I want to continue my struggle against slavery here in Appalachee."

"Oh, yes. Using your knack to meddle with the cloth, aren't you?" said Becca. "Do you know where it leads?"

"To liberty for the slaves, I hope."

"Perhaps," she said. "But the sure thing is this: It leads to war."

Peggy looked up grimly. "I see warsigns down all the paths. Before I started doing this, I saw those signs." Grieving mothers. The terror of battle in young men's lives.

"It begins as a civil war in Appalachee, but it ends as a war between the King on the one side and the United States on the other. Brutal, bloody, cruel . . ."

"Are you saying I should stop? That I should let these monsters continue to rule over the Blacks they kidnapped and all their children forever?"

"Not at all," said Becca. "The war comes because of a million different choices. Your actions push things that way, but you aren't the only cause. Do you understand? If war is the only way to free the slaves, then isn't the war worth all the suffering? Are lives wasted, when they end for such a cause?"

"I can't judge this sort of thing," said Peggy.

"But that's not true," said Becca. "Only you are fit to judge, because only you see the outcomes that might result. By the time I see things they've become inevitable."

"If they're inevitable, then why are you bothering to tell me to try to change them?"

"Almost inevitable. Again, I spoke imprecisely. I can't meddle with the threads on a grand scale. I can't foresee the consequences of change. But a single thread—sometimes I can move it without undoing the whole fabric. I didn't know a way to move Calvin that would make a difference. But I could move you. I could bring the judge here, the one who sees with the blindfold over her eyes. So I've done that."

"I thought you said your sister did it."

"Well, she's the one who decided it must be done. But only I could touch the thread."

"I think you spend a lot of your time lying and concealing things."

"Quite possibly."

"Like the fact that the western door leads into Ta-Kumsaw's land west of the Mizzipy."

"I never lied about that, or concealed it either."

"And the eastern door, where does that lead?"

"It opens in my auntie's house in Winchester, back in England. See? I conceal nothing."

"You have but one daughter," said Peggy, "and she's already got a loom of her own. Who will take your place here?"

"None of your business," said Becca.

"Nothing is none of my business now," said Peggy. "Not after you picked up my thread and moved it here."

"I don't know who will take my place. Maybe I'll be here forever. I'm not my mother. I won't quit and force this on an unwilling soul."

"When it comes time to choose, look at the boy," said Peggy. "He's wiser than you think."

"A boy's hands on the loom?" Becca's face bore an expression that suggested she had just tasted something awful.

"Before any talent for weaving," said Peggy, "doesn't the weaver have to care about the threads coming into the cloth? He may have killed a squirrel, but I don't think he loves death."

Becca regarded her steadily. "You take too much upon yourself."

"As you said. I'm a judge."

"You'll do it, then?"

"What, watch Alvin? Yes. Though I know I'll have a broken heart six times over before I bury him, yes, I'll turn my eyes back to that boy."

"That man."

"That Maker," said Peggy.

"And the other?"

"I'll meddle if I can find a way."

Becca nodded. "Good." She nodded again. "We're done, now. The doors will lead you out of the house."

That was all the good-bye that Peggy got. But what Becca said was true. Where once Peggy couldn't see a way out, now every corridor led to a door standing open, with the daylight outside. She didn't want to go through the doors back into her own world, though. She wanted to pass through the doors in the old cabin. The east door, into England. The west door, into Red country. Or the south door—where did it lead?

Nevertheless, it was this time and place where she belonged. There was a carriage waiting for her, and work to do, stirring up war by encouraging compassion for the slaves. She could live with that, yes, as Becca had said. Didn't Jesus himself say that he came to bring, not peace, but war? Turning brother against brother? If that's what it takes to remove the stain of slavery from this land, then so be it. I speak only of peaceful change—if others choose to kill or die rather than let the slaves go free, that is their choice, and I didn't cause it.

Just as I didn't cause my mother to take up the gun and kill the Finder who was, after all, only obeying the law, unjust as the law might be. He wouldn't have found Arthur Stuart, hidden as he was in my house, his very smell changed by Alvin's Making, and his presence hidden behind all the hexes Alvin had put there. I didn't kill her. And even if I could have prevented what she did, it wouldn't have changed who she was. She was the woman who would make such a choice as that. That was the woman I loved, her fierce angry courage along with everything else. I am not guilty of her death. The man who shot her was. And she was the one, not I, who placed her in harm's way.

Peggy strode out into the sunlight feeling invigorated, light of step. The air tasted sweet to her. The place with no heartfires had rekindled her own.

She got back into the carriage and it took her without further distractions to an inn well north of Chapman Valley. She spent the night there, and then the next day rode on to Baker's Fork. Once there, she held her master classes, teaching schoolmasters and gifted students, and in between conversing with this man or that woman about slavery, making comments, scorning those who mistreated slaves, declaring that as long as anyone had such power over other men and women, there would be mistreatment, and the only cure for it was for all men and women to be free. They nodded. They agreed. She spoke of the courage it would take, how the slaves themselves bore the lash and had lost all; how much would White men and women suffer in order to free them? What did Christ suffer, for the sake of others? It was a strong and measured performance that she gave. She did not retreat from it one bit, even though she knew now that it would lead to war. Wars have been fought for foolish causes. Let there be one, at last, in a good cause, if the enemies of decency refuse to soften their hearts.

Amid all the teaching and all the persuasion, she did find time, a scrap of an hour to herself, sitting at the writing desk in one old plantation widow's home. It was the very desk where, moments before, the woman had manumitted all her slaves and hired them on as free workingmen and workingwomen. Peggy saw in her heartfire when the choice was made that she would end up with her barns burnt and her fields spoiled. But she would lead these newfreed Blacks northward, despite all harassment and danger. Her courage would become legendary, a spark that would inspire other brave hearts. Peggy knew that in the end, the woman would not miss her fine house and lovely lands. And someday twenty thousand Black daughters would be given the woman's name. Why am I named Jane? they would ask their mothers. And the answer would come: Because once there was a woman by that name who freed her slaves and protected them all the way north, and then hired and looked after them until they learned the ways of free men and women and could stand on their own. It is a name of great honor. No one would know of the schoolteacher who came one day and gave open words to the secret longings of Jane's heart.

At that writing desk, Peggy took the time to write a letter and address it. Vigor Church, in the state of Wobbish. It would get to him, of course. As she sealed it, as she handed it over to the postal rider, she looked at long last toward the heartfire that she knew best, knew even better than her own. In it she saw the familiar possibilities, the dire consequences. But they were different now, because of the letter. Different . . . but better? She couldn't guess. She wasn't judge enough to know. Right and wrong were easy for her. But good and bad, better and worse, those were still too tricky. They kept sliding past each other strangely and changing before her eyes. Perhaps there was no judge who could know that; or if there was, he wasn't talking much about it.

The messenger took the letter and carried it north, where in another town he handed it to a rider who paid him what he thought the letter might be worth on delivery, minus half. The second rider took it on north, in his meandering route, and finally he stood in a store in the town of Vigor Church, where he asked about a man named Alvin Smith.

"I'm his brother-in-law," said the storekeeper. "Armor-of-God Weaver. I'll pay you for the letter. You don't want to go any farther into the town, or up there, either. You don't want to listen to the tale those people have to tell."

The tone of his voice convinced the rider. "Five dollars, then," he said.

"I'll wager you only paid the rider who gave it to you a single dollar, thinking the most you could get from me was two. But I'll pay you the five, if you still ask for it, because

I'm willing to be cheated by a man who can live with himself after doing it. It's you that'll pay most, in the end."

"Two dollars, then," said the rider. "You didn't have to get personal about it."

Armor-of-God took out three silver dollars and laid them in the man's hand. "Thank you for honest riding, friend," he said. "You're always welcome here. Stay for dinner with us."

"No," the man said. "I'll be on my way."

As soon as he was gone, Armor-of-God laughed and told his wife, "He only paid fifty cents for that letter, I'll wager. So he still thinks he cheated me."

"You need to be more careful with our money, Armor," she answered.

"Two dollars to cause a man a little spiritual torment that perhaps could change his life for the better? Cheap enough bargain, I'd say. What is a soul worth to God? Two dollars, do you think?"

"I shudder to think what some men's souls will be marked down to when God decides to close the shop," said his wife. "I'll take the letter up to Mother's house. I'm going there today anyway."

"Measure's boy Simon comes down for the mail," said Armor-of-God.

She glared at him. "I wasn't going to read it."

"I didn't say you were." But still he didn't hand her the letter. Instead he laid it on the counter, waiting for Measure's oldest boy to come and fetch it up the hill to the house where Alvin was teaching people to be Makers. Armor-of-God still wasn't happy about it. It seemed unreligious to him, improper, against the Bible. And yet he knew Alvin was a good boy, grown to be a good man, and whatever powers of witchery he had, he didn't use them to do harm. Could it be truly against God and religion for him to have such powers, if he used them in a Christian way? After all, God created the world and all things in it. If God didn't want there to be Makers, he didn't have to create any of them. So what Alvin was doing must be in line with the will of God.

Sometimes Armor-of-God felt perfectly at peace with Alvin's doings. And sometimes he thought that only a devil-blinded fool would think even for a moment that God was happy with any sort of witchery. But those were all just thoughts. When it came to action, Armor-of-God had made his decision. He was with Alvin, and against whoever opposed him. If he was damned for it, so be it. Sometimes you just had to follow your heart. And sometimes you just had to make up your mind and stick with it, come hell or high water.

And nobody was going to mess with Alvin's letter from Peggy Larner. Especially not Armor-of-God's wife, who was a good deal too clever with hexery herself.

Far away in another place, Peggy saw the changes in the heartfires and knew the letter was now in Alvin's family. It would do its work. The world would change. The threads in Becca's loom would move. It is unbearable to watch without meddling, thought Peggy. And then it is unbearable to watch what my meddling causes.

✤ 4 ✤

Quest

EVEN BEFORE MISS Larner's letter came, Alvin was feeling antsy.
Things just wasn't going the way he planned. After months of
trying to turn his family and neighbors into Makers, it was
looking like a job for six lifetimes, and try as he might, Alvin
couldn't figure out how he was going to have more than one
lifetime to work with.

Not that the teaching was a failure—he couldn't call it an
outright bust, not yet, considering that some of them really
were learning how to do some small Makings. It's just that
Making wasn't their knack. Alvin had figured out that there
wasn't no knack that another person couldn't learn, given time
and training and wit enough and plain old stick-to-it-iveness.
But what he hadn't taken into account was that Making was
like a whole bunch of knacks, and while some of them could
grasp this or that little bit of it, there was hardly any who
seemed to show a sign of grasping the whole of it. Measure
sometimes showed a glimmer. More than a glimmer, really.
He could probably be a Maker himself if only he didn't keep

getting distracted. But the others—there was no way they were going to be anything like what Alvin was. So if there was no hope of success, what was the point of trying?

Whenever he got to feeling discouraged like that, though, he'd just tell himself to shut his mouth and stick to his work. You don't get to be a Maker by changing your plan every few minutes. Who can follow you then? You stick to it. Even when Calvin, the only natural born Maker among them, even when he refused to learn anything and finally took himself off to do who knows what sort of mischief in the wide world, even then you don't give up and go off in search of him because, as Measure pointed out to the men who wanted to get up a search party, "You can't force a man to be a Maker, because forcing folks to do things is to Unmake them."

Even when Alvin's own father said, "Al, I marvel at what you can do, but it's enough for me that you can do it. My part was done when you were born, it seems to me. Ain't no man alive but what he isn't proud to have his son pass him up, which you done handily, and I don't aim to get back into the race." Even then, Alvin determined grimly to go on teaching while his father went back to the mill and began to clean it up and get it ready to grind again.

"I can't figure out," said Father, "if my milling is Making or Unmaking. The stones grind the grain and break it apart into dust, so that's Unmaking. But the dust is flour, and you can use it to make bread and cake that the maize or wheat can't be made into, so milling might be just a step along the road to Making. Can you answer me that, Alvin? Is grinding flour Making or Unmaking?"

Well, Alvin could answer it glib enough, that it was Making for sure, but it kept nagging at him, that question. I set out to make Makers out of these people, my family, my neighbors. But am I really just grinding them up and Unmaking them? Before I started trying to teach them, they were all content with their own knacks or even their own lack of a knack, when you come down to it. Now they're frustrated and they feel like failures and why? Is it Making to turn people into something that they weren't born to be? To be a Maker is good—I know it, because I am one. But does that mean it's the only good thing to be?

He asked Taleswapper about it, of course. After all, Taleswapper didn't show up for no reason, even if the old coot had no notion what the reason was himself. Maybe he was there to give Alvin some answers. So one day when the two of them were chopping wood out back, he asked, and Taleswapper answered like he always did, with a story.

"I heard a tale once about how a man who was building a wall as fast as he could, but somebody else was tearing it down faster than he could build it up. And he wondered how he could keep the wall from being torn down completely, let alone ever finish it. And the answer was easy: You can't build it alone."

"I remember that tale," said Alvin. "That tale is why I'm here, trying to teach these folks Making."

"I just wonder," said Taleswapper, "if you might be able to stretch that story, or maybe twist it a little and wring a bit more useful truth out of it."

"Wring away," said Alvin. "We'll find out whether the story is a wet cloth or a chicken's neck when you're done wringing."

"Well maybe what you need isn't a bunch of other stonemasons, cutting the stone and mixing the mortar and plumbing the wall and all those jobs. Maybe what you need is just a lot of cutters, and a lot of mortar mixers, and a lot of surveyors, and so on. Not everybody has to be a Maker. In fact, maybe all you need is just the one Maker."

The truth of what Taleswapper was saying was obvious; it had already occurred to Alvin many times, in other guises. What took him by surprise was how tears suddenly came to his own eyes, and he said softly, "Why does that make me so desperate sad, my friend?"

"Because you're a good man," said Taleswapper. "An evil man would delight to find out that he was the only one who could rule over a great many people working in a common cause."

"More than anything I don't want to be alone anymore," said Alvin. "I've been alone. Almost my whole time as a prentice in Hatrack River, I felt like there was nobody to take my part."

"But you were never alone the whole time," said Taleswapper.

"If you mean Miss Larner looking out for me—"

"Peggy is who I meant. I can't see why you still call her by that false name."

"That's the name of the woman I fell in love with," said Alvin. "But she knows my heart. She knows I killed that man and I didn't have to."

"The man who murdered her mother? I don't think she holds it against you."

"She knows what kind of man I am and she doesn't love me, that's what," said Alvin. "So I *am* alone, the minute I leave this place. And besides, leaving here is like lining up all these people and slapping their faces and saying, You failed so I'm gone."

At that Taleswapper just laughed. "That is plain foolishness and you know it. Truth is you've already taught them everything, and now it's just a matter of practice. They don't need you here anymore."

"But nobody needs me anywhere else," said Alvin.

Taleswapper laughed again.

"Stop laughing and tell me what's funny."

"A joke you have to explain isn't going to be funny anyway," said Taleswapper, "so there ain't no point in explaining it."

"You're no help," said Alvin, burying the head of his axe in the chopping stump.

"I'm a great help," said Taleswapper. "You just don't want to be helped yet."

"Yes I do! I just don't need riddles, I need answers!"

"You need somebody to tell you what to do? That's a surprise.

Still an apprentice then, after all? Want to turn your life over to somebody else? For how long, another seven years?"

"I may not be a prentice anymore," said Alvin, "but that don't mean I'm a master. I'm just a journeyman."

"Then hire on somewhere," said Taleswapper. "You've still got things to learn."

"I know," said Alvin. "But I don't know where to go to learn it. There's that crystal city I saw in the twister with Tenskwa-Tawa. I don't know how to build it. I don't know *where* to build it. I don't even know *why* to build it, except that it ought to exist and I ought to make it exist."

"There you are," said Taleswapper. "Like I said, you've already taught everybody here everything you know, twice over. All you're doing now is helping them practice—and cheating now and then by helping them, don't think I haven't noticed."

"When I use my knack to help them, I tell them I helped," said Alvin, blushing.

"And then they feel like failures anyway, figuring that your help was all that made anything happen, and nothing of their own doing. Alvin, I think I *am* giving you your answer. You've done what you can here. Leave Measure to help them, and the others who've learned a bit of it here and there. Let them work things out on their own, the way you did. Then you go out into the world and learn more of the things you need to know."

Alvin nodded, but in his heart he still refused to believe it. "I just can't see what good it is to go out to try to learn when you know as well as I do there's not another Maker in the world right now, unless you count Calvin which I don't. Who am I going to learn from? Where am I going to go?"

"So you're saying that there's no use in just wandering around, seeing what happens and learning as you can?"

Taleswapper's face was so wry as he said this that Alvin knew at once there was a double meaning. "Just because *you* learn that way doesn't mean *I* can. You're just collecting stories, and there's stories everywhere."

"There's Making almost everywhere, too," said Taleswapper.

"And where there isn't Making, there's still old made things being torn down, and you can learn from them, too."

"I can't go," said Alvin. "I can't go."

"Which is to say, you're afraid."

Alvin nodded.

"You're afraid you'll kill again."

"I don't think so. I know I won't. Probably."

"You're afraid you'll fall in love again."

Alvin hooted derisively.

"You're afraid you'll be alone out there."

"How could I be alone?" he asked. "I'd have my golden plow with me."

"That's another thing," said Taleswapper. "That living plow. What did you make it for, if you keep it in darkness all the time and never use it?"

"It's gold," said Alvin. "People want to steal it. Many a man would kill for that much gold."

"Many a man would kill for that much tin, for that matter," said Taleswapper. "But you remember what happened to the man who was given a talent of gold, and buried it in the earth."

"Taleswapper, you're plumb full of wisdom today."

"Brimming over," said Taleswapper. "It's my worst fault, splashing wisdom all over other people. But most of the time it dries up real fast and doesn't leave a stain."

Alvin grimaced at him. "Taleswapper, I'm not ready to leave home yet."

"Maybe folks have to leave home *before* they're ready, or they never get ready at all."

"Was that a paradox, Taleswapper? Miss Larner taught me about paradox."

"She's a fine teacher and she knows all about it."

"All I know about paradox is that if you don't shovel it out of the stable, the barn gets to stinking real bad and fills up with flies."

Taleswapper laughed at that, and Alvin joined in laughing, and that was the end of the serious part of the conversation.

Only it clung to Alvin, the whole thing, knowing that Taleswapper thought he should leave home, and him not having a clue where he would go if he did leave, and not being willing to admit failure, either. All kinds of reasons for staying. Most important reason of all was simply being home. He'd spent half his childhood away from his family, and it was good to sit down at his mother's table every day. Good to see his father standing at the mill. Hear his father's voice, his brothers' voices, his sisters' voices laughing and quarreling and telling and asking, his mother's voice, his mother's sharp sweet voice, all of them covering his days and nights like a blanket, keeping him warm, all of them saying to him, You're safe here, you're known here, we're your people, we won't turn on you. Alvin had never heard him a symphony in his life, or even more than two fiddles and a banjo at the same time, but he knew that no orchestra could ever make a music more beautiful than the voices of his family moving in and out of their houses and barns and the millhouse and the shops in town, threads of music binding him to this place so that even though he knew Taleswapper was right and he ought to leave, he couldn't bring himself to go.

How did Calvin ever do it? How did Calvin leave this music behind him?

Then Miss Larner's letter came.

Measure's boy Simon brought it, him being five now and old enough to run down to Armor-of-God's store to pick up the post. He could do his letters now, too, so he didn't just give the letter over to his grandma or grandpa, he took it right to Alvin himself and announced at the top of his lungs, "It's from a woman! She's called Miss Larner and she makes real purty letters!"

"*Pretty* letters," Alvin corrected him.

Simon wasn't to be fooled. "Oh, Uncle Al, you're the only person around here as says it like that! I'd be plumb silly to fall for a joke like that!"

Alvin pried up the sealing wax and unfolded the letter. He

knew her handwriting from the many hours he had tried to imitate it, studying with her back in Hatrack River. His hand was never as smooth, could never flow the way hers did. Nor was he as eloquent. Words weren't his gift, or at least not the formal, elegant words Miss Larner—Peggy—used in writing.

Dear Alvin,

You've overstayed in Vigor Church. Calvin's a great danger to you, and you must go find him and reconcile with him; if you wait for him to come back to you, he will bring the end of your life with him.

I can almost hear you answer me: I ain't afraid to see my life end. (I know you still say ain't, just to spite me.) Go or stay, that's up to you. But I can tell you this. Either you will go now, of your own free will, or you will go soon anyway, but not freely. You're a journeyman smith—you will have your journey.

Perhaps in your travels we shall encounter each other. It would please me to see you again.

Sincerely,
Peggy

Alvin had no idea what to make of this letter. First she bosses him around like a schoolboy. Then she talks teasingly about how he still says *ain't*. Then she as much as asks him to come to her, but in such a cold way as to chill him to the bone—"It would please me to see you again" indeed! Who did she think she was, the Queen? And she signed the letter "sincerely" as if she was a stranger, and not the woman that he loved, and that once said she loved him. What was she playing at, this woman who could see so many futures? What was she trying to get him to do? It was plain there was more going on than she was saying in her letter. She thought she was so wise, since she knew more about the future than other folks, but the fact was that she could make mistakes like anybody else and he didn't want her telling him what to *do*, he wanted her to tell him what she *knew* and let him make up his own mind.

One thing was certain. He wasn't going to drop everything and take off in search of Calvin. No doubt she knew exactly where he was and she hadn't bothered to tell him. What was *that* supposed to accomplish? Why should he go off searching for Calvin when she could send him a letter and tell him, not where Calvin was right now, but where Calvin would *be* by the time Alvin caught up with him? Only a fool takes off on foot trying to follow the flight of a wild goose.

I know I've got to leave here sometime. But I'm not going to leave in order to chase down Calvin. And I'm not going to leave because the woman I almost married sends me a bossy letter that doesn't even hint that she still loves me, if she ever really did. If Peggy was so sure that he'd go soon anyway, because he had to, well, then he might as well just wait around and see what it was that would make him go.

⌖ 5 ⌖

Twist

AMERICA WAS TOO small a country for Calvin. He knew that now. It was all too new. The powers of a land took time to ripen. The Reds, they knew the land, but they were gone. And the Whites and Blacks who lived here now, they had only shallow powers, knacks and hexes, spells and dreams. Nothing like the ancient music that Alvin had talked about. The greensong of the living forest. Besides, the Reds were gone, so whatever it was they knew, it must have been weak. Failure was proof enough of that.

Even before Calvin knew in his mind where he was headed, his feet knew. East. Sometimes a bit north, sometimes a bit south, but always east. At first he thought he was just going to Dekane, but when he got there he just worked for a day or two to get a bit of coin and some bread in his belly, and then he was off over the mountains, following the new railroad into Irrakwa, where he could sneer a little at men and women who were Red in body but White in dress and speech and soul. More work, more coin, more practice at using his Making here and there. Pranks, mostly, because he didn't dare use his knack out in the open where folks would take notice and spread word of him. Just little favors for houses where they treated him good, like driving all the mice and roaches off their property. And a little bit of getting even with those who turned him away. Sending a rat to die in a well. Causing a leak in the roof over a flour barrel. That one was hard, making the wood swell and then shrink. But he could work with the water. The water lent itself to his use better than any other element.

Turned out that Irrakwa wasn't where his feet were taking him, either. He worked his way across Irrakwa to New Holland, where the farmers all spoke Dutch, and then down the Hudson to New Amsterdam.

He thought when he came to the great city on the tip of Manhattan Island that this might be the place he was looking for. Biggest city in the U.S.A. And it wasn't hardly Dutch anymore. Everybody spoke English for business, and on top of that Calvin counted a dozen languages before he stopped caring how many. Not to mention strange accents of English from places like York and Glasgow and Monmouth. Surely all the lores of the world were gathered here. Surely he could find teachers.

So he stayed for days, for a week. He tried the college farther up the island, but they wanted him to study intellectual things instead of the lore of power, and soon enough Calvin figured out that none of them high-toned professors knew anything useful anyhow. They treated him like he was crazy. One old coot with a white goat-beard spent half an hour trying to convince Calvin to let the man study *him*, like as if he was some strange specimen of bug. Calvin only stayed for the whole half hour so he'd have time to loosen all the bindings of all the books on the man's shelves. Let him wonder about Calvin's kind of madness as the pages of every book he picked up fell out and scattered on the floor.

If the professors weren't worth nothing, the street wasn't much better. Oh, he heard about loremasters and wizards and such. Gypsies bragged on some cursemonger. Irishmen knew of a priest who had special ways. Frenchmen and Spaniards heard of witches or child-saints or whatever. One Portugee told of a free Black woman who could make your enemy's crotch turn as smooth and blank as an armpit—which, according to the story, was how she got her freedom, after doing that to her master's firstborn son and threatening to do it next to him. But every one of them kept retreating out of sight. He'd find out who knew the loremaster, and then go to that person and find out that he only knew somebody else who knew the powerful one, and so on and so on, like constables searching through the night for a fugitive who kept slipping away into alleys.

In the meantime, though, Calvin learned to live in a city and he liked it. He liked the way that you could disappear right out in the open. Nobody knew you. Nobody expected anything from you. You were what you wore. When he arrived he dressed like a rube from the country, and so people expected him to be stupid and awkward and, what the hell, he was. But in a few days he realized how his clothes gave him away and he bought some city garb from a used-garment house. That was when people started being willing to talk to him. And he learned to change his speech a little, too. Talk faster, get rid of some of the drawl. Shake off the country twang. He knew he gave himself away with every word he said, but he was getting better. People didn't ask him to repeat himself as much. And by the end of the week, he was no more out of place than any of the other immigrants. That was as good as it got—it wasn't as if anybody was actually *from* New Amsterdam. Except maybe for some old Dutch landlords hiding in their mansions up-island.

Rumors of wisdom, but no wisdom to be had in this town. Well, what did he expect? Anybody who really knew the powers of the old world would hardly have to board some miserable boat and sail west at risk of life and limb in order to come live in some sinkhole of a slum in New Amsterdam. No, the people of Europe who understood power were still in Europe—because they were running things there, and didn't have no reason to leave.

And who was the most powerful one of all? Why, the man whose victories had caused all these people of the dozen languages to flock to American shores. The man who drove the aristocrats out of France, and then conquered Spain and the Holy Roman Empire and Italy and Austria and then for some reason stopped at the Russian border and the English Channel, declared peace and held on, iron-fisted but, as they said, tender-hearted, so that pretty soon nobody in Italy or Austria or the low countries or anywhere, really, was wishing for their old rulers to come back. That was the man who understood power. That was the man who was fit to teach Calvin what he needed to know.

Only trouble was, why would a man so powerful ever agree to speak to a poor farmboy from Wobbish? And how was that poor farmboy ever going to find passage across the ocean? If only Alvin had bothered to teach him how to turn iron into gold. Now *that* would be useful. Imagine a whole steam locomotive turned to solid gold. Fire up the engine and the whole damn thing would melt down—but it would melt down into pools of gold. Just put in a dipper and draw it out and there was passage to France, and not in no steerage, neither. First-class passage, and a fine hotel in Paris. Fine clothes, too, so that when he walked into the American embassy the flunkies would bow and scrape and take him straight to the ambassador and the ambassador would take him straight to the imperial palace where he would be presented to Napoleon himself and Napoleon would say, Why should I meet with you, an ordinary citizen of a second-rate country in the wild lands of the west? And Calvin would take three dipperfuls of gold out of his pockets and set them heavily in Napoleon's hands and say, How much of this do you want? I know how to make more. And Napoleon would say, I have all the taxes of Europe to buy me gold. What do I need with your pathetic handfuls? And Calvin would say, Now you have a bit more gold than you had before. Look at your buttons, sir. And Napoleon would look at the brass buttons on his coat and they would be gold, too, and he would say, What do you want from me, sir? That's right, he'd call Calvin "sir" and Calvin would say, All I want is for you to teach me the ways of power.

Only if Calvin knew how to turn iron or brass into gold, he sure as hell wouldn't need no help from Napoleon Bonaparte, Emperor of Earth or whatever fool title the man had given himself in his latest promotion. It was one of those circular dilemmas that he always kept running into. If he had enough power to attract Napoleon's attention, he wouldn't need Napoleon. And, because he needed Napoleon, there was no chance that any of his underlings would let Calvin come anywhere near him.

Calvin wasn't stupid. He wasn't no rube, whatever the city people thought. He knew that powerful men didn't let just anybody come in and chat.

But I do have some powers, thought Calvin. I do have some powers, and I can wangle a way, once I get across the pond. That's what the sophisticated people called the Atlantic Ocean—the pond. Once I get across the pond. Might have to learn French, but they say Napoleon speaks English, too, from his days as a general in Canada. One way or another, I'll get to see him and he'll take me on as his apprentice. Not apprenticed like to take over his empire after him, but instead to do the same thing in America. Bring the Crown Colonies and New England and the United States all under one flag. And Canada, too. And Florida. And then maybe he'd turn his eyes across the Mizzipy and see how good a job old Tenskwa-Tawa would do at holding back a *Maker* who wanted to cross and conquer Red country.

All dreams. All stupid foolish dreams of a boy sleeping in a cheap boardinghouse and doing lousy odd jobs to earn a few cents a day. Calvin knew that, but he also knew that if he couldn't turn a knack like his into money and power he didn't deserve nothing better than those lousy beds and wormy meals and backbreaking jobs.

One thing, though. Folks on the street were getting used to the idea that Calvin was searching for something, and finally the old woman he bought apples from—the one who'd given him an apple his first day there when he was out of money, since she was a country girl herself, she said; the one who from that day to this found no more worms or flies in her fruit—she said to him, "Well I hope you've talked to the Bloody Man, he knows stuff."

"Bloody Man?"

"You know, the one as tells horrible stories or when he can't find nobody new to tell it to, his hands are dripping with blood. Everybody knows the Bloody Man. He come here because the curse on him is, he has to find new people every day to tell his story to, and where you going to find a good supply of new people all the time?"

Of course Calvin knew by now exactly who she was talking about. "Harrison is *here*?"

"You know him?"

"Know *of* him. He called hisself—himself—governer of Wobbish for a while. Slaughtered Tenskwa-Tawa's people at Tippy-Canoe."

"That's the one. Dreadful story. Thank heaven I only had to hear it the once. But there's some kind of power in the fact that his hands get all bloody. I mean, that's strange, ain't it? All them other folks you hear about, you never actually see them do nothing, if you know what I mean. But you can see the blood. That's power, I reckon."

"Reckon so." Again he corrected himself. "I think so."

"Might as well say, 'I imagine so,' if you're trying to get all highfalutin."

"Just don't want to sound country, that's all."

"Then you'd better learn French. All the high-tone folks do. Here we are in a Dutch city where everybody speaks English, and they go into their toney restaurants and order their food in French! What did the *French* ever have to do with New Amsterdam? You want to eat in French, you go to Canada, that's what I say!"

He listened to her diatribe until he could finally get free— which meant when she finally got a customer—and then he set out to find Harrison. White Murderer Harrison. Calvin knew all about the curse on him, from the stories told by his own father and neighbors, and he'd sometimes imagined Harrison walking country roads from town to town, folks throwing him out before he could come in and start telling his awful tale. It never occurred to him that Harrison would come to the city, but it made sense, once you thought about it. Bloody Man.

He found him in an alleyway behind a restaurant where he got fed every night by a manager who didn't want him accosting his customers. "It's a stiff punishment," said the manager. "I had a landlord in Kilkenny who believed in that kind of justice. Punishments that went on forever. Permanent shame. I think it's wrong. I don't care much what the man did. Let him without sin among you, and all that. So he eats back of my restaurant. Long as he doesn't hurt trade."

"Aren't you the generous one," said Calvin.

"You got a mouth on you, boy. In fact I *am* generous, and open-minded, too, and just because I know it and take credit for it doesn't make it any less true. So you can take your little winking sort of wit and leave my establishment if you're going to eat my food and then sit in judgment on me."

"I haven't eaten your food."

"But you will," said the man, "because, as I said, I *am* generous, and you look hungry. Now get back to the kitchen and you can tell the cook to give you something for yourself and something for Bloody Man out in the alley. If you come with his food, he'll talk to you, right enough. He'll probably tell you his story, for that matter."

"I know his story."

"Everybody might know a story, but it's never the same story they know. Now get away from my door, you look like a street rat."

Calvin looked down at his clothes and realized, yes, he had bought clothing to blend in, but what he blended in with was the street, not the city. He'd have to do something about that before he went to Paris. Have to become, if not a gentleman, then at least a tradesman. Not a street rat.

He didn't like people who called themselves generous, but the fact was the food in the kitchen was good. The cook didn't give him no scraps or scrapings. He got food that was decent and there was plenty. How did this manager stay in business, being so generous to the poor? No doubt he was cheating his boss. He could afford to be generous, since he didn't have to pay for it himself. Most virtues were like that. People could take pride in how virtuous they were, but the fact was that as soon as virtue got expensive or inconvenient, it was amazing how fast it gave way to practical concerns.

The man's generosity got him this much: No roaches or mice in his kitchen.

Out in the alleyway, Bloody Man was sipping from a wine bottle. He saw Calvin and his eyes went hungry. Calvin laughed. "I hear you've got a story to tell."

"They still sending boys like you to find me, as a prank?"

"No prank. I know your story, mostly. Just wanted to meet you my own self, I guess."

Harrison offered him the wine bottle. "Best thing about this place," he said. "Besides that they don't run me off in the first place. When somebody opens a bottle of wine and doesn't finish it at the table, the manager refuses to pour from that bottle to anyone else. So it comes out into the alley."

"The big surprise," said Calvin, "is that there ain't ten dozen other hungry drunks here."

Harrison laughed. "They used to. But they got sick of hearing me tell my story and now I have the alley to myself. That's how I like it."

But Calvin could hear it in his voice that it was a lie. He didn't like it that way. He was hungry for company.

"Might as well start telling me the story. Between bites, if you want," said Calvin.

Harrison started eating. Calvin could see a remnant of table manners. Once he had been a civilized man.

Between bites, Harrison told the tale. All of it: How he had some Reds from south of the Hio come and kidnap two White boys in order to blame it on Tenskwa-Tawa, the so-called Red Prophet. Only the boys were rescued somehow and fell in with the Prophet's brother, Ta-Kumsaw. But that didn't matter because Harrison still used the kidnapping to rile up the White folks in the northern part of Wobbish, the ones as lived nearest to the Prophet's village at Tippy-Canoe. So Harrison was able to raise an army to go wipe out Prophetstown. And then at the last minute, who shows up but one of the kidnapped boys. Well, Harrison sees nothing for it but to have the boy killed, and everything seems to be working. The Reds just stand there, letting the musketfire and the grapeshot mow them down until nine out of ten of them was dead, the whole meadow a sheet of blood flowing down into the Tippy-Canoe, only it was too much for those White men—they *called* themselves men— because they all stopped shooting before the job was done, and then up comes that boy who was supposed to be dead and he wasn't even injured, and he tells the truth to everybody and then the Red Prophet puts a curse on all of them there and the worst curse on Harrison, including that he has to tell a new person every day and . . .

"You're telling it all wrong," said Calvin.

Harrison looked at him angrily. "You think after all these years I don't know how to tell the tale? If I tell it any other way, I get blood on my hands and believe me, it looks bad. People throw up when they see me. Looks like I stuck my hands in a corpse up to my elbows."

"Telling it *your* way has you living in an alley, eating from charity and drinking leftover wine," said Calvin.

Harrison squinted at him. "Who *are* you?"

"The boy you tried to kill is my brother Measure. The other boy you had them kidnap is my brother Alvin."

"And you came to gloat?"

"Do I look like I'm gloating? No, I left home because I got sick of their righteousness, knowing everything and not having respect for nobody else."

Harrison winked. "I never liked people like that."

"You want to hear how you *ought* to tell your tale?"

"I'm listening."

"The Reds were at war with the Whites. They weren't using the land but they didn't want White farmers to use it, either. They just couldn't share even though there was plenty of room. Tenskwa-Tawa claimed to be peaceful, but you knew that he was gathering all those thousands of Reds together in order to be Ta-Kumsaw's army. You had to do *something* to rile up the Whites there to put a stop to this menace. So yes, you had two boys kidnapped, but you never gave orders for anybody to be killed—"

"If I say *that* the blood just leaps onto my hands on the spot—"

"I'm sure you've thought of all the possible lies, but hear me out," said Calvin.

"Go on."

"You didn't order anybody killed. That was just lies your enemies told about you. Lies originating with Alvin Miller Junior, now called Alvin Smith. After all, Alvin was the Boy Renegado, the White boy who went everywhere with Ta-Kumsaw for a year. He was Ta-Kumsaw's friend—we'll use the word *friend* because we're in decent company—so of course he lied about you. It was your battle at Tippy-Canoe that broke the back of Ta-Kumsaw's plans. If you hadn't struck then and there, Ta-Kumsaw would have been victorious later at Fort Detroit, and Ta-Kumsaw would have driven all the civilized folks out of the land west of the Appalachees and Red armies would be descending on the cities of the east, raiding out of the mountains and—why, thanks to you and your courage at Tippy-Canoe, the Reds have been driven west of the Mizzipy. You opened up all the western lands to safe colonization."

"My hands would be dripping before I said all that."

"So what? Hold them up and say, 'Look what the Red Witch Tenskwa-Tawa did to punish me. He covered my hands with blood. But I'm glad to pay that price. The blood on my hands is the reason why White men are building civilization right to the shores of the Mizzipy. The blood on my hands is the reason why people in the east can sleep easy at night, without so much as a thought about Reds coming and raping and killing the way those savages always did.' "

Harrison chuckled. "Every word you've said is the profoundest bull hockey, my boy, I hope you know that."

"You just need to decide whether you're going to let Tenskwa-Tawa have the final victory over you."

"Why are you telling me this? What's in it for you?"

"I don't know. I came looking for you thinking you might know something of power, but when I heard you tell that weaselly weakling tale I knew that you didn't know nothing that a *man* could use. In fact, I knew more than *you*. So, seeing how I was going to ask you to share, it seemed only fair to share right back."

"How kind of you." His sarcasm was inescapable.

"I don't think so. I just picture the look on my brother Alvin's face when you tell everbody he was the Boy Renegado. You say *that*, and nobody'll believe him if he testifies against you. In fact, he'll have to hide himself, when you think of all the terrible things folks believe about the Boy Renegado. How he was the cruelest Red of them all, killing and torturing so even the Shaw-Nee puked."

"I remember those tales."

"You hold up those bloody hands, my friend, and then make them mean what *you* want them to mean."

Harrison shook his head. "I can't live with the blood."

"So you *have* a conscience, eh?"

Harrison laughed. "The blood gets in my *food*. It stains my clothes. It makes people sick."

"If I were you, I'd eat with gloves on and I'd wear dark clothes."

Harrison was through eating. So was Calvin.

"So you want me to do this to hurt your brother."

"Not hurt him. Just keep him silent and out of sight. You've spent, what, eight years living like a dog. Now it's his turn."

"There's no going back," said Harrison. "Once I tell lies, I'll have bloody hands till the day I die."

Calvin shrugged. "Harrison, you're a liar and a murderer, but you love power more than life. Unfortunately you're piss-poor at getting it and keeping it. Ta-Kumsaw and Alvin and Tenskwa-Tawa played you for a sucker. I'm telling you how to undo what they done to you. How to set yourself free. I don't give a rat's front teeth whether you do what I said or not." He got up to go.

Harrison half-rose and clutched at Calvin's pantlegs. "Someone told me that Alvin, he's a Maker. That he has real power."

"No he doesn't," said Calvin. "Not for you to worry about. Because, you see, my friend, he can only use his power for *good*, never to harm nobody."

"Not even me?"

"Maybe he'll make an exception for you." Calvin grinned wickedly. "I know *I* would."

Harrison withdrew his hands from Calvin's clothing. "Don't look at me like that, you little weasel."

"Like what?" asked Calvin.

"Like I'm scum. Don't *you* judge *me*."

"Can you tell me a single good reason why not?"

"Because whatever else I did, boy, I never betrayed my own brother."

Now it was Calvin's turn to look into the face of contempt. He spat on the ground near Harrison's knees. "Eat pus and die," he said.

"Was that a curse?" asked Harrison jeeringly as Calvin walked away. "Or merely a friendly warning?"

Calvin didn't answer him. He was already thinking of other things. How to raise the money to get passage east, for one thing. First class. He was going to go first class. Maybe what he needed to do was see if his knack extended to causing money to fall out of some shopkeeper's moneybag as he carried his earnings to the bank. If he did it right, no one would see. He wouldn't get caught. And even if someone saw the money fall out and him pick it up, they could only accuse him of finding dropped money, since he never laid a hand on the bag. That would work. It would be easy enough. So easy that it was stupid that Alvin had never done it before. The family could have used the money. There were some hard years. But Alvin was too selfish ever to think of anybody but himself, or anything but his stupid plan of trying to teach Making to people with no knack for it.

First-class passage to England, and from there across the channel to France. New clothes. It wouldn't take much to get that kind of money. A lot of money changed hands in New Amsterdam, and there was nothing to stop some of it from falling onto the street at Calvin's feet. God had given him the power, and that meant that it must be the will of God for him to do it.

Wouldn't it be a hoot if Harrison actually took Calvin's advice?

⚜ 6 ⚜

True Love

AMY SUMP DIDN'T care what her friends or anybody said. What she felt for Alvin Maker was love. Real love. True, deep, abiding love that would withstand the test of time.

If only he would pay any attention to her openly, so others could see it. Instead all he ever did was give her those glances that made her heart flutter so within her. She worried sometimes that maybe it was just his Makerness, his knack or whatever it was. Worried that he was somehow reaching inside her chest and making her heart turn over and her whole body quiver. But no, that wasn't the sort of thing that Makers did. In fact maybe he didn't even *know* about her love for him. Maybe his glances were really searching looks, hoping to see in her face some sign of her love. That was why she no longer tried to hide her maidenly blushes when her heart beat so fast and her face felt all hot and tingly. Let him see how his gaze transforms me into a quivering mass of devoted worshipfulness.

How Amy longed to go to the teaching sessions where Alvin worked with a dozen or so grownups at once, telling them how a Maker had to see the world. How she would love to hear his voice for hours on end. Then she would discover the true knack within her, and both she and her beloved Alvin would rejoice to discover that she was secretly a Maker herself, so that the two of them together would be able to remake the world and fight off the evil nasty Unmaker together. Then they would have a dozen babies, all of them Makers twice over, and the love of Alvin and Amy Maker would be sung for a thousand generations throughout the whole world, or at least America, which was pretty much the same thing as far as Amy cared.

But Amy's parents wouldn't let her go. "How could Alvin possibly concentrate on teaching anybody anything with you making cow-eyes at him the whole time?" her mother said, the heartless old hag. Not as cruel as her father, though, telling her, "Get some control over yourself, girl! Or I'm going to have to get you some love diapers to keep you from embarrassing yourself in public. Love diapers, do you understand me?" Oh, she understood him, the nasty man. Him of the cranks and pulleys, pipes and cables. Him of pumps and engines and machinery, who had no understanding of the human heart. "The heart's just a pump itself, my girl," he said, which showed him to be a deeply totally impossibly eternally abysmally ignorant machine of a man his own self but said nothing about the truth of the universe. It was her beloved Alvin who understood that all things were alive and had feelings—all things *except* her father's hideous dead machines, chugging away like walking corpses. A steam-powered lumbermill! Using fire and water to cut wood! What an abomination before the Lord! When she and Alvin were married, she'd get Alvin to stop her father from making any more machines that roared and hissed and chugged and gave off the heat of hell. Alvin would keep her in a sylvan wonderland where the birds were friends and the bugs didn't bite and they could swim naked together in clear pools of water and he would swim to her in real life instead of just in her dreams and he would reach out and embrace her and their naked bodies would touch under the water and their flesh would meet and join and . . .

"No such thing," said her friend Ramona.

Amy felt herself grow hot with anger. Who was Ramona to decide what was real and what wasn't? Couldn't Amy tell her dreams to *somebody* without having to keep saying it was just a dream instead of pretending that it was real, that his arms had been around her? Didn't she remember it as clearly—no, far *more* clearly—than anything that had ever happened to her in real life?

"Did so happen. In the moonlight."

"When!" said Ramona, her voice dripping with contempt.

"Three nights ago. When Alvin *said* he was going out into the woods to be alone. He was really going to be with me."

"Well where is there a pool of clear water like that? Nothing like that around here, just rivers and streams, and you *know* Alvin never goes into the Hatrack to swim or nothing."

"Don't you know *anything*?" said Amy, trying to match her best friend's disdain. "Haven't you heard of the greensong? How Alvin learned from them old Reds how to run through the forest like the wind, silent and not even so much as bending a branch? He can run a hundred miles in an hour, faster than any railroad train. It wasn't any kind of pool around *here*, it was so far away that it would take anybody from Vigor Church three days to get there on a good horse!"

"Now I know you're just lying," said Ramona.

"He can do that *any day*," insisted Amy hotly.

"*He* can, but *you* can't. You screech when you brush up into a spiderweb, you dunce."

"I'm not a dunce I'm the best student in the school *you're* the dunce," said Amy all in a breath—it was an epigram she had often used before. "I held Alvin's *hand* is what, and he carried me along, and then when I got tired he picked me up in those blacksmith's arms of his and carried me."

"And then I'm *sure* he really took off all his clothes and you took off all of yours, like you was a couple of weasels or something."

"Muskrats. Otters. Creatures of water. It wasn't nakedness, it was naturalness, the freeness of two kindred souls who have no secrets from each other."

"Well, what a bunch of beautifulness," said Ramona. "Only I think if it really happened it would be *disgustingness* and *revoltingness*, him coming up and hugging you in your complete and utter *starkersness*."

Amy knew that Ramona was making fun of her but she wasn't sure why making up words like *disgustingness* made the idiotic girl laugh and almost fall off the tree branch where they were sitting.

"You have no appreciation of beauty."

"You have no appreciation of *truth*," said Ramona. "Or should I say, of 'truthfulness.' "

"You calling me a liar?" said Amy, giving her a little push.

"Hey!" cried Ramona. "No fair! I'm farther out on the branch so there's nothing for me to grab onto."

Amy pushed her again, harder, and Ramona wobbled, her eyes growing wide as she clutched at the branch.

"Stop it you little liar!" cried Ramona. "I'll tell what lies you've been saying."

"They *aren't* lies," said Amy. "I remember it as clearly as . . . as clearly as the sunlight over the fields of green corn."

"As clearly as the grunting of the hogs in my father's sty," said Ramona, in a voice that matched Amy's for dreaminess.

"Of course true love would be beyond your ability to imagine."

"Yes, my imaginingness is the epitaph of feebleness."

"Epitome, not epitaph," Amy said.

"Oh, if only I could have your sublimeness of correctness, your wiseness."

"Stop *ness*ing all the time."

"*You* stop."

"I don't do that."

"Do so."

"Do not."

"Eat worms," said Ramona.

"On brain salad," said Amy. And now that they were back to familiar playful argument, they both broke into laughter and talked about other things for a while.

And if things had stayed that way, maybe nothing would have happened. But on the way back home in the gathering dusk, Ramona asked one last time, "Amy, telling truth, cross your heart, friend to friend, swear to heaven, remember forever, tell me that you didn't really actually with your own flesh and blood go swimming naked with Alvin Smith—"

"Alvin *Maker*."

"Tell me it was a dream."

Almost Amy laughed and said, Of course it was a dream, you silly girl.

But in Ramona's eyes she saw something: wide-eyed wonder at the idea that such things were possible, and that someone Ramona actually knew might have done something so wicked and wonderful. Amy didn't want to see that look of awe change to a look of knowing triumph. And so she said what she knew she shouldn't say. "I wish it was a dream, I honestly do, Ramona. Because when I think back on it I long for him all the more and I wonder when he'll dare to speak to my father and tell him that he wants me for his wife. A man who's done a thing like that with a girl—he's got to marry her, doesn't he?"

There. She had said it. The most secret wonderful dream of her heart. Said it right out.

"You've got to tell your papa," said Ramona. "He'll see to it Alvin marries you."

"I don't want him to be forced," said Amy. "That's silly. A man like Alvin can only be enticed into marriage, not pushed into it."

"Everybody thinks you're all goo-goo over Alvin and he doesn't even see you," said Ramona. "But if he's going off with you a swimming starkers in some faraway pond that only he can get to, well, I don't think that's right. I honestly don't."

"Well, I don't care what you think," said Amy. "It *is* right and if you tell I'll cut off all your hair and tat it into a doily and *burn* it."

Ramona burst out laughing. "Tat it into a *doily?* What kind of power does *that* have?"

"A six-sided doily," said Amy portentously.

"Oh, I'm trembling. Made out of my own hair, too. Silly, you can't do things like that, that's what Black witches do, make things out of hair and burn them or whatever."

As if that was an argument. Alvin did Red magic; why couldn't Amy learn to do Black magic, when her Makering knack was finally unlocked? But there was no use arguing about that sort of thing with Ramona. Ramona thought she knew better than anybody. It was a marvel that Amy even bothered to keep her as a best friend.

"I'm going to tell," said Ramona. "Unless you tell me right now that it's all a lie."

"If you tell I'll kill you," said Amy.

"Tell me it's a lie, then."

Tears sprang unbidden to Amy's eyes. It was *not* a lie. It was a dream. A true dream, of true love, a dream that came from the paths of secretness within her own and Alvin's hearts. He dreamed the same dream at the same time, she knew it, and he felt her flesh against his as surely as she felt his against hers. That made it true, didn't it? If a man and a woman both remembered the realness of each other's bodies pressing against each other, then how was that anything but a true experience? "I love Alvin too much to lie about such a thing. Cut my tongue out if any part of it is false!"

Ramona gasped. "I never believed you till now."

"But you tell *no* one," said Amy. Her heart swelled with satisfaction over her victory. Ramona finally believed her. "Swear."

"I swear," said Ramona.

"Show me your fingers!" cried Amy.

Ramona brought her hands out from behind her. The fingers weren't crossed, but that didn't prove they weren't crossed a few moments ago.

"Swear again now," said Amy. "When I can see your hands."

"I *swear*," said Ramona, rolling her eyes.

"It's our beautiful secret," said Amy, turning and walking away.

"Ours and Alvin's," said Ramona, uncrossing her ankles and following her.

7

Booking Passage

IT DIDN'T TAKE Calvin too long to figure out that it was going to take a powerful long time to earn enough money to buy passage to Europe as a gentleman. A long time and a lot of work. Neither idea sounded attractive.

He couldn't turn iron into gold, but there was plenty of things he *could* do, and he thought about them long and hard. He wasn't sure, but he didn't reckon them banks could keep him out of their vaults for long if he got to working on what all was holding them together. Still, there was a chance of being caught, and that would be the ruination of all his dreams. He thought of putting out his shingle as a Maker, but that would bring a kind of fame and attention that wouldn't stand in his favor later, not to mention all the accusations of charlatanry that would be bound to come. He was already hearing rumors of Alvin—or rather, of some prentice smith out west who turned an iron plow into gold. Half those who told the tale did it with rolled eyes, as if to say, I'm sure some western farmboy has a Maker's knack, that's likely, yes!

Sometimes Calvin wished it was a different knack he had. For instance, he could do with a torch's knack about now. Seeing the future—why, he could see which property to buy, or which ship to invest in! But even then he'd have to have a partner to put up the money, since he had nothing now. And hanging around New Amsterdam getting rich wasn't what he wanted. He wanted to learn Makering, or whatever it was that Napoleon could teach him. Having set his sights so high, the petty businessmen of Manhattan were hardly the partners he wanted.

There's more than one way to skin a cat, as the saying went. If he couldn't easily get the money for his first-class voyage, why not go direct to the source of all voyages? So it was that he found himself walking the wharfs of Manhattan, along the Hudson and the East River. It was entertaining in its own right, the long, sleek sailing ships, the clunky, smoky steamers, the stevedores shouting and grunting and sweating, the cranes swinging, the ropes and pulleys and nets, the stink of fish and the bawling of the gulls. Who would have guessed, when he was a boy rowdying in a millhouse in Vigor Church, that one day he would be here on the edge of the land, drinking in the liquorous scents and sounds and sights of the life of the sea.

Calvin wasn't one to get lost in reverie and contemplation, though. He had his eye out for the right ship, and from time to time stopped to ask a stevedore of a loading ship what the destination might be. Those as were bound for Africa or Haiti or the Orient were no use to him, but them with European destinations got a thorough looking-over. Until at last he found the right one, a bright and tall-masted English ship with a captain of some breeding who didn't seem to raise his voice at all, though all the men did his will, working hard and working smart under his eye. Everything was clean, and the cargo included trunks and parcels carefully loaded up the ramp instead of being tossed around carelesslike.

Naturally, the captain wouldn't think of talking to a boy

Calvin's age, wearing Calvin's clothes. But it wasn't hard for Calvin to think of a plan to get the captain's attention.

He walked up to one of the stevedores and said, "Scuse me, sir, but there's a sharp leak a-going near the back of the boat, on the further side."

The stevedore looked at him oddly. "I'm not a sailor."

"Neither am I, but I think the captain'll thank them as warns him of the problem."

"How can you see it, if it's under the water?"

"Got a knack for leaks," said Calvin. "I'd hurry and tell him, if I were you."

Saying it was a knack was enough for the stevedore, him being an American, even if he *was* a Dutchman by his accent. The captain, of course, wouldn't care diddly about knacks, being an Englishman, which under the Protectorate had a law against knacks. Not against having them, just against believing they existed or attempting to use them. But the captain was no fool, and he'd send somebody to check, knack or no knack.

Which is how it happened. The stevedore talking to his foreman; the foreman to some ship's officer; each time there was a lot of pointing at Calvin and staring at him as he nonchalantly whistled and looked down at the waterline of the ship. To Calvin's disappointment, the officer didn't go to the captain, but instead sent a sailor downstairs into the dark cellar of the ship. Calvin had to provide something for him to see, so now he sent out his doodlebug and got into the wood, right where he'd said the leak was. It was a simple thing to let the planks get just a little loose and out of position under the waterline, which sent a goodly stream of water spurting into the cellar of the ship. Just for the fun of it, when he figured the sailor must be down there looking at it, Calvin opened and closed the gap, so the leak was sometimes a fine spray, sometimes a gush of water, and sometimes just a trickle. Like blood seeping from a wound with an intermittent tourniquet. Bet he never saw no leak like that before, thought Calvin.

Sure enough, in a few minutes the sailor was back, acting

all agitated, and now the officer barked orders to several seamen, then went straight to the captain. This time, though, there wasn't no finger-pointing. The officer wasn't going to give Calvin none of the credit for finding the leak. That really got Calvin's goat, and for a minute he thought of sinking the boat then and there. But that wouldn't do him no good. Time enough to put that greedy ambitious officer in his place.

When the captain went below, Calvin put on a fine show for him. Instead of causing one leak to spurt and pulse, Calvin shifted the leak from one place to another—a gush here, a gush there. By now it had to be obvious that there wasn't nothing natural about that leak. There was a good deal of stirring on the deck, and a lot of sailors started rushing below. Then, to Calvin's delight, a fair number started rushing back onto the deck and onto the gangplank, heading for dry land where there wasn't no strange powers causing leaks in the boat.

Finally the captain came on deck, and this time the officer wasn't taking all the credit for himself. He pointed to the foreman, who pointed to the stevedore, and pretty soon they were all pointing at Calvin.

Now, of course, Calvin could stop fiddling with the leak. He stopped it cold. But he wasn't done. As the captain headed for the gangplank, Calvin sent his bug to seek out all the nearby rats that he could sense lurking under the wharf and among the crates and barrels and on the other ships. By the time the captain got halfway down the gangplank, a couple of dozen rats were racing up the very same bridge, heading for the ship. The captain tried in vain to shoo them back, but Calvin had filled them with courage and grim determination to reach the deck—food, food, Calvin was promising them—and they merely dodged and went on. Dozens more were streaming across the planking of the pier, and the captain was fairly dancing to avoid tripping on rats and falling on his face. On deck, sailors with mops and bowling pins were striking at the rats, trying to knock or sweep them off into the sea.

Then, as suddenly as he had launched the rats, Calvin sent

them a new message: Get off this ship. Fire, fire. Leaks. Drowning. Fear.

Squealing and scurrying, all the rats that he had sent aboard came rushing back down the gangplank and all the lines and cables connecting the ship to the shore. And all the rats that had already been aboard, lurking in the cargo hold and in the dark wet cellar and in the hidden caves in the joints and beams of the ship, they also gushed up out of the hatches and portholes like water bubbling out of a new spring. The captain stopped cold to watch them leave. Finally, when all the rat traffic had disappeared into their hiding places on the wharf and the other ships, the captain turned toward Calvin and strode to him. Through it all the man had never lost his dignity—even while dancing to avoid the rats. My kind of man, thought Calvin. I must watch him to learn how gentlemen behave.

"How did you know there was a leak on my ship?" asked the captain.

"You're an Englishman," said Calvin. "You don't believe in what I can see and do."

"Nevertheless, I believe in what *I* can see, and there was nothing natural about that leak."

"I'd say them rats might have been doing it. Good thing for you they all left your ship."

"Rats and leaks," said the captain. "What do you want, boy?"

"I want to be called a man, sir," said Calvin. "Not a boy."

"Why do you wish harm to me and my ship? Has someone of my crew done you an offense?"

"I don't know what you're talking about," said Calvin. "I reckon you're not such a fool as to blame the one as told you you had a leak."

"I'm also not such a fool as to think you knew of anything you didn't have the power to cause or cure at will. Were the rats your doing as well?"

"I was as surprised as you were by their behavior," said Calvin. "Didn't seem natural, all them rats rushing *onto* a sinking ship. But then they seemed to come to their senses and leave again. Every single rat, I daresay. Now, that would be an interesting voyage, wouldn't it—to cross the ocean without any loss of your food supply to the nibbling of rats."

"What do you want from me?" asked the captain.

"I stopped to do you a favor, with no thought of benefit to my own self," said Calvin, trying to sound like an educated Englishman and knowing from the expression on the captain's face that he was failing pathetically. "But it happens that I am in need of first-class passage to Europe."

The captain smiled thinly. "Why in the world would you want to book passage on a leaking ship?"

"But sir," said Calvin, "I've got a sort of knack for spotting leaks. And I can promise you that if I were aboard your ship, during the whole voyage there'd be not a single leak, even in the stoutest storm." Calvin had no idea whether he could keep a ship tight during all the stresses of a storm at sea, but odds were that he'd never have to find out, either.

"Correct me if I'm wrong," said the captain, "but am I to guess that if I take you on my ship, first class, without your paying a farthing, I'll find no problem with leaks and not a rat on my ship? While if I refuse, I'll find my ship at the bottom of the harbor?"

"That would be a rare disaster," said Calvin. "How could such a well-made ship possibly sink faster than your boys could pump?"

"I saw how the leak moved from place to place. I saw how strangely the rats behaved. I may not believe in your American knacks, but I know when I'm in the presence of unaccountable power."

Calvin felt pride flush through his body like ale.

Suddenly he felt the barrel of a pistol just under his breastbone. He looked down to see that the captain had somehow come up with a weapon.

"What's to stop me from blowing a hole in your belly?" asked the captain.

"The likelihood of your dancing on the end of an American

rope," said Calvin. "There ain't no law against knacks here, sir, and saying that somebody was doing witchery ain't cause enough to kill him the way it is in England."

"But it's to England you're going," said the captain. "What's to stop me from taking you on my ship, then having you arrested the moment you step ashore?"

"Nothing," said Calvin. "You could do that. You could even kill me in my sleep during the voyage and cast my body overboard into the sea, telling all the others that you had to dispose of the body of a plague victim as quickly as possible. You think I'm a fool, not to think of that stuff?"

"So go away and leave me and my ship alone."

"If you killed me, what would keep the planks from pulling free of the beams of your boat? What would stop your boat from turning into scraps of lumber bobbing on the water?"

The captain eyed him curiously.

"First-class passage is ludicrous for you. The other first-class passengers would snub you at once, and no doubt they'd assume I'd brought you aboard as my catamite. It would ruin my career anyway, to permit an uncouth, unlettered ruffian like you to sail among my gentle passengers. To put it plainly, young master, you may have power over rats and planks, but you have none over rich men and women."

"Teach me," said Calvin.

"There aren't enough hours in the day or days in the week."

"Teach me," said Calvin again.

"You come here threatening me with destruction of my ship by the evil powers of Satan, and then dare to ask me to teach you to be a gentleman?"

"If you believed my powers were from the devil," said Calvin, "then why didn't you once say a prayer to ward me off?"

The captain glared at him for a moment, then smiled, grimly but not without genuine mirth. "Touché," he said.

"Whatever the devil *that* means," said Calvin.

"It's a fencing term," said the captain.

"I must've put up ten miles of fences in my life," said Calvin.

"Post and rail, stone, wire, and picket, every kind, and I never heard of no tooshay."

The captain's smile broadened. "There is something attractive in your challenge. You may have some interesting . . . what do you call them . . . knacks? But you're still a poor boy from the farm. I've taken many a peasant lad and turned him into a first-rate seaman. But I've never taken a boy who wasn't a gentleman born and turned him into something that could pass for civilized."

"Consider me the challenge of your life."

"Oh, believe me, I already do. I haven't altogether decided not to kill you, of course. But it seems to me that since you mean to cause me trouble anyway, why not accept the challenge and see if I can work a miracle just as inexplicable and impossible as any of the nasty pranks you've played on me this morning?"

"First class, not steerage," Calvin insisted.

The captain shook his head. "Neither one. You'll travel as my cabin boy. Or rather, my cabin boy's boy. Rafe is a good three years younger than you, I imagine, but he knows from birth all that you are so desperate to learn. With you to help him, perhaps he'll have enough free time to teach you. And I'll oversee you both. On several conditions, though."

Calvin didn't see as how the captain was in much of a position to set conditions, but he listened civil-like all the same.

"No matter what powers you have, survival at sea depends on instant and perfect obedience from everyone on board the ship. Obedience to *me*. You know nothing of the sea and I gather you don't care about learning seamanship, either. So you will do nothing that interferes with my authority. And you will obey me yourself. That means that when I say piss, you don't even look for a pot, you just whip it out and pee."

"In front of others, I'll do a fine show of obedience, unless you command me to kill myself or some such foolishness."

"I'm not a fool," said the captain.

"All right, I'll do like you say."

"And you'll keep your mouth shut until you learn—in *private*—to talk in some way approximating gentlemanly speech. Right now if you open your mouth you confess your low origins and you will embarrass yourself and me in front of my crew and the other officers and passengers."

"I know how to keep my mouth shut when I need to."

"And when you reach England, our deal is done and you leave no curse on my ship."

"Now you've asked too much," said Calvin. "What I need is your introduction to other high-class people. And passage to France."

"To France! Aren't you aware that England is at war with France?"

"You *have* been ever since Napoleon conquered Austria and Spain. What's that to me?"

"In other words, reaching England doesn't mean I'll be rid of you."

"That's right," said Calvin.

"So why don't I just kill myself now and spare myself all this adventure before you send me to an early grave?"

"Because them as is my friends will prosper in this world and there ain't nothing much bad that can happen to them."

"And all I have to do is maintain my status as your friend, is that it?"

Calvin nodded.

"But someday, isn't it going to occur to you that if the only reason I'm kind to you is out of terror that you'll destroy my ship, I'm not really your friend at all?"

Calvin smiled. "That just means you'll have to try extra hard to convince me that you really mean it."

The officer who had first heard Calvin's message now approached the captain diffidently. "Captain Fitzroy," he said. "The leaking seems to have stopped, sir."

"I know," said the captain.

"Thank you sir," said the officer.

"Get everyone back to work, Benson," said the captain.

"Some of the American stevedores and sailors won't get back on that ship no matter what we say, sir."

"Pay them off and hire others," said the captain. "That will be all, Benson."

"Yes sir." Benson turned around and headed back toward the gangplank.

Calvin, in the meantime, had heard the air of crisp command in Captain Fitzroy's voice and wondered how a man could learn to use his voice like a sharp hot knife, slicing through other men's will like warm butter.

"I would say you've already caused me more trouble than you're worth," said Captain Fitzroy. "And I personally doubt that you have it in you to learn to be a gentleman, though heaven knows there are plenty that have the title who are every bit as ignorant and boorish as you. But I will accept your coercive agreement, in part because I find you fascinating as well as despicable."

"I don't know what all them words mean, Captain Fitzroy, but I know this—Taleswapper once told us how when kings have bastards, the babies get the last name 'Fitzroy.' So no matter what I am, your name says you're a son of a bitch."

"In my case, the great-great-grandson of a bitch. The second Charles sowed his wild oats. My great-great-grandmother, a noted actress of semi-noble origins, entered into a liaison with him and managed to get her child recognized as royal before the parliament deprived him of his head. My family has had its ups and downs since the end of the monarchy, and there have been Lords Protector who thought that our association with the royal family made us dangerous. But we managed to survive and even, in recent years, prosper. Unfortunately, I'm the younger son of a younger son, so I had the choice of the church or the army or the sea. Until meeting you, I did not regret my choice. Do you have a name, my young extortionist?"

"Calvin," he said.

"And are you of such a benighted family that you have but the one name to spend as your patrimony?"

"Maker," said Calvin. "Calvin Maker."

"How deliciously vague. Maker. A general term that can be construed in many ways while promising no particular skill. A Calvin of all trades. And master of none?"

"Master of rats," said Calvin, smiling. "And leaks."

"As we have seen," said Captain Fitzroy. "I will have your name enrolled as part of the ship's company. Have your gear aboard by nightfall."

"If you have someone follow me to kill me, your ship—"

"Will dissolve into sawdust, yes, the threat has already been made," said Fitzroy. "Now you only have to worry about how much I actually care for my ship."

With that, Fitzroy turned his back on Calvin and headed up the gangplank. Calvin almost made him slip and take a pratfall, just to pierce that dignity. But there was a limit, he knew, to how far he could push this man. Especially since Calvin hadn't the slightest idea how to carry out his threat to make the ship fall apart if they killed him. Either he could make the ship leak or stop leaking, but either way he had to be there and alive to do it. If Fitzroy ever realized that his worst threats were pure bluff, how long would he let Calvin live?

Get used to it, Calvin, he told himself. Plenty of people have wanted Alvin dead, too, but he got through it all. We Makers must have some kind of protection, it's as simple as that. All of nature is looking out for us, to keep us safe. Fitzroy won't kill me because I can't be killed.

I hope.

⭓ 8 ⭔

Leavetaking

FOR SOME REASON Alvin's classroom of grownup women just wasn't going well today. They were distracted, it seemed like, and Goody Sump was downright hostile. It finally came to a head when Alvin started working with their herb boxes. He was trying to help them find their way into the greensong, the first faintest melody, by getting their sage or sorrel or thyme, whatever herb they chose, to grow one specially long branch. This was something Alvin reckoned to be fairly easy, but once you mastered it, you could pretty much get into harmony with any plant. However, only a couple of the women had had much success, and Goody Sump was not one of them. Maybe that was how come she was so testy—her laurel wasn't even thriving, let alone showing lopsided growth on one branch.

"The plants don't make the same music they did back when the Reds were tending the woods," Alvin said. He was going to go on and explain how they could do, in a small way, what the Reds did large, but he didn't get a chance, because that was the moment Goody Sump chose to erupt.

She leapt from her chair, strode over to the herb table, and brought her fist right down on top of her own laurel, capsizing the pot and spattering potting soil and laurel leaves all over the table and her own dress. "If you think them Reds was so much better why don't you just go live with *them* and carry off *their* daughters to secret randy views!"

Alvin was so stunned by her unprovoked rage, so perplexed by her inscrutable words, that he just looked at her gape-mouthed as she pulled what was left of her laurel out of what was left of the soil, pulled off a handful of leaves, and threw them in his face, then turned and stalked out of the room.

As soon as she was gone, Alvin tried to make a joke out of it. "I reckon there's some folks as don't take natural to agriculture." But hardly anybody laughed.

"You got to overlook her behavior, Al," said Sylvy Godshadow. "A mother's got to believe her own daughter, even if everybody else knows she's spinning moonbeams."

Since Goody Sump had five daughters, and Alvin had heard nothing significant about any of them lately, this information wasn't much help. "Is Goody Sump having some trouble at home?" he asked.

The women all looked around at each other, but not a one would meet his eyes.

"Well, it looks to me like everybody here knows somewhat as hasn't yet found its way to my ears," said Alvin. "Anybody mind explaining?"

"We're not gossips," said Sylvy Godshadow. "I'm surprised you'd think to accuse us." With that, she stood up and started for the door.

"But I didn't call nobody a gossip," said Alvin.

"Alvin, I think before you criticize others, you'd comb the lice out of your own hair," said Nana Pease. And she was up and off, too.

"Well, what are the rest of you waiting for?" said Alvin. "If you all wanted a day off of class, you only had to ask. It's a sure thing *I'm* done for the day."

Before he could even get started sweeping up the spilt soil, the other ladies had all flounced out.

Alvin tried to console himself by muttering things he'd heard his own father mutter now and then over the years, things like "Women" and "Can't do nothing to please 'em" and "Might as well shoot yourself first thing in the morning." But none of that helped, because this *wasn't* just some normal display of temper. These were levelheaded ladies, every one of them, and here they were up in arms over plain nothing, which wasn't natural.

It wasn't till afternoon that Alvin realized something serious was wrong. A couple of months ago, Alvin had asked Clevy Sump, Goody Sump's husband, to teach them all how to make a simple one-valve suction pump. It was part of Alvin's idea to teach folks that making is making, and everybody ought to know everything they can possibly learn. Alvin was teaching them hidden powers of Making, but they ought to be learning how to make with their hands as well. Secretly Alvin also hoped that when they saw how tricky and careful it was to make fine machinery like Clevy Sump did, they'd realize that what Alvin was teaching wasn't much harder if it was harder at all. And it was working well enough.

Except that today, after the noon bread and cheese, he went on out to the mill to find the men gathered around the wreckage of the pumps they'd been making. Every one of them was broke in pieces. And since the fittings were all metal, it must have took some serious work to break it all up. "Who'd do a thing like this?" Alvin asked. "There's a lot of hate goes into something like *this*." And thinking of hate, it made Alvin wonder if maybe Calvin hadn't come back secretly after all.

"There's no mystery who done it," said Winter Godshadow. "I reckon we ain't got us a pump-making teacher no more."

"Yep," said Taleswapper. "This looks like a specially thorough way of telling us, 'Class dismissed.'"

Some of the men chuckled. But Alvin could see that he wasn't the only one angry at the destruction. After all, these pumps were nearly completed, and all these men had put serious work into making them. They counted on them at their own houses. For many of them, it meant the end of drawing water, and Winter Godshadow in particular had got him a plan to pipe the water right into the kitchen, so his wife wouldn't even have to go outdoors to fetch it. Now their work was undone, and some of them weren't taking kindly to it.

"Let me talk to Clevy Sump about this," said Alvin. "I can't hardly believe it was him, but if it was, whatever's the problem I bet it can be set to rights. I don't want none of you getting angry at him before he's had his say."

"We ain't angry at *Clevy*," said Nils Torson, a burly Swede. His heavy-lidded gaze made it clear who he *was* angry at.

"Me?" said Alvin. "You think *I* done this?" Then, as if he could hear Miss Larner's voice in his ear, he corrected himself: "*Did* this?"

Murmurs from several of the men assented to the proposition.

"Are you crazy? Why would I go to all this trouble? I'm not an Unmaker, boys, you know that, but if I was, don't you think I could tear up these pumps a lot more thoroughly without taking half so much trouble?"

Taleswapper cleared his throat. "Perhaps you and I ought to talk alone about this, Alvin."

"They're accusing me of wrecking all their hard work and it ain't so!" said Alvin.

"Ain't nobody accusin' nobody of nothin'," said Winter Godshadow. "God follows all. God sees all deeds."

Usually when Winter got into his God-talking moods, the others would sort of back off and pretend to be busy paring their nails or something. But not this time—this time they were nodding and murmuring their agreement.

"Like I said, Alvin, let's you and me have a word. In fact, I think we ought to go on up to the house and talk to your father and mother."

"Talk to me right here," said Alvin. "I'm not some little boy to be taken out behind the woodshed and given a licking in private. If I stand accused of something that everybody knows about except me . . ."

"We ain't accusing," said Nils. "We're pondering."

"Pondering," echoed a couple of the others.

"Tell me here and now what you're pondering," said Alvin. "Because whatever I'm accused of, if it's true I want to make it right, and if it's false I want to set it straight."

They looked at each other back and forth, until finally Alvin turned to Taleswapper. "*You* tell me."

"I only repeat tales that I believe to be true," said Taleswapper. "And this one I believe to be a flat-out lie told by a dreamy-hearted girl."

"Girl? What girl?" and then, putting together Goody Sump's behavior and what Clevy Sump had done to the pumps, and remembering the dreamy expression in one girl's eyes when she sat there in the children's class paying no intelligent attention to a thing that Alvin said, he jumped to a certain conclusion and whispered her name. "Amy."

To Alvin's consternation, some of the men took the fact that he came up with her name as proof that Amy was telling the truth about whatever it was she had said. "See?" they murmured. "See?"

"I'm done with this," said Nils. "I'm done. I'm a farmer. Corn and hogs, that's my knack if I have me any." When he left, several other men went with him.

Alvin turned to the others. "I *don't* know what I'm accused of, but I can promise you this, I've done nothing wrong. In the meantime, it's plain there's no use in holding class today, so let's all go home. I reckon there's a way to salvage every one of these pumps, so your work isn't lost. We'll get back to it tomorrow."

As they left, some of the men touched Alvin's shoulder or punched his arm to show their support. But some of the support was of a kind he didn't much like. "Can't hardly blame you, pretty little calf-eyed thing like that." "Women is always reading more into things than a man means."

Finally Alvin was alone with Taleswapper.

"Don't look at me," said Taleswapper. "Let's go on up to the house and see if your father's heard the stories yet."

When they got there, it was like a family council was already in session. Measure, Armor-of-God, and Father and Mother were all gathered around the kitchen table. Arthur Stuart was kneading dough—small as he was, he was good with bread and liked doing it, so Mother had finally given in and admitted that a woman could still be mistress of her own house even if somebody else made the bread.

"Glad you're here, Al," said Measure. "You'd think a piece of silliness like this would just get laughed out of town. I mean, these folks should *know* you."

"Why should they?" asked Mother. "He's been gone most of the past seven years. When he left he was a scrub-size boy who'd just spent a year running around the countryside with a Red warrior. When he come back he was full of power and majesty and scared the pellets out of all the bunny-hearts around here. What do they know of his character?"

"Would somebody please tell me what this is *about*?" Alvin said.

"You mean they haven't?" asked Father. "They were powerful quick to tell your mother and Measure and Armor-of-God."

Taleswapper chuckled. "Of course they didn't tell Alvin. Those who believe the tale assume he already knows. And those who don't believe it are plain ashamed that anyone could say such silly slander."

Measure sighed. "Amy Sump told her friend Ramona, and Ramona told her mama, and her mama went straight to Goody Sump, and she went straight to her husband, and he like to went crazy because he can't conceive that every male creature larger than a mouse isn't hottin' up after his nubian daughter."

"Nubile," Alvin corrected him.

"Yeah yeah," said Measure. "I know, you're the one who reads the books, and now's *sure* the time to correct my grammar."

"Nubians are Black Africans," said Alvin. "And Amy ain't no Black near as I can figure."

"This might be a good time to shut up and listen," said Measure.

"Yes *sir*," said Alvin.

"If only you had left when that torch girl sent you that warning," said Mother. "It's a plain fool who stays inside a burning house because he wants to see the color of the flames."

"What's Amy saying about me?" asked Alvin.

"Pure nonsense," said Father. "About you running off in the Red way, a hundred miles in a night through the woods, taking her to a secret lake where you swum nekkid and other such indecencies."

"With *Amy*?" asked Alvin, incredulous.

"Meaning that you'd do it with someone else?" asked Measure.

"I'd do such a thing with nobody," said Alvin. "Ain't decent, and besides, there ain't enough unbroken living forest these days to *get* a hundred miles in a night. I can't make half so good a speed through fields and farms. The greensong gets noisy and busted up and I get too tired trying to hear it and *why* is anybody believing such silliness?"

"Because they think you can do anything," said Measure.

"And because a good number of these men have noticed Amy filling out of late," said Armor-of-God, "and they know that if *they* had the power, and if Amy was as moony toward them as she plainly is toward you, they'd have her naked in a lake in two seconds flat."

"You're too cynical about human nature," said Taleswapper. "Most of these fellows are the wishing kind. But they know Alvin is a doer, not just a wisher."

"I hardly noticed her except to think she was sure slow to learn, considering how tight she seemed to pay attention," said Alvin.

"To *you* she was paying attention. Not to what you said or taught," said Measure.

"Well it ain't so. I didn't do anything to her or with her, and . . ."

"And even if you did it would be plain disaster if you married her," said Mother.

"*Married* her!" cried Alvin.

"Well of course if it was true, you'd have to marry her," said Father.

"But it *ain't* true."

"You got any witnesses of that?" asked Measure.

"Witnesses of what? How can I have witnesses that it didn't happen? Everybody's my witness—everybody didn't see any such thing."

"But she says it happened," said Measure. "And you're the only other one who knows whether she's lying or not. So either she's a plain liar and you're innocently accused, or she's a brokenhearted lied-to seduced girl and you're the cad who got the use of her and now won't do the decent thing, and nobody can prove either way."

"So *you* don't even believe me?"

"Of course we believe you," said Father. "Do you think we're insane? But our believing you ain't any kind of evidence. Measure's been reading law, and he explained it to us."

"Law?" asked Alvin.

"Well, afore you come home from Hatrack River, anyway. And now and then since. I reckon somebody in the family ought to know something about the law."

"But you mean you think this might come to court?"

"Might," said Measure. "That's what the Sumps were saying. Get them a lawyer from Carthage City instead of one of the frontier lawyers as has a shingle out here in Vigor Church. Lots of publicity."

"But they can't convict me of anything!"

"Breach of promise. Indecent liberties with a child. All depends on how many jurors think that where there's smoke, there's fire."

"Indecent liberties with a . . ."

"That one's a hanging offense, all right," said Measure. "But I hear that's the charge that Clevy wants to bring."

"Doesn't matter if they convict you or not," said Taleswapper.

"Matters to *me*," said Mother.

"Either way, the tale will spread. Alvin the so-called Maker, taking advantage of young girls. You can't let this go to trial," said Taleswapper.

Alvin saw at once how such rumors, such publicity as a trial would bring, it would bring down his work, make it impossible to attract others to come and learn Making at Vigor Church.

Not that he was doing much good teaching Making anyway.

"Miss Larner," murmured Alvin.

"Yep," said Taleswapper. "She warned you. Leave now freely, or leave later because you have to."

"Why should he be driven from his own home just because a horny lying little . . ." Mother's voice trailed off.

Alvin sat in the ensuing silence, recognizing his foolishness. "I spose I'm a plain fool for not heeding Miss Larner." And then, stiffening his back, he closed his eyes and said, "There's another way. So I don't have to leave at all."

"What's that?" asked Measure.

"I could marry her."

"No!" cried Mother and Father at once.

"Why not just sign a confession?" asked Armor-of-God.

"You can't marry her," said Measure.

"It's what she wants," said Alvin. "You can bet she'd say yes, and her father and mother would have to agree to it."

"Agree to it—and then despise you ever after," said Father.

"Doesn't matter about his reputation or what people think of him or anything, compared to this," said Measure. "Waking up every morning and seeing Amy Sump in bed next to you, and knowing the only reason she's there is because she slandered you—tell me what kind of home you'll make, the two of you, for your babies?"

Alvin thought about that for a moment and nodded. "I guess

marriage ain't much of a solution. More like starting a whole new set of problems."

"Ah, good," said Father. "I was afraid we'd raised us a fool."

"So I sneak off like a thief, and everybody reckons Amy was telling the truth and I ran off."

"Not likely," said Measure. "We'll let it be known that you left because your work is too important to be distracted by this nonsense. You'll be back when Amy starts telling the truth, and in the meantime, you'll be studying up on . . . whatever. Learning something."

"Learning how to build the Crystal City," murmured Taleswapper.

They all looked at him.

"You don't know how, do you, Alvin?" asked Taleswapper. "While you're busy trying to make Makers out of these people, you don't even know yourself what the Crystal City really is, or how to make it."

Alvin nodded. "That's right."

"So . . . it isn't even a lie," said Taleswapper. "You *do* have much to learn, and you're overdue to learn it. Why, you're even grateful to Amy for showing you that you've been hanging around here far too long. Measure's been learning right good. He's far enough ahead of the others that he can go on teaching in your absence. And him being a married man, no schoolgirl's going to get some foolish notion about *him*."

"I don't know," said Measure. "I'm pretty cute."

"You have my bags packed yet, Taleswapper?" asked Alvin.

"Ain't as if you need much luggage," said Taleswapper. "You're going to be traveling small and fast. I reckon there's only one burden that will weigh you down much. A certain farm implement."

"I couldn't leave it here?" asked Alvin.

"Not safe," said Taleswapper. "Not safe for your family, to have the rumor get about that the Maker is gone but he left the golden plow behind."

"Not safe for *him* to have the rumor say he took it with him," said Mother.

"Nobody on this planet is safer than Alvin, if he wants to be," said Measure.

"So I just pick up the plow, put it in a gunnysack, and head on out?" asked Alvin.

"That's about the best plan," said Armor-of-God. "Though I bet your ma will insist on you taking some salt pork with you, and a change of clothes."

"And me."

They all turned to the source of the small piping voice.

"He's taking me with him," said Arthur Stuart.

"You'd only slow him down, boy," said Father. "You got a good heart, but short legs."

"He ain't in no hurry," said Arthur, "specially figuring as he don't know where he's going."

"The point is you'd be in the way," said Armor-of-God. "He'd always have to be thinking of you, trying to keep you out of harm's way. There's plenty of places in this land where a free half-Black boy is going to get folks' dander up, and that won't be much help to Alvin either."

"You're talking like you think you got a choice," said Arthur. "But if Alvin goes, I go, and that's it. You can lock me in a closet, but someday I'll get out and then I'll follow him and find him or die trying."

They all looked at him in consternation. Arthur Stuart had been near silent since coming to Vigor after his adopted mother was murdered back in Hatrack River. Silent but hardworking, cooperative, obedient. This was a complete surprise, this attitude from him.

"And besides," said Arthur Stuart, "while Alvin's busy looking after the whole world, I'll be there to look after *him*."

"I think the boy should go," said Measure. "The Unmaker plainly ain't done with Alvin yet. He needs somebody to watch his back. I think Arthur's got it in him."

And that was pretty much it. Nobody could size up a fellow like Measure could.

Alvin walked to the hearth and pried up four stones. Nobody would have guessed that anything was hid under them, because until he raised the stones there wasn't so much as a crack in the mortar. He didn't dig in the earth under the stones; the plow was buried eight feet deep, and shoveling would have taken all day, not to mention the dismantling of the entire hearth. No, he just held out his hands and called to the plow, and willed the earth to float it up to him. A moment later, the plow bobbed to the surface of the soil like a cork on a still pond. Alvin could hear a couple of sharp breaths behind him— it still got to folks, even his own family, when he showed his knack so openly. Also, the gold had such a luster to it. As if, even in the pitch black of the darkest moonless stormy night, that plow would still be visible, the gold burning its way even through your closed eyelids to imprint its shining life straight onto your eyes, straight into your brain. The plow trembled under Alvin's hand.

"We got us a journey to take," Alvin murmured to the warm gold. "And maybe along the way we'll figure out what I made you for."

An hour later, Alvin stood at the back door of the house. Not that it took him an hour to pack—he'd spent most of the time down at the mill, fixing the pumps. Nor had he spent any of the time on farewells. They hadn't even sent word to any of the family that he was going, because word would get out and the last thing Alvin needed was for folks to be lying in wait for him when he headed into the forest. Mother and Father and Measure and Armor would have to carry his words of love and Godblessyou to his brothers and sisters and nieces and nephews.

Alvin hitched the bag with the plow and his change of clothes in it over his shoulder. Arthur Stuart took his other hand. Alvin scanned the hexes he'd laid in place around the house and made sure they were still perfect in their sixness, undisturbed by wind or meddling. All was in order. It was the only thing he could do for his family in his absence, was to keep wardings about to fend off danger.

"Don't you worry about Amy, neither," said Measure. "Soon as you're gone, she'll notice some other strapping boy and pretty soon the dreams and stories will be about *him* and folks'll realize that you never done nothing wrong."

"Hope you're right," said Alvin. "Because I don't intend to stay away for long."

Those words hung in the silence for a moment, because they all knew it was quite possible that this time Alvin might be gone for good. Might never come home. It was a dangerous world, and the Unmaker had plainly gone to some trouble to get Alvin out of here and onto the road.

He kissed and hugged all around, taking care not to let the heavy plow smack into anybody. And then he was off for the woods behind the house, sauntering so as to give anyone watching him the impression that this was just a casual errand he was on, and not some life-changing escape. Arthur Stuart had ahold of his left hand again. And to Alvin's surprise, Taleswapper fell into step right beside him.

"You coming with me, then?" asked Alvin.

"Not far," said Taleswapper. "Just to talk a minute."

"Glad to have you," said Alvin.

"I just wondered if you've given any thought to finding Peggy Larner," said Taleswapper.

"Not even for a second," said Alvin.

"What, are you mad at her? Hell, boy, if you'd just listened to her . . ."

"You think I don't know that? You think I haven't been thinking of that this whole time?"

"I'm just saying that you two was on the verge of marrying back there in Hatrack River, and you could do with a good wife, and she's the best you'll ever find."

"Since when do you meddle?" asked Alvin. "I thought you just collected stories. I didn't think you made them happen."

"I was afraid you'd be angry at her like this."

"I'm not angry at her. I'm angry at myself."

"Alvin, you think I don't know a lie when I hear it?"

"All right, I *am* angry. She knew, right? Well, why didn't she just *tell* me? Amy Sump is going to tell lies about you and force you to leave, so get out now before her childish imaginings ruin everything."

"Because if she said that, you wouldn't have left, would you, Alvin? You would have stayed, figuring you could make everything work out fine with Amy. Why, you would have taken her aside and told her not to love you, right? And *then* when she started talking about you, there'd be witnesses who remembered how she stayed after class one day and was alone with you, and then you *would* be in trouble because even *more* people would believe her story and—"

"Taleswapper, I wish you sometime would learn the knack of shutting up!"

"Sorry," said Taleswapper. "I just don't have any gift for that. I just blather on, annoying people. The fact is that Peggy told you as much as she could without making things worse."

"That's right. In her judgment, she decided how much I was entitled to know, and that's all she told me. And then you have the gall to tell me I should go *marry* her?"

"I'm not following your logic here, Al," said Taleswapper.

"What kind of marriage is it, when my wife knows *everything* but she never tells me enough to make up my own mind! Instead she always makes up my mind for me. Or tells me exactly what she needs to tell me in order to get me to do what *she* thinks I ought to do."

"But you didn't do what she said you ought to do. You stuck around."

"So that's the life you want for me? Either to obey my wife in everything, or wish I had!"

Taleswapper shrugged. "I'm still not getting your objection."

"It's this simple: A grownup man doesn't want to be married to his mother. He wants to make his own decisions."

"I'm sure you're right," said Taleswapper. "And who's this grownup man you're talking about?"

Alvin refused to be baited. "I hope someday it's me. But it'll never be me if I tie myself to a torch. I owe much to Miss Larner. And I owe even more to the girl she was before she became a teacher, the girl who watched over me and saved my life again and again. No wonder I loved her. But marrying her would have been the worst mistake of my life. It would have made me weak. Dependent. My knack might have remained in my hands, but it would be entirely at her service, and that's no way for a man to live."

"A *grownup* man, you mean."

"Mock me all you want, Taleswapper. I notice *you* got no wife."

"I must be a grownup, then," said Taleswapper. But now there was an edge to his voice, and after gazing at Alvin for just another moment, he turned and walked back the way they'd come together.

"I never seen Taleswapper mad like that before," said Arthur Stuart.

"He doesn't like it when folks throw his own advice back in his face," said Alvin.

Arthur Stuart said nothing. Just waited.

"All right, let's go."

At once Arthur turned and started walking.

"Well, wait for me," said Alvin.

"Why?" said Arthur Stuart. "You don't know where we're going, either."

"Reckon not, but I'm bigger, so I get to choose which nowhere we head for."

Arthur laughed a little. "I bet there's not a single direction you can choose where there isn't *somebody* standing in your road, somewhere. Even if it's halfway around the world."

"I don't know about that," said Alvin. "But I know for sure that no matter which way we go, eventually we'll run into the ocean. Can you swim?"

"Not an ocean's worth I can't."

"So what good are *you*, then?" said Alvin. "I was counting on you to tow me across."

Hand in hand they plunged deeper into the woods. And even though Alvin didn't know where he was going, he did know this: The greensong might be weak and jumbled these days, but it was still there, and he couldn't help but fall into it and start moving in perfect harmony with the greenwood. The twigs leaned out of his way; the leaves were soft under his feet, and soon he was soundless, leaving no trail behind him and making no disturbance as he went.

That night they camped on the shore of Lake Mizogan. If you could call it camping, since they made no fire and built no shelter. They broke of the woods late in the afternoon and stood there on the shore. Alvin remembered being at this lake—not quite this spot, but not far off either—when Tenskwa-Tawa had called a whirlwind and cut his feet and walked out on the bloody water, taking Alvin with him, drawing him up into the whirlwind and showing him visions. It was then that Alvin first saw the Crystal City and knew that he would build it someday, or rather rebuild it, since it had existed once before, or maybe more than once. But the storm was gone, a distant memory; Tenskwa-Tawa and his people were gone, too, most of them dead and the rest of them in the west. Now it was just a lake.

Once Alvin would have been afraid of the water, for it was water that the Unmaker had used to try to kill him, over and over, when he was a child. But that was before Alvin grew into his knack and became a true Maker that night in the forge, turning iron into gold. The Unmaker couldn't touch him through water anymore. No, the Unmaker's tool would be more subtle now. It would be people. People like Amy Sump, weak-willed or greedy or dreamy or lazy, but all of them easily used. It was people who held danger for him now. Water was safe enough, for them as could swim, and that was Alvin.

"How about a dip in the water?" Alvin asked.

Arthur shrugged. It was when they dipped together in the water of the Hio that the last traces of Arthur's old self got washed away. But there'd be none of that now. They just stripped down and swam in the lake as the sun set, then lay down in the grass to dry off, the moonlight making the water shine, a breeze making the humid air cool enough for sleeping. In the whole journey they hadn't said a word till they got to the shore of the lake, just moved in perfect harmony through the wood; even now as they swam, they still said nothing, and hardly splashed they were so much in harmony with everything, with each other. So it startled Alvin when Arthur spoke to him, lying there in the dark.

"This is what Amy dreamed of, ain't it?"

Alvin thought of that for a moment. Then he got up and put on his clothes. "I reckon we're dry now," he said.

"You think maybe she had a true dream? Only it wasn't her, it was me?"

"I didn't do no hugging or unnatural things when we was naked in the water," said Alvin.

Arthur laughed. "Ain't nothin' unnatural about what *she* dreamed of."

"It wasn't no true dream."

Arthur got up and put his clothes on, too. "I heard the greensong this time, Alvin. Three times I let go of your hand, and I still heard it for the longest time before it started fading and I had to catch your hand or get left behind."

Alvin nodded as if that was what he expected. But it wasn't. In all his teaching of the folks of Vigor Church, he hadn't even *tried* to teach Arthur Stuart much, sending him instead to the schoolhouse to learn reading and ciphering. But it was Arthur who might well be his best student after all.

"You going to become a Maker?" asked Alvin.

Arthur shook his head. "Not me," he said. "Just going to be your friend."

Alvin didn't say aloud the thought of his heart: To be my

friend, you might just have to be a Maker. He didn't have to say it. Arthur already understood.

The wind rose a little in the night, and far away, out over the lake, lightning brightened the underside of distant clouds. Arthur breathed softly in his sleep; Alvin could hear him in the stillness, louder than the whisper of distant thunder. It should have made him feel lonely, but it didn't. The breaths in the darkness beside him could have been Ta-Kumsaw on their long journey so many years ago, when Alvin had been called the Boy Renegado and the fate of the world seemed to hang in the balance. Or it might have been his brother Calvin when as boys they shared a room; Alvin remembered him as a baby in a cradle, then in a crib, the child's eyes looking up to him as if he were God, as if he knew something no other human knew. Well, I did know it, but I lost Calvin anyway. And I saved Ta-Kumsaw's life, but couldn't do a thing to save his cause, and he is lost to me also, across the river in the fog of the Red west.

And the breathing could have been a wife, instead of just a dream of a wife. Alvin tried to imagine Amy Sump there in the darkness, and even though Measure was right that it would have been a miserable marriage, the fact was that her face was pretty, and in this moment of solitary wakefulness Alvin could imagine that her young body was sweet and warm to the touch, her kiss eager and full of life and hope.

Quickly he shrugged off that image. Amy was not for him, and even to imagine her like that felt akin to some kind of awful crime. He could never marry someone who worshipped him. Because his wife would not be married to the Maker named Alvin; his wife would be married to the man.

It was Peggy Larner he thought of then. He imagined leaning up on one elbow and looking at her when the low distant lightning cast a brush of light across her face. Her hair loose and tousled in the grass. Her ladylike hands no longer controlled and graceful with studied gestures, but now casually flung out in sleep.

To his surprise tears came to his eyes. In a moment he realized why: She was as impossible for him as Amy, not because she would worship him, but because she was more committed to his cause than he was. She loved, not the Maker, and certainly not the man, but rather the Making and the thing made. To marry her would be a kind of surrender to fate, for she was the one who saw futures that might arise out of all possible present choices, and if he married her he would be no man at all, not because she would mean to unman him, but because he himself would not be so stupid as not to follow her advice. Freely he would follow her, and thus freely lose his freedom.

No, it was Arthur lying there beside him, this strange boy who loved Alvin beyond all reason and yet demanded nothing from him; this boy who had lost a part of himself in order to be free, and had replaced it with a part of Alvin.

The parallel was suddenly obvious to Alvin, and for a moment he was ashamed. I did to Arthur just what I fear that Peggy Larner might do to me. I took away a part of him and replaced it with myself. Only he was so young and his danger so great that I didn't ask him or explain, nor could he have understood me if I tried. He had no choice. I still have one.

Would I be as content as Arthur, if once I gave myself to Peggy?

Perhaps someday, Alvin thought. But not now. I'm not ready yet to give myself to someone, to surrender my will. The way Arthur has to me. The way parents do to their children, giving their lives over to the needs of helpless selfish little ones. The road is open before me, all roads, all possibilities. From this grassy bed beside Lake Mizogan I can go anywhere, find all that is findable, do all that is doable, make all that can be made. Why should I build a fence around myself? Leash myself to one tree? Not even a horse, not even a dog was loyal enough to do such a mad thing to itself.

From infancy on his knack had captured him. Whether as a child in his family, as Ta-Kumsaw's traveling companion, as a prentice smith, or as a teacher of would-be Makers, he had been hobbled by his knack. But not now.

The lightning flashed again, farther off this time. There would be no rain here tonight. And tomorrow he would get up and go south, or north, or west, or east, as the idea struck him, seeking whatever goal seemed desirable. He had left home to get away, not to go toward anything. There was no greater freedom than that.

❖ 9 ❖

Cooper

PEGGY LARNER KEPT watch on both of those bright heartfires: Alvin as he wandered through America, Calvin as he made his way to England and prepared for his audience with Napoleon. There was little change in the possible futures that she saw, for neither man's plan was one whit altered.

Alvin's plan, of course, was no plan at all. He and Arthur Stuart, traveling afoot, made their way westward from Mizogan, past the growing town of Chicago and on until the dense fogs of the Mizzipy turned them back. Alvin had entertained a vague hope that he, at least, would be permitted to pass to the Mizzipy and beyond, but if such a thing would ever be possible, it certainly was not possible now. So he went north all the way to High Water Lake, where he boarded one of the new steamboats that was carrying iron ore to Irrakwa, where it would be loaded on trains and carried the rest of the way to the coal country of Suskwahenny and Pennsylvania, to feed into the new steel mills. "Is that Making?" asked Arthur Stuart, when Alvin explained the process to him. "Turning iron into steel?"

"It's a sort of Making," said Alvin, "where earth is forced by fire. But the cost is high, and the iron aches when it's been transformed like that. I've seen some of the steel they've made. It's in the rails. It's in the locomotives. The metal screams all the time, a soft sound, very high, but I can hear it."

"Does that mean it's evil to use steel?" asked Arthur Stuart.

"No," said Alvin. "But we should only use it when it's worth the cost of such suffering. Maybe someday we'll find a better way to bring the iron up to strength. I *am* a smith. I won't deny the forgefire or refuse the hammer and the anvil. Nor will I say that the foundries of Dekane are somehow worse than my small forge. I've been inside the flame. I know that the iron can live in it too, and come out unhurt."

"Maybe that's what we're wandering for," said Arthur Stuart. "For you to go to the foundries and help them make steel more kindly."

"Maybe," said Alvin, and they rode the train to Dekane and Alvin applied for work in a foundry and learned by watching and doing all the things there was to know about the making of steel, and in the end he said, "I found a way, but it takes a Maker to do it, or pretty close." And there it was: If Alvin was to change the world, it required him to do what he had already half-failed at doing back in Vigor Church, which was to make more Makers. They left the steeltowns and went on east and as Peggy watched Alvin's heartfire she saw no change, no change, no change. . . .

And then one day, of a sudden, for no reason she could see in Alvin's life, a thousand new roads opened up and down every one of them was a man that she had never seen before. A man who called himself Verily Cooper and spoke like a book-learned Englishman and walked beside Alvin every step of his life for years. Down that path the golden plow was fixed with a perfect handle and leapt to life under human hands. Down that path the Crystal City rose skyward and the fog at the Mizzipy shore cleared for a few miles and Red folk stood on the western shore and gladly greeted White folk come on coracles and rafts to trade with them and speak to them and learn from them.

But where did this Verily Cooper come from, and why had he now so suddenly appeared in Alvin's life?

Only later in the day did it occur to Peggy that it was none of Alvin's doing that brought this man to him, but rather some-one else. She looked to Calvin's heartfire—so far away she had to look deep through the ground to see him in England, around the curve of the Earth—and there she saw that it was he who had made the change, and by the simplest of choices. He took the time to charm a Member of Parliament who invited him to tea, and even though Calvin knew that this man had nothing for him, on a whim, the merest chance, he decided he would go. That decision transformed Calvin's own futures only slightly. Nothing much was changed, except this: Down almost every road, Calvin spent an hour at the tea sitting beside a young barrister named Verily Cooper, who listened avidly to all that Calvin had to say.

Was it possible, then, that Calvin was part of Alvin's making after all? He went to England with the undoing of all of Alvin's works in his heart; and yet, by whim, by chance—if there was such a thing as chance—he would have an encounter that would almost surely bring Verily Cooper to America. To Alvin Smith. To the golden plow, the Crystal City, the opening of the Mizzipy fog.

Arise Cooper was an honest hardworking Christian. He lived his life as close to purity as he could, given the finite limits of the human mind. Every commandment he learned of, he obeyed; every imperfection he could imagine, he purged from his soul. He kept a detailed journal every day, tracking the doings of the Lord in his life.

For instance, on the day his second son was born, he wrote: "Today Satan made me angry at a man who insisted on measuring the three kegs I made him, sure that I had given him short measure. But the Spirit of God kindled forgiveness within my heart, for I realized that a man might become suspicious because he had been so often cheated by devilish men. Thus I saw that the Lord had trusted me to teach this man that not all men will cheat him, and I bore his insult with patience. Sure enough, as Jesus taught, when I answered vileness with kindness the stranger did part from my coopery as my friend instead of my enemy, and with a wiser eye about the workings of the Lord among men. Oh how great thou art, my beloved God, to turn my sinful heart into a tool to serve thy purposes in this world! At nightfall entered into the world my second son, whom I name Verily, Verily, I Say Unto You, Except Ye Become As A Little Child Ye Shall In No Wise Enter Into The Kingdom Of Heaven."

If anyone thought the name a bit excessive, they said nothing to Arise Cooper, whose own name was also a bit of scripture: Arise And Come Forth. Nor did the child's mother, whose own name was the shortest verse in scripture: He Wept. They all knew that the baby's whole name would almost never be used. Instead he was known as Verily, and as he grew up the name would often be shortened to Very.

It was not the name that was Verily Cooper's heaviest burden. No, there was something much darker that cast its shadow upon the boy very early in his life.

Arise's wife, Wept, came to him one day when Verily was only two years old. She was agitated. "Arise, I saw the boy playing with scraps today, building a tower of them."

Arise cast his mind through all the evil that one might do with wood scraps from the cooper's trade and could think of only one. "Was it a representation of the tower of Babel?"

Wept looked puzzled. "It might be, or might not. What would I know of that, since the boy speaks not a word yet?"

"What, then?" asked Arise, impatient now because she had not got straight to the point. No, no, he was impatient because he had guessed wrong and now was a bit ashamed of himself. It was a sin to try to put the blame on her for ill feelings of his own causing. In his heart he prayed for forgiveness even as she went on.

"Arise, he built high with the scraps, but they fell over, again and again. I saw him and thought, The Lord of heaven teaches our little one that the works of man are all futility, and only the works of God can last. But then he gets on his face this look of grim determination, and now he studies each scrap of wood as he builds with it, laying it in place all careful-like. He builds and he builds and he builds, until the last scrap is higher than his own head, and still it stands."

Arise was uncertain what she meant by this, or why it troubled her.

"Come, husband, and see the working of our baby's hand."

Arise followed her into the kitchen. No one else was there, though this was the busiest cooking time of the day. Arise could see why they had all fled. For the pile of scrap wood rose higher than reason or balance should have allowed. The blocks lay every which way, balanced perfectly no matter how odd or precarious the fit with the blocks above and below.

"Knock it down at once," said Arise.

"Do you think that didn't occur to me?" asked Wept. She flung out her arm and dashed the tower to the ground. It fell, but all in one motion, and even lying on the ground the blocks remained attached to each other as surely as if they were glued.

"He must have been playing with the mucilage," said Arise, but he knew even as he said it that it wasn't so.

He knelt beside the supine tower and tried to separate a block from the end. He couldn't pry it away. He picked up the whole tower and dashed it across his knee. It bruised him but did not break. Finally, by standing on the middle of it and lifting one end with all his strength, he broke the tower, but it took as much force as if he were breaking a sturdy plank. And when he examined the torn ends, he saw that the tower had broken in the middle of a block, and not at the joint between them.

He looked at his wife, and knew what he should say to her. He should tell her that it was obvious her son had been possessed by Satan, to such a point that the lad was now fully empowered with extraordinary witchery. When such a word was said, there would be no choice but to take the boy to the magistrate, who would administer the witch tests. The boy, being too young and speechless to confess or recant, would burn as the court's sentence, if he did not drown during the trial.

Arise had never questioned the rightness of the laws that kept England pure of witchery and the other dark doings of Satan. No more would they exile witches to America—the only result of that old policy had been a nation possessed by the Devil. The scripture was clear, and there was no room for mercy: Thou shalt not suffer a witch to live.

And yet Arise did not say to his wife the words that would force them to give their baby to the magistrate for discipline. For the first time in his life, Arise Cooper, knowing the truth, did not act upon it.

"I say we burn this odd-shaped board," said Arise. "And forbid the child to play with blocks. Watch him close, and teach him to live each moment in close obedience to the laws of God. Until he has learned, let no other woman look after him out of your presence."

He looked his wife in the eye, and Wept looked back at him. At first her eyes were wide with surprise at his words; then surprise gave way to relief, and then to determination. "I will watch him so close that Satan will have no opportunity to whisper in his ear," she said.

"We can afford to have a cook to supervise the work of the serving girls from now on," said Arise. "The raising of this most difficult son is in our hands. We *will* save him from the Devil. No other work is more important than this."

Thus it was that Verily Cooper's upbringing became difficult and interesting. He was beaten more than any other child in the family, for his own good, for Arise well knew that Satan had made an inroad in the child's heart at an early age. Thus all signs of rebellion, disrespect, and sin must be driven out vigorously.

If little Verily was resentful of the special discipline he received compared to his older brother and his younger sisters, he said nothing of it—perhaps because complaint always resulted in swift blows from a birch rod. He learned to live with such punishment and even, after a little while, to take some pride in it, for the other children looked at him in awe, seeing how much beating he took without so much as crying— and for offenses which, in them, would have brought no more than a sharp look from their parents.

Verily was quick to learn. The birch rod taught him which of his actions were merely the normal mischief of a growing boy, and which were regarded as signs that Satan was laboring mightily for possession of his soul. When the neighborhood boys were building a snow fort, for instance, if he built sloppily and carelessly like they did, there was no punishment. But when he took special care to make the blocks fit smoothly and seamlessly together, he got such a caning that his buttocks bled. Likewise, when he helped his father in the shop, he learned that if he joined the staves of a barrel loosely, as other men did it, barely holding them together inside the hoops, relying on the liquid the barrel would eventually hold to swell the wood and make the joints truly airtight, then it was all right. But if he chose the wood carefully and concentrated to fit them so the wood joined perfectly, and the barrel held air as tight as a pig's bladder, his father beat him with the sizing tool and drove him from the shop.

By the time he was ten, Verily no longer went openly into his father's shop, and it seemed that his father didn't mind having him stay away. Yet still it galled him to see the work that the shop turned out without his help, for Verily could sense the roughness, the looseness of the fit between the staves of the kegs and the barrels and the butts. It grated on him. It made him tingle between the shoulder blades just to think of it, until he could hardly stand it. He took to rising in the middle of the night and going into the shop and rebuilding the worst of the barrels. No one guessed what he had done, for he left no scraps behind. All he did was unhoop the barrel, refit the staves, and draw the hoops back on, more tightly than before.

The result was, first, that Arise Cooper got a name for making the best barrels in the midlands; second, that Verily was often sleepy and lazy-seeming during the day, which led to more beatings, though nothing like as severe as the ones he got when he really concentrated on making things fit together; and third, that Verily learned to live with constant deception, hiding what he was and what he saw and what he felt and what he did from everyone around him. It was only natural that he should be drawn to the study of law.

Lazy as Verily sometimes seemed, he had a sharp mind with his studies—Arise and Wept both saw it, and instead of contenting themselves with the local taxpaid teacher, they sent him to an academy that was normally only for the sons of squires and rich men. The taunting and mockery that Verily endured from the other boys because of his rough accent and homely clothing was hardly noticeable to Very—such poundings as the boys inflicted on him were nothing compared to the beatings he was inured to, and any abuse that didn't cause physical pain didn't even enter Very's consciousness. All he cared about was that at school he didn't have to live in fear all the time, and the teachers loved it when he studied carefully and saw how ideas fit together. What he could only do in secret with his hands, he could do openly with his mind.

And it wasn't just ideas. He began to learn that if he concentrated on the boys around him, really listening to them, watching how they acted, he could see them as clearly as he saw bits of wood, seeing exactly where and how each boy might fit well with each other boy. Just a word here and there, just an idea tossed into the right mind at the right time, and he made the boys of his dormitory into a cohesive band of loving friends. As much as they were willing, that is. Some were filled with deep rage that made it so that the better they fit, the more surly and suspicious they became. Verily couldn't help that. He couldn't change a boy's heart—he could only help him find where his natural inclinations would make him fit most comfortably with the others.

No one saw it, though—no one saw that it was Verily who made these boys into the tightest group of friends that had ever passed through this school. The masters saw that they were friends, but they also saw that Verily was the one misfit who never quite belonged. They could not have imagined that he was the cause of the others' extraordinary closeness. And that was fine with Very. He suspected that if they knew what he was doing, it would be like being home with Father again, only now it wouldn't be birch rods.

For in his studies, particularly in religion class, Verily finally came to understand what the beatings were all about. Witchery. Verily Cooper had been born a witch. No wonder his father looked haunted all the time. Arise Cooper had suffered a witch to live, and those canings, far from being an act of rage or hatred, were really designed to help Verily learn to disguise the evil born in him so that no one would ever know that Arise and Wept Cooper had concealed a witchchild in their own home.

But I'm not a witch, Verily finally told himself. Satan never came to me. And what I do causes no harm. How can it be against God to make barrels tight, or help boys find the best chance of friendship between them? How have I ever used my powers except to help others? Was that not what Christ taught? To be the servant of all?

By the time Verily was sixteen, a sturdy and rather good-looking young man of some education and impeccable manners, he had become a thoroughgoing skeptic. If the dogmas about witchery could be so hopelessly wrong, how could any of the teachings of the ministers be relied upon? It left Verily Cooper at loose ends, intellectually speaking, for all his teachers spoke as if religion were the cornerstone of all other learning, and yet all of Very's actual studies led him to the conclusion that sciences founded upon religion were uncertain at best, utterly bogus at worst.

Yet he breathed no word of these conclusions. You could be burned as an atheist just as fast as you could be burned as a witch. And besides, he wasn't sure he didn't believe in *anything*. He just didn't believe in what the ministers said.

If the preachers had no idea of what was good or evil, where could he turn to learn about right and wrong? He tried reading philosophy at Manchester, but found that except for Newton, the best the philosophers had to offer was a vast sea of opinion with a few blocks of truth floating here and there like wreckage from a sunken ship. And Newton and the scientists who followed him had no soul. By deciding that they would study only that which could be verified under controlled conditions, they had merely limited their field of endeavor. Most truth lay outside the neat confines of science; and even within those boundaries, Verily Cooper, with his keen eye for things which did not fit, soon found that while the pretense of impartiality was universal, the fact of it was very rare. Most scientists, like most philosophers and most theologians, were captives of received opinion. To swim against the tide was beyond their powers, and so truth remained scattered, unassembled, waterlogged.

At least lawyers knew they were dealing with tradition, not truth; with consensus, not objective reality. And a man who understood how things fit together might make a real contribution. Might save a few people from injustice. Might even, in some far distant year, strike a blow or two against the witchery laws and spare those few dozen souls a year so incautious as to be caught manipulating reality in unapproved ways.

As for Arise and Wept, they were deeply gratified when their son Verily left home expressing no interest in the family business. Their oldest child, Mocky (full name: He Will Not Be Mocked Cooper) was a skilled barrelmaker and popular both inside and outside the family. He would inherit everything. Verily would go to London and Arise and Wept would no longer be responsible for him. Verily even gave them a quit-claim against the family estate, though they hadn't asked for it. When Arise accepted the document, twenty-one-year-old Verily took

122 • Orson Scott Card

the birch rod from where it hung on the wall, broke it over his
knee, and fed it into the kitchen fire. There was no further
discussion of the matter. All understood: What Verily chose to
do with his powers was his own business now.

Verily's talents were immediately noticed. He was invited to
join several law firms, and finally chose the one that gave
him the greatest independence to choose his own clients. His
reputation soared as he won case after case; but what impressed
the lawyers who truly understood these things was not the
number of victories, but rather the even larger number of cases
that were settled—justly—without even going to trial. By the
time Verily turned twenty-five, it was becoming a custom several times a month for both parties in hotly contested lawsuits
to come to Verily and beg him to be their arbiter, completely
sidestepping the courts: such was his reputation as a wise and
just man. Some whispered that in due course he would become
a great force in politics. Some dared to wish that such a man
might someday be Lord Protector, if that office were only filled
by election, like the presidency of the United States.

The United States of America—that motley, multilingual,
mongrel, mossbacked republic that had somehow, kingless and
causeless, arisen by accident between the Crown Lands and
New England. America, where men wearing buckskin were
said to walk the halls of Congress along with Reds, Dutchmen,
Swedes, and other semi-civilized specimens who would have
been ejected from Parliament before they could speak a word
aloud. More and more Verily Cooper turned his eyes to that
country; more and more he yearned to live in a place where
his gift for making things fit together could be used to the
fullest. Where he could join things together with his hands, not
just with his mind and with his words. Where, in short, he
could live without deception.

Maybe in such a land, where men did not have to lie about
who they were in order to be granted the right to live, maybe
in such a land he could find his way to some kind of truth,

some kind of understanding about what the universe was for. And, failing that, at least Verily could be free there.

The trouble was, it was English law that Verily had studied, and it was English clients who were on the way to making him a rich man. What if he married? What if he had children? What kind of life would he make for them in America, amid the forest primeval? How could he ask a wife to leave civilization and go to Philadelphia?

And he wanted a wife. He wanted to raise children. He wanted to prove that goodness wasn't beaten into children, that fear was not the fount from which virtue flowed. He wanted to be able to gather his family in his arms and know that not one of them dreaded the sight of him, or felt the need to lie to him in order to have his love.

So he dreamed of America but stayed in London, searching in high society to find the right woman to make a family with. By now his homely manners had been replaced by university fashion and finally with courtliness that made him welcome in the finest houses. His wit, never biting, always deep, made him a popular guest in the great salons of London, and if he was never invited to the same dinners or parties as the leading theologians of the day, it was not because he was thought to be an atheist, but rather because there were no theologians regarded as his equal in conversation. One had to place Verily Cooper with at least one who could hold his own with him— everyone knew that Very was far too kindhearted to destroy fools for public entertainment. He simply fell silent when surrounded by those of dimmer wit; it was a shameful thing for a host when word spread that Verily Cooper had been silent all night long.

Verily Cooper was twenty-six years old when he found himself at a party with a remarkable young American named Calvin Miller.

Verily noticed him at once, because he didn't fit, but it wasn't because of his Americanness. In fact, Verily could see at once that Calvin had done a good job of acquiring a veneer of manners that kept him from the most egregious faux pas that bedevilled most Americans who attempted to make their way in London. The boy was going on about his effort to learn French, joking about how abominably untalented he was at languages; but Verily saw (as did many others) that this was all pretense. When Calvin spoke French each phrase came out with splendid accents, and if his vocabulary was lacking, his grammar was not.

A lady near Verily murmured to him, "If he's bad at languages, I shudder to imagine what he's *good* at."

Lying, that's what he's good at, thought Verily. But he kept his mouth shut, because how could he possibly know that Calvin's every word was false, except because he knew that nothing fit when Calvin was speaking? The boy was fascinating if only because he seemed to lie when there was no possible benefit from lying; he lied for the sheer joy of it.

Was this what America produced? The land that in Verily's fantasies was a place of truth, and this was what was spawned there? Maybe the ministers were not wholly wrong about those with hidden powers—or "knacks," as the Americans quaintly called them.

"Mr. Miller," said Verily. "I wonder, since you're an American, if you have any personal knowledge of knacks."

The room fell silent. To speak of such things—it was only slightly less crude than to speak of personal hygiene. And when it was rising young barrister Verily Cooper doing the asking . . .

"I beg your pardon?" asked Calvin.

"Knacks," said Verily. "Hidden powers. I know that they're legal in America, and yet Americans profess to be Christian. Therefore I'm curious about how such things are rationalized, when here they are considered to be proof of one's enslavement to Satan and worthy of a sentence of death."

"I'm no philosopher, sir," said Calvin.

Verily knew better. He could tell that Calvin was suddenly more guarded than ever. Verily's guess had been right. This

Calvin Miller was lying because he had much to hide. "All the better," said Verily. "Then there's a chance that your answer will make sense to a man as ignorant of such matters as I am."

"I wish you'd let me speak of other things," said Calvin. "I think we might offend this company."

"Surely you don't imagine you were invited here for any reason other than your Americanness," said Verily. "So why do you resist talking about the most obvious oddity of the American people?"

There was a buzz of comment. Who had ever seen Verily be openly rude like this?

Verily knew what he was doing, however. He hadn't interviewed a thousand witnesses without learning how to elicit truth even from the most flagrant habitual liar. Calvin Miller was a man who felt shame sharply. That was why he lied—to hide himself from anything that would shame him. If provoked, however, he would respond with heat, and the lies and calculation would give way to bits of honesty now and then. In short, Calvin Miller had a dander, and it was up.

"Oddity?" asked Calvin. "Perhaps the odd thing is not having knacks, but rather denying that they exist or blaming them on Satan."

Now the buzz was louder. Calvin, by speaking honestly, had shocked and offended his pious listeners more than Verily's rudeness had. Yet this *was* a cosmopolitan crowd, and there *were* no ministers present. No one left the room; all watched, all listened with fascination.

"Take that as your premise, then," said Verily. "Explain to me and this company how these occult knacks came into the world, if not caused by the influence of the Devil. Surely you won't have us believe that we Englishmen burn people to death for having powers given to them by God?"

Calvin shook his head. "I see that you want merely to provoke me, sir, into speaking in ways that are against the law here."

"Not so," said Verily. "There are three dozen witnesses in this salon right now who would testify that far from initiating this conversation, you were dragged into it. Furthermore, I am not asking you to preach to us. I'm merely asking you to tell us, as scientists, what Americans believe. It is no more a crime to tell about American beliefs concerning knacks than it is to report on Muslim harems and Hindu widow-burning. And this is a company of people who are eager to learn. If I'm wrong, please, let me be corrected."

No one spoke up to correct him. They were, in fact, dying to hear what the young American would say.

"I'd say there's no consensus about it," said Calvin. "I'd say that no one knows what to think. They just use the knacks that they have. Some say it's against God. Some say God made the world, knacks included, and it all depends on whether the knacks are used for righteousness or not. I've heard a lot of different opinions."

"But what is the wisest opinion that you've heard?" insisted Verily.

He could feel it the moment Calvin decided on his answer: It was a kind of surrender. Calvin had been flailing around, but now he had given in to the inevitable. He was going to tell, if not the truth, then at least a true reporting of somebody else's truth.

"One fellow says that knacks come because of a natural affinity between a person and some aspect of the world around him. It's not from God *or* Satan, he says. It's just part of the random variation in the world. This fellow says that a knack is really a matter of winning the trust of some part of reality. He reckons that the Reds, who don't believe in knacks, have found the truth behind it all. A White man gets it in his head he has a knack, and from then on all he works on is honing that particular talent. But if, like the Reds, he saw knacks as just an aspect of the way all things are connected together, then he wouldn't concentrate on just one talent. He'd keep working on all of them. So in this fellow's view, knacks are just the result of too much work on one thing, and not enough work on all the rest. Like a hodsman who carries bricks only on his right shoulder. His body's going to get twisted. You have to study it all, learn it all. Every knack is within our power to acquire it, I reckon, if only we . . ."

His voice trailed off.

When Calvin spoke again, it was in the crisp, clear, educated-sounding way he must have learned since reaching England. Only then did Verily and the others realize that his accent had changed during that long speech. He had shed the thin coating of Englishness and shown the American.

"Who is this man who taught you all this lore?" asked Verily.

"Does it matter? What does such a rough man know of nature?" Calvin spoke mockingly; but he was lying again, Verily knew it.

"This 'rough man,' as you call him. I suspect he says a great deal more than the mere snippet you've given us today."

"Oh, you can't stop him from talking, he's so full of his own voice." The bitterness in Calvin's tone was a powerful message to Verily: This is sincere. Calvin resents whoever this frontier philosopher is, resents him deeply. "But I'm not about to bore this company with the ravings of a frontier lunatic."

"But you don't think he's a lunatic, do you, Mr. Miller?" said Verily.

A momentary pause. Think of your answer quickly, Calvin Miller. Find a way to deceive me, if you can.

"I can't say, sir," said Calvin. "I don't think he knows half as much as he lets on, but I wouldn't dare call my own brother a liar."

There was a sudden loud eruption of buzzing. Calvin Miller had a brother who philosophized about knacks and said they weren't from the Devil.

More important to Verily was the fact that Calvin's words obviously didn't fit in with the world he actually believed in. Lies, lies. Calvin obviously believed that his brother was very wise indeed; that he probably knew *more* than Calvin was willing to admit.

At this moment, without realizing it himself, Verily Cooper

made the decision to go to America. Whoever Calvin's brother was, he knew something that Verily wanted desperately to learn. For there was a ring of truth in this man's ideas. Maybe if Verily could only meet him and talk to him, he could make Verily's own knack clear to him. Could tell him why he had such a talent and why it persisted even though his father tried to beat it out of him.

"What's your brother's name?" asked Verily.

"Does that matter?" asked Calvin, a faint sneer in his voice. "Planning a visit to the backwoods soon?"

"Is that where you're from? The backwoods?" asked Verily.

Calvin immediately backtracked. "Actually, no, I was exaggerating. My father was a miller."

"How did the poor man die?" asked Verily.

"He's not dead," said Calvin.

"But you spoke of him in the past tense. As if he were no longer a miller."

"He still runs a mill," said Calvin.

"You still haven't told me your brother's name."

"Same as my father's. Alvin."

"Alvin Miller?" asked Verily.

"Used to be. But in America we still change our names with our professions. He's a journeyman smith now. Alvin Smith."

"And you remain Calvin Miller because . . ."

"Because I haven't chosen my life's work yet."

"You hope to discover it in France?"

Calvin leapt to his feet as if his most terrible secret had just been exposed. "I have to get home."

Verily also rose to his feet. "My friend, I fear my curiosity has made you feel uncomfortable. I will stop my questioning at once, and apologize to this whole company for having broached such difficult subjects tonight. I hope you will all excuse my insatiable curiosity."

Verily was at once reassured by many voices that it had been most interesting and no one was angry with or offended by anyone. The conversation broke into many smaller chats.

In a few moments, Verily managed to maneuver himself close to the young American. "Your brother, Alvin Smith," he said. "Tell me where I can find him."

"In America," said Calvin; and because the conversation was private, he did not conceal his contempt.

"Only slightly better than telling me to search for him on Earth," said Verily. "Obviously you resent him. I have no desire to trouble you by asking you to tell me any more of his ideas. It will cost you nothing to tell me where he lives so I can search him out myself."

"You'd make a voyage across the ocean to meet with a boy who talks like a country bumpkin in order to learn what he thinks about knacks?"

"Whether I make such a voyage or merely write him a letter is no concern of yours," said Verily. "In the future I'm bound to be asked to defend people accused of witchery. Your brother may have the arguments that will allow me to save a client's life. Such ideas can't be found here in England because it would be the ruin of a man's career to explore too assiduously into the works of Satan."

"So why aren't you afraid of ruining your own career?" said Calvin.

"Because whatever he knows, it's true enough to make a liar like you run halfway around the world to get away from the truth."

Calvin's expression grew ugly with hate. "How dare you speak to me like that! I could . . ."

So Verily had guessed right about the way Calvin fit into his own family back home. "The name of the town, and you and I will never have to speak again."

Calvin paused for a moment, weighing the decision. "I take you at your word, Mr. Rising Young Barrister Esquire. The town is Vigor Church, in Wobbish Territory. Near the mouth of Tippy-Canoe Creek. Go find my brother if you can. Learn from him—if you can. Then you can spend the rest of your life wondering if maybe you wouldn't have been better off trying to learn from *me*."

Verily laughed softly. "I don't think so, Calvin Miller. I already know how to lie, and alas, that's the only knack you have that you've practiced enough to be truly accomplished at it."

"In another time I would have shot you dead for that remark."

"But this is an age that loves liars," said Verily. "That's why there are so many of us, acting out lives of pretense. I don't know what you're hoping to find in France, but I can promise you, it will be worthless to you in the long run, if your whole life up to that moment is a lie."

"Now you're a prophet? Now you can see into a man's heart?" Calvin sneered and backed away. "We had a deal. I told you where my brother lives. Now stay away from me." Calvin Miller left the party, and, moments later, so did Verily Cooper. It was quite a scandal, Verily's acting so rudely in front of the whole company like that. Was it quite safe to invite him to dinners and parties anymore?

Within a week that question ceased to matter. Verily Cooper was gone: resigned from his law firm, his bank accounts closed, his apartment rented. He sent a brief letter to his parents, telling them only that he was going to America to interview a fellow about a case he was working on. He didn't add that it was the most important case of his life: his trial of himself as a witch. Nor did he tell them when, if ever, he meant to return to England. He was sailing west, and would then take whatever conveyance there was, even if it was his own feet on a rough path, to meet this fellow Alvin Smith, who said the first sensible thing about knacks that Verily had ever heard.

On the very day that Verily Cooper set sail from Liverpool, Calvin Miller stepped onto the Calais ferry. From that moment on, Calvin spoke nothing but French, determined to be fluent before he met Napoleon. He wouldn't think of Verily Cooper again for several years. He had bigger fish to fry. What did he care about what some London lawyer thought of him?

⊠ 10 ⊠

Welcome Home

LEFT TO HIMSELF, Alvin likely wouldn't have come back to Hatrack River. Sure, it was his birthplace, but since his folks moved on before he was even sitting up by himself he didn't have no memories of the way it was then. He knew that the oldest settlers in that place were Horace Guester and Makepeace Smith and old Vanderwoort, the Dutch trader, so when he was born the roadhouse and the smithy and the general store must have been there already. But he couldn't conjure up no pictures in his memory of such a little place.

The Hatrack River he knew was the village of his prentice-ship, with a town square and a church with a preacher and Whitley Physicker to tend the sick and even a post office and enough folks with enough children that they got them up a subscription and hired them a schoolteacher. Which meant it was a real town by then, only what difference did that make to Alvin? He was stuck there from the age of eleven, bound over to a greedy master who squeezed the last ounce of work out of "his" boy while teaching him as little as possible, as late as possible. There was scarce any money, and neither time to get any pleasure from it nor pleasures to be bought if you had the time.

Even so, miserable as his prenticeship was, he might have looked back on Hatrack River with some fondness. There was Makepeace's shrewish wife Gertie, who nevertheless was a fine cook and had a spot of kindness for the boy now and then. There was Horace and Old Peg Guester, who remembered his birth and made him feel welcome whenever he had a moment to visit with them or do some odd job to help them out. And as Alvin got him a name for making perfect hexes and doing better ironwork than his master, there was plenty of visits from all the other folks in town, asking for this, asking for that, and all sort of pretending they didn't know Alvin was the true master in that smithy. Wouldn't want to rile up old Makepeace, cause then he'd take it out on the boy, wouldn't he? But he was a good one with his hands, that boy Alvin.

So Alvin might have made him some happy memories of the place, the way folks always finds a way to dip into their own past and draw out wistful moments, even if those very moments was lonely or painful or downright hellish to live through at the time.

For Alvin, though, all those childish and youthish memories was swallowed up in the way it ended. Right at the happiest time, when he was falling in love with Miss Larner while trying to pick up some decent book learning, them Slave Finders came for little Arthur Stuart and everything went ugly. They even forced Alvin to make the manacles that Arthur would wear back into slavery. Then Alvin and Horace Guester took their life in their hands and went to fetch back the boy, and Alvin changed Arthur Stuart deep inside and washed away his old self in the Hio, so the Finders could never match him up with the bits of hair and flesh in their cachet. So even then, it might have still been hopeful, a good memory of a bad time that turned out fine.

Then that last night, standing in the smithy with Miss Larner,

Alvin told her he loved her and asked her to marry him and she might have said yes, she had a look in her eyes that said yes, he thought. But at that very moment Old Peg Guester killed one Finder and got herself killed by the other. Only then did Alvin find out that Miss Larner was really Little Peggy, Peg's and Horace's long-lost daughter, the torch girl who saved Alvin's life when he was a little baby. What a thing to find out about the woman you love, in the exact moment that you're losing her forever.

But he wasn't really thinking of losing Miss Larner then. All he could think of was Old Peg, gruff and sharp-tongued and loving old Peg, shot dead by a Slave Finder, and never mind that she shot one of them first, they was in her house without leave, trespassing, and even if the law gave them the right to be there, it was an evil law and they was evil to make their living by it and it didn't none of it matter then, anyway, because Alvin was so angry he wasn't thinking straight. Alvin found the one as killed Old Peg and snapped his neck with one hand, and then he beat his head against the ground until the skull inside the skin was all broke up like a pot in a meal sack.

When Alvin's fury died, when the white-hot rage was gone, when deep justice stopped demanding the death of the killer of Old Peg, all that was left was the broken body in his arms, the blood on his apron, the memory of murder. Never mind that nobody in Hatrack River would ever call him a killer for what he done that night. In his own heart he knew that he had Unmade his own Making. For that moment he had been the Unmaker's tool.

That dark memory was why none of the other memories could ever turn light in Alvin's heart. And that's why Alvin probably wouldn't never have come back to Hatrack River, left to himself.

But he wasn't left to himself, was he? He had Arthur Stuart with him, and to that little boy the town of Hatrack River was nothing but pure golden childhood. It was setting and watching Alvin work in the smithy, or even pumping the bellows sometimes. It was listening to the redbird song and knowing the words. It was hearing all the gossip in the town and saying it back all clever so the grownups clapped their hands and laughed. It was being the champion speller of the whole town even though for some reason they wouldn't let him into the school proper. And yes, sure, the woman he called Mother got herself killed, but Arthur didn't see that with his own eyes, and anyway, he *had* to go back, didn't he? Old Peg his adopted mother who killed a man to save him and died her own self, she lay buried on a hill behind the roadhouse. And in a grave on the same hill lay Arthur's true mother, a little Black slavegirl who used her secret African powers to make wings for herself so she could fly with the baby in her arms, she could fly all the way north to where her baby would be safe, even though she herself died from the journey. How could Arthur Stuart not return to that place?

Don't go thinking that Arthur Stuart ever asked Alvin to go there. That wasn't the way Arthur thought about things. He was going along with Alvin, not telling Alvin where to go. It was just that when they talked, Arthur kept going on about this or that memory from Hatrack River until Alvin reached his own conclusion. Alvin reckoned that it would make Arthur Stuart happy to go back to Hatrack River, and then it never crossed Alvin's mind that his own sadness might outweigh Arthur's happiness. He just up and left Irrakwa, where they happened to be that week in late August of 1820. Up and left that land of railroads and factories, coal and steel, barges and carriages and men on horseback going back and forth on urgent errands. Left that busy place and came through quiet woods and across whispering streams, down deer paths and along rutted roads until the land started looking familiar and Arthur Stuart said, "I've been here. I know this place." And then, in wonder: "You brung me home, Alvin."

They came from the northeast, passing the place where the railroad spur was fixing to pass near Hatrack River and cross the Hio into Appalachee. They came across the covered bridge over the Hatrack that Alvin's own father and brothers built, like a monument to their dead oldest brother Vigor, who got mashed by a tree carried on a storm flood while he was crossing the river. They came into town on the same road his family used. And, just like Alvin's family, they passed the smithy and heard the ringing of hammer on iron on anvil.

"Ain't that the smithy?" asked Arthur Stuart. "Let's go see Makepeace and Gertie!"

"I don't think so," said Alvin. "In the first place, Gertie's dead."

"Oh, that's right," said the boy. "Blew out a blood vein screaming at Makepeace, didn't she?"

"How'd you hear that?" asked Alvin. "You don't miss much gossip, do you, boy?"

"I can't help what people talk about when I'm right there," said Arthur Stuart. And then, back to his original idea: "I reckon it wouldn't be proper anyway, to visit Makepeace before seeing Papa."

Alvin didn't tell him that Horace Guester hated it when Arthur called him Papa. Folks got the wrong impression, like maybe Horace himself was the White half of that mixup boy, which wasn't so at all but folks will talk. When Arthur got older, Alvin would explain to him that he ought to not call Horace Papa anymore. For now, though, Horace was a man and a man would have to bear the innocent offense of a well-meaning boy.

The roadhouse was twice as big as before. Horace had built on a new wing that doubled the front, with the porch continuing all along it. But that wasn't hardly the only difference—the whole thing was faced with clapboards now, whitewashed and pretty as you could imagine against the deep green of the forest that still snuck as close to the house as it dared.

"Well, Horace done prettied up the place," said Alvin.

"It don't look like itself no more," said Arthur Stuart.

"Anymore," Alvin corrected him.

"If you can say 'done prettied up' then I can say 'no more,' " said Arthur Stuart. "Miss Larner ain't here to correct us no more anyhow."

"That should be 'no more nohow,' " said Alvin, and they both laughed as they walked up onto the porch.

The door opened and a somewhat stout middle-aged woman stepped through it, almost running into them. She carried a basket under one arm and an umbrella under the other, though there wasn't a sign of rain.

"Excuse me," said Alvin. He saw that she was hedged about with hexes and charms. Not many years ago, he would have been fooled by them like any other man (though he would always have seen where the charms were and how the hexes worked). But he had learned to see past hexes of illusion, and that's what these were. These days, seeing the truth came so natural to him that it took real effort to see the illusion. He made the effort, and was vaguely saddened to see that she was almost a caricature of feminine beauty. Couldn't she have been more creative, more *interesting* than this? He judged at once that the real middle-aged woman, somewhat thick-waisted and hair salted with grey, was the more attractive of the two images. And it was a sure thing she was the more interesting.

She saw him staring at her, but no doubt she assumed it was her beauty that had him awed. She must have been used to men staring at her—it seemed to amuse her. She stared right back at him, but *not* looking for beauty in him, that was for sure.

"You were born here," she said, "but I've never seen you before." Then she looked at Arthur Stuart. "But you were born away south."

Arthur nodded, made mute by shyness and by the overwhelming force of her declaration. She spoke as if her words were not only true, but superseded all other truth that had ever been thought of.

"He was born in Appalachee, Missus. . . ." In vain Alvin waited for her reply. Then he realized that he was supposed to assume, seeing her young beautiful false image, that she was a Miss rather than a Missus.

"You're bound for Carthage City," said the woman, speaking to Alvin again, and rather coldly.

"I don't think so," said Alvin. "Nothing for me there."

"Not yet, not yet," she said. "But I know you now. You must be Alvin, that prentice boy old Makepeace is always going on about."

"I'm a journeyman, ma'am. If Makepeace isn't saying that part, I wonder how much of what he says *is* true."

She smiled, but her eyes weren't smiling. They were calculating. "Aha. I think there's the makings of a good story in that. Just needs a bit of stirring."

At once Alvin regretted having said so much to her. Why *had* he spoken up so boldly, anyway? He wasn't a one to babble on to strangers, especially when he was more or less calling another fellow a liar. He didn't want trouble with Makepeace, but now it looked pretty sure he was going to get it anyway. "I wish you'd tell me who you are, ma'am."

It wasn't *her* voice that answered. Horace Guester was in the doorway now. "She's the postmistress of Hatrack River, on account of her uncle's brother-in-law being the congressman from some district in Susquahenny and he had some pull with the president. We're all hoping to find a candidate in the election this fall who'll promise to throw her out so we can vote for him for president. Failing that, we're going to have to up and hang her one of these days."

The postmistress got a sort of half-smile on her face. "And to think Horace Guester's knack is to make folks feel welcome!"

"What would the charge be, in the hanging?" asked Alvin.

"Criminal gossip," said Horace Guester. "Rumor aforethought. Sniping with malice. Backbiting with intent to kill. Of course I mean all that in the nicest possible way."

"I do no such thing," said the postmistress. "And my name, since Horace hasn't deigned to utter it yet, is Vilate Franker. My grandmother wasn't much of a speller, so she named my mother Violet but spelled it Vilate, and when my mother grew up she was so ashamed of grandmama's illiteracy that she changed the pronunciation to rhyme with 'plate.' However, I am *not* ashamed of my grandmother, so I pronounce it 'Violet,' as in the delicate flower."

"To rhyme," said Horace, "with Pilate, as in Pontius the handwasher."

"You sure talk a lot, ma'am," said Arthur Stuart. He spoke in all innocence, simply observing the facts as he saw them, but Horace hooted and Vilate blushed and then, to Alvin's shock, clicked with her tongue and opened her mouth wide, letting her upper row of teeth drop down onto the lower ones. False teeth! And such a horrible image—but neither Arthur nor Horace seemed to see what she had done. Behind her wall of illusion, she apparently thought she could get away with all kinds of ugly contemptuous gestures. Well, Alvin wasn't going to disabuse her. Yet.

"Forgive the boy," said Alvin. "He hasn't learned when's the right time to speak his mind."

"He's right," she said. "Why shouldn't he say so?" But she dropped her teeth at the boy again. "I find it irresistible to tell stories," she went on. "Even when I know my listeners don't care to hear them. It's my worst vice. But there are worse ones—and I thank the good Lord I don't have *those*."

"Oh, I like stories, too," said Arthur Stuart. "Can I come listen to you talk some more?"

"Any time you like, my boy. Do you have a name?"

"Arthur Stuart."

It was Vilate's turn to hoot with laughter. "Any relation to the esteemed king down in Camelot?"

"I was named after him," he said, "but far as I know we ain't no kin."

Horace spoke up again. "Vilate, you won yourself a convert cause the poor boy's got no guile and less sense, but kindly stand aside of this door and let me welcome in this man who was born in my house and this boy who grew up in it."

"There's obviously parts of this story that I haven't heard yet," said Vilate, "but don't trouble yourself on my account— I'm sure I'll get a much fuller version from others than I would ever get from you. Good day, Horace! Good day, Alvin! Good day, my young kingling. Do come see me, but don't bring me any of Horace's cider, it's sure to be poisoned if he knows it's for me!" With that she bustled off the porch and out onto the hard-packed dirt of the road. Alvin saw the illusions dazzle and shimmer as she went. The hexes weren't quite so perfect from the rear. He wondered if others ever saw through her when she was going away.

Horace watched her grimly as she walked up the road. "We pretend that we're only pretending to hate each other, but in fact we really do. The woman's evil, and I mean that serious. She has this knack of knowing where something or somebody's from and where they're bound to end up, but she uses that to piece together the nastiest sort of gossip and I swear she reads other people's mail."

"Oh, I don't know," said Alvin.

"That's right, my boy, you ain't been here for the past year and you *don't* know. A lot of changes since you left."

"Well, let me in, Mr. Guester, so I can set down and maybe eat some of today's stew and have a drink of something—even poisoned cider sounds good about now."

Horace laughed and embraced Alvin. "Have you been gone so long you forgot my name is Horace? Come in, come in. And you too, young Arthur Stuart. You're always welcome here."

To Alvin's relief, Arthur Stuart said nothing at all, and so naturally among the things he didn't say was "papa."

They followed him inside and from then on till they laid down for naps in the best bedroom, they were in Horace's hospitable care. He fed them, gave them hot water for washing their hands and feet and faces, took their dirty clothes for laundering, stuffed more food in them, and then personally tucked them into bed after making them watch him put clean sheets on the bed "just so you *know* I still keep my dear Peg's high standards of cleanliness even if I am just an old widower living alone."

The mention of his late wife was all it took, though, to bring memory flooding back. Tears came into Arthur Stuart's eyes. Horace at once began to apologize, but Alvin stilled him with a smile and a gesture. "He'll be all right," he said. "It's coming home, and her not here. Those are good tears and right to shed them."

Arthur reached out and patted Horace's hand. "I'll be all right, Papa," he said.

Alvin looked at Horace's face and was relieved to see that instead of annoyance, his eyes showed a kind of rueful gladness at hearing the name of Papa. Maybe he was thinking of the one person who had the true right to call him that, his daughter Peggy, who had come home in disguise and was too soon gone, and who knew if he'd ever see her again. Or maybe he was thinking of the one who taught Arthur Stuart to call him Papa, the dear wife whose body lay in the hilltop plot behind the roadhouse, the woman who was always faithful to him even though he never deserved her goodness, being (as only he in all the world believed) a man of evil.

Soon Horace backed on out of the room and closed the door, and Arthur Stuart quietly cried himself to sleep in Alvin's arms. Alvin lay there, wanting to doze, too, for a little while. It was good to be home, or as near to home as Alvin could figure in these days when he wondered what home even was. Carthage City was where he was bound to end up, eh? Why would he go there to live? Or would he only go there to die? What did this Vilate Franker actually know, anyway? He lay there, sleepless, wondering about her, wondering if she could really be as evil as Horace Guester said. Alvin had met true evil in his life, but he still persisted in thinking it was awful rare, and the word was bandied about too much by those who didn't understand what real badness was.

What he could not let himself think of was the only other

woman he had known who fenced herself around with hexes. Rather than remember Miss Larner, who was really little Peggy, he finally drifted into sleep.

What an interesting boy, thought Vilate as she walked away from the roadhouse. Not at all like the shifty little weasel I expected after the things Makepeace Smith has said. But then, nobody trusts shifty little weasels well enough to be betrayed by them—it's strong, fine-looking men as tricks folks into thinking they're as open-hearted as they are open-faced. So maybe every word Makepeace said was true. Maybe Alvin did steal some precious hoard of gold that he found while digging a well. Maybe Alvin did fill up the well where the gold was found and dig another a few yards off, hoping nobody'd notice. Maybe he did shape it like a plow and pretend that he had turned iron into gold so he could run off with Makepeace's treasure trove. What's that to me? thought Vilate. It wasn't my gold, and never could be, as long as Makepeace had it. But if it happens to be a golden plow that Alvin has in that bag he carries over his shoulder, why, then it might end up being anybody's gold.

Anybody strong enough might take it away by brute force, for instance. Anybody cruel enough might kill Alvin and take it from the corpse. Anybody sneaky enough could take it out of Alvin's room as he slept. Anybody rich enough could hire lawyers to prove something against Alvin in court and take it away by force of law. All kinds of ways to get that plow, if you want it bad enough.

But Vilate would never stoop to coercion. She wouldn't even *want* that golden plow, if it existed, unless Alvin gave it to her of his own free will. As a gift. A love-gift, perhaps. Or . . . well, she'd settle for a guilt gift, if it came to that. He looked like a man of honor, but the way he was staring at her . . . well, she knew that look. The man was smitten. The man was hers, if she wanted him.

Play this right, Vilate, she told herself. Set the stage. Make *him* come after you. Let no one say you set your cap for him.

Her best friend was waiting for her in the kitchen shed back of the post office when she got there. "So what do you think of that Alvin?" she asked, before Vilate even had time to greet her.

"Trust you to get the news before I can tell you myself." Vilate set to work stoking up the fine cast-iron stove with a bread oven in it that made her the envy of the women in Hatrack River.

"Five people saw you on the roadhouse porch greeting him, Vilate, and the word reached me before your foot touched the street, I'm sure."

"Then those are idle people, I'd say, and the devil has them."

"No doubt you'd know—I'm sure the devil gives you a new list every time he makes another recruit."

"Of course he does. Why, everyone knows the devil lives right here in my fancy oven." Vilate cackled with glee.

"So . . ." said her best friend impatiently. "What do you think of him?"

"I don't think he's that much," said Vilate. "Workingman's arms, of course, and tanned like any low-class boy. His talk is rather coarse and country-like. I wonder if he can even read."

"Oh, he can read all right. Teacher lady taught him when he lived here."

"Oh, yes, the fabled Miss Larner who was so clever she got her prize student to win a spelling bee, which caused the slave finders to get wind of a half-Black boy and ended up killing Horace Guester's wife, Miss Larner's own mother. A most unnatural woman."

"You do find a way to make the story sound right ugly," said her friend.

"Is there a pretty version of it?"

"A sweet love story. Teacher tries to transform the life of a half-Black boy and his rough-hewn friend, a prentice smith. She falls in love with the smith boy, and turns the half-Black lad into a champion speller. Then the forces of evil take notice—"

"Or God decides to strike down her pride!"

"I do think you're jealous of her, Vilate. I do think that."

"Jealous?"

"Because she won the heart of Alvin Smith, and maybe she still owns it."

"Far as I can tell, his heart's still beating in his own chest."

"And is the gold still shining in his croker sack?"

"You talk sweet about Miss Larner, but you always assume *I* have the worst motives." Vilate had the stove going nicely now, and put on a teapot to boil as she began cutting string beans and dropping them in a pan of water.

"Because I know you so well, Vilate."

"You *think* you know me, but I'm full of surprises."

"Don't you drop your teeth at *me*, you despicable creature."

"They dropped by themselves," said Vilate. "I never do it on purpose."

"You're such a liar."

"But I'm a beautiful liar, don't you think?" She flashed her best smile at her friend.

"I don't understand what men see in women anyway," her friend answered. "Hexes or no hexes, as long as a woman has her clothes on a man can't see what he's interested in anyhow."

"I don't know about *all* men," said Vilate. "I think some men love me for my character."

"A character of sterling silver, no doubt—never mind a little tarnish, you can wipe *that* off with a little polish."

"And some men love me for my wit and charm."

"Yes, I'm sure they do—if they've been living in a cave for forty years and haven't seen a civilized woman in all that time."

"You can tease me all you want, but I know you're jealous of me, because Alvin Smith is already falling in love with me, the poor hopeless boy, while he'll never give a look at you, not a single look. Eat your heart out, dear."

Her best friend just sat there with a grumpy face. Vilate had really hit home with that last one. The teapot sang. As always, Vilate set out two teacups. But, as always, her best friend sniffed the tea but never drank it. Well, so what? Vilate never failed in her courtesy, and that's what mattered.

"Makepeace is going to take him to court."

"Ha," said Vilate. "You heard *that* already, too?"

"Oh, no. I don't know if Makepeace Smith even knows his old prentice is back in town—though you can bet that if the word reached *me* that fast, it got to him in half the time! I just know that Makepeace has been bragging so much on how Alvin robbed him that if he don't serve papers on the boy, everybody's going to know it was just empty talk. So he's *got* to bring the boy to trial, don't you see?"

Vilate smiled a little smile to herself.

"Already planning what you're going to bring to him in jail?" asked her friend.

"Or something," said Vilate.

Alvin woke from his nap to find Arthur Stuart gone and the room half-dark. The traveling must have taken more out of him than he thought, to make him sleep the afternoon away.

A knock on the door. "Open up, now, Alvin," said Horace. "The sheriff's just doing his job, he tells me, but there's no way out of it."

So it must have been a knock on the door that woke him in the first place. Alvin swung his legs off the bed and took the single step that got him to the door. "It wasn't barred," he said as he opened it. "You only had to give it a push."

Sheriff Po Doggly looked downright sheepish. "Oh, it's just Makepeace Smith, Alvin. Everybody knows he's talking through his hat, but he's gone and got a warrant on you, to charge you with stealing his treasure trove."

"Treasure?" asked Alvin. "I never heard of no treasure."

"Claims you dug up the gold digging a well for him, and moved the well so nobody'd know—"

"I moved the well cause I struck solid stone," said Alvin.

"If I found gold, why would that make me move the well? That don't even make sense."

"And that's what you'll say in court, and the jury will believe you just fine," said Sheriff Doggly. "Everybody knows Makepeace is just talking through his hat."

Alvin sighed. He'd heard the rumors flying hither and yon about the golden plow and how it was stolen from a blacksmith that Alvin prenticed with, but he never thought Makepeace would have the face to take it to court, where he'd be proved a liar for sure. "I give you my word I won't leave town till this is settled," said Alvin. "But I've got Arthur Stuart to look after, and it'd be right inconvenient if you locked me up."

"Well, now, that's fine," said Doggly. "The warrant says you have a choice. Either you surrender the plow to me for safekeeping till the trial, or you sit in jail *with* the plow."

"So the plow is the only bail I can pay, is that it?" asked Alvin.

"Reckon that's the long and short of it."

"Horace, I reckon you'll have to look after the boy," said Alvin to the innkeeper. "I didn't bring him here to put him back in your charge, but you can see I got small choice."

"Well, you could put the plow in Po's keeping," said Horace. "Not that I mind keeping the boy."

"No offense, Sheriff, but you wouldn't keep the plow safe a single night," said Alvin, smiling wanly.

"Reckon I could do just fine," said Po, looking a mite offended. "I mean, even if I lock you up, you don't think I'd let you keep the plow in the cell with you, do you?"

"Reckon you *will*," said Alvin mildly.

"Reckon not," said Po.

"Reckon you think you could keep it safe," said Alvin. "But what you don't know is how to keep folks safe from the plow."

"So you admit you have it."

"It was my journeypiece," said Alvin. "There are witnesses of that. This whole charge is nonsense, and you and everybody else knows it. But what'll the charge be if I give you this plow and somebody opens the sack and gets struck blind? What's the charge then?"

"Blind?" asked Po Doggly, glancing at Horace, as if his old friend the innkeeper could tell him whether he was having his leg pulled.

"You think you can tell your boys not to look in the sack, and that's going to be enough?" said Alvin. "You think they won't just try to take a peek?"

"Blind, eh?" said Po.

Alvin picked up the sack from where it had lain beside him on the bed. "And who's going to carry the plow, Po?"

Sheriff Doggly reached out to take it, but no sooner had his hands closed around the sack than he felt the hard metal inside shift and dance under his hands, sliding away from him. "Stop doing that, Alvin!" he demanded.

"I'm just holding the top of the sack," said Alvin. "What shelf you going to keep this on?"

"Oh, shut up, boy," said Doggly. "I'll let you keep it in the cell. But if you plonk somebody over the head with that thing and make an escape, I'll find you and the charge won't be no silly tale from Makepeace Smith, I promise you."

Alvin shook his head and smiled.

Horace laughed out loud. "Po, if Al wanted to escape from your jail, he wouldn't have to do no head plonking."

"I'm just telling you, Al," said the sheriff. "Don't push your luck with me. There's a outstanding extradition order from Appalachee about standing trial for the death of a certain dead Slave Finder."

Suddenly Horace's genial manner changed, and in a quick movement he had the sheriff pressed into the doorjamb so tight it looked like it might make a permanent difference in his posture. "Po," said Horace, "you been my dearest friend for many a year. We done in the dark of night what would get us kilt for doing in daylight, and trusted each other's life through it all. If you ever bring a charge or even *try* to extradite this boy for killing the *Slave Finder* who killed my Margaret in my own house, I will do a little justice on you with my own two hands."

Po Doggly squinted and looked the innkeeper in the eye. "Is that a threat, Horace? You want me to break my oath of office for you?"

"How can it be a threat?" said Horace. "You know I meant it in the nicest possible way."

"Just come along to jail, Alvin," said Doggly. "I reckon if the town ladies don't have meals for you, Horace here will bring you roadhouse stew every night."

"I keep the plow?" asked Alvin.

"I ain't coming near that thing," said the sheriff. "*If* it's a plow. *If* it's gold." Doggly gestured him to pass through the door and come into the hall. Alvin complied. The sheriff followed him down the narrow hall to the common room, where about two dozen people were standing around waiting to see what the sheriff had been after. "Alvin, nice to see you," several of them greeted him. They looked kind of embarrassed, seeing how Alvin was in custody. "Not much of a welcome, is it?" said Ruthie Baker, her face grim. "I swan, that Makepeace Smith has bit himself a tough piece of gristle with this mischief."

"Just bring me some of them snickerdoodles in jail," said Alvin. "I been hankering for them the whole way here."

"You can bet the ladies'll be quarreling all day about who's to feed you," said Ruth. "I just wish dear old Peg had been here to greet you." And she burst into quick, sentimental tears. "Oh, I wish I didn't cry so easy!"

Alvin gave her a quick hug, then looked at the sheriff. "She ain't passing me no file to saw the bars with," he said. "So is it all right if I . . ."

"Oh, shut up, Alvin," said Sheriff Doggly. "Why the hell did you even come back here?"

At that moment the door swung open and Makepeace Smith himself strode in. "There he is! The thief has been apprehended at last! Sheriff, make him give me my plow!"

Po Doggly looked him in the eye. Makepeace was a big

man, with massive arms and legs like tree trunks, but when the sheriff faced him Makepeace wilted like a flower. "Makepeace, you get out of my way right now."

"I want my plow!" Makepeace insisted—but he backed out the door.

"It ain't your plow till the court says it's your plow, if it ever does," said the sheriff.

Horace Guester chimed in. "It ain't your plow till you show you know how to make one just like it."

But Alvin himself said nothing to Makepeace. He just walked on out of the roadhouse, pausing in the doorway only to tell Horace, "You let Arthur Stuart visit me all he wants, you hear?"

"He'll want to sleep right in the cell with you, Alvin, you know that!"

Alvin laughed. "I bet he can fit right through the bars, he's so skinny."

"I made those bars!" Makepeace Smith shouted. "And they're too close together for anyone to fit through!"

Ruth Baker shouted back, just as loudly. "Well, if you made those bars, little Arthur can no doubt *bend* them out of the way!"

"Come on now, folks," Sheriff Doggly said. "I'm just making a little arrest here, so stand clear and let me bring the prisoner on through. While you, Makepeace, are exactly three words away from being arrested your own self for obstructing justice and disturbing the peace."

"Arrest *me!*" cried Makepeace.

"Now you're just *one* word away," said Sheriff Doggly. "Come on, any word will do. Say it. Let me lock you up, Makepeace. You know I'm dying to."

Makepeace knew he was. He clamped his mouth shut and took a few steps away from the roadhouse porch. But then he turned to watch, and let himself smile as he saw Alvin getting led away down the street toward the courthouse, and the jail out back.

❧ 11 ❧

Jail

CALVIN'S FRENCH WAS awful—but that was hardly his worry. Talking he had done in England, and plenty of it, until he learned to imitate the cultured accents of a refined gentleman. But here in Paris, talking was useless—harmful, even. One did not become a figure of myth and rumor by chatting. That's one thing Calvin had learned from Alvin, all right, even though Alvin never meant to teach it. Alvin never tooted his own horn. So every Tom, Dick, and Sally tooted it for him. And the quieter he got, the more they bragged on him. That was what Calvin did from the moment he arrived in Paris, kept his silence as he went about healing people.

He had been working on healing—like Taleswapper said, that was a knack people would appreciate a lot more than a knack for killing bugs. No way could Calvin do the subtle things that Alvin talked about, seeing the tiny creatures that spread disease, understanding the workings of the little bits of life out of which human bodies were built. But there *were* things within Calvin's grasp. Gross things, like bringing the edges of open wounds together and getting the skin to scar over—Calvin didn't rightly understand how he did it, but he could sort of squinch it together in his mind and the scarstuff would grow.

Getting skin to split, too, letting the nasty fluids spew out— that was impressive indeed, especially when Calvin did it with beggars on the city streets. Of course, a lot of the beggars had phony wounds. Calvin could hardly heal *those*, and he wouldn't make himself many friends by making the painted scars slide off beggars' faces. But the real ones—he could help some of them, and when he did, he was careful to make sure plenty of people could see exactly what happened. Could see the healing, but could not hear him brag or boast, or even promise in advance what would happen. He would make a great show of it, standing in front of the beggar, ignoring the open hand or the proffered cup, looking down instead at the wound, the sore, the swelling. Finally the beggar would fall silent, and so would the onlookers, their attention at last riveted on the spot that Calvin so intently watched. By then, of course, Calvin had the wound clearly in mind, had explored it with his doodling bug, had thought through what he was going to do. So in that exact moment of silence he reached out with his bug and gave the new shape to the skin. The flesh opened or the wound closed, whatever was needed.

The onlookers gasped, then murmured, then chattered. And just when someone was about to engage him in conversation, Calvin turned and walked away, shaking his head and refusing to speak.

The silence was far more powerful than any explanation. Rumors of him spread quickly, he knew, for in the cafe where he supped (but did no healing) he heard people speaking of the mysterious silent healer, who went about doing good as Jesus did.

What Calvin hoped would not get spread about was the fact that he wasn't exactly healing people, except by chance. Alvin could get into the deep hidden secrets of the body and do real healing, but Calvin couldn't see that small. So the wound might drain and close, but if there was a deep infection it would come right back. Still, some of them might be healed, for all he knew. Not that it would really help them—how would they beg, without a wound? If they were smart, they'd get away from him before he could take away the coin they used to buy compassion. But no, the ones with real injury wanted to be healed more than they wanted to eat. Pain and suffering did that to people. They could be wise and careful when they felt fine. Add a little pain to the mix, though, and all they wanted was whatever would make the pain go away.

It took a surprisingly long time before one of the Emperor's secret police came to see him. Oh, a gendarme or two had witnessed what he did, but since he touched no one and said nothing, they also did nothing, said nothing to him. And soldiers—they were beginning to seek him out, since so many veterans had injuries from their days in service, and half the cripples Calvin helped had old companions from the battle lines they went to see, to show the healing miracle that Calvin had brought them. But no one with the furtive wariness of the secret police was ever in the crowd, not for three long weeks—weeks in which Calvin had to keep moving his operation from one part of the city to another, lest someone he had already healed come back to him for a second treatment. What good would all this effort do if the rumor began to get about that the ones he healed didn't stay healed?

Then at last a man came, a middle-sized man of bourgeois clothing and modest demeanor, but Calvin saw the tension, the watchfulness—and, most important, the brace of pistols hidden in the pockets of his coat. This one would report to the Emperor. So Calvin made quite sure that the secret policeman was in a good position to see all that transpired when he healed a beggar. Nor did it hurt that even before the silence fell and he did the healing, everyone was murmuring things like, "Is he the one? I heard he healed that one-legged beggar near Montmartre," though of course Calvin had never even attempted to heal someone with a missing limb. Even Alvin might not be able to do something as spectacular as *that*. But it didn't hurt that such a rumor was about. Anything to get him into the presence of the Emperor, for everyone knew that he suffered agonies from the gout. Pain in the legs—he will bring me to him to end the pain in his legs. For the pain, he'll teach me all he knows. Anything to remove the pain.

The healing ended. Calvin walked away, as usual. To his surprise, however, the secret policeman left by quite another route. Shouldn't he follow me? Whisper to me that the Emperor needs me? Would I come and serve the Emperor? Oh, but I'm not sure I can be of help. I do what I can, but many wounds are stubborn and refuse to be fully healed. Oh, that's right, Calvin meant to promise *nothing*. Let his deeds speak for themselves. He would make the Emperor's leg feel better for a while—he was sure he could do that—but no one would ever be able to say that Calvin Miller had promised that the healing would be permanent, or even that there would be any kind of healing at all.

But he had no chance to say these things, for the secret policeman went another way.

That evening, as he waited for his supper at the cafe, four gendarmes came into the cafe, laughing as if they had just come off duty. Two went toward the kitchen—apparently they knew someone there—while the other two jostled, clumsy and laughing, among the tables. Calvin smiled a moment and then looked out the window.

The laughing stopped. Harsh hands seized his arms and lifted him out of his chair. All four gendarmes were around him now, not laughing at all. They bound his wrists together and hobbled his legs. Then they half-dragged him from the cafe.

It was astonishing. It was impossible. This had to be a response to the report of the secret policeman. But why would they arrest him? What law had he broken? Was it simply that he spoke English? Surely they understood the difference between an Englishman and an American. The English were still at war with France, or something like war, anyway, but the Americans were neutral, more or less. How dare they?

For a moment, painfully hobbling along with the gendarmes at the too-brisk pace they set for him, Calvin toyed with the idea of using his Makering power to loose the bonds and stand free of them. But they were all armed, and Calvin had no desire to tempt them to use their weapons against an escaping prisoner.

Nor did he waste effort, after the first few minutes, trying to persuade them that some terrible mistake was underway. What was the point? They knew who he was; someone had told them to arrest him; what did they care whether it was a mistake or not? It wasn't *their* mistake.

Half an hour later, he found himself stripped and thrown into a miserable stinking cell in the Bastille.

"Welcome to the Land of the Guillotine!" croaked someone farther up the corridor. "Welcome, O pilgrim, to the Shrine of the Holy Blade!"

"Shut up!" cried another man.

"They sliced through another man's neck today, the one who was in the cell you're in now, new boy! That's what happens to Englishmen here in Paris, once somebody decides that you're a spy."

"But I'm not English!" Calvin cried out.

This was greeted with gales of laughter.

Peggy set down her pen in weariness, closed her eyes in disgust. Wasn't there some kind of plan here? The One who sent Alvin into the world, who protected him and prepared him for the great work of building the Crystal City, didn't that One have some kind of plan? Or was there no plan? No, there had to be some meaning in the fact that this very day, in Paris, Calvin was locked up in prison, just as Alvin was in prison in Hatrack River. The Bastille, of course, was a far cry from a second-story room in the back of the courthouse, but jail was jail— they were both locked in, for no good reason, and with no idea of how it would all come out.

But Peggy knew. She saw all the paths. And, finally, she closed up her pen, put away the papers she had been writing on, and got up to tell her hosts that she would have to leave earlier than she expected. "I'm needed elsewhere, I think."

Bonaparte's nephew was a weasel who thought he was an ermine. Well, let him have his delusion. If men didn't have delusions, Bonaparte wouldn't be Emperor of Europe and Lawgiver of Mankind. Their delusions were his truth; their hungers were his heart's desire. Whatever they wanted to believe about themselves, Bonaparte helped them believe it, in exchange for control over their lives.

Little Napoleon, the lad called himself. Half of Bonaparte's nephews had been named Napoleon, in an effort to curry favor, but only this one had the effrontery to use the name in court. Bonaparte wasn't quite sure if this meant that Little Napoleon was bolder than the others, or simply too stupid to realize how dangerous it was to dare to use the Emperor's own name, as if to assert one's claim to succeed him. Seeing him now, marching in here like a mechanical soldier—as if he had some secret military accomplishment that no one knew about but which entitled him to strut about playing the general—Bonaparte wanted to laugh in his face and expose in front of all the world Little Napoleon's dreams of sitting on the throne, ruling the world, surpassing his uncle's accomplishments. Bonaparte wanted to look him in the eye and say, "You couldn't even fill my pisspot, you vainglorious mountebank."

Instead he said, "What good wind blows you here, my little Napoleon?"

"Your gout," said the lad.

Oh, no. Another cure. Cures found by fools usually did more harm than good. But the gout was a curse, and . . . let's see what he has.

"An Englishman," said Little Napoleon. "Or, to speak more accurately, an American. My spies have watched him—"

"*Your* spies? These are different spies from the spies I pay?"

"The spies you assigned to me for supervision, Uncle."

"Ah, those spies. They do still remember they work for me, don't they?"

"Remember it so well that instead of simply following orders and watching for enemies, they have also watched for someone who might help you."

"Englishmen in Europe are all spies. Someday after some notable achievement when I'm very very popular I will round them all up and guillotine them. Monsieur Guillotin—now *that* was a useful fellow. Has he invented anything else lately?"

"He's working on a steam-powered wagon, Uncle."

"They already exist. We call them locomotives, and we're laying track all over Europe."

"Ah, but *he* is working on one that doesn't have to run on rails."

"Why not a steam-powered balloon? I can't understand why that has never worked. The engine would propel the craft, and the steam, instead of being wastefully discharged into the atmosphere, would fill the balloon and keep the craft aloft."

"I believe the problem, Uncle, is that if you carry enough fuel to travel more than twenty or thirty feet, the whole thing weighs too much to get off the ground."

"That's why inventors exist, isn't it? To solve problems like that. Any fool could come up with the basic idea—*I* came up with it, didn't I? And when it comes to such matters I'm plainly a fool, as most men are." Bonaparte had long since learned that such modest remarks always got repeated by onlookers in the court and did much to endear him to the people. "It's Monsieur Guillotin's job to . . . well, never mind, the machine that bears his name is enough of a contribution to mankind. Swift, sure, and painless executions—a boon to the unworthiest of humans. A very Christian invention, showing kindness to the least of Jesus' brethren." The priests would repeat that one, and from the pulpit, too.

"About this Calvin Miller," said Little Napoleon.

"And my gout."

"I've seen him drain a swollen limb just by standing on the street staring at a beggar's pussing wound."

"A pussing wound isn't the gout."

"The beggar had his trousers ripped open to show the wound, and this American stood there looking for all the world as if he were dozing off, and then suddenly the skin erupted with pus and all of it drained out, and then the wound closed without a single stitch. Neither he nor any man touched the leg. It was quite a demonstration of remarkable healing powers."

"You saw this yourself?"

"With my own eyes. But only the once. I can hardly go about secretly, Uncle. I look too much like your esteemed self."

No doubt Little Napoleon imagined that this was flattery. Instead it sent a faint wave of nausea through Bonaparte. But he let nothing show in his face.

"You now have this healer under arrest?"

"Of course. Waiting for your pleasure."

"Let him sweat."

Little Napoleon cocked his head a moment, studying Bonaparte, probably trying to figure out what plan his uncle had for the healer, and why he didn't want to see him right away. The one thing he would never think of, Bonaparte was quite sure, was the truth: that Bonaparte hadn't the faintest idea what to do about a healer who actually had power. It made him uneasy thinking about it. And he remembered the young white boy who had come with the Red general, Ta-Kumsaw, to visit him in Fort Detroit. Could this American be the same one?

Why should he even make such a connection? And why would that boy in Detroit matter, after all these years? Bonaparte was uncertain about what it all meant, but it felt to him as if forces were at work, as if this American in the Bastille were someone of great importance to him. Or perhaps not to him. To someone, anyway.

Bonaparte's leg throbbed. Another episode of gout was starting. "Go away now," he said to Little Napoleon.

"Do you want information from the American?" asked Little Napoleon.

"No," said Bonaparte. "Leave him alone. And while you're at it, leave *me* alone, too."

Alvin had a steady stream of visitors in the courthouse jail. It seemed like they all had the same idea. They'd sidle right up to the bars, beckon him close, and whisper (as if the deputy didn't know right well what they was talking about), "Don't you have some way to slip on out of here, Alvin?"

What, they believed he hadn't thought of it? Such a simple matter, to soften the stone and pull one of the bars out. Or, for that matter, he could make the metal of a bar flow away from the stone it was embedded in. Or dissolve the bar entirely. Or push against the stone and press on through, walking through the wall into freedom. Such things would be easy enough for Alvin. As a child he had played with stone and found softness and weakness in it; as a prentice blacksmith, he had come to understand iron from the heart out. Hadn't he crawled into the forgefire and turned an iron plowshare to living gold?

Now, locked in this prison, he thought of leaving, thought of it all the time. Thought of hightailing it off into the woods, with or without Arthur Stuart—the boy was happy here, so why take him away? Thought of the sun on his back, the wind in his face, the greensong of the forest now so faint to him through stone and iron that he could hardly hear it.

But he told himself what he told those friendly folk who meant so well. "I need to be shut of this whole affair before I go off. So I mean to stand trial here, get myself acquitted, and then go on without fear of somebody tracking me down and telling the same lies on me again."

And then they always did the same thing. Having failed to persuade him to escape, they'd eye his knapsack and whisper, "Is it in there?"

And the boldest of them would say what they were all wishing. "Can I see it?"

His answer was always the same. He'd ask about the weather. "Think it's a hard winter coming on?" Some picked up slower than others, but after a while they all realized he wasn't going to answer a blame thing about the golden plow or the contents of his knapsack, not a word one way or the other. Then they'd make some chat or take up his used dishes, them as brought food, but it never took long and soon they was on their way out of the courthouse to tell their friends and family that Alvin was looking sad kind of but he still wasn't saying a thing about that gold plow that Makepeace claimed was his own gold treasure stolen by the boy back in his prentice days.

One day Sheriff Doggly brought in a fellow that Alvin recognized, sort of, but couldn't remember why or who. "That's the one," said the stranger. "Got no respect for any man's knack except his own." Then Alvin recollected well enough—it was the dowser who picked the spot for Alvin to dig a well for Makepeace Smith. The spot where Alvin dug right down to a sheet of thick hard rock, without finding a drop of water first. No doubt Makepeace meant to use him as a witness that Alvin's well wasn't in the spot the dowser chose. Well, that was true enough, no disputing it. The dowser fellow wasn't going to testify to anything that Alvin wouldn't have admitted freely his own self. So let them plot their plots. Alvin had the truth with him, and that was bound to be enough, with twelve jurors of Hatrack River folk.

The visits that really cheered him were Arthur's. Two or three times a day, the boy would blow in from the square like a leaf getting tucked into an open door by a gust of wind. "You just got to meet that feller John Binder," he'd say. "Ropemaker. Some folks is joking how if they decide to hang you, he'll be the one as makes the rope, but he just shuts 'em right up, you should hear him, Alvin. 'No rope of mine is going to hang no Maker,' he says. So even though you never met him I count him as a friend. But I tell you, they say his ropes *never* unravel, never even *fray*, no matter where you cut em. Ain't that some knack?"

And later in the same day, he'd be on about someone else. "I was out looking for Alfreda Matthews, Sophie's cousin, she's the one lives in that shack down by the river, only the river's a long windy thing and I couldn't find her and in fact it was getting on toward dark and I couldn't rightly find myself, and then here I am face to face with this Captain Alexander, he's a ship's captain only who knows what he's doing so far from the sea? But he lives around here doing tinkering and odd fixing, and Vilate Franker says he must have done some terrible crime to have to hide from the sea, or maybe there was some great sea beast that swallowed up his ship and left only him alive and now he daresn't go back to sea for fear the beast— she calls it La Vaya Than, which Goody Trader says is Spanish for 'Ain't this a damn lie,' do you know Goody Trader?"

"Met her," says Alvin. "She brung me some horehound drops. Nastiest candy I ever ate, but I reckon for them as loves horehound they were good enough. Strange lady. Squatted right outside the door here pondering for the longest time until she finally gets up and says 'Humf, you're the first man I ever met what didn't need *nothing* and here you are in jail.'"

"They say that's her knack, knowing what a body needs even when he don't know himself," said Arthur. "Though I *will* say that Vilate Franker says that Goody Trader is a humbug just like the alligator boy in the freak show in Dekane, which you wouldn't take me to see cause *you* said if he was real, it was cruel to gawk at him, and—"

"I remember what I said, Arthur Stuart. You don't have to gossip to me about *me*."

"Anyway, what was I talking about?"

"Lost in the woods looking for old drunken Freda."

"And I bumped into that sea captain, anyway, and he looks me in the eye and he says, 'Follow me,' and I go after him about ten paces and he sets me right in the middle of a deer track and he says, 'You just go along this way and when you reach the river again, you go upstream about three rods.' And you know what? I did what he said and you know what?"

"You found Freda."

"Alfreda Matthews, and she was stone drunk of course but I splashed her face with some water and I done what you said folks ought to do, I emptied her jug out and boy howdy, she was spitting mad, I like to had to out-dance the devil just to keep from getting hit by them rocks she threw!"

"Poor lady," said Alvin. "But it won't do no good as long as there's folks to give her another jug."

"Can't you do like you did with that Red Prophet?"

Alvin looked at him sharp. "What do you think you know about *that*?"

"Just what your own mama told me back in Vigor Church, about how you took a drunken one-eyed Red and made a prophet out of him."

Alvin shook his head. "No sir, she got it wrong. He was a prophet all along. And he wasn't a drunk the way Freda's a drunk. He took the likker into him to drown out the terrible black noise of death. That's what I fixed, and then he didn't need that likker no more. But Freda—there's something else in her that hungers for it, and I don't understand it yet."

"I told her to come to you though, so I reckon you oughta know and that's why I told you she's a-coming to get healed."

Alvin shook his head.

"Did I do wrong?"

"No, you done right," said Alvin. "But there's nothing I can do for her beyond what she oughta do for herself. She knows the likker's eating her up, stealing her life away from her. But I'll talk to her and help her if I can."

"They say she can tell you when rain's coming. If she's sober."

"Then how would anybody know she has such a knack?" asked Alvin.

Arthur just laughed and laughed. "I reckon she must have been sober *once*, anyway. And it was raining!"

When Arthur Stuart left, Alvin pondered the tales he told. Some of Arthur's chat was just gossip. There was some powerful gossips in Hatrack River these days, and the way Alvin figured it, the two biggest gossips was Vilate Franker, who Alvin had met and knew she was living inside a bunch of lying hexes, and Goody Trader, who he didn't really know yet except for what he gleaned from her visit. Her real name was either Chastity or Charity—Vilate said it was Chastity, but other folks said the other. She went by Goody, short for Goodwife, seeing how she'd been married three times and kept all them husbands happy till they croaked, accidental every time, though again Vilate managed to give Arthur the impression that they wasn't truly accidental. Them two women was at war all the time, that much was plain—hardly a word one said as wasn't contradicted flat out by the other. Now, neither one of these ladies invented gossip, nor was it so that Hatrack River didn't have rumors and tales before the two of them moved here. But it was plain that Arthur was visiting both of them every day, and both of them was filling him full of tales until Alvin could hardly make sense of it and it was a sure thing that Arthur didn't really understand the half of what he'd been told.

Alvin knew for himself that Vilate was deceptive and spiteful. But Goody might be just the same or worse, only she was better at it so Alvin couldn't see it so plain. Hard to tell. And that business with Goody Trader saying Alvin didn't need nothing—well, what was *that*?

But behind all the gossip and quarreling, there was something else that struck Alvin as pretty strange. Mighty knacks was thick underfoot in Hatrack River. Most towns might have somebody with something of a knack that you might notice. Most knacks, though, was pretty plain. A knack for soup. A knack for noticing animal tracks. Useful, but nothing to write a letter to your daddy about. A lot of folks had no idea what their own knack was, because it was so easy for them and not all that remarkable in the eyes of other folks. But here in Hatrack River, the knacks was downright astonishing. This sea captain who could help you find your way even when you didn't know you was lost. And Freda—Alvin pooh-poohed it to Arthur Stuart, but there was folks in town as swore she didn't just *predict* rain, if you sobered her up in a dry season she could *bring* it. And Melýn, a Welsh girl who can harp and sing so you forget everything while she's doing it, forget it all and just sit there with a stupid smile on your face because you're so happy— she came and played for Alvin and he could feel how the sound that flowed from her could reach inside him like a doodlebug scooting through the earth, reach inside and find all the knots and loosen them up and just make him feel good.

It was power like he'd been trying to teach the folks back in Vigor, only they could hardly understand it, could hardly get but a glimmer of it now and then, and here it was so thick on the ground you could rake it up like leaves. Maggie who helped out in Goody Trader's store, she could ride any horse no matter how wild, plenty of witnesses of that. And one who scared Alvin a little, a girl named Dorcas Bee who could draw portraits of folks that not only looked like their outward face, but also showed everything that was inside them—Alvin didn't know what to make of her, and even with his eyes he couldn't rightly understand how she did it.

Any one of these folks would be remarkable in whatever town they lived in, no matter if it was as big as New Amsterdam or Philadelphia. Yet here they were living in the middle of nowhere, Hatrack River of all places, swelling the numbers of the town but yet nobody seemed to find it remarkable at all that so many knacks was gathered here.

There's a reason for it, Alvin thought. Got to be a reason for it. And I have to know it, because there's going to be a jury of these knacky folks, and they're going to decide whether Makepeace Smith is a plain liar—or I am. Only this town is full of lies, since the things Vilate Franker says and the things Goody Trader says can't all be true at the same time. Full of lies and, yes, miseries. Alvin could feel that there was something of the Unmaker going on, but couldn't lay hands on it or find who it was. Hard to find the Unmaker when the Unmaker didn't want to be found. Especially hard from a jail cell, where all you got was rumor and brief visits.

Well, they wasn't *all* brief. Vilate Franker herself came and stayed sometimes half an hour at a time, even though there wasn't no place to sit down. Alvin couldn't figure what she wanted. She didn't gossip with him, rightly speaking—all of *her* gossip Alvin got secondhand from Arthur Stuart. No, Vilate came to him to talk about philosophy and poetry and such, things that no man or woman had talked to him about since Miss Larner. Alvin wondered if maybe Vilate was trying to charm him, but since he couldn't see the beauty-image from her hexes, he didn't rightly know. She sure wasn't pretty to *him*. But the more she talked, the more he liked her company, till he found himself looking forward to her coming every day. More than anybody except Arthur Stuart, truth be known, and as they talked, Alvin would lie down on the cot in the cell and he'd close his eyes and then he didn't have to see either her unprettiness *or* her hexery, he could just hear the words and think the ideas and see the visions that she conjured in him. She'd say poetry and the words had music inside him. She'd talk of Plato and Alvin understood and it made him feel wise in a way that the adulation of folks back in Vigor Church never did.

Was this some knack of hers? Alvin didn't know, just plain couldn't tell. He only knew that it was only during her visits that he could completely forget that he was in jail. And it dawned on him, after a week or so, that he might just be falling in love. That the feelings that he had only ever had toward Miss Larner were getting waked up, just a little, by Vilate Franker. Now wouldn't that beat all? Miss Larner had been pretty and young, using knacks to make herself look plain and middle-aged. Now here was a woman plain and middle-aged using knacks that made other folks think she was pretty and young. How opposite could you be? But in both cases, it was the mature woman without obvious beauties that he delighted in.

And yet, even as he wondered if he was falling in love with Vilate, every now and then, in his lonely hours especially after dark, he would think of another face entirely. A young girl back in Vigor, the girl whose lies had driven him from home in the first place, the girl who claimed he had done forbidden things with her. He found himself thinking of those forbidden things, and there was a place in his heart where he wished he *had* done them. If he had, of course he would have married her. In fact, he would have married her before doing them, because that was right and the law and Alvin wasn't no kind of man to do wrong by a woman or break no law if he could help it. But in his imaginings in the dark there wasn't no law nor right and wrong neither, he just woke up sweating from a dream in which the girl wasn't no liar after all, and then he was plain ashamed of himself, and couldn't figure out what was wrong with him, to be falling in love with a woman of words and ideas and experience during the day, but then to be hot with passion for a stupid lying girl who just happened to be pretty and flat-out in love with him once upon a time back home.

I am an evil man, thought Alvin at times like that. Evil and unconstant. No better than them faithless fellows who can't leave women alone no matter what. I am the kind of man that I have long despised.

Only even that wasn't true, and Alvin knew it. Because he hadn't done a blamed thing wrong. Hadn't *done* anything. Had only imagined it. Imagined . . . and enjoyed. Was that enough to make him evil? "As a man thinketh in his heart, so is he," said the scripture. Alvin remembered it because his mother quoted it all the time till his father barked back at her, "That's just your way of saying that all men are devils!" and Alvin wondered if it was true—if all men had evil in their hearts, and those men as were good, maybe they were simply the ones who controlled theirselves so well they could act contrary to their heart's desire. But if that were so, then no man was good, not one.

And didn't the Holy Book say that, too?

No man good, not one. Not me, neither. Maybe me least of all.

And that was his life in that jail in Hatrack River. Darker and darker thoughts about his own worthiness, falling in love with two women at once, caught up in the gossip of a town where the Unmaker was surely at work, and where knacks abounded.

Calvin was pretty good with stone—he always did all right with that. Well, not always. He wasn't *born* finding the natural weaknesses of stone. But after Alvin went off to be a prentice to a smith, Calvin started trying to do what he saw or heard of his big brother doing. In those days he was still hoping to show Alvin how good he was at Makering when he got back, to hear his brother say to him, "Calvin, why, you're most as good as I am!" Which Alvin never said, nor even close to it. But it was true, at least about stone. Stone was easy, really, not like flesh and bone. Calvin could find his way into the stone, part it, shift it.

Which is what he started doing right away with the Bastille, of course. He didn't know why the secret police had put him inside those walls, clammy and cold. It wasn't a dungeon, not like in those stories, where the prisoner never sees any light except when a guard comes down with a torch, so he can go blind without knowing it. There was light enough, and a chair to sit on and a bed to lie on and a chamber pot that got emptied every day, once he figured out he was supposed to leave it by the door.

It was still a prison, though.

It took Calvin about five minutes to figure out that he could pretty much dissolve the whole locking mechanism, but he remembered just in time that getting out of his cell wasn't exactly the same thing as getting out of the Bastille. He couldn't make himself invisible, and Maker or not, a musket ball would knock him down or maim him or kill him like any other man.

He'd have to find another way out. And that meant going

right through the wall, right through stone. Trouble was, he didn't have any idea whether he was forty feet up or twenty feet under the street level. Or if the wall at the back of his cell opened on the outside or into an inner courtyard. Who might see if a gap appeared in the wall? He couldn't just remove a stone—he had to remove it in once piece, so he could put it back after if he had to.

He waited till night, then began working on a stone block right near floor level. It was heavy, and he didn't know of any way to make it lighter. Nor was there some subtle way to make stone move across stone. Finally he just softened the stone, plunged his fingers into it, then let it harden around his fingers, so he had a grip right in the middle of the stone block. Now, as he pulled on it, he made a thin layer of the stone turn liquid on the bottom and sides, so it was easier to pull it out, once he got it moving. It also made it silent as rock slid across rock. Except for the loud thud as the back of the stone dropped out of the hole and fell the few inches to the floor.

A breeze came through the cell, making it all the cooler. He slid the stone out of the way and then lay down and thrust his head and shoulders into the gap.

He was maybe twelve feet above the ground and directly over the head of a group of a dozen soldiers marching from somewhere to somewhere. Fortunately, they didn't look up. But that didn't keep Calvin's heart from beating halfway out of his chest. Once they were past, though, he figured he could go feetfirst through the hole and drop safely down to the ground and just walk away into the streets of Paris. Let them wonder how he got a stone out of the wall. That'd teach them to lock up folks who heal beggars.

He was all set to go, his feet already going into the hole, when it suddenly dawned on him that escaping was about as dumb a thing as he could do. Wasn't he here to see the Emperor? If he became a fugitive, that wasn't going to be too helpful. Bonaparte had powers that even Alvin didn't know about. Calvin *had* to learn them, if he could. The smart thing to do was sit tight here and see if somehow, someone in the chain of command might realize that a fellow who could heal beggars might be able to help with Bonaparte's famous gout.

So he got his back into it and hefted the stone back up into the gap and shoved it into place. He left the finger holes in it—it was dark at the back of the cell and besides, maybe if they noticed those holes in the stone they'd have more respect for his powers.

Or maybe not. How could he know? Everything was out of his control now. He hated that. But if you want to get something, you got to put yourself in the way of getting it.

Now that he wasn't trying to escape—but knew that he could if he wanted to—Calvin spent the days and nights lying on his cot or pacing his cell. Calvin wasn't good at being alone. He'd learned that on his trek through the woods after leaving Vigor. Alvin might be happy running along like a Red, but Calvin soon abandoned the forest tracks and got him on a road and hitched a ride on a farmer's wagon and then another and another, making friends and talking for company the whole way.

Now here he was stuck again, and even if the guards had been willing to talk to him, he didn't know the language. It hadn't bothered him that much when he was free to walk the streets of Paris and feel himself surrounded by the bustle of busy city life. Here, though, his inability to so much as ask a guard what day it was . . . it made him feel crippled.

Finally he began to amuse himself with mischief. It was no trouble at all to get his doodle bug inside the lock mechanism and ruin the guard's key by softening it when he inserted it. When the guard took the key back out, it had no teeth and the door was still locked. Angry, the guard stalked off to get another key. This time Calvin let him open the door without a problem— but what was it that made the first key lose its teeth?

And it wasn't just his own lock. He began to search far and wide with his doodle bug until he located the other occupied cells. He played games with their locks, too, including fusing a couple of them shut so no key could open them, and ruining a couple of others so they couldn't be locked at all. The shouting, the stomping, the running, it kept Calvin greatly entertained, especially as he imagined what the guards must be thinking. Ghosts? Spies? Who could be doing these strange things with the locks in the Bastille?

He also learned a few things. Back in Vigor, whenever he sat down for long he'd either get impatient and get up and move again, or he'd start thinking about Alvin and get all angry. Either way, he didn't spend all that much time testing the limits of his powers, not since Alvin came home. Now, though, he found that he could send his doodle bug right far, and into places that he'd never seen with his own eyes. He began to get used to moving his bug through the stone, feeling the different textures of it, sensing the wooden frames to the heavy doors, the metal hinges and locks. Damn, but he was good at this!

And he explored his own body with that doodle bug, and the bodies of the other prisoners, trying to find what it was that Alvin saw, trying to see deep. He experimented a little on the other prisoners' bodies, too, making changes in their legs the way he'd have to change Bonaparte's leg. Not that any of them had gout, of course—that was a rich man's disease, and nobody in prison was rich, even if they had money on the outside. Still, he could get a mental chart of what a more-or-less healthy leg looked like, on the inside. Get some idea of what he needed to do to get the Emperor's leg back in good shape.

Truth to tell, though, he didn't understand much more about legs after a week of this than he did at the beginning.

A week. A week and a half. Every day, more and more often, he'd walk to the wall, squat down, and put his fingers into those finger holes. He'd pull the stone a little bit, or maybe sometimes more, and once or twice all the way out of the wall, wanting to slide through the hole and walk away to freedom. Always, after a little thought, he put it back. But it took more thought every day. And the longing to be gone got stronger and stronger.

It was a blame fool plan anyway, like all his plans, when

you came right down to it. Calvin was a fool to think they'd let some unknown American boy have access to the Emperor.

He had the stone out of the wall for what he thought might well be the last time, when he heard the steps in the corridor. Nobody ever came along here this late at night! No time to get the stone back in place, either. So . . . was it go, or stay? They'd see the stone out of the wall no matter what he did. So did he want to face the consequences, which might include seeing the Emperor, but might just as easy mean facing the guillotine; or did he duck through the hole and get out into the street before they got the door open?

Little Napoleon grumbled to himself. All these days, the Emperor could have asked about the American healer any time. But no, it had to be in the middle of the night, it had to be *tonight*, when Little Napoleon had reserved the best box for the opening of a new opera by some Italian, what's-his-name. He wanted to tell the Emperor that tonight was *not* convenient, he should find another toady to do his bidding. But then the Emperor smiled at him and suggested that he had others who could do such a menial job, and he shouldn't waste his nephew's time on such unimportant matters . . . and what could Little Napoleon do? He couldn't let the Emperor realize that he could be replaced by some flunky. No, he insisted, No, Uncle, I'll go myself, it'll be my pleasure.

"I just hope he can do what you promised," Bonaparte said.

The bastard was playing with him, that was the truth. He knew as well as Little Napoleon did that there was no promise of anything, just a report. But if it pleased the Emperor to make his nephew sweat with fear that maybe he'd be made a fool of, well, Emperors were allowed to toy with other people's feelings.

The guard made a great noise about marching down the stone corridor and fumbling a long time with the keys.

"What, fool, are you giving the prisoner time to stop digging his tunnel and hide the evidence?"

"There be no tunnels from this floor, my lord," the turnkey said.

"I know that, fool. But what's all the fumble with the keys?"

"Most of them are new, my lord, and I don't recognize which one opens which door, not as easy as I used to."

"Then get the old keys and don't waste my time!"

"The old keys been stripped, or the locks was broken, my lord. It's been crazy, you wouldn't believe it."

"I *don't* believe it," said Little Napoleon grumpily. But he did, really—he had heard something about some sabotage or some kind of rare lock rust or something in the Bastille.

The key finally slid into the lock, and the door creaked open. The turnkey stepped in and shone his lantern about, to make sure the prisoner was in his place and not poised to jump him and take the keys. No, this one, the American boy, he was sitting far from the door, leaning against the opposite wall.

Sitting on what? The turnkey took a step or two closer, held the lantern higher.

"Mon dieu," murmured Little Napoleon.

The American was sitting on a large stone block from the wall, with a gap that led right out to the street. No man could have lifted such a block out of the wall with his bare hands— how could he even get hold of it? But having moved it somehow, what did this American fool do but sit down and wait! Why didn't he escape?

The American grinned at him, then stood up, still smiling, still looking at Little Napoleon—and then plunged his hands into the stone right up to his elbows, as easy as if the stone had been a water basin.

The turnkey screeched and ran for the door.

The American pulled his hands back out of the stone—except that one of them was in a fist now. He held out the stone to Little Napoleon, who took it, hefted it. It was stone, as hard as ever—but it was shaped with the print of the inside of a man's palms and fingers. Somehow this fellow could reach into solid rock and grab a lump of stone as if it were clay.

Little Napoleon reached into his memory and pulled out some English from his days in school. "What are your name?" he asked.

"Calvin Maker," said the American.

"Speak you the French?"

"Not a word," said Calvin Maker.

"Go *avec* me," said Little Napoleon. "*Avec . . .*"

"With," said the boy helpfully. "Go with you."

"*Oui.* Yes."

The Emperor had finally asked for the boy. But now Little Napoleon had serious misgivings. There was nothing about the healing of beggars to suggest the boy might have power over solid stone. What if this Calvin Maker did something to embarrass him? What if—it was beyond imagining, but he had to imagine it—what if he killed Uncle Napoleon?

But the Emperor had asked for him. There was no undoing *that*. What was he going to do, go tell Uncle that the boy he'd brought to heal his gout just *might* decide to plunge his hands into the floor and pull up a lump of marble and brain him with it? That would be political suicide. He'd be living on Corsica tending sheep in no time. If he didn't get to watch the world tumble head over heels as his head rolled down into the basket from the guillotine.

"Go go go," said Little Napoleon. "Wiss me."

The turnkey was huddled in a far corner of the corridor. Little Napoleon aimed a kick in his direction. The man was so far gone that he didn't even dodge. The kick landed squarely, and with a whimper the turnkey rolled over like a cabbage.

The American boy laughed out loud. Little Napoleon didn't like his laugh. He toyed with the idea of drawing his knife and killing the boy on the spot. But the explanation to the Emperor would be dangerous. "So you tried for weeks to get me to see him, and he was an assassin all along?" No, whatever happened, the American would see the Emperor.

Calvin Maker would see Napoleon Bonaparte . . . while Little Napoleon would see if God would answer a most fervent prayer.

❖ 12 ❖

Lawyers

"YOU KNOW THE miller's boy, Alvin, is in jail up in Hatrack River." The stranger leaned on the counter and smiled.

"I reckon we heard about it," said Armor-of-God Weaver.

"I'm here to help get the truth about Alvin, so the jury can make the right judgment up in Hatrack. They don't know Alvin as well as folks around here are bound to. I just need to get some affidavits about his character." The stranger smiled again.

Armor-of-God nodded. "I reckon this is the place for affidavits, if the truth about Alvin is what you're after."

"That I am. I take it you know the young man yourself?"

"Well enough." Armor-of-God figured if he was going to find out what this fellow was doing, it was best not to say he was married to Alvin's sister. "But I reckon you don't know what you're getting into up here, friend. You'll get more than the affidavits you're after."

"Oh, I've heard tell about the massacre at Tippy-Canoe, and the curse that folks here are under. I'm a lawyer. I'm used to hearing grim stories from people I'm defending."

"Defending, eh?" asked Armor. "You a lawyer as defends people, is that it?"

"That's what I'm best known for, in my home in Carthage City."

Armor nodded again. He might live in Carthage City now, but his accent said New England. And he might try some folksy talk, but it was a lawyer's version of it, to put folks off guard. This man could talk like the Bible if he wanted to. He could talk like Milton. But Armor didn't let on that he didn't trust the man. Not yet. "So when folks here tell you how they slaughtered Reds what never done nobody no harm, you can hear that without batting an eye, is that it?"

"I can't guarantee I won't do any eye-batting, Mr. Weaver. But I'll listen, and when it's done, I'll get on with the business that brought me here."

Now it's time. "And what business is that?" asked Armor.

The man blinked. Already batting an eye, thought Armor. That was right quick.

"I told you, Mr. Weaver. Getting affidavits about Alvin the miller's son."

"In order to tell people in Hatrack River about his true character, I remember. The thing is, out of the last eight years, Alvin spent seven in Hatrack, and only one here in Vigor Church. We knowed him as a child, you bet, but lately I'd say it's the people of Hatrack River as knows him best. So the way I see it, you're here to get a picture of Alvin that folks in Hatrack *don't* know. And the only reason for that is because you need to change their point of view about the boy. And since I know for a fact that Alvin is respected in Hatrack, you can only be here to try to dig up some dirt on the boy in order to do him harm. Have I just about got it? Friend?"

The lawyer's sudden lack of a cheerful smile was all the confirmation Armor needed. "Dirt is the farthest thing from my mind, Mr. Weaver. I come here with an open mind."

"An open mind, and free talk about how you defend people and all so as to make folks think you're on Alvin's side, instead of being hired to do your best to destroy folks' good opinion of him. So I reckon the fact that you're here means that Alvin's friends better get somebody else to go around collecting affidavits in his favor, since you won't be satisfied until you dig up some lies."

The man stiffened and stepped back. "I see that you're rather a partisan about the matter. I hope you can tell me what I said to give offense."

"Why, the only offense you gave was thinking that because I'm not a lawyer I must be dumb as a dog's butt."

"Well, no matter what conclusion you have reached, I assure you that as an officer of the court I seek nothing more than the simple truth."

"Officer of the court, is it? Well, I happen to know that *all* lawyers is called officers of the court. Even when they're hired by a private party to do mischief, because you sure as God lives wasn't hired by the county attorney down in Hatrack, because *he* would've give you a letter of introduction and you wouldn't have tried none of these pussyfooting prevaricating misrepresenting shenanigans."

The stranger put his hat back on his head and pushed it down right firm. Armor suppressed the impulse to reach out and push it down still firmer. As the stranger reached the door, Armor called out one last question. "Do you have a name, so we can inquire with the state bar association about any outstanding actions against you?"

The lawyer turned and smiled, even broader than when he was trying to fool Armor. "My name is Daniel Webster, Mr. Weaver, and my client is truth and justice."

"Truth and justice must pay a damn sight better in New England than it does out here," said Armor. "You *are* from New England, aren't you?"

"I was born there, and raised there, but saw no future for myself in that benighted backward place. So I came to the United States, where the laws are founded on the rights of man instead of the dynastic claims of monarchs or the worn-out theology of Puritans."

"Ah. So nobody's paying you?"

"I didn't say that, Mr. Weaver."

"Who's paying you, then? Ain't the county, and it ain't the state. And it sure can't be Makepeace Smith, since he's got him hardly four bits to rub together."

"I'm representing a consortium of concerned citizens of Carthage City, who are determined to see that justice prevails even in the benighted backwaters of the state of Hio."

"A consortium. That anything like a public house? Or a brothel?"

"How amusing."

"Name me a name, Mr. Webster. I happen to be mayor of this town, such as it is, and you're here practicing law, after a fashion, and I think I have a right to know who's sending lawyers up here to collect lies about our respected citizens."

"Do you own a gun of any kind, Mr. Weaver?"

"I do, friend."

"Then why should I reveal the names of my clients to an armed and angry man of a town that is so proud of being a nest of murderers that they brag out the whole story to any unfortunate visitor who happens by? Also, mayors have no right to inquire about anything from an attorney about his relations with his clients. Good day, Mr. Weaver."

Armor watched the Webster fellow out the door, then put on his hat, called out to his oldest boy to leave off soapmaking and watch the store, and took off at a jog up and over the hill to his in-laws' house. His wife would be there, since she was the best of the women at doing Alvin's Makery stuff and so was in much demand as a teacher and a fashioner of—much as Armor hated it—hexes. The family needed to know what was going on, that Alvin had enemies from the capital who were spending money on a lawyer to come dig up dirt about the boy. There was no way around it now—they had to get them a lawyer for Alvin, somehow. And not no country cousin, either. It had to be a city lawyer who knew all the same tricks as this Webster fellow. Armor vaguely remembered having heard of this man somewhere. He was spoke of with awe in some circles, and having talked to him and heard his golden voice and his quick answers and the way he made a lie sound like the natural truth even to someone who knew it was deception—well, Armor knew it would take some finding to get them a lawyer who could best him. And finding was going to be complicated by another problem—paying.

Calvin had no idea what he was supposed to do upon meeting the Emperor. The man's title was a throwback to ancient Rome, to Persia, to Babylon. But there he sat in a straight-back chair instead of a throne, his leg up on a cushioned bench; and instead of courtiers there were only secretaries, each scribbling away on a writing desk until an order or letter or edict was finished, then leaping to his feet and rushing from the room as the next secretary began to scribble furiously as Bonaparte dictated in a continuous stream of biting, lilting, almost Italian-sounding French.

As the dictation proceeded, Calvin, with guards on either side of him (as if that could stop him from making the floor collapse under the Emperor if he felt like it), watched silently. Of course they did not invite him to sit down; even Little Napoleon, the Emperor's nephew, remained standing. Only the secretaries could sit, it seemed, for it was hard to imagine how they could write without a lap.

At first Calvin simply took in the surroundings; then he studied the face of the Emperor, as if that slightly pained expression contained some secret which, if only examined long enough, would yield the secrets of the sphinx. But soon Calvin's attention drifted to the leg. It was the gout that he had to cure, if he was to make any headway. And Calvin had no idea what caused the gout or even how to figure it out. That was Alvin's province.

For a moment it occurred to Calvin that maybe he ought to

beg permission to write to his brother so he could get Alvin over here to cure the Emperor and win Calvin's freedom. But he immediately despised himself for the cowardly thought. Am I a Maker or not? And if a Maker, then Alvin's equal. And if Alvin's equal, why should I summon him to bail me out of a situation which, for all I know right now, might need no bailing?

He sent his doodling bug into Napoleon's leg.

It wasn't the sort of swelling that Calvin was used to in the festering sores of beggars. He didn't understand what the fluids were—not pus, that was certain—and he dared not simply make them flow back into the blood, for fear that they might be poisons that would kill the very man he came to learn from.

Besides, was it really in Calvin's best interests to cure this man? Not that he knew how to do it—but he wasn't sure he really ought to try. What he needed was not the momentary gratitude of a cured man, but the continuing dependence of a sufferer who needed Calvin's ministration for relief. Temporary relief.

And this was something Calvin *did* understand, to a point. He had learned long ago how to find the nerves in a dog or squirrel and give them a sort of tweak, an invisible pinch. Sometimes it set the animal to squealing and screeching till Calvin almost died from laughing. Other times the creature didn't show pain, but limped along as if that pinched limb didn't even exist. One time a perfectly healthy dog dragged around its hindquarters till its belly and legs were rubbed raw in the dirt and Father was all set to shoot the poor thing to put it out of its misery. Calvin took mercy on the beast then and unpinched the nerve so it could walk again, but after that it never did walk right, it sort of sidled, though whether that was from the pinch Calvin gave it or from the damaged caused by dragging its butt through the dirt for most of a week Calvin had no way to guess.

What mattered was that pinching of the nerve, to remove all feeling—Bonaparte might limp, but it would take away the pain. Relief, not a cure.

Which nerve? It wasn't like Calvin had them all charted out. That sort of methodical thinking was Alvin's game. In England, Calvin had realized that this was one of the crucial differences between him and his brother. There was a new word a fellow just coined at Cambridge for people who were ploddingly methodical like Alvin: *scientist.* While Calvin, with dash and flair and verve and, above all, the spirit of improvisation, *he* was an artist. Trouble was, when it came to getting at the nerves in Bonaparte's leg, Calvin couldn't very well experiment. He didn't think a strong friendship would develop between the Emperor and him if it began with the Emperor squealing and screeching like a tortured squirrel.

He pondered that for a while until, watching a secretary rise up and rush from the room, it occurred to him that Bonaparte's weren't the only legs around. Now that it mattered that Calvin find out exactly which nerve did what, and that his pinch deadened pain instead of provoking it, he had to play the scientist and test many legs until he got it right.

He started with the secretary who was next in line, a shortish fellow (smaller even than the Emperor, who was a man of scant stature) who fidgeted a little in his chair. Uncomfortable? Calvin asked him silently. Then let's see if we can find you some relief. He sent his bug into the man's right leg, found the most obvious nerve, and pinched.

Not a wince, not a grimace. Calvin was annoyed. He pinched harder. Nothing.

Then the current secretary jumped to his feet and rushed from the room. It was now the turn of the short fellow Calvin had pinched. The man tried to shift his body in his chair, to adjust the position of the lapdesk, but to Calvin's delight a look of astonishment came over the man's face, followed by a blush as he had to reach down and move his right leg with his hands. So. That large nerve—or was it a bundle of very fine nerves?— had nothing to do with feeling. Instead they seemed to control movement. Interesting.

The fellow wrote in silence, but Calvin knew that all he was really thinking about was what would happen when he had to jump up and run from the room. Sure enough, when the edict ended—it was about the granting of a special tax exemption to certain vintners in southern France because of a bad harvest—the man leapt up, spun around, and sprawled on the floor, his right leg tangled with his left like the fishing lines of children.

Every eye turned to the poor fellow, but not a word was spoken. Calvin watched with amusement as he got up on his hands and his left knee, while the right leg hung useless. The knee bent well enough, of course, and the man got it under his body so it *looked* like it might work, but twice he tried to put weight on it and twice he fell again.

Bonaparte, looking annoyed, finally spoke to him. "Are you a secretary, sir, or a clown?"

"My leg, sir," said the miserable clerk. "My right leg seems not to work just now."

Bonaparte turned sharply to the guards detaining Calvin. "Help him out of here. And fetch someone to clean up the spilled ink."

The guards hauled the man to his feet and started to move him toward the door. Now it was time for Little Napoleon to assert himself. "Take his desk, fools," said the Emperor's nephew. "And the inkwell, and the quill, and the edict, if it isn't spoiled."

"And how will they do all that?" asked Bonaparte testily. "Seeing they have to hold up this one-legged beggar?" Then he looked expectantly at Little Napoleon's face.

It took a moment for Little Napoleon to realize what the Emperor wanted of him, and an even longer moment for him to swallow his pride enough to do it. "Why, of course, Uncle," he said, with careful mildness. "I shall gladly pick it up myself, sir."

Calvin suppressed a smile as the proud man who had arrested him now knelt down and gathered up papers, lapdesk, quill, and inkwell, carefully avoiding getting a single drop of ink on himself. By now the secretary Calvin had pinched was out of the room. He thought of sending out his bug to find the man and unpinch the nerve, but he wasn't sure where he had gone and anyway, what did it matter? It was just a secretary.

When Little Napoleon was gone, Bonaparte resumed dictating, but now his delivery was not rapid and biting. Rather he halted, corrected himself now and then, and sometimes lapsed into silence for a time, as the secretary sat with pen poised. At such moments Calvin would cause the ink on the quill to flow to the tip and drop off suddenly onto the paper—ah, the flurry of blotting! And of course this only served to distract the Emperor all the more.

There remained, however, the matter of legs. Calvin explored each secretary in turn, finding other nerves to pinch, ever so slightly. He left the nerves of movement alone now; it was the nerves of pain that he was finding now, charting his progress by the widened eyes, flushed faces, and occasional gasps of the unfortunate secretaries. Bonaparte was not unaware of their discomfort—it distracted him all the more. Finally, when a man gasped at a particularly sharp pinch—Calvin's touch was not always precise with such slender things as nerves—Bonaparte turned himself in his chair, wincing at the pain in his own leg, and said, as best Calvin could understand his French, "Do you mock me with these pains and moans? I sit here in agony, making no sound, while you, with no more pain than that of sitting too long to take letters, moan and gasp and wince and sigh until I can only imagine I am trapped with a choir of hyenas!"

At that moment Calvin finally got it right, giving just the right amount of pressure to a secretary's pain nerve that all feeling vanished, and instead of the man wincing, his face relaxed in relief. That's it, thought Calvin. That's how it's done.

He almost sent his bug right into Bonaparte's leg to do that same little twist and make the Emperor's pain go away. Fortunately he was distracted by the opening of the door. It was a scullery maid with a bucket and rags to clean up the ink from the marble floor. Bonaparte glared at her, and she almost dropped her things and fled, except that he at once softened his expression. "My rage is at my pain, girl," he said to her. "Come in and do your work, no one minds."

With that she gathered her courage, scurried to the drying ink, set down the bucket with a clank and a slosh, and set to work scrubbing.

By now Calvin had come to his senses. What good would it do to take away Bonaparte's pain if the Emperor didn't *know* that it was Calvin doing it? Instead he practiced the soothing twist of the nerves on all the secretaries, to their undoubted relief, and as he did he began to sense a sort of current, a humming, a vibration on the nerves that were actually carrying pain at the instant he twisted them, so that he could get even more precise, taking away not all the feeling in a leg, but just the pain itself. Finally he got to the scullery maid, to the pain she always felt in her knees as she knelt on hard cold floors to do her work. So sudden was the relief, and so sharp and constant had been the pain, that she cried aloud, and again Bonaparte glared at the interruption.

"Oh sir," she said, "forgive me, but I suddenly felt no pain in my knees."

"Lucky you," said Bonaparte. "Along with this miracle, do you also find that you see no ink on the floor?"

She looked down. "Sir, with all my scrubbing, I can't get up the whole stain. I'm afraid it's gone down into the stone, sir."

Calvin at once sent his doodling bug into the surface of the marble and discovered that the ink had, indeed, penetrated beyond the reach of her scrubbing. Now was the chance to have Bonaparte notice him, not as a prisoner—even his guards were gone—but as a man of power. "Perhaps I can help," he said.

Bonaparte looked at him as if seeing him for the first time, though Calvin was quite aware that the Emperor had sized him up several times over the past half-hour. Bonaparte spoke to him in accented English. "Was it for scullery work you came to Paris, my dear American friend?"

"I came to serve you, sir," said Calvin. "Whether with a stained floor or a pained leg, I care not."

"Let's see you with floors first," said Bonaparte. "Give him the rags and bucket, girl."

"I don't need them," said Calvin. "I've already done it. Have her scrub again, and this time the stain will come right up."

Bonaparte glowered at the idea of serving as interpreter for an American prisoner and a scullery maid, but his curiosity got the better of his dignity and he gave the girl the order to scrub again. This time the ink came right up, and the stone was clean again. It had been child's play for Calvin, but the awe in the girl's face was the best possible advertisement for his wondrous power. "Sir," she said, "I had only to pass the rag over the stain and it was gone!"

The secretaries were eyeing Calvin carefully now—they weren't fools, and they clearly suspected him of causing both their discomfort and their relief, though some of them were pinching the legs to try to restore feeling after Calvin's first, clumsier attempts at numbing pain. Now Calvin went back into their legs, restored feeling, and then gave the more delicate twist that removed pain. They watched him warily, as Bonaparte looked back and forth between his clerks and his prisoner.

"I see you have been busy playing little jokes on my secretaries."

Without an answer, Calvin reached into the Emperor's leg and, for just a moment, removed all pain. But only for a moment; he soon let it come back.

Bonaparte's face darkened. "What kind of man are you, to take away my pain for a moment and then send it back to me?"

"Forgive me, sir," said Calvin. "It's easy to cure the pain I caused myself, in your men. Or even the pain from hours of kneeling, scrubbing floors. But the gout—that's hard, sir, and I know of no cure, nor of any relief that lasts more than a little while."

"Longer than five seconds, though—I'll wager you know how to do *that*."

"I can try."

"You're the clever one," said Bonaparte. "But I know a lie. You can take away the pain and yet you choose not to. How dare you hold me hostage to my pain?"

Calvin answered in mild tones, though he knew he took his life in his hands to say such a bold thing in *any* tone: "Sir, you have held my whole body prisoner this whole time, when I was free before. I come here and find you already a prisoner of pain, and you complain to *me* that I do not set *you* free?"

The secretaries gasped again, but not in pain this time. Even the scullery maid was shocked—so much so that she knocked her bucket over, spilling soapy, inky water over half the floor.

Calvin quickly made the water evaporate from the floor, then made the residue of ink turn to fine, invisible dust.

The scullery maid went screaming from the room.

The secretaries, too, were on their feet. Bonaparte turned to them. "If I hear any rumor of this, you will all go to the Bastille. Find the girl and silence her—by persuasion or imprisonment, she deserves no torture. Now leave me alone with this extortionist, while I find out what he wants to get from me."

They left the room. As they were going, Little Napoleon and the guards returned, but Bonaparte sent them away as well, to his nephew's ill-concealed fury.

"All right, we're alone," said Bonaparte. "What do you want?"

"I want to heal your pain."

"Then heal it and have done."

Calvin took the challenge, twisted the nerves just right, and saw Bonaparte's face soften, losing the perpetual wince. "Such a gift as that," murmured the Emperor, "and you spend it cleaning floors and taking stones from prison walls."

"It won't last," said Calvin.

"You mean you choose not to make it last," said Bonaparte.

Calvin took the unusual step of telling the plain truth, sensing that Bonaparte would know if anything he said was a lie. "It's not a cure. The gout is still there. I don't understand the gout and I can't cure it. I can take away the pain."

"But not for long."

Truthfully, Calvin answered, "I don't know how long."

"And for what payment?" asked Bonaparte. "Come on, boy, I know you want something. Everyone does."

"But you're Napoleon Bonaparte," said Calvin. "I thought you knew what every man wanted."

"God doesn't whisper it in my ear, if that's what you think. And yes, I know what you want but I have no idea why you've come to me for it. You're hungry to be the greatest man on Earth. I've met men with ambition like yours before—and women, too. Unfortunately I can't easily bend such ambition into subservience to my interests. Generally I have to kill them, because they're a danger to me."

Those words went like a knife through Calvin's heart.

"But you're different," said Bonaparte. "You mean me no harm. In fact, I'm just a tool to you. A means of gaining advantage. You don't want my kingdom. I rule all of Europe, northern Africa, and much of the ancient East, and yet you want me only to tutor you in preparation for a much greater game. What game, on God's green Earth, might that be?"

Calvin never meant to tell him, but the words came blurting out. "I have a brother, an older brother, who has a thousand times my power." The words galled him, burned his throat as he said them.

"And a thousand times your virtue, too, I think," said Bonaparte. But those words had no sting for Calvin. Virtue, as Alvin defined it, was waste and weakness. Calvin was proud to have little of it.

"Why hasn't your brother challenged me?" asked Bonaparte. "Why hasn't he shown his face to me in all these years?"

"He's not ambitious," said Calvin.

"That is a lie," said Bonaparte, "even though in your ignorance you believe it. There is no such thing as a living human being without ambition. St. Paul said it best: Faith, ambition, and love, the three driving forces of human life."

"I believe it was hope," said Calvin. "Hope and charity."

"Hope is the sweet weak sister of ambition. Hope is ambition wishing to be liked."

Calvin smiled. "That's what I've come for," he said.

"Not to heal my gout."

"To ease your pain, as you ease my ignorance."

"With powers like yours, what do you need with my small world-conquering gifts?" Bonaparte's irony was plain and painful.

"My powers are nothing compared to my brother's, and he is the only teacher I can learn them from. So I need other powers that he doesn't have."

"Mine."

"Yes."

"Then how do I know that you won't turn on me and try to take my empire?"

"If I wanted it I could have it now," said Calvin.

"It's one thing to terrify people with displays of power," said Bonaparte. "But terror only gets you obedience when you're there. I have the power to hold men obedient to me even when my back is turned, even when there's no chance I'd ever catch them in wrongdoing. They love me, they serve me with their whole hearts. Even if you sent every building in Paris crashing to the street, it wouldn't win the people's loyalty."

"That's why I'm here, because I know that."

"Because you want to win the loyalty of your brother's friends," said Bonaparte. "You want them to spurn your brother and put you in his place."

"Call me Cain if you want, but yes," said Calvin. "Yes."

"I can teach you that," said Bonaparte. "But no pain. And no little games with the pain, either. If the pain comes back, I'll have you killed."

"You can't even hold me in a prison if I don't want to stay there."

"When I decide to kill you, boy, you won't even see it coming."

Calvin believed him.

"Tell me, boy—"

"Calvin."

"Boy, don't interrupt me, don't correct me." Bonaparte smiled sweetly. "Tell me, Calvin, weren't you afraid that I would win *your* loyalty and put your gifts to use in my service?"

"As you said," Calvin answered, "your powers have scant effect on people with ambition as great as your own. It's only really the goodness in people that you turn against them to control them. Their generosity. Isn't that right?"

"In a sense, though it's much more complicated than that. But yes."

Calvin smiled broadly. "Well, then, you see? I knew I was immune."

Bonaparte frowned. "Are you so sure of that? So proud to be a man utterly devoid of generosity?"

Calvin's smile faded just a little. "Old Boney, the terror of Europe, the toppler of empires—Old Boney is shocked at *my* lack of compassion?"

"Yes," said Bonaparte. "I never thought I'd see the like. A man I'll never have power over . . . and yet I will let you stay with me, for the sake of my leg, and I'll teach you all that can be taught. For the sake of my leg."

Calvin laughed and nodded. "Then you've got a deal."

Only later, as he was being shown to a luxurious apartment in the palace, did it occur to Calvin to wonder if, perhaps, Bonaparte's admission that Calvin could not be controlled might not be just a ploy; if, perhaps, Bonaparte already had control over Calvin but, like all the Emperor's other tools, Calvin continued to think that he was free.

No, he told himself. Even if it's true, what good will it do me to think about it? The deed's done or it's not done, and either way I'm still myself and still have Alvin to deal with. A thousand times more powerful than me! A thousand times more virtuous! We'll see about that when the time comes, when I take your friends away from you, Alvin, the way you stole my birthright from *me*, you thieving Esau, you pit-digging Reuben, you jealous taunting Ishmael. God will give me my birthright, and has given me Bonaparte to teach me how to accomplish something with it.

Alvin didn't realize he was doing it. Daytimes he thought he was bearing his imprisonment right well, putting on a cheerful face for his visitors, singing now and then—harmonizing with the jailors when they knew the song and joined in. It was a jaunty sort of imprisonment, and everyone was saying that it was a shame for Alvin to be all cooped up, but wasn't he taking it like a soldier?

In his sleep, though, his hatred for the jail walls, for the sameness and lifelessness of the place, it came out in another kind of song, an inward music that harmonized with the greensong that once had filled this part of the world. It was the music of the trees and the lesser plants, of the insects and spiders, of the furred and finny creatures that dwelt in the leaves, on the ground, in the earth, or in the cold streams and unstoppable rivers. And Alvin's inner voice was tuned to it, knew all the melodies, and instead of harmonizing with jailors his heart sang with free creatures.

And they heard his song that went unheard by human ears. In the tattered remnants of the ancient woods, in the new growth where a few abandoned fields were four or ten years fallow, they heard him, the last few bison, the still deer, the hunting cats and the sociable coyotes and the timber wolves. The birds above all heard him, and they came first, in twos, in tens, in flocks of hundreds, visiting the town and singing with his music for a while, daybirds coming in the nighttime, until the town was wakened by the din of so many songs all at once. They came and sang an hour and left again, but the memory of their song lingered.

First the birds, and then the song of coyotes, the howl of

wolves, not so near as to be terrifying, but near enough to fill the untuned hearts of most folks with a kind of dread, and they woke with nightsweats. Raccoon prints were all over, and yet there was no tearing or thievery, and no more than the usual number of chickens were taken, though foxfeet had trodden on every henhouse roof. Squirrels a-gathering their nuts ran fearlessly through the town to leave small offerings outside the courthouse. Fish leapt in the Hatrack and in other nearby streams, a silver dance in the sparkling moonlit water, the drops like stars falling back into the stream.

Through it Alvin slept, and most folks also slept, so only gradually did the word spread that the natural world was all a-flutter, and then only a few began to link it with Alvin being in jail. Logical folks said there couldn't be no connection. Dr. Whitley Physicker boldly said, when asked (and sometimes when no one asked at all), "I'm the first to say it's wrong to have that boy locked up. But that doesn't imply that the swarming of harmless unstinging bees through the town last night meant anything at all except that perhaps this will be a hardish winter. Or perhaps a mild one. I'm not a great reader of bees. But it's *nothing* to do with Alvin in jail because nature hardly concerns itself with the legal disputes of human beings!"

True enough, but, as a lawyer might say, irrelevant. It wasn't Alvin in jail that disturbed nature, it was Alvin singing in his dreams that drew them. And those few in town who could hear some faint echo of his song—ones like John Binder, for instance, and Captain Harriman, who had heard such silent stirrings all their lives—why, they didn't wake up to the birdsong and the coyotes yipping and the wolves howling and the patter of squirrel feet on shingles. Those things just fit into their own dreams, for to them it all belonged, it all fit, and Alvin's song and the natural greensong of the world spoke peace to them deep in their hearts. They heard the rumors but didn't understand the fuss. And if Drunken Freda drank a little less and slept a little better, who would notice it besides herself?

* * *

Verily Cooper came to Vigor Church the hard way, but then everybody did. What with the town's reputation for making travelers listen to a hard dark story, it's no wonder nobody put a stagecoach route there. The railroad wasn't out that far west yet, but even if it was, it wasn't likely there'd be a Vigor Station or even a spur. The town that Armor-of-God Weaver once expected to be the gateway to the west was now a permanent backwater.

So it was railroad—shaky and stinky, but fast and cheap—to Dekane, and stagecoach from there. By sheerest chance, Verily's route took him right through the town of Hatrack River, where the man he was coming to meet, Calvin's brother Alvin, was locked up. But this was the express coach and it didn't stop in Hatrack for a leisurely meal at Horace Guester's roadhouse, where no doubt Verily would have heard talk that stopped his journey right there. Instead he rode on to Carthage City, changed to a slow coach heading northwest into Wobbish, and then got out at a sleepy little ferry town and bought him a horse and a saddle and a pack mule for his luggage, which wasn't all that much but more than he wanted to have on the horse he was riding. From there it was a simple matter of riding north all day, stopping at a farmhouse at night, and riding another day until, late in the afternoon, just as the sun was setting, he came to Armor's general store, where lamps were lit and Verily hoped he might find a night's lodging.

"I'm sorry," said the man at the door. "We don't take in lodgers—not much call for them in this town. The miller's family up the road takes in such lodgers as we get, but . . . well, friend, you might as well come in. Because most of the miller's family is right here in my store, and besides, there's a tale they have to tell you before you or they can go to bed tonight."

"I've been told of it," said Verily Cooper, "and I'm not afraid to hear it."

"So you came here on purpose?"

"With those signs on the road, warning travelers away?" Verily stepped through the doorway. "I have a horse and a mule to attend to—"

His words were heard by the people gathered on stools and chairs and leaning on the store counter. Immediately two young men with identical faces swung themselves over the counter. "I've got the horse," said one.

"Which gives me the mule—and his baggage, no doubt."

"And I've got the saddle," said the first. "I think it comes out even."

Verily Cooper stuck out his hand in the forthright American manner he had already learned. "I'm Verily Cooper," he said.

"Wastenot Miller," said one of the boys.

"And I'm Wantnot," said the other.

"Puritans, from the naming of you," said Verily.

"Not on a bet," said a thick-bodied middle-aged man who was sitting on a stool in the corner. "Naming babies for virtues ain't no monopoly of religious fanatics from New England."

For the first time Verily felt suspicion in the air, and he realized that they had to be wondering who he was and what his business was here. "There's not more than one miller in town, is there?" he asked.

"Only me," said the thickset man.

"Then you must be Alvin Miller, Senior," said Verily, striding up to him and thrusting out his hand.

The miller took it warily. "You've got me pegged, young feller, but all I know about you is that you come here late in the day, nobody knew you was coming, and you talk like a highfalutin Englishman with a lot of education. Had us a preacher here for a while who talked like you. Not anymore though." And from the tone of his voice, Verily gathered that the parting hadn't been a pleasant one.

"My name is Verily Cooper," he said. "My father's trade is barrelmaking, and I learned the trade as a boy. But you're right, I did get an education and I'm now a barrister."

The miller looked puzzled. "Barrelmaker to barrister," he said. "I got to say I don't rightly know the difference."

The man who greeted him at the door helped out. "A barrister is an English lawyer."

The dry tone of his voice and the way everyone stiffened up told Verily that they had something against lawyers here. "Please, I assure you, I left that profession behind when I left England. I doubt that I'd be allowed to practice law here in the United States, at least not without some kind of examination. I didn't come here for that, anyway."

The miller's wife—or so Verily guessed from her age, for she wasn't sitting by the man—spoke up, and with a good deal less hostility in her voice than her husband had had. "A man comes from England especially to come to the town in America that lives every day in shame. I admit I'm curious, lawyer or no lawyer. What *is* your business here?"

"Well, I met a son of yours, I think. And what he told me—"

It was almost comic, the way they all suddenly leaned forward. "You saw Calvin?"

"The very one," said Verily. "An interesting young man."

They reserved comment.

Well, if there was one thing Verily had learned as a lawyer, it was that he didn't have to fill every silence with his own speech. He couldn't be sure of this family's attitude toward Calvin—after all, Calvin was such an accomplished liar he must have practiced the art here at home before trying to use it to make his way in the world. So he might be hated. Or he might be loved and yearned for. Verily didn't want to make a mistake.

Finally, predictably, it was Calvin's mother who spoke up. "You saw my boy? Where was he? How was he?"

"I met him in London. He has the language and bearing of quite a clever young man. Seems to be in good health, too."

They nodded, and Verily saw that they seemed to be relieved. So they did love him, and had feared for him.

A tall, lanky man of about Verily's age stretched out his long legs and leaned back on his stool. "I'm pretty near certain that you didn't come all this way just to tell us Calvin was a-doing fine, Mr. Cooper."

"No, indeed not. It was something Calvin said." Verily looked around at them again, this large family that was at once welcoming and suspicious of a stranger, at once concerned and wary about a missing son. "He spoke of a brother of his." At this Verily looked at the lanky one who had just spoken. "A son with talents that exceeded Calvin's own."

The lanky one hooted and several others chuckled. "Don't go telling us no stories!" he said. "Calvin wouldn't never speak of Alvin that way!"

So the lanky one wasn't Alvin Junior after all. "Well, let's just say that I read between the lines, so to speak. You know that in England, the use of hidden powers and arcane arts is severely punished. So we Englishmen remain quite ignorant of such matters. I gathered, however, that if there was one person in the world who could teach me how to understand such things, it might well be Calvin's brother Alvin."

They all agreed with that, nodding, some even smiling.

But the father remained suspicious. "And why would an English lawyer be looking to learn more about such things?"

Verily, to his own surprise, was at a loss for words. All his thought had been about finding Alvin the miller's son—but of course they would have to know why he cared so much about hidden powers. What could he say? All his life he had been forced to hide his gift, his curse; now he found he couldn't just blurt it out, or even hint.

Instead, he strode to the counter and picked up a couple of large wooden spools of thread that were standing there, presumably so that customers could reel off the length of thread they wanted and wind it onto a smaller spool. He put the ends of the spools together, and then found the perfect fit for them, so that no man could pull them apart.

He handed the joined spools to the miller. At once the man

tried to pull them apart, but he didn't seem surprised when he failed. He looked at his wife and smiled. "Lookit that," he said. "A lawyer who knows how to do something useful. That's a miracle."

The spools got passed around, mostly in silence, until they got to the lanky young man leaning back on his stool. Without a moment's reflection, he pulled the spools apart and set them on the counter. "Spools ain't no damn good stuck together like that," he said.

Verily was stunned. "You *are* the one," he said. "You *are* Alvin."

"No, sir," said the young man. "My name is Measure, but I've been learning somewhat of my brother's skill. That's his main work these days, is teaching folks how to do the same Makering stuff that he does, and I reckon I'm learning it about as good as anybody. But you—I *know* he'd want to meet you."

"Yes," said Verily, making no effort to hide his enthusiasm. "Yes, that's what I've come for. To learn from him—so I'm glad to hear that he wants to teach."

Measure grinned. "Well, he wants to teach, and you want to learn. But I got a feeling you two are going to have to do each other a different kind of service before that can happen."

Verily was not surprised. Of course there would be some kind of price, or perhaps a test of loyalty or trustworthiness. "I'll do whatever it takes to have a Maker teach me what my gift is for and how to use it well."

Mrs. Miller nodded. "I think you just might do," she said. "I think perhaps God brought you here."

Her husband snorted.

"It would be enough if he brought you to teach my husband manners, but I fear that may be beyond even the powers of a benevolent God," she said.

"I hate it when you talk like old Reverend Thrower," said the miller grumpily.

"I know you do, dear," said his wife. "Mr. Cooper, suppose you *did* need to practice law, not in Wobbish, but in the state of Hio. How long would it take you to prepare to take the test?"

"I don't know," he said. "It depends on how far American legal practice has diverged from English common law and equity. Perhaps only a few days. Perhaps much longer. But I assure you, I didn't come here to practice law, but rather to study higher laws."

"You want to know why you found us all down here at Armor's store?" asked the miller. "We were having a meeting, to try to figure out how to raise the money to hire us a lawyer. We knew we needed a good one, a first-rate one, but we also knew that some rich and secret group in Carthage had already hired them the best lawyers in Hio to work against us. So the question was, who could we hire, and how in the world could we pay him? My wife thinks God brung you, but my own opinion is that you brung your own self, or in another way of looking at it, my boy Alvin brung you. But who knows, I always say. You're here. You're a lawyer. And you want something from Alvin."

"Are you proposing an exchange of services?" asked Verily.

"Not really," Measure interrupted, rising from his stool. Verily had always thought of himself as rather a tall man, but this young farmer fairly towered over him. "Alvin would teach you for free, if you want to learn. The thing is, you pretty much *got* to do us that legal service before Alvin can take you on as a pupil. That's just the way it is."

Verily was baffled. Either it was barter or it wasn't.

The storekeeper spoke up from behind him, laughing. "We're all talking at each other every whichaway. Mr. Cooper, the legal service we need from you is to defend Alvin Junior at his trial. He's in jail over in Hatrack River, charged with stealing a man's gold and my guess is they're going to pile on a whole bunch of other charges, too. They're out to put that boy in prison for a long time, if not hang him, and you coming along here just now—well, you got to see that it looks mighty fortunate to us."

"In jail," Verily said.

"In Hatrack River," said Armor.

"I just rode through there not a week ago."

"Well, you passed by the courthouse where they got him locked up."

"Yes, I'll do it. When is the trial?"

"Oh, pretty much whenever you want. The judge there is a friend of Alvin's, as are most of the townfolk, or most of them as amount to much, anyway. They can't just let him go, much as they'd like to. But they'll delay the trial as long as you need to get admitted to the bar."

Verily nodded. "Yes, I'll do it. But ... I'm puzzled. You have no idea whether I'm a *good* lawyer or not."

Measure hooted with laughter. "Come on, friend, you think we're blind? Look at your clothes! You're rich, and you didn't get that way from barrelmaking."

"Besides," said Armor, "you have that English accent, those gentlemanly airs. The jury in Hatrack River will mostly be on Alvin's side. Everything you say is going to sound powerful clever to them."

"You're saying that I don't actually have to be very good. I just have to be English, an attorney-at-law, alive, and present in the courtroom."

"Pretty much, yep," said Armor.

"Then you have an attorney. Or rather, your son does. If he wants me, that is."

"He wants to get out of jail and have his name cleared," said Measure solemnly. "And he wants to teach folks how to be Makers. I think you'll fit right in with what he wants."

"Come here!" The command came from Mrs. Miller, and Verily obediently walked to her. She reached out and took his right hand and held it in both of hers. "Mr. Verily Cooper," she said, "will you be a true friend to my son?"

He realized that it was an oath she was asking for, an oath with his whole heart in it. "Yes, ma'am. I will be his true friend."

It wasn't quite silence that followed his promise. There was the sound of breaths long pent being released. Verily had never been the answer to anyone's heartfelt wish before. It was rather exhilarating. And a bit terrifying, too.

Wastenot and Wantnot came back in. "Horse and mule are unloaded, fed, watered, and stabled."

"Thank you," said Verily.

The twins looked around. "What's everybody grinning for?"

"We got us a lawyer for Alvin," said Measure.

Wastenot and Wantnot grinned, too. "Well, heck, then let's go home to bed!"

"No," said the miller. "One more item of business we got to do."

At once the cheerful mood faded.

"Have a seat, Mr. Cooper," said the miller. "We have a tale to tell you. A sad one, and it ends with all the men of this town, except Armor here, and Measure—it ends with all of us in shame."

Verily sat down to listen.

⋈ 13 ⋈

Maneuvers

VILATE BROUGHT HIM another pie. "I couldn't finish the last one," Alvin said. "You think my stomach is a bottomless pit?"

"A man of your size and strength needs something to keep the meat on his bones," said Vilate. "And I haven't figured out yet how to make half a pie."

Alvin chuckled. But as she slid the pie under the iron-barred door of the cell, Alvin noticed that she had some new hexes on her, not to mention a come-hither and a beseeching. Most hexes he recognized right off—he'd made a few of them in his own time, for protection or warding, and even for conceal-ment and mildness of heart, which made for a deeper kind of safety but were much harder to make. What Vilate had today, though, was beyond Alvin's ken. And since they probably wouldn't work on him, or not too well, he couldn't rightly tell what they'd be for. Nor could he ask her.

Some kind of concealment, maybe. It seemed related to an overlook-me hex, which was always very subtle and usually worked only in one direction.

Alvin bent down, picked up the pie, and set it on the small table they'd allowed him.

"Alvin," she said softly.

"Yes?" he answered.

"Sh."

He looked up, wondering what the secrecy was about.

"I don't want to be heard," she said. She glanced toward the half-open door leading to the sheriff's office, where the guard was no doubt eavesdropping. She beckoned to Alvin.

What went through his mind then made him a little shy. Was she perhaps thinking some of the same romantic thoughts about him that he had thought about her on some of these lonely nights? Maybe she knew somehow that he alone could see past her false charms of beauty and liked her for who she really was. Maybe she thought of him as someone she could come to love, as he had wondered sometimes about her, seeing as how his first love was lost to him.

He came closer. "Alvin, do you want to escape from here?" she whispered. She leaned her forehead on the bars. Her face was so close. Was she, in some shy way, offering a kiss?

He reached down and touched her chin, lifted her face. Did she want him to kiss her? He smiled ruefully. "Vilate, if I wanted to escape, I—"

He didn't get to finish his sentence, didn't get to say, I reckon I could walk on out of here any old day. Because at that moment the deputy swung the door open and looked into the jail. He immediately got a frantic look on his face, and scanned right past them as if he didn't see them at all. "How in the hell!" he cried, then rushed from the jail. Alvin heard his feet pounding down the hall as he called out, "Sheriff! Sheriff Doggly!"

Alvin looked down at Vilate. "What was *that* all about?" he asked.

Vilate dropped her teeth at him, then smiled. "How should I know, Alvin? But I reckon this is a dangerous time to be talking about what I come to talk about." She picked up her skirts and rushed from the jail.

Alvin had no idea what her visit had been about, but he knew this much: Whatever her new hexes did, they were involved with the deputy and what he saw when he came in. And since there was a come-hither and a beseeching, Vilate might well have been the reason the deputy came into the room in the first place, and the reason he panicked so fast and rushed out without investigating any further.

She dropped the upper plate of her teeth to show contempt for me, thought Alvin. Just like she did to Horace, her enemy. Somehow I've become her enemy.

He looked at the pie sitting on the cot. He picked it up and slid it back under the door.

Five minutes later, the deputy came back with the sheriff and the county attorney. "What the hell was this all about!" Sheriff Doggly demanded. "There he is, just like always! Billy Hunter, you been drinking?"

"I swear there wasn't a soul here," said the deputy. "I saw Vilate Franker go in with a pie—"

"Sheriff, what's he talking about?" said Alvin. "I saw him come in here not five minutes ago and start yelling and running down the hall. It scared poor Vilate so she took on out of here like she had a bear after her."

"He was *not* here, I'd swear to that before God and all the angels!" said Billy Hunter.

"I was right here by the door," said Alvin.

"Maybe he was bending over to get the pie and you didn't see him," said the sheriff.

"No sir," said Alvin, unwilling to lie. "I was standing right up. There's the pie—you can have it if you want, I told Miz Vilate that I didn't finish the last one."

"I don't want none of your pie," said Billy. "Whatever you did, you made me look like a plain fool."

"It don't take no help from Alvin to make you look that way," said Sheriff Doggly. Marty Laws, the county attorney, hooted at the joke. Marty had a way of laughing at just the right time to make everything worse.

Billy glared at Alvin.

"Now, Alvin, we got to put you on your parole," said Marty. "You can't just go taking jaunts out of the jail whenever you feel like it."

"So you *do* believe me," said the deputy.

Marty Laws rolled his eyes.

"*I* don't believe nobody," said Sheriff Doggly. "And Alvin ain't taking no jaunts, are you, Alvin?"

"No sir," said Alvin. "I have not stirred from this cell."

None of them bothered to pretend that Alvin *couldn't* have escaped whenever he wanted.

"You calling me a liar?" asked Billy.

"I'm calling you mistaken," said Alvin. "I'm thinking maybe somebody fooled you into thinking what you thought and seeing what you saw."

"Somebody's fooling somebody," said Billy Hunter.

They left. Alvin sat on the cot and watched as an ant canvassed the floor of the jail, looking for something to eat. There's a pie right there, just a little that way . . . and sure enough, the ant turned, heeding Alvin's advice though of course the words themselves were just too hard a thing to fit into an ant's tiny mind. No, the ant just got the message of food and a direction, and in a minute or two it was up the pie dish and walking around on the crust. Then it headed out to find its friends and bring them for lunch. Might as well somebody get some good out of that pie.

Vilate's hexes were for concealment, all right, and they were aimed at the door. She had got him to stand close so that he'd be included in her strong overlook-me, so Billy Hunter had looked and couldn't see that anybody was there.

But why? What possible good could she accomplish from such a bit of tomfoolery as that?

Underneath all his puzzlement, though, Alvin was mad. Not so much at Vilate as he was mad at himself for being such a plain fool. Getting all moony-eyed about a woman with false teeth and vanity hexes, for pete's sake! Liking her even when he knew she was a plain gossip and suspected that half the tales she told him weren't true.

And the worst thing was, when he saw Peggy again—*if* he saw Peggy again—she'd know just how stupid he was, falling for a woman that he knew was all tricks and lies.

Well, Peggy, when I fell in love with *you* you were all tricks and lies, too, you know. Remember *that* when you're thinking I'm the biggest fool as ever lived.

The door opened and Billy Hunter came back in, stalked over to the cell door, and picked up the pie. "No sense this going to waste even if you are a liar," said Billy.

"As I said, Billy, you're welcome to it. Though I sort of half-promised it to an ant a minute ago."

Billy glared at him, no doubt thinking that Alvin was making fun of him instead of telling the plain truth. Well, Alvin was, kind of. Making fun out of the situation, anyway. He'd have to talk this over with Arthur Stuart when the boy came back, see if he had any idea what Vilate might have meant by this charade.

The ant came back, leading a line of her sisters. All they found was a couple of crumbs of crust. But those were something, weren't they? Alvin watched as they struggled to maneuver the big chunks of pastry. To help them out, he sent his doodlebug to break the pieces into smaller loads. The ants made short work of them then, carrying out the crumbs in a line. A feast in the anthill tonight, no doubt.

His stomach growled. Truth to tell, he could have used that pie, and might not have left much behind, neither. But he wasn't eating nothing that came from Vilate Franker, never again. That woman wasn't to be trusted.

Dropped her teeth at me, he thought. Hates me. Why?

There was no way around it. Even with the best possible luck in choosing a jury, even with this new English fellow as Alvin's lawyer, Little Peggy saw no better than a three-in-four chance of him being acquitted, and that wasn't good enough odds. She would have to go to him. She would have to be available to testify. Even with all the newcomers in Hatrack, one thing was certain: If Peggy the torch said a thing was true, she would be believed. The people of Hatrack knew that she saw the truth, and they also knew—sometimes to their discomfiture—that she never said what wasn't true, though they were grateful enough that she didn't tell every truth she knew.

Only Peggy herself could count how many terrible or shameful or mournful secrets she had left unmentioned. But that was neither here nor there. She was used to carrying other people's secrets around inside her, used to it from the earliest time of her life, when she had to face her father's dark secret of adultery. Since then she had learned not to judge. She had even come to love Mistress Modesty, the woman with whom her father, old Horace Guester, had been unfaithful. Mistress Modesty was like another mother to her, giving her, not the life of the body, but the life of the mind, the life of mannered society, the life of grace and beauty that Peggy valued perhaps too highly.

Perhaps too highly, because there wasn't going to be too much of grace and beauty in Alvin's future, and like it or not, Peggy was tied to that future.

What a lie I tell myself, she thought. "Like it or not" indeed. If I chose to, I could walk away from Alvin and not care whether he stayed in jail or got himself drowned in the Hio or whatnot. I'm tied to Alvin Smith because I love him, and I love what he can be, and I want to be part of all that he will do. Even the hard parts. Even the ungraceful, unmannered, stupid parts of it.

So she headed for Hatrack River, one stage at a time.

On a certain day she passed through the town of Wheelwright in northern Appalachee. It was on the Hio, not far upriver from where the Hatrack flowed into it. Close enough to home that she might have hired a wagon and taken the last ferry, trusting that the moonlight and her ability as a torch would get her home safely. Might have, except that she stopped for dinner at a restaurant she had visited before, where the food was fresh, the flavors good, and the company reputable—a welcome change in all three categories, after long days on the road.

While she was eating, she heard some kind of tumult outside—a band playing, rather badly but with considerable enthusiasm; people shouting and cheering. "A parade?" she asked her waiter.

"You know the presidential election's only a few weeks off," said the waiter.

She knew, but had scarcely paid attention. Somebody was running against somebody else for some office or other in every town she passed through, but it hardly mattered, compared to the matter of stopping slavery, not to mention her concerns about Alvin. It made no difference to her, up to now, who won these elections. In Appalachee, as in the other slave states, there wasn't a soul dared to run openly as an anti-slavery candidate— that would be a ticket for a free suit of tar and feathers and a rail ride out of town, if not worse, for those as loved slavery were violent at heart, and those as hated it were mostly timid, and wouldn't stand together. Yet.

"Some sort of stump speech?" she asked.

"I reckon it's old Tippy-Canoe," said the waiter.

She blanched, knowing at once whom the man referred to. "Harrison?"

"Reckon he'll carry Wheelwright. But not farther south, where the Cherriky tribe is right numerous. They figure him to be the man to try to take away their rights. Won't amount to much in Irrakwa, neither, that being Red country. But, see, White folks isn't too happy about how the Irrakwa control the railroads and the Cherriky got them toll roads through the mountains."

"They'd vote for a murderer, out of nothing more than envy?"

The waiter smiled thinly. "There's them as says just because a Red witch feller put a spell on Tippy-Canoe don't mean he did nothing wrong. Reds get mad over any old thing."

"Slaughtering thousands of innocent women and children— silly of them to take offense."

The waiter shrugged. "I can't afford to have strong opinions on politics, ma'am."

But she saw that he *did* have strong opinions, and they were not the same as hers.

Paying for the meal—and leaving two bits on the table for the waiter, for she saw no reason to punish a man in his livelihood because of his political views—she made haste outside to see the fuss. A few rods up the street, a wagon had been made over into a sort of temporary rostrum, decked out with the red, white, and blue bunting of the flag of the United States. Not a trace of the red and green colors of the old flag of independent Appalachee, before it joined the Union. Of course not. Those had been the Cherriky colors—red for the Red people, green for the forest. Patrick Henry and Thomas Jefferson had adopted them as the colors of a free Appalachee; it was for that flag that George Washington died. But now, though other politicians still invoked the old loyalties, Harrison could hardly want to bring to mind the alliance between Red and White that won freedom for Appalachee from the King at Camelot. Not with those bloody hands.

Hands that even now dripped blood as they gripped the podium. Peggy, standing on the wooden sidewalk across the street, looked over the heads of the cheering crowd to watch William Henry Harrison's face. She looked in his eyes first, as any woman might study any man, to see his character. Quickly enough, though, she looked deeper, into the heartfire, seeing the futures that stretched out before him. He had no secrets from her.

She saw that every path led to victory in the election. And not just a slight victory. His leading opponent, a hapless lawyer named Andrew Jackson from Tennizy, would be crushed and humiliated—and then suffer in the ignominious position of vice-president into which the leading loser in each election was always forced. A cruel system, Peggy had always thought, the political equivalent of putting a man in the stocks for four years. It was significant that both candidates were from the

new states in the west; even more significant that both were
from territories that permitted slavery. Things were taking a
dark turn indeed. And darker yet were the things she saw in
Harrison's mind, the plans he and his political cronies meant
to carry out.

Their most extravagant ideas had little hope of success—
only a few paths in Harrison's heartfire led to the union with
the Crown Lands that he hoped for; he would never be a duke;
what a pathetic dream, she thought. But he would certainly
succeed in the political destruction of the Reds in Irrakwa and
Cherriky, because the Whites, especially in the west, were ready
for it, ready to break the power of a people that Harrison dared
to speak of as savages. "God didn't bring the Christian race to
this land in order to share it with heathens and barbarians!"
cried Tippy-Canoe, and the people cheered.

Harrison would also succeed in spreading slavery beyond its
present locale, permitting slave owners to bring slaves to property in the free states and continue to own them and force them
to serve on such property—as long as the slave owner continued
to own any amount of land in a slave state and cast his vote
there. It was precisely to achieve this end that most of Harrison's
backers were behind him. It was the matter of Reds that would
sweep Tippy-Canoe into office, but once there, it was the matter
of slavery that would give him his power base in Congress.

This was unbearable. Yet she bore it, watching on into the
afternoon as he ranted and exhorted, periodically lifting his
bloody hands skyward to remind the crowd. "*I* have tasted the
treacherous wrath of the secret powers of the Red man, and
I'll tell you, if this is all they can do, well, that's good, because
it ain't much! Sure, I can't keep a shirt clean"—and they
laughed at that, over and over, each variation on the tedious
details of life with bloody hands—"and ain't a soul willing to
lend me a hankie"—laughter again—"but they can't stop me
from telling you the plain truth, and they can't stop a Christian
people from electing the one man proven to be willing to stand
up against the Red traitors, the barbarians who dress like White

men but secretly plan to own everything the way they own the railroads and the mountain toll roads and . . ."

And on and on. Confounded nonsense, all of it, but the crowd only grew as the afternoon passed, and by dark, when Harrison finally climbed down from his pulpit, he was carried away on the shoulders of his supporters to be watered with beer and stuffed with some sort of rough food, whatever would make the crowd think of him as one of them, while Peggy Larner stood gripping the rail on the sidewalk, seeing down every path that this man was the undoing of all her work, that this man would be the cause of the death and suffering of countless more Reds than had already died or suffered at his hands.

If she had had a musket in her hands at that moment, she might have gone after him and put a ball through his heart.

But the murderous rage passed quickly and shamefully. I am not a one who kills, she thought. I am one who frees the slave if I can, not one who murders the master.

There had to be a way to stop him.

Alvin would know. She had to get to Hatrack River all the more urgently, not just to help with Alvin's trial, but to get his help in stopping Harrison. Perhaps if he went to Becca's house and used the doorways in her ancient cabin to let him visit with Tenskwa-Tawa—surely the Red Prophet would do something to make his curse against White Murderer Harrison more effective. Though she didn't see such an outcome down any of the paths in Alvin's heartfire, she never knew when some act of hers or of someone else's might open up new paths that led to better hopes.

It was too late that day, though. She would have to spend the night in Wheelwright and finish her journey to Hatrack River the next day.

"I come to you, sir, with the good wishes of your family," said the stranger.

"I confess I didn't catch your name," said Alvin, unfolding himself from his cot. "It's pretty late in the evening."

"Verily Cooper," said the stranger. "Forgive my late arrival. I thought it better that we speak tonight, since the first matter of your defense before the court is in the morning."

"I know the judge is finally going to start choosing him a jury."

"Yes, that's important, of course. But under the advice of an outside lawyer, a Mr. Daniel Webster, the county attorney has introduced some unpleasant motions. As, for instance, a motion requiring that the contested property be placed under the control of the court."

"The judge won't go for that," said Alvin. "He knows that the second this plow is out of my hands, some rough boys from the river, not to mention a few greedier souls from town, will move heaven and earth to get their hands on it. The thing's made of gold—that's all they know and care about it. But who are you, Mr. Cooper, and what does all this have to do with you?"

"I'm your attorney, Mr. Smith, if you'll have me." He handed Alvin a letter.

Alvin recognized Armor-of-God's handwriting at once, and the signatures of his parents and his brothers and sisters. They all signed, affirming that they found Mr. Cooper to be a man of good character and assuring him that someone was paying a high-powered lawyer from New England named Daniel Webster to sneak around and collect lies from anyone as had a grievance against him in Vigor Church. "But I've done no harm to anyone there," said Alvin, "and why would they lie?"

"Mr. Smith, I have to—"

"Call me Alvin, would you? 'Mr. Smith' always sounds to me like my old master Makepeace, the fellow whose lies got me into this fix."

"Alvin," said Cooper again. "And you must call me Verily."

"Whatever."

"Alvin, it has been my experience that the better a man you are, the more folks there are who resent you for it, and find occasion to get angry at you no matter how kindly meant your deeds may be."

"Well then, I'm safe enough, not being such a remarkable good man."

Cooper smiled. "I know your brother Calvin," he said.

Alvin raised an eyebrow. "I'd like to say that any friend of Calvin's is a friend of mine, but I can't."

"Calvin's hatred of you is, I believe, one of the best recommendations of your character that I could think of. It's because of his account of you that I came to meet you. I met him in London, you see, and determined then and there to close my legal practice and come to America and see the man who can teach me who and what I am, and what it's for."

With that, Cooper bent down and took up Alvin's Testament, the book that lay open on the floor beside his cot. He closed it, then handed it back to Alvin.

Alvin tried to thumb it open, but the pages were fused shut as tight as if the book were one solid block of wood with a leather cover.

Verily took it back from him for only a moment, then returned it yet again. This time the book fell open to the exact page that Alvin had been reading. "I could have died for that in England," said Verily. "It was the wisdom of my parents and my own ability to learn to hide these powers that kept me alive all these years. But I have to know what it is. I have to know why God lets some folks have such powers. And what to do with them. And who you are."

Alvin lay back on his cot. "Don't this beat all," he said. "You crossed an ocean to meet me?"

"I had no idea at the time that I might be of service to you. In fact, I must say that it occurs to me that perhaps some providential hand led me to the study of law instead of following my father's trade as a cooper. Perhaps it was known that one day you would face the silver tongue of Daniel Webster."

"You got you a tongue of gold, then, Verily?" asked Alvin.

"I hold things together," said Verily. "It's my . . . knack, as you Americans call it. That is what the law does. I use the law to hold things together. I see how things fit."

"This Webster fellow—he's going to use the law to try to tear things apart."

"Like you and the plow."

"And me and my neighbors," said Alvin.

"Then you understand the dilemma," said Verily. "Up till now you've been known as a man of generosity and kindness to all. But you have a plow made of gold that you won't let anyone see. You have fantastic wealth which you share with no one. This is a wedge that Webster will attempt to use to split you from your community like a rail from a log."

"When gold comes into it," said Alvin, "folks start to finding out just how much love and loyalty is worth to them, in cash money."

"And it's rather shameful, don't you think, how cheap the price can be sometimes." Verily smiled ruefully.

"What's *your* price?"

"When you get free of this place, you let me go with you, to learn from you, to watch you, to be part of all you do."

"You don't even know me, and you're proposing marriage?"

Verily laughed. "I suppose it sounds like that, doesn't it."

"Without none of the benefits, neither," said Alvin. "I'm right comfortable taking Arthur Stuart along with me because he knows when to keep silent, but I don't know if I can take having a fellow who wants to pick my brains tagging along with me every waking minute."

"I'm a lawyer, so my trade is talk, but I promise you that if I didn't know when and how to keep silence, I'd never have lived to adulthood in England."

"I can't give you no promises," said Alvin. "So I reckon you ain't my attorney after all, since I can't make your fee."

"There's one promise you can make me," said Verily. "To give me an honest chance."

Alvin studied the man's face and decided he liked the look of him, though he wished as more than once before that he had

Peggy's knack of seeing inside a fellow's mind instead of just being able to check out the health of his organs.

"Yes, I reckon I can make that promise, Verily Cooper," said Alvin. "An honest chance you'll have, and if that's fee enough for you, then you're my attorney."

"Then the deed is done. And now I'll let you go back to sleep, excepting only for one question."

"Ask it."

"This plow—how vital is it to you that the plow remain in your hands, and no one else's?"

"If the court demands that I give it up, I'll buck this jail and live in hiding the rest of my days before I'll let any other hand touch the plow."

"Let's be precise. Is it the possession of it that matters, or the very seeing and touching of it?"

"I don't get your question."

"What if someone else could see and touch it in your presence?"

"What good would that do?"

"Webster will argue that the court has the right and duty to determine that the plow exists and that it's truly made of gold, in order to make just compensation possible, if the court should determine that you need to pay Mr. Makepeace Smith the cash value of the plow."

Alvin hooted. "It never crossed my mind, in all this time in jail, that maybe I could buy old Makepeace off."

"I don't think you can," said Verily. "I think it's the plow he wants, and the victory, not the money."

"True enough, though I reckon if the money's all he can get . . ."

"So tell me, as long as the plow is in your possession . . ."

"I guess it depends on who's doing the looking and the touching."

"If you're there, nobody can steal it, am I right?" asked Verily.

"Reckon that's true," said Alvin.

"So how free a hand do I have?"

"Makepeace can't be the one to touch it," said Alvin. "Not out of any meanness on my part, but here's the thing: The plow's alive."

Verily raised an eyebrow.

"It don't breathe and it don't eat or nothing like that," said Alvin. "But the plow is alive under a man's hand. Depending on the man. But for Makepeace to touch the plow while he's living in the midst of a black lie—I don't know what would happen to him. I don't know if it'd be safe for him ever to touch metal again. I don't know what the hammer and anvil would do to him, if his hands touched the plow with his heart so black."

Verily leaned his face against the bars, closed his eyes.

"Are you unwell?" asked Alvin.

"Sick with the thrill of at last staring knowledge in the face," said Verily. "Sick with it. Faint with it."

"Well, don't puke on the floor, I'll have to smell it all night." Then Alvin grinned.

"I was thinking more of fainting," said Verily. "Not Makepeace, or anyone else who's living in a . . . black lie. Makes me wonder about my opponent, Mr. Daniel Webster."

"Don't know him," said Alvin. "Might be an honest man, for all I know. A lying man might have an honest attorney, don't you think?"

"He might," said Verily. "But such a combination would only work to destroy the lying man in the end."

"Well hell, Verily, a lying man destroys himself in the end every time anyway."

"Do you know that? I mean, the way you know the plow is alive?" asked Verily.

"I reckon not," said Alvin. "But I have to believe it's true, or how could I trust anybody?"

"I think you're right, in the long run," said Verily. "In the long run, a lie ties itself in knots and eventually people come to see that it's a lie. But the long run is very, very long. Longer than life. You could be long dead before the lie dies, Alvin."

"You warning me of something in particular?" asked Alvin.

"I don't think so," said Verily. "The words just sounded like something I had to say and you had to hear."

"You said them. I heard them." Alvin grinned. "Good night, Verily Cooper."

"Good night, Alvin Smith."

Peggy Larner got to the ferry bright and early in the morning, wearing her urgency like a tight corset so she could hardly breathe. White Murderer Harrison was going to be president of the United States. She had to talk to Alvin, and this river, this Hio, was standing in her way.

But the ferry was on the other side of the river, which made perfect sense, since the farmers on the other side would need to have it earliest, to bring their goods to market. So she had to wait, urgency or not. She could see the ferry already being poled along, tied to a metal ring that slid along the cable that crossed the river some forty feet overhead. Only that frail connection kept the whole thing from being washed downriver; and she imagined that when the river was in flood they didn't run the ferry at all some days, since even if the cable were strong enough, and the ring, and the rope, there'd be no trees strong enough to tie the ends to without fear of one or the other of them pulling out of the ground. Water was not to be tamed by cables, rings, or ropes, any more than dams or bridges, hulls or rafts, pipes or gutters, roofs or windows or walls or doors. If she had learned anything in her early years of looking out for Alvin, it was the untrustworthiness of water, the sneakiness of it.

There was the river to be crossed, though, and she would cross it.

As so many others had crossed. She thought of how many times her father had snuck down to the river and taken a boat across to rescue some runaway slave and bring him north to safety. She thought of how many slaves had come without help to this water, and, not knowing how to swim, had either despaired and waited for the Finders or the dogs to get them, or struck out anyway, breasting the water until their feet found no purchase on the bottom mud and they were swept away. The bodies of such were always found on some downriver bank or bar or snag, made white by the water, bloated and horrible in death; but the spirit, ah, the spirit was free, for the owner who thought he owned the woman or the man, that owner had lost his property, for his property would not be owned whatever it might cost. So the water killed, yes, but just reaching this river meant freedom of one kind or another to those who had the courage or the rage to take it.

Harrison, though, would take away all meaning from this river. If his laws came to be, the slave who crossed would still be a slave no matter what; only the slave who died would be free.

One of the ferrymen, the one poling on this side, he looked familiar to her. She had met him before, though he'd not been missing an ear then, nor had he any kind of scar on his face. Now a gash marked him with a faint white line, a little puckering and twisting at the eyebrow and the lip. It had been a wicked fight. Once no one had been able to lay a hand of harm on this rough man, and in the sure knowledge of that he had been a bully. But someone took that lifelong hex away from him. Alvin had fought this man, fought him in defense of Peggy herself, and when the fight was done, this river rat had been undone. But not completely; and he was alive still, wasn't he?

"Mike Fink," she said softly when he stepped ashore.

He looked sharp at her. "Do I know you, ma'am?"

Of course he didn't. When they met before, not two years ago, she was covered in hexes that made her look many years older. "I don't expect you to remember me," she said. "You must take many thousands of people a year across the river."

He helped her hoist her traveling bags onto the ferry. "You'll want to sit in the middle of the raft, ma'am." She sat down on the bench that ran the middle of the raft. He stood near her, waiting, while another couple of people sauntered over to the ferry—locals, obviously, since they had no luggage.

"A ferryman now," she said.

He looked at her.

"When I knew you, Mike Fink, you were a full-fledged river rat."

He smiled wanly. "You was that lady," he said. "Hexed up six ways to Tuesday."

She looked at him sharply. "You saw through them?"

"No ma'am. But I could feel them. You watched me fight that Hatrack River boy."

"I did."

"He took away my mother's hex," said Mike.

"I know."

"I reckon you know damn near everything."

She looked at him again. "You seem to be abundant in knowledge yourself, sir."

"You're Peggy the torch, of Hatrack River town. And the boy as whupped me and stole my hex, he's in jail in Hatrack now, for stealing gold off'n his master when he was a prentice smith."

"And I suppose that pleases you?" asked Peggy.

Mike Fink shook his head. "No ma'am."

And in truth, as she looked into his heartfire, she saw no future in which he harmed Alvin.

"Why are you still here? Not ten miles from Hatrack Mouth, where he shamed you?"

"Where he made a man of me," said Mike.

She was startled then, for sure. "That's how you think of it?"

"My mother wanted to keep me safe. Tattooed a hex right into my butt. But what she never thought of was, what kind of man does it make a fellow, to never get hurt no matter what harm he causes to others? I've killed folks, some bad, but some not so bad. I've bit off ears and noses and broken limbs, too, and all the time I was doing it, I never cared a damn, begging your pardon, ma'am. Because nothing ever hurt me. Never touched me."

"And since Alvin took away your hex, you've stopped hurting people?"

"Hell no!" Mike Fink said, then roared with laughter. "Why, you sure don't know a thing about the river, do you! No, every last man I ever beat in a fight had to come find me, soon as word spread that a smith boy whupped me and made me howl! I had to fight every rattlesnake and weasel, every rat and pile of pigshit on the river all over again. You see this scar on my face? You see where my hair hangs straight one side of my head? That's two fights I damn near lost. But I won the rest! Didn't I, Holly!"

The other ferryman looked over. "I wasn't listening to your brag, you pitiful scab-eating squirrel-fart," he said mildly.

"I told this lady I won every fight, every last one of them."

"That's right enough," said Holly. "Course, mostly you just shot them dead when they made as if to fight you."

"Lies like that will get you sent to hell."

"Already got me a room picked out there," said Holly, "and you to empty my chamberpot twice't a day."

"Only so's you can lick it out after!" hooted Mike Fink.

Peggy felt repulsed by their crudity, of course; but she also felt the spirit of camaraderie behind their banter.

"What I don't understand, Mr. Fink, is why you never sought vengeance against the boy who beat you."

"He wasn't no boy," said Fink. "He was a man. I reckon he was probably born a man. *I* was the boy. A bully boy. He knew pain, and I didn't. He was fighting for right, and I wasn't. I think about him all the time, ma'am. Him and you. The way you looked at me, like I was a crusty toad on a clean bedsheet. I hear tell he's a Maker."

She nodded.

"So why's he letting them hold him in jail?"

She looked at him quizzically.

"Oh, come now, ma'am. A fellow as can wipe the tattoo off my butt without touching it, he can't be kept in no natural jail."

True enough. "I imagine he believes himself to be innocent, and therefore he wants to stand trial to prove it and clear his name."

"Well he's a damn fool, then, and I hope you'll tell him when you see him."

"And why will I give him this remarkable message?"

Fink grinned. "Because I know something he don't know. I know that there's a feller lives in Carthage City who wants Alvin dead. He plans to get Alvin exerdited to Kenituck—"

"Extradited?"

"That means one state tells another to give them up a prisoner."

"I know what it means," said Peggy.

"Then what was you asking, ma'am?"

"Go on with your story."

"Only when they take Alvin in chains, with guards awake and watching him day and night, they'll never take him to Kenituck for no trial. I know some of the boys they hired to take him. They know that on some signal, they're to walk away and leave him alone in chains."

"Why haven't you told the authorities?"

"I'm telling *you*, ma'am," said Mike Fink, grinning. "And I already told myself and Holly."

"Chains won't hold him," said Peggy.

"You reckon not?" said Mike. "There was some reason that boy took the tattoo off my butt. If hexes had no power over him, I reckon he never would've had to clean mine off, do you think? So if he needed to get rid of my hex, then I reckon them as understands hexes right good might be able to make chains that'd hold him long enough for somebody to come with a shotgun and blow his head off."

But she had seen nothing of the kind in his future.

"Course it'll never happen," said Mike Fink.

"Why not?" she asked.

"Cause I owe that boy my life. My life as a man, anyway, a man worth looking at in the mirror, though I ain't half so pretty as I was before he dealt with me. I had a grip on that boy in my arms, ma'am. I meant to kill him, and he knowed it. But he didn't kill me. More to the point, ma'am, he broke both my legs in that fight. But then he took pity on me. He had mercy. He must've knowed I wouldn't live out the night with broke legs. I had too many enemies, right there among my friends. So he laid hands on my legs and he fixed them. Fixed my legs, so the bones was stronger than before. What kind of man does that to a man as tried to kill him not a minute before?"

"A good man."

"Well, many a good man might wish to, but only one good man had the power," said Mike. "And if he had the power to do that, he had the power to kill me without touching me. He had the power to do whatever he damn well pleased, begging your pardon. But he had mercy on me, ma'am."

That was true—the only surprise to Peggy was that Mike Fink understood it.

"I aim to pay the debt. As long as I'm alive, ma'am, ain't no harm coming to Alvin Smith."

"And that's why you're here," she said.

"Came here with Holly as soon as I found out what was getting plotted up."

"But why here?"

Mike Fink laughed. "The portmaster at Hatrack Mouth knows me real good, and he don't trust me, I wonder why. How long you reckon it'd be afore the Hatrack County sheriff was on my back like a sweaty shirt?"

"I suppose that also explains why you haven't made yourself known to Alvin directly."

"What's he going to think when he sees me, but that I've come to get even? No, I'm watching, I'm biding my time, I ain't showing my hand to the law nor to Alvin neither."

"But you're telling me."

"Because you'd know it anyway, soon enough."

She shook her head. "I know this: There's no path in your future that has you rescuing Alvin from thugs."

His face grew serious. "But I got to, ma'am."

"Why?"

"Because a good man pays his debts."

"Alvin won't think you're in his debt, sir."

"Don't matter to me what he thinks about it, I feel the debt so the debt's going to be paid."

"It's not just debt, is it?"

Mike Fink laughed. "Time to push this raft away and get it over to the north shore, don't you think?" He hooted twice, high, as if he were some kind of steam whistle, and Holly hooted back and laughed. They set their poles against the floating dock and pushed away. Then, smooth as if they were dancers, he and Holly poled them across the river, so smoothly and deftly that the line that tied them to the cable never even went taut.

Peggy said nothing to him as he worked. She watched instead, watched the muscles of his arms and back rippling under the skin, watched the slow and graceful up-and-down of his legs as he danced with the river. There was beauty in it, in him. It also made her think of Alvin at the forge, Alvin at the anvil, his arms shining with sweat in the firelight, the sparks glinting from the metal as he pounded, the muscles of his forearms rippling as he bent and shaped the iron. Alvin could have done all his work without raising a hand, by the use of his knack. But there was a joy in the labor, a joy from making with his own hands. She had never experienced that—her life, her labors, all were done with her mind and whatever words she could think of to say. Her life was all about knowing and teaching. Alvin's life was all about feeling and making. He had more in common with this one-eared scar-faced river rat than he had with her. This dance of the human body in contest with the river, it was a kind of wrestling, and Alvin loved to wrestle. Crude as Fink was, he was Alvin's natural friend, surely.

They reached the other shore, bumping squarely against the

floating dock, and the shoreman lashed the upstream corner of the raft to the wharf. The men with no luggage jumped ashore at once. Mike Fink laid down his pole and, sweat still dripping down his arms and from his nose and grizzled beard, he made as if to pick up her bags.

She laid a hand on his arm to stop him. "Mr. Fink," she said. "You mean to be Alvin's friend."

"I had in mind more along the lines of being his champion, ma'am," he said softly.

"But I think what you really want is to be his friend."

Mike Fink said nothing.

"You're afraid that he'll turn you away, if you try to be his friend in the open. I tell you, sir, that he'll *not* turn you away. He'll take you for what you are."

Mike shook his head. "Don't want him to take me for that."

"Yes you do, because what you are is a man who means to be good, and undo the bad he's done, and that's as good as any man ever gets."

Mike shook his head more emphatically, making drops of sweat fly a little; she didn't mind the ones that struck on her skin. They had been made by honest work, and by Alvin's friend.

"Meet him face to face, Mr. Fink. Be his friend instead of his rescuer. He needs friends more. I tell you, and you know that I know it: Alvin will have few true friends in his life. If you mean to be true to him, and never betray him, so he can trust you always, then I can promise you he may have a few friends he loves as much, but none he loves more than you."

Mike Fink knelt down and turned his face away toward the river. She could see from the glinting that his eyes were awash with tears. "Ma'am," he said, "that's not what I was daring to hope for."

"Then you need more courage, my friend," she said. "You need to dare to hope for what is good, instead of settling for what is merely good enough." She stood up. "Alvin has no need of your violence. But your honor—that he can use." She lifted both her bags herself.

At once he leapt to his feet. "Please ma'am, let me . . ."

She smiled at him. "I saw you take such joy from wrestling with the river just now. It made me want to do a little physical work myself. Will you let me?"

He rolled his eyes. "Ma'am, in all the tales of you I've heard around here, I never heard you was *crazy*."

"You have something to add to the legend, then," she said, winking. She stepped onto the floating dock, bags in hand. They were heavy, and she almost regretted turning down his help.

"I heard all you said," Mike told her, coming up behind her. "But please don't shame me by letting me be seen empty-handed while a fine lady carried her own luggage."

Gratefully she turned and handed the bags to him. "Thank you," she said. "I think some things must be built up to."

He grinned. "Maybe I'll build up to going to see Alvin face to face."

She looked into his heartfire. "I'm sure of it, Mr. Fink."

As Fink put her bags into the carriage in which the men who had crossed with them impatiently waited for her, she wondered: I just changed the course of events. I brought Mike Fink closer than he would ever have come on his own. Have I done something that will save Alvin in the end? Have I given him the friend that will confound his enemies?

She found Alvin's heartfire almost without trying. And no, there was no change, no change, except for a day when Mike Fink would go away from a prison cell in tears, knowing that Alvin would surely die if he wasn't there, but knowing also that Alvin refused to have him, refused to let him stand guard.

But it was not the jail in Hatrack River. And it was not anytime soon. Even if she hadn't changed the future much, she'd changed it a little. There'd be other changes, too. Eventually one of them would make the difference. One of them would turn

Alvin away from the darkness that would engulf the end of his life.

"God be with you, ma'am," said Mike Fink.

"Call me Miss Larner, please," said Peggy. "I'm not married."

"So far, anyway," he said.

Even though he hardly slept the night before, Verily was too keyed up to be sleepy as he entered the courtroom. He had met Alvin Smith, after all these weeks of anticipation, and it was worth it. Not because Alvin had overawed him with wisdom— time enough to learn from him later. No, the great and pleasant surprise was that he liked the man. He might be a bit rough-hewn, more American and more countrified than Calvin. What of that? He had a glint of humor in his eyes, and he seemed so direct, so open . . .

And I am his attorney.

The American courtroom was almost casual, compared to the English ones in which Verily had always litigated up to now. The judge had no wig, for one thing, and his robe was a little threadbare. There could hardly be any majesty of law here; and yet law was law, and justice was not utterly unconnected to it, not if the judge was honest, and there was no reason to think he wouldn't be.

He called the court into session and asked for motions. Marty Laws rose quickly. "Motion to have the golden plow removed from the prisoner and placed into the custody of the court. It doesn't make any sense for the very item in question to remain in the possession of the prisoner when . . ."

"Didn't ask for arguments," said the judge. "I asked for motions. Any others?"

"If it please the court, I move for dismissal of all charges against my client," said Verily.

"Speak up, young man, I couldn't hear a word you said."

Verily repeated himself, more loudly.

"Well, wouldn't that be nice," said the judge.

"When the court is ready for argument, I'll be glad to explain why."

"Explain now, please," said the judge, looking just a little annoyed.

Verily didn't understand what he had done wrong, but he complied. "The point at issue is a plow that all agree is made of solid gold. Makepeace Smith has not a scintilla of evidence that he was ever in possession of such a quantity of gold, and therefore he has no standing to bring a complaint."

Marty Laws pounced at once. "Your Honor, that's what this whole trial is designed to prove, and as for evidence, I don't know what a scintilla is, unless it has something to do with *The Odyssey*—"

"Amusing reference," said the judge, "and quite flattering to me, I'm sure, but please sit back down on your chairybdis until I ask for rebuttal, which I won't have to ask for because the motion to dismiss is denied. Any other motions?"

"I've got one, your honor," said Marty. "A motion to postpone the matter of extradition until after—"

"Extradition!" cried the judge. "Now what sort of nonsense is this!"

"It was discovered that there was an outstanding warrant of extradition naming the prisoner, demanding that he be sent to Kenituck to stand trial for the murder of a Slave Finder in the act of performing his lawful duty."

This was all news to Verily. Or was it? The family had told him some of the tale—how Alvin had changed a half-Black boy so the Finders could no longer identify him, but in their search for the boy they got into the roadhouse where his adopted parents lived, and there the boy's mother had killed one of the Finders, and the other had killed her, and then Alvin had come up and killed the one that killed her, but not until after the Finder had shot him, so it was obviously self-defense.

"How can he be tried for this?" asked Verily. "The determination of Pauley Wiseman, who was sheriff at the time, was that it was self-defense."

Marty turned to the man sitting, up to now silently, beside him. The man arose slowly. "My learned friend from England is unaware of local law, Your Honor. Do you mind if I help him out?"

"Go ahead, Mr. Webster," said the judge.

So . . . the judge had already had dealings with Mr. Webster, thought Verily. Maybe that meant he was already biased; but which way?

"Mr.—Cooper, am I right?—Mr. Cooper, when Kenituck, Tennizy, and Appalachee were admitted to the union of American states, the Fugitive Slave Treaty became the Fugitive Slave Law. Under that law, when a Slave Finder engaged in his lawful duty in one of the free states is interfered with, the defendant is tried in the state where the owner of the slave being pursued has his legal residence. At the time of the crime, that state was Appalachee, but the owner of the slave in question, Mr. Cavil Planter, has relocated in Kenituck, and so that is where by law Mr. Smith will have to be extradited to stand trial. If it is found there that he acted in self-defense, he will of course be set free. Our petition to the court is to set aside the matter of extradition until after the conclusion of this trial. I'm sure you'll agree that this is in the best interests of your client."

So it seemed, on the surface. But Verily was no fool—if it *was* in the best interest of Alvin Smith, Daniel Webster would not be so keen on it. The most obvious motive was to influence the jury. If people in Hatrack, who mostly liked Alvin, came to believe that by convicting him of stealing Makepeace's plow they might keep him from being extradited to a state where he would surely be hanged, they might convict him for his own good.

"Your Honor, my client would like to oppose this motion and demand an immediate hearing on the matter of extradition, so it may be cleared up before he stands trial on the charges here."

"I don't like that idea," said the judge. "If we have the hearing and approve the extradition, then this trial takes second place and off he goes to Kenituck."

Marty Laws whispered to Verily, "Don't be daft, boy! I'm

the one as pushed Webster into agreeing to this, it's crazy to send him to Kenituck."

For a moment Verily wavered. But by now he had some understanding of how Webster and Laws fit together. Laws might believe that he had persuaded Webster to put off the extradition, but Verily was pretty sure the reality went the other way. Webster wanted extradition postponed. Therefore Verily didn't.

"I'm quite aware of that," said Verily, a statement that had become true not five seconds before. "Nevertheless, we wish an immediate hearing on the matter of extradition. I believe that is my client's right. We don't wish the jury to be aware of a matter of extradition hanging over him."

"But *we* don't want the defendant leaving the state while still in possession of Makepeace Smith's gold!" cried Webster.

"We don't know whose gold it is yet," said the judge. "This is all pretty darn confusing, I must say. Sounds to me like the prosecution is pleading the defense's cause, and vice-versa. But on general principles I'm inclined to give the capital charge precedence over a matter of larceny. So the extradition hearing will be—how long do you boys need?"

"We could be ready in this afternoon," said Marty.

"No you can't," said Verily. "Because you have to obtain evidence that at present is almost certainly in Kenituck."

"Evidence!" Marty looked genuinely puzzled. "Of what? All the witnesses of Alvin's killing that Finder fellow live right here in town."

"The crime for which extradition is mandatory is not killing a Finder, plain and simple. It's interfering with a Finder who is in pursuit of his lawful duty. So you must not only prove that my client killed the Finder—you must prove the Finder was in lawful pursuit of a particular slave." The thread that Verily was holding to was what the Miller family back in Vigor had told him about Alvin changing the half-Black boy so the Finders couldn't Find him anymore.

Marty Laws leaned close to Daniel Webster and they conferred for a moment. "I believe we'll have to bring us a Slave Finder over the river from Wheelwright," said Laws, "and fetch the cachet. Only that's in Carthage City, so . . . by horse and then by train . . . day after tomorrow?"

"That works for me," said the judge.

"If it please the court," said Webster.

"Nothing has pleased me much so far today," said the judge. "But go ahead, Mr. Webster."

"Since there is some considerable history of people hiding the slave in question, we'd like him taken into custody immediately. I believe the boy is in this courtroom right now." He turned and looked straight at Arthur Stuart.

"On the contrary," said Verily Cooper. "I believe the boy Mr. Webster is indicating is the adopted son of Mr. Horace Guester, the owner of the roadhouse in which I have taken lodging, and therefore he has presumptive rights as a citizen of the state of Hio, which decrees that he is presumed to be a free man until and unless it is proven otherwise."

"Hell's bells, Mr. Cooper," said Marty Laws, "we all know the Finders picked the boy out and took him back across the river in chains."

"It is my client's position that they did so in error, and a panel of impartial Finders will be unable, using only the cachet, to pick the boy out from a group of other boys if his race is concealed from them. We propose this as the first matter for the court to demonstrate. If the panel of Finders cannot pick out the boy, then the Finders who died in this town were *not* pursuing their lawful business, and therefore Kenituck has no jurisdiction because the Fugitive Slave Law does not apply."

"You're from England and you don't know diddly about what these Finders can do," said Marty, quite upset now. "Are you trying to get Arthur Stuart sent off in chains? And Alvin hanged?"

"Mr. Laws," said the judge, "you are the state's attorney in this matter, not Mr. Smith's or Mr. Stuart's."

"For crying out loud," said Marty.

"And if the Fugitive Slave Law does not apply, then I submit to the court that Alvin Smith has already been determined by the sheriff and attorney of Hatrack County to have acted in self-defense, and therefore to bring charges now would put him in double jeopardy, which is forbidden by—"

"I know exactly who and what forbids double jeopardy," said the judge, now getting a little edgy with Verily.

What am I doing wrong? Verily wondered.

"All right, since it's Mr. Smith's neck that's on the line, I'll deny the prosecution's motion and grant the defense motion to set up a blind test of a panel of Finders. Let's add another day—we'll meet on Friday to see if they can identify Arthur Stuart. As for putting Arthur in custody, I'll ask the boy's adopted father—is old Horace in the court today?"

Horace stood up. "Here I am, sir," he said.

"You going to make my life difficult by hiding this boy, so I have to lock you up for the rest of your natural life for contempt of court? Or are you going to keep him in plain sight and bring him to court for that test?"

"I'll bring him," said Horace. "He ain't going nowheres as long as Alvin's in jail, anyhow."

"Don't get cute with me, Horace, I'm just warning you," said the judge.

"Got no intention of being cute, dammit," murmured Horace as he sat back down.

"Don't curse in my courtroom, either, Mr. Guester, and don't insult me by assuming that my grey hair means I'm deaf." The judge rapped with his gavel. "Well, that does it for motions and—"

"Your Honor," said Verily.

"That's me," said the judge. "What, you got another motion?"

"I do," said Verily.

"And there's the matter of arguments on the motion to produce the plow," offered Marty Laws helpfully.

"Dammit," muttered the judge.

"I heard that, judge!" cried Horace Guester.

"Bailiff, put Mr. Guester outside," said the judge.

They all waited while Horace Guester got up and hurried out of the courtroom.

"What's your new motion, Mr. Cooper?"

"I respectfully request to know the position of Mr. Webster in this courtroom. He seems not to be an official of the county of Hatrack or the state of Hio."

"Ain't you co-counsel or some other fool thing?" asked the judge of Daniel Webster.

"I am," said Webster.

"Well, there you have it."

"Begging your pardon, Your Honor, but it seems plain to me that Mr. Webster's fees are not being paid by the county. I respectfully request to know who *is* paying him, or if he is acting out of the goodness of his heart."

The judge leaned on his desk and cocked his head to look at Daniel Webster. "Now that you mention it, I do recall never seeing you represent anybody as wasn't either very rich or very famous, Mr. Webster. I'd like to know myself who's paying you."

"I'm here volunteering my services," said Webster.

"So if I put you under oath and ask you to tell me if your time and expenses here are or are not being paid by someone other than your own self, you would say that you are receiving no payment? Under oath?"

Webster smiled faintly. "I'm on retainer, and so my expenses are paid, but not for this case specifically."

"Let me ask it another way. If you don't want the bailiff to put you out with Mr. Guester, tell me who's paying you."

"I am on retainer with the Property Rights Crusade, located at 44 Harrison Street in the city of Carthage in the state of Wobbish." Webster smiled thinly.

"Does that answer your respectful request, Mr. Cooper?" the judge asked.

"It does, Your Honor."

"Then I'll declare this—"

"Your Honor!" cried Marty Laws. "The matter of possession of the plow."

"All right, Mr. Laws," said the judge. "Time for brief arguments."

"It's absurd for the defendant to remain in possession of the property in question, that's all," said Marty.

"Since the defendant himself is in the custody of the county jail," said Verily Cooper, "and the plow is in his possession, then, like his clothing and his pen and ink and paper and everything else in his possession, the plow is obviously in the custody of the county jail as well. The state's motion is moot."

"How do we know that the defendant even *has* the plow?" asked Marty Laws. "Nobody's seen it."

"That's a point," said the judge, looking at Verily.

"Because of special properties of the plow," said Verily, "the defendant feels it unwise to let it out of his sight. Nevertheless, if the state wishes to designate three officers of the court to see it . . ."

"Let's keep it simple," said the judge. "Mr. Laws, Mr. Cooper, and I will go see this plow today, as soon as we finish here."

Verily noticed with pleasure that Daniel Webster flushed with anger as he realized he was not going to be treated as an equal and invited along. Webster tugged at Laws' coat and then whispered in his ear.

"Um, Your Honor," said Laws.

"What message are you delivering for Mr. Webster?" asked the judge.

"We can't exactly call me, you, and Mr. Cooper as witnesses, us being, um, what we are," said Laws.

"I thought the point of this was to make sure the plow existed," said the judge. "If you and me and Mr. Cooper see it, then I think we can fairly well assure everybody it exists."

"But in the trial, we'll want people other than the defendant and Mr. Makepeace Smith to be able to testify about the plow."

"Plenty of time for worrying about that later. I'm sure we

can get a few witnesses to see it by then, too. How many do you want?"

Another whispered conference. "Eight will do fine," said Laws.

"You and Mr. Cooper get together in the next while and decide which eight people you'll settle on as witnesses. In the meantime, the three of us will go visit Mr. Alvin Smith in prison and get an eyeful of this marvelous legendary mythical golden plow that has—how did you put it, Mr. Cooper?"

"Special properties," said Verily.

"You Englishmen have such a fine way with words."

Once again, Verily could sense some kind of nastiness directed toward him from the judge. As before, he had no idea what he had done to provoke it.

Still, the judge's inexplicable annoyance aside, things had gone rather well.

Unless, of course, the Millers had been all wrong and the Slave Finders *could* identify Arthur Stuart as the wanted runaway. Then there'd be problems. But . . . the nicest thing about this case was that if Verily performed quite badly, making it certain that Alvin would be hanged or Arthur Stuart returned to slavery, Alvin, being a Maker, could always just take the boy and go away; and not a soul could stop them if Alvin didn't want to be stopped, or find them if Alvin didn't want to be found.

Still, Verily had no intention of doing badly. He intended to win spectacularly. He intended to clear Alvin's name of all charges so the Maker would be free to teach him all that he wanted to know. And another, deeper motive, one which he did not try to hide from himself though he would never have admitted it to another: He wanted the Maker to respect him. He wanted Alvin Smith to look him in the eye and say, "Well done, friend."

That would be good. Verily Cooper wanted that good thing.

❧ 14 ❧

Witnesses

ALL THE TIME of waiting hadn't been so bad, really. Nothing was happening in the jail, but Alvin didn't mind being alone and doing nothing. It gave him thinking time. And thinking time was making time, he reckoned. Not like he used to do as a boy, making bug baskets out of pulled-up grass to keep the Unmaker back. But making things in his head. Trying to remember the Crystal City as he saw it in the waterspout with Tenskwa-Tawa. Trying to figure how such a place was made. Can't teach folks how to make it if I don't know what it is myself.

Outside the jail he knew that the Unmaker was moving in the world, tearing down a little here, knocking over a little there, setting a wedge in every tiny crack it found. And there were always people searching for the Unmaker, for some awful destructive power outside themselves. Poor fools, they always thought that Destruction was merely destruction, they were using it and when they were done with it, they'd set to building. But you don't build on a foundation of destruction. That's the dark secret of the Unmaker, Alvin thought. Once he sets you to tearing down, it's hard to get back to building, hard to get your own self back. The digger wears out the ground *and* the spade. And once you let yourself be a tool in the Unmaker's hand, he'll wear you out, he'll tear you down, he'll dull you and hole you and all the time you'll be thinking you're so sharp and fine and bright and whole, and you never know till he lets go of you, lets you drop and fall. What's that clatter? Why, that was me. That was me, sounding like a wore-out tool. What you leaving me for? I still got use left in me!

But you don't, not when the Unmaker's got you.

What Alvin figured out was that when you're Making, you don't use people like tools. You don't wear them out to achieve *your* purpose. You wear yourself out helping them achieve *theirs*. You wear yourself out teaching and guiding, persuading and listening to advice and letting folks persuade *you*, when it happens they're right. So instead of one ruler and a bunch of wore-out tools, you got a whole city of Makers, all of them free fellow-citizens, hard workers every one . . .

Except for one little problem. Alvin couldn't teach Making. Oh, he could get people to sort of set their minds right and their work would be enhanced a little. And a few people, like Measure, mostly, and his sister Eleanor, they learned a thing or two, they caught a glimmer. But most was in the dark.

And then there comes a one like this lawyer from England, this Verily Cooper, and he was just born knowing how to do in a second what Measure could only do after a whole day's struggle. Sealing a book shut like it was a single block of wood and cloth, and then opening it again with no harm to any of the pages and the letters still stuck on the surfaces. That was some Making.

What did he have to teach Verily? He was born knowing. And how could he hope to teach those as wasn't born knowing? And anyway how could he teach anything when he didn't know how to make the crystal out of which the city would be made?

You can't build a city of glass; it'll break, it can't hold weight.

You can't build out of ice, either, because it ain't clear enough and what about summer? Diamonds, they're strong enough, but a city made of diamond, even if he could find or make so much of it—no way would they be allowed to use such rich stuff for building, there'd be folks to tear it down in no time, each one stealing a bit of wall to make hisself rich, and pretty soon the whole thing would be like a Swiss cheese, more hole than wall.

Oh, Alvin could spin himself through these thoughts and wonderings, through memories and words of books he read when Miss Larner—when Peggy—was teaching him. He could keep his mind occupied in solitude and not mind it a bit, though he also sure didn't mind when Arthur Stuart came to talk to him about goings on.

Today, though, things were happening. Verily Cooper would be fending off motions for this and that, and even if he was a good lawyer, he was from England and he didn't know the ways here, he could make mistakes, but there wasn't a blame thing Alvin could do about it even if he did. He just had to put his trust in other folks and Alvin hated that.

"Everyone hates it," said a voice, a so-familiar voice, a dreamed-of, longed-for voice with which he had had many a debate in his memory, many a quarrel in his imagination; a voice that he dreamed of whispering gently to him in the night and in the morning.

"Peggy," he whispered. He opened his eyes.

There she was, looking just as she would if he had conjured her up, only she was real, he hadn't done no conjuring.

He remembered his manners and stood up. "Miss Larner," he said. "It was kind of you to come and visit me."

"Not so much kind as necessary," she said, her tone business-like.

Businesslike. He sighed inwardly.

She looked around for a chair.

He picked up the stool that stood inside the cell and impulsively, thoughtlessly handed it right through the bars to her.

He hardly even noticed how he made the bits of iron bar and the strands of woodstuff move apart to let each other through; only when he saw Peggy's wide, wide eyes did he realize that of course she'd never seen anybody pass wood and iron right through each other like that.

"Sorry," he said. "I've never done that before, I mean without warning or nothing."

She took the stool. "It was very thoughtful of you," she said. "To provide me with a stool."

He sat down on his cot. It creaked under him. If he hadn't toughened up the material, it would have given way under his weight days ago. He was a big man and he used furniture kind of rough; he didn't mind if it complained out loud now and then.

"They're doing pretrial motions in court today, I understand."

"I watched part of it. Your lawyer is excellent. Verily Cooper?"

"I think he and I ought to be friends," Alvin said. He watched for her reaction.

She nodded, smiled thinly. "Do you really want me to tell you what I know about the possible courses your friendship might take?"

Alvin sighed. "I do, and I don't, and you know it."

"I'll tell you that I'm glad he's here. Without him you'd have no chance of getting through this trial."

"So now I'll win?"

"Winning isn't everything, Alvin."

"But losing is nothing."

"If you lost the case but kept your life and your life's work, then losing would be better than winning, and dying for it, don't you think?"

"I'm not on trial for my life!"

"Yes you are," said Peggy. "Whenever the law gets its hands on you, those who use the law to their own advantage will also turn it against you. Don't put your trust in the laws of men,

Alvin. They were designed by strong men to improve their power over weaker ones."

"That's not fair, Miss Larner," said Alvin. "Ben Franklin and them others as made the first laws—"

"They meant well. But the reality for you is that whenever you put yourself in jail, Alvin, your life is in grave danger every moment."

"You came to tell me that? You know I can walk out of here whenever I want."

"I came so I could tell you when to walk away, if the need comes."

"I want my name cleared of Makepeace's lies."

"I also came to help with that," she said. "I'm going to testify."

Alvin thought of that night when Goody Guester died, Peggy's mother, though he hadn't known that Miss Larner was really Peggy Guester until she knelt weeping over her mother's ruined body. Right till the moment they heard the first gunshot, he and Peggy had been on the verge of declaring their love for each other and deciding to marry. And then her mother killed the Finder, and the other Finder killed her, and Alvin got there way too late to heal her from the shotgun blast, and all he could do was kill the man that shot her, kill him with his bare hands, and what did that do? What good did that do? What kind of Making was that?

"I don't want you to testify," he said.

"I wasn't looking forward to it myself," she said. "I won't do it if it's not needed. But you have to tell Verily Cooper what and who I am, and tell him that when he's all done with his other witnesses, he's to look to me, and if I nod, he's to call me as a witness, no arguments. Do you understand me? I'll know better than either of you whether my testimony is necessary or not."

Alvin heard what she said and knew he'd go along, but there was a part of him that was seething with anger even though he didn't know why—he'd been longing to see her for more than a year now, and suddenly she was here and all he wanted to do was yell at her.

Well, he didn't yell. But he did speak up in a voice that sounded less than kind. "Is that what you come back for? To tell poor stupid Alvin and his poor stupid lawyer what to do?"

She looked sharp at him. "I met an old friend of yours at the ferry."

For a moment his heart leapt within him. "Ta-Kumsaw?" he whispered.

"Goodness no," she said. "He's out west past the Mizzipy for all I know. I was referring to a fellow who once had a tattoo on an unmentionable part of his body, a Mr. Mike Fink."

Alvin rolled his eyes. "I guess the Unmaker's assembling all my enemies in one place."

"On the contrary," said Peggy. "I think he's no enemy. I think he's a friend. He swears he means only to protect you, and I believe him."

He knew she meant him to take that as proof that the man could be trusted, but he was feeling stubborn and said nothing.

"He came to the Wheelwright ferry in order to be close enough to keep an eye on you. There's a conspiracy to get you extradited to Kenituck under the Fugitive Slave Law."

"Po Doggly told me he wasn't going to pay no mind to that."

"Well, Daniel Webster is here precisely to see to it that whether you win or lose here, you get taken to Kenituck to stand trial."

"I won't go," said Alvin. "They'd never let me get to trial."

"No, they never would. That's what Mike Fink came to watch out for."

"Why is he on my side? I took away his hex of protection. It was a strong one. Near perfect."

"And he's suffered a few scars and lost an ear since then. But he's also learned compassion. He values the exchange. And you healed his legs. You left him with a fighting chance."

Alvin thought about that. "Well, you never know, do you. I thought of him as a stone killer."

"I think that a good person can sometimes do wrong out of ignorance or weakness or wrong thinking, but when hard times come, the goodness wins out after all. And a bad person can often seem good and trustworthy for a long time, but when hard times come, the evil in him gets revealed."

"So maybe we're just waiting for hard enough times to come in order to find out just how bad I am."

She smiled thinly. "Modesty is a virtue, but I know you too well to think for a minute you believe you're a bad man."

"I don't think much about whether I'm good or bad. I think a lot about whether I'm going to be worth a damn or not. Right now I reckon myself to be worth about six bits."

"Alvin," she said, "you never used to swear in front of me."

He felt the rebuke but he rather liked the feeling of annoying her. "It's just the bad in me coming out."

"You're very angry with me."

"Yes, well, you know all, you see all."

"I've been busy, Alvin. You've been doing your life's work, and I've been doing mine."

"Once upon a time I hoped it might be the same work," said Alvin.

"It will never be the same work. Though our labors may complement each other. I will never be a Maker. I only see what is there to be seen. While you imagine what might be made, and then make it. Mine is by far the lesser gift, and mostly useless to you."

"That's the purest nonsense I ever heard."

"I don't speak nonsense," she said sharply. "If you don't think my words sound true, then think again until you understand them."

He imagined her as he used to see her, the severe-looking teacher lady at least ten years older than Peggy really was; she still knew how to use her voice like a rap across the knuckles. "It ain't useless to me to know what's coming in the future."

"But I don't *know* what's coming. I only know what *might* come. What seems likely to come. There are so many paths the future might take. Most people stumble blindly along, plunging into this or that path that I see in their heartfire, heading for disaster or delight. Few have your power, Alvin, to open up a new path that did not exist. There was no future in which I saw you push that stool through the bars of the cell. And yet it was an almost inevitable act on your part. A simple expression of the impulsiveness of a young man. I see in people's heartfires the futures that are possible for them in the natural course of events. But you can set aside the laws of nature, and so you can't be properly accounted for. Sometimes I can see clearly; but there are deep gaps, dark and wide."

He got up from the cot and came to the bars, held them, knelt down in front of her. "Tell me how I find out how to make the Crystal City."

"I don't know how you do it. But I've seen a thousand futures in which you do."

"Tell me where I look then, in order to learn!"

"I don't know. Whatever it is, it doesn't follow the laws of nature. Or at least I think that's why I can't see it."

"Vilate Franker says my life ends in Carthage City," said Alvin.

She stiffened. "How does she know such a thing?"

"She knows where things come from and where they'll end up."

"Don't go to Carthage City. Never go there."

"So she's right."

"Never go there," she whispered. "Please."

"I got no plans for it," he said. But inside his heart he thought: She cares for me after all. She still cares for me.

He might have said something about it, or she might have talked a bit more tenderly and less businesslike. *Might* have, but then the door opened and in trooped the sheriff and the judge and Marty Laws and Verily Cooper.

"Scuse us," said Sheriff Doggly. "But we got us a courtroom thing to do here."

"I'm at your service, gentlemen," said Alvin, rising at once to his feet. Peggy also rose, then stooped to move the stool out of the way of the door.

The sheriff looked at the stool.

"It was so kind of you to allow Alvin's stool to be placed outside the bars for me," said Peggy.

Po Doggly looked at her. He hadn't given any such order, but he decided not to argue the point. Alvin was Alvin.

"Explain things to your client," said the judge to Verily Cooper.

"As we discussed last night," said Verily, "we'll need to have various witnesses view the plow. The three of us will be enough to ascertain that the plow exists, that it appears to be made of gold, and . . ."

"That's all right," said Alvin.

"And we've agreed that after the jury is empaneled, we'll select eight more witnesses who can testify to the existence and nature of the plow in open court."

"As long as the plow stays in here with me," said Alvin. He glanced toward Sheriff Doggly.

"The sheriff already knows," said the judge, "that he is *not* one of the designated witnesses."

"Blame it all, Your Honor!" said Doggly. "It sets in here for weeks in my jail and I can't even *see* it?"

"I don't mind if he stays," said Alvin.

"I do," said the judge. "It's better if he doesn't regale his deputies with tales of how big and how gold the thing is. I know we can trust Mr. Doggly. But why exacerbate the temptation that must already afflict at least some of his deputies?"

Alvin laughed.

"What's so funny, Mr. Smith?" asked the judge.

"How everybody's all pretending they know what in hell the word *exacerbate* means." They all joined him in laughter.

When it died down, Sheriff Doggly was still in the room. "I'm waiting to escort the lady out," he said.

Alvin rolled his eyes. "She saw the plow on the night that it was made."

"Nevertheless," said the judge, "three witnesses on this official occasion. You can show it to every visitor in the jail if you want to, but on this occasion, we have agreed to three, and three it is."

Peggy smiled at the judge. "You are a man of extraordinary integrity, sir," she said. "I'm glad to know you're presiding at this trial."

When she was gone and the sheriff had closed the door to the jail, the judge looked at Alvin. "That was Peggy Guester? The torch girl?"

Alvin nodded.

"She grew up prettier than I ever expected," said the judge. "I just wish I knew whether she was being sarcastic."

"I don't think so," said Alvin. "But you're right, she has a way of saying even nice things as if she's only barely holding back from telling a bunch of stuff that ain't so nice."

"Whoever marries that one," said the judge, "he better have a thick skin."

"Or a stout stick," said Marty Laws, and then he laughed. But he laughed alone, and soon fell silent, vaguely embarrassed, uncertain why his joke had fallen so flat.

Alvin reached under the cot and slid out the burlap bag that held the plow. He pulled back the mouth of the sack, so the plow sat exposed, surrounded by burlap, shining golden in the light from the high windows.

"I'll be damned," said Marty Laws. "It really is a plow, and it really is gold."

"*Looks* gold," said the judge. "I think if we're to be honest witnesses, we have to touch it."

Alvin smiled. "I ain't stopping you."

The judge sighed and turned to the county attorney. "We forgot to get the sheriff to open the cell door."

"I'll fetch him," said Marty.

"Please cover the plow, Mr. Smith," said the judge.

"Don't bother," said Alvin. He reached over and opened the

cell door. The latch didn't even so much as make a sound; nor did the hinges squeak. The door just opened, silent and smooth.

The judge looked down at the latch and lock. "Is this broken?" he asked.

"Don't worry," said Alvin. "It's working fine. Come on in and touch the plow, if you want."

Now that the door was open, they hung back. Finally Verily Cooper stepped in, the judge after him. But Marty held back. "There's something about that plow," he said.

"Nothing to be worried about," said Alvin.

"You're just bothered because the door opened so easy," said the judge. "Come on in, Mr. Laws."

"Look," said Marty. "It's trembling."

"Like I told you," said Alvin, "it's alive."

Verily knelt down and reached out a hand toward the plow. With no one touching it yet, the plow slid toward him, dragging the burlap with it.

Marty yelped and turned his back, pressing his face into the wall opposite the cell door.

"You can't be much of a witness with your back turned," said the judge.

The plow slid to Verily. He laid his hand on the top of it. It slowly turned under his hand, turned and turned, around and around, smooth as an ice skater.

"It *is* alive," he said.

"After a fashion," said Alvin. "But it's got a mind of its own, so to speak. I mean, it's not like I've tamed it or nothing."

"Can I pick it up?" asked Verily.

"I don't know," said Alvin. "Nobody but me has ever tried."

"It would be useful," said the judge, "if we could heft it to see if it weighs like gold, or if it's some other, lighter alloy."

"It's the purest gold you'll ever see in your life," said Alvin, "but heft it if you can."

Verily squatted, got his hands under the plow, and lifted. He grunted at the weight of it, but it stayed in his hands as he lifted it. Still, there was some struggle with it. "It wants to turn," said Verily.

"It's a plow," said Alvin. "It reckon it wants to find good soil."

"You wouldn't actually plow with this, would you?" said the judge.

"I can't think why else I made it, if it ain't for plowing. I mean, if I was making a bowl I got the shape wrong, don't you think?"

"Can you hand it to me?" asked the judge.

"Of course," said Verily. He stepped close to the judge and held the plow as the older man wrapped his hands around it. Then Verily let go.

At once the plow began to buck in the judge's hands. Before the judge could drop it, Alvin reached out and rested his right hand on the plow's face. Immediately it went still.

"Why didn't it do that with Mr. Cooper?" asked the judge, his voice trembling a little.

"I reckon it knows Verily Cooper is my attorney," said Alvin, grinning.

"While I am impartial," said the judge. "Perhaps Mr. Laws is correct not to handle it."

"But he has to," said Verily. "He's the most important one to see it. He has to assure Mr. Webster and Makepeace Smith that it's the real plow, the gold plow, and that it's safe here in the jailhouse."

The judge handed the plow to Alvin, then left the cell and put his hand on Marty Laws' shoulder. "Come now, Mr. Laws, I've handled it, and even if it bucks a bit, it won't harm you."

Laws shook his head.

"Marty," said Alvin. "I don't know what you're afraid of, but I promise you that the plow won't hurt you, and you won't hurt it."

Marty turned sideways. "It was so bright," he said. "It hurt my eyes."

"Just a glint of sunlight," said the judge.

"No sir," said Marty. "No, your honor. It was bright. It was bright from way down deep inside itself. It shone right into me. I could feel it."

The judge looked at Alvin.

"*I* don't know," said Alvin. "It's not like I've been showing it to folks."

"I know what he means," said Verily. "I didn't see it as light. But I felt it as warmth. When the bag fell open, the whole place felt warmer. But there's no harm in it, Mr. Laws. Please—I'll hold it with you."

"As will I," said the judge.

Alvin held the plow out to them.

Marty slowly turned so he could watch, his head partly averted, as the other two witnesses got their hands on and under the plow. Only then did he sidle forward and gingerly lay his fingertips on and under the golden plowshare. He was sweating something awful, and Alvin felt plain sorry for him, but couldn't begin to understand what the man was going through. The plow had always felt comfortable and friendly-like to him. What did it mean to Marty?

When the thing didn't hurt him, Marty gained confidence, and shifted his hands to get some of the weight of the plow. Still his eyes were squinted and he looked sidelong, as if to protect one eye in case the other one was suddenly blinded. "I can hold it alone, I guess," he said.

"Let Mr. Smith keep his hand on it, so it doesn't buck," said the judge.

Alvin left his hand, but the others took their hands away, and Marty held the plow alone.

"I reckon it weighs like gold," said Marty.

Alvin reached under the plow and got hold of it. "I got it now, Marty," he said.

Marty let go—reluctantly, it seemed to Alvin.

"Anyway, I reckon you can see why I don't just let anyone have a grab at it," said Alvin.

"I'd hate to think what shape I'd be in if I dropped it on my toe," said the judge.

"Oh, it lands easy," said Alvin.

"It really is alive," said Verily softly.

"You're a bold fellow," said the judge to Alvin. "Your attorney was quite adamant about having a hearing on the extradition matter before we even empanel a jury about the larceny business."

Alvin looked at Verily. "I reckon my attorney knows what he's doing."

"I told them," said Verily, "that my defense would be that the finder was not engaged in lawful business, since by the cachet they carried, Arthur Stuart could not possibly be identified."

Alvin knew that this was more a question than a statement. "They walked right by Arthur Stuart that night," said Alvin.

"We are going to bring a group of Slave Finders from Wheelwright to see if they can pick Arthur Stuart from a group of boys about his age," said Verily. "Their faces and hands will be hidden, of course."

"Make sure," said Alvin, "to get a couple of Mock Berry's boys in the group, along with whatever White boys you settle on. I reckon those as spends their whole lives looking for Black folks might have some ways of spotting which is which, even if they got gloves on and bags over their heads."

"Mock Berry?" asked the judge.

"He's a Black fellow," explained Marty. "Free Black, mind you. Him and Anga his wife, they've got a passle of young folks in a cabin in the woods not far from the roadhouse."

"Well, that's a good idea, to have some Black boys in the mix," said the judge. "And maybe I'll see to a few others things to make things stay fair." He reached out to the plow, which Alvin still held in his hands. "Mind if I touch it one more time?"

He did; the plow trembled under his hand.

"If the jury should decide that this is truly Makepeace Smith's gold," said the judge, "I wonder how he's going to get it home?"

"Your Honor," Marty protested.

The judge glared at him. "Don't you even for a *moment* imagine that I'm going to be anything but completely fair and impartial in the conduct of this trial."

Marty shook his head and held out his hands as if to ward off the very *thought* of impartiality.

"Besides," said the judge. "You saw what you saw, too. You going to turn the trial over to Mr. Webster, now that you seen it move and shine and whatnot?"

Marty shook his head. "The point at issue is whether Alvin Smith made the plow with gold that belonged to Makepeace. What the plow is like, its other properties—I don't see but what that's completely irrelevant."

"Exactly," said the judge. "All we needed to verify right now is that it exists, it's gold, and it should remain in Alvin's custody while Alvin remains in the custody of the sheriff. I think we've determined all three points to everyone's satisfaction. Right, gentlemen?"

"Right," said Marty.

Verily smiled.

Alvin put the plow back in the burlap bag.

As they left the cell, the judge carefully closed the door until the latch clicked. Then he tried to open it and couldn't. "Well, I'm glad to see the jail is secure." He didn't grin when he said it. He didn't have to.

Po Doggly looked beside himself with curiosity as they emerged from the jail into the outer office. In moments he was inside the jail, looking through bars at Alvin, hoping to catch a glint of gold.

"Sorry, Sheriff," said Alvin. "All put away."

"You got no sense of sport, Alvin," said Doggly. "You couldn't even leave the top open a little bit?"

"I won't mind a bit if you're one of the eight," said Alvin. "Let's see what happens."

"Not a bad idea," said Doggly. "And thank you for not minding. I won't do that, though. Better to use eight ordinary citizens, instead of a public official. I'm just curious, you know. Never saw that much gold in all my life, and I'd like to be able to tell my grandchildren."

"So would I," said Alvin. And then: "Sheriff Doggly, Peggy Larner wouldn't still be out there, would she?"

"No. Sorry, Al. She's gone. Reckon she went on home to say howdy to her pa."

"Reckon so," said Alvin. "No matter."

Arthur Stuart would never have called himself a spy. He couldn't help it that he was short. He couldn't help it that his skin was dark and that, being shy, he tended to stand in shadows and hold very, very still so people overlooked him quite easily. He wasn't aware that some of the greensong from his long journeys with Alvin still lingered with him, a melody in the back of his mind, so that his step was unusually quiet, twigs tended to bend out of his way, and boards didn't often squeak under his step.

But when it came to his visit to Vilate's house, well, it wasn't no accident she didn't see him. In fact, he made it a point not to step on the porch of the post office, so he couldn't very well walk through the front door and make the bell ring. Nor, when he got around to the back of Vilate Franker's house, did he knock on her back door or ask her permission before climbing up on her rain barrel and leaning over to look through her window into her kitchen, where the teapot simmered on the stove and Vilate sat drinking tea and carrying on quite a lively conversation with . . .

With a salamander.

Not a lizard—even from the window, Arthur Stuart could see there were no scales. Besides, you didn't have to be some kind of genius to know a salamander from a lizard at five paces. Arthur Stuart was a boy, and boys tended to know such things. Moreover, Arthur Stuart had been an unusually solitary and inquisitive boy, and he had a way with animals, so even if some other boy might make a mistake, Arthur Stuart never would. It was a salamander.

Vilate would say something, and then sip her tea, glancing up from the cup now and then to nod or murmur something— "Mm-hm"; "I know"; "Isn't it just awful?"—as if the salamander was saying something.

But the salamander didn't say nothing. Didn't even look at her, most of the time, though truth to tell you never quite knew for sure what a salamander was looking at, because if one eye was looking there, the other might be looking here and how would you know? Still and all, Arthur was pretty sure it looked right at him. Knew he was there. But didn't seem to get alarmed or nothing, so Arthur just kept on looking and listening.

"A man shouldn't trifle with a lady's affections," she was saying. "Once a man goes down that road, the lady has a right to protect herself as best she can."

Another sip. Another nod.

"Oh, I know. And the worst of it is, people are going to think so badly of me. But everyone knows that Alvin Smith has hidden powers. Of course I couldn't help myself."

Another sip. And then, abruptly, tears streamed out of her eyes.

"Oh, my dear, dear soul, my friend, my beloved trusted friend, how can I do this? I really do care for the boy. I really do care for him. Why oh why couldn't he have loved me? Why did he have to spurn me and make me do this?"

And so it went. Arthur wasn't no dummy. He knew right off that Vilate Franker was planning some kind of devilment against Alvin, and he sort of hoped she might mention what it was, though that wasn't too likely, since all she talked about was how bad she felt and how she hated to do it but it was a lady's right to defend her honor even though it might involve giving the appearance of having *no* honor but that's why it was so good having such a good, true, wonderful *friend*.

Ah, the tears that flowed. Ah, the sighs. Ah, the quart of

tea she consumed while Arthur leaned on the sill, watching, listening.

Oddly, though, as soon as the tears were done, her face just went clean. Not a streak. Not a trace of redness around the eyes. Not a sign that she had even shed a tear.

The tea eventually took its toll. Vilate slid her chair back and rose to her feet. Arthur knew where the privy was; he immediately jumped from the rain barrel and ran around the front of the house before the door even opened leading out to the back. Then, knowing she couldn't possibly hear the bell, he opened the post office door, went inside, clambered over the counter, and made his way into the kitchen from the front of the house. There was the salamander, licking a bit of tea that had spilled from the saucer. As Arthur entered, the salamander lifted its head. Then it scurried back and forth, making a shape on the table. One triangle. Another triangle crossing it.

A hex.

Arthur moved to the chair where Vilate had been sitting. Standing, his head was just about at the height her head was at when she was seated. And as he leaned over her chair, the salamander changed.

No, not really. No, the salamander disappeared. Instead, a woman was sitting in the chair across from him.

"You're an evil little boy," the woman said with a sad smile.

Arthur hardly even noticed what she said. Because he knew her. It was Old Peg Guester. The woman he called Mother. The woman who was buried under a certain stone marker on the hill behind the roadhouse, near his real mother, the runaway slave girl he never met. Old Peg was there.

But it wasn't Old Peg. It was the salamander.

"And you imagine things, you nasty boy. You make up stories."

Old Peg used to call him her "nasty boy," but it was a tease. It was when he repeated something someone else had said. She would laugh and call him nasty boy and give him a hug and tell him not to repeat *that* remark to anyone.

But this woman, this pretend Old Peg, she meant it. She thought he was a nasty boy.

He moved away from the chair. The salamander was back on the table and Old Peg was gone. Arthur knelt by the table to look at the salamander at eye level. It stared into his eyes. Arthur stared back.

He used to do this for hours with animals in the forest. When he was very little, he understood them. He came away with their story in his mind. Gradually that ability faded. Now he caught only glimmers. But then, he didn't spend as much time with animals anymore. Maybe if he tried hard enough . . .

"Don't forget me, salamander," he whispered. "I want to know your story. I want to know who taught you how to make them hexes on the table."

He reached out a hand, then slowly let a single finger come to rest on the salamander's head. It didn't recoil from him; it didn't move even when his finger made contact. It just looked at him.

"What are you doing indoors?" he whispered. "You don't like it indoors. You want to be outside. Near the water. In the mud. In the leaves. With bugs."

It was the kind of thing Alvin did, murmuring to animals, suggesting things to them.

"I can take you back to the mud if you want. Come with me, if you want. Come with me, if you can."

The salamander raised a foreleg, then slowly set it down. One step closer to Arthur.

And from the salamander he thought he felt a hunger, a desire for food, but more than that, a desire for . . . for freedom. The salamander didn't like being a prisoner.

The door opened.

"Why, Arthur Stuart," said Vilate. "Imagine you coming to visit."

Arthur had sense enough not to jump to his feet as if he was doing something wrong. "Any letters for Alvin?" he asked.

"Not a one."

Arthur didn't even mention the salamander, which was just as well, because Vilate never even looked at it. You'd think that if a lady was caught with a live salamander—or even a dead one, for that matter—on her kitchen table, she'd at least offer some explanation.

"Want some tea?" she asked.

"Can't stay," said Arthur.

"Oh, next time then. Give Alvin my love." Her smile was sweet and beautiful.

Arthur reached out his hand, right in front of her, and touched the salamander's back.

She didn't notice. Or at least she gave no sign of noticing.

He moved away, backed out of the room, hopped the counter, and ran out the front door, hearing the bell ring behind him as he went.

If the salamander was a prisoner, who had captured it? Not Vilate—the salamander was making hexes to fool her into seeing somebody there. Though Arthur was willing to bet that it wasn't Old Peg Guester that Vilate saw. But the salamander wasn't fooling her out of its own free will, because all it wanted was to be free to go back to being an ordinary salamander again.

He'd have to tell Alvin about this, that was sure. Vilate was planning to do something rotten to him, and the salamander that walked out hexes on the kitchen table, it had something to do with the plot.

How could Vilate be so stupid that she didn't even see me touching her salamander? Why didn't she get upset when she saw me in the kitchen when she got back from the privy?

Maybe she wanted me to see the salamander. Or maybe someone else wanted me to see it.

Wanted me to see Mother.

For a moment, walking along the dusty main street of Hatrack River, he lost control of himself, almost let himself cry thinking about Mother, thinking about seeing her sitting across from him.

It wasn't real, he told himself. It was all fakery. Humbug. Hoaxification. Whoever was behind all this was a liar, and a mean liar at that. Nasty boy indeed. Evil boy. He wasn't no evil boy. He was a good boy and the real Peg Guester would know that, she wouldn't say nothing like that to him. The real Peg Guester would hug him up tight and say, "My good boy, Arthur Stuart, you are my own good boy."

He walked it off. He walked the tears right out of his eyes, and when the sad feelings went away, another feeling came in its place. He was plain mad. Got no right making him see Mama. Got no right. I hate you, whoever you are, making me see my Mama calling me names like that.

He trotted up the stairs into the courthouse. The only good thing about Alvin being in jail was that Arthur Stuart always knew where he was.

It was hard for Napoleon to believe that he had once come *this* close to killing the American boy Calvin. Hard to remember how frightened he had been to see the boy's power. How for the first few days, Napoleon had watched him closely, had hardly slept for fear that the boy would do something to him in the night. Remove his legs, for instance. That would be a cure for the gout! It only occurred to him because of the number of times he had wished, in the throes of agony, that in one of his battles a cannonball had severed his leg. Stumping around on sticks couldn't be worse than this. And the boy brought such relief. Not a cure . . . but a cessation of the pain.

In exchange for that, Napoleon was content to let Calvin manipulate him. He knew who was really in control, and it wasn't an upstart, ignorant American boy. Who cared if Calvin thought he was clever, doling out a day's relief from pain in exchange for another lesson on how to govern men? Did he really imagine Napoleon would teach him anything that would give him the upper hand? On the contrary, with every hour, every day they spent together, Napoleon's control over a boy who *could* have been uncontrollable grew stronger, deeper. And Calvin had no idea.

They never understood, none of them. They all thought they served Napoleon out of love and admiration, or out of greed and self-interest, or out of fear and discretion. Whatever motive drove them, Napoleon fed it, got control of it. Some were impelled by shame, and some by guilt; some by ambition, some by lust, some even by their excess of piety—for when the occasion demanded, Napoleon could convince some spiritually starved soul that he was God's chosen servant on Earth. It wasn't hard. None of it was hard, when you understood other people the way Napoleon did. They gave off their desires like sweat, like the smell of an athlete after the contest or a soldier after a battle, like the smell of a woman—Napoleon didn't even have to think, he simply said the word, the exact words they needed to hear to win them to him.

And on those rare occasions when someone was immune to his words, when they had some sort of protective amulet or hex, each one more clever than the last—well, that's what guards were for. That's why there was a guillotine. The people knew that Napoleon was not a cruel man, that few indeed were ever punished under his rule. They knew that if a man was sent to the guillotine, it was because the world would be better off with that particular mouth detached from those lungs, with those hands unconnected to that head.

Calvin? Ah, the boy could have been dangerous. The boy had the power to save himself from the guillotine, to stop the blade from striking his neck. The boy might have been able to prevent anything that didn't come as a complete surprise. How would the Emperor have defeated him? Perhaps a little opium to dull him; he had to sleep sometime. But it didn't matter. No need to kill after all. Only a little study, a little patience, and Napoleon had him.

Not as his servant—no, this American boy was clever, he was watching for that, he was careful not to allow himself to succumb to any attempt by Napoleon to turn him into a slave, into one of those servants who looked at their Emperor with adoring eyes. Now and then Napoleon made a remark, a sort of feint, so Calvin would *think* he was fending off the Emperor's best strokes. But in fact, Napoleon had no need for this boy's loyalty. Just his healing touch.

This boy was driven by envy. Who would have guessed it? All that innate power, such gifts from God or Nature or whatever, and the boy was wasting it all because of envy for his older brother Alvin. Well, he wasn't about to tell Calvin he had to stop letting those feelings control him! On the contrary, Napoleon fed them, subtly, with little queries now and then about how Alvin might have done this or that, or comments about how awful it was having to put up with younger brothers who simply haven't the ability to measure up to one's own ability. He knew how this would rankle, how it would fester in Calvin's soul. A worm, twisting its way through the boy's judgment, eating tunnels in it. I have you, I have you. Look across the ocean, your gaze fixed upon your brother; you might have challenged me for the empire here, for half the world, but instead all you can think about is some useless fellow in homespun or deerskin or whatever who can make polished stone with his bare hands and heal the sick.

Heal the sick. That's the one that Napoleon was working on now. He knew perfectly well that Calvin was deliberately not healing him; he also knew that if Calvin ever got the idea that Napoleon was really in command, he'd probably flee and leave him with the gout again. So he had to keep a delicate balance: Taunt him because his brother could heal and he couldn't; at the same time, convince him that he'd already learned all the Emperor had to teach, that it was just a matter of practice now before he was as good at controlling other men.

If it worked out well, the boy, filled with confidence that he had squeezed the last drop of knowledge from Napoleon's mind, would finally show off that he was a match for his brother after all. He would heal the Emperor, then leave the court at once and sail back to America to challenge his brother—to attempt, using Napoleon's teachings, to get control over him.

Of course, if he got there and nothing he learned from the Emperor worked, well, he'd be back for vengeance! But Napoleon really was teaching him. Enough to play on the weaknesses of weak men, the fears of fearful men, the ambitions of proud men, the ignorance of stupid men. What Calvin didn't notice was that Napoleon wasn't teaching him any of the truly difficult arts: how to turn the virtues of good men against them.

The most hilarious thing was that Calvin was surrounded by the very best men, the most difficult ones that Napoleon had won over. The Marquis de La Fayette, for instance—he was the servant who bathed the boy, just as he bathed the Emperor. It would never occur to Calvin that Napoleon would keep his most dangerous enemies near him, oblivious to how he humiliated them. If Calvin only understood, he would realize that this was *real* power. Evil men, weak men, fearful men—they were so easy to control. It was only when men of virtue fell under Napoleon's control that he felt at last the confidence to reach for power, to unseat the king and take his place, to conquer Europe and impose his peace upon the warring nations.

Calvin never sees that, because he is himself a fearful and ambitious man, and does not realize that others might be fearless and generous. No wonder he resents his older brother so much! From what Calvin said of him, it seemed to Napoleon that Alvin would be a very difficult case indeed, a very hard one to break. In fact, knowing that Calvin's brother existed was enough to cause Napoleon to hold off on his plan of building up his armies in Canada with an eye to conquering the three English-speaking nations of America. No reason to do anything to make Alvin Smith turn his eyes eastward. That was a contest Napoleon did not want to embark on.

Instead he would send Calvin home, armed with great skill at subversion, deception, corruption, and manipulation. He'd have no control over Alvin, of course, but he would surely be able to deceive him, for Napoleon well knew that just as evil, weak, and fearful people saw their own base motives in other people's actions, so also the virtuous tended to assume the noblest of motives for other people's acts; why else were so many awful liars so successful at bilking others? If good people weren't so trusting of bad ones, the human race would have died out long ago—most women never would have let most men near them.

Let the brothers battle it out. If anyone can get rid of the threat of this Alvin Smith, it's his own brother, who can get close to him—not me, with all my armies, with all my skill. Let them fight.

But not until my leg is healed.

"My dear Leon, you mustn't drift off with the covers down like that."

It was La Fayette, checking on him before sleep. Napoleon let the fellow pull his blanket up. It was a coolish night; it was good to have such tender concern from a loving man of great responsibility, dependability, creativity. I have in my hands the best of men, and under my thumb the worst of them. My record is much better than God's. Clearly the old fellow chose the wrong son to make his only begotten. If I'd been in Jerusalem in the place of that dullard Jesus, I'd never have been crucified. I would have had Rome under my control in no time, and the whole world converted to my doctrine.

Maybe that's what this Alvin was—God's second try! Well, Napoleon would help with the script. Napoleon would send Alvin Smith his Judas.

"You need your sleep, Leon," said La Fayette.

"My mind is so full," said Napoleon.

"Of happy things, I pray."

"Happy indeed."

"No pain in your leg? It's good to have that American boy here, if he keeps you from that dreadful suffering."

"I know that when I'm in pain I'm so difficult to live with," said Napoleon.

"Not at all, never. Don't even think it. It's a joy to be with you."

"Do you ever miss it, my Marquis? The armies, the power? Government, politics, intrigues?"

"Oh, Leon! How could I miss it? I have it all through you. I watch what you do and I marvel. I never could have done so well. I'm at school with you every day; you are the superb master."

"Am I?"

"The master. The master of all is my dear Leon. How truly they named your house in Corsica, my dear. Buona Parte. Good parts. You are truly the lion of good parts."

"How sweet of you to say so, my Marquis. Good night."

"God bless you."

The candle retreated from the room, and moonlight returned its dim light through the curtains.

I know you're studying me, Calvin. Sending your doodling bug, as you so quaintly call it, into my legs, to find the cause of the gout. Figure it out. Be as smart as your brother about this one thing, so I can finally get rid of you and the pain both.

Verily had known debased men in his life; he had been offered large sums of money to defend one now and then, but his conscience was not for sale. He remembered one of them who, thinking that his minions had not been clear about just how *much* money he was offering, came to see Verily in person. When he finally realized that Verily was not simply holding out for a higher price, he looked quite hurt. "Really, Mr. Cooper, why isn't my money as good as anyone else's?"

"It isn't your money, sir," said Verily.

"What, then? What is your objection?"

"I keep imagining: What if, through some gross miscarriage of justice, I won?"

Livid, the man hurled vile threats at him and left. Verily never knew whether it was this man or another who sent an assassin after him—a pathetic attempt, knifework in the dark.

Verily saw the blade and the assassin's vicious smile—obviously the fellow had chosen a profession that allowed him to satisfy his own predilections—and caused the blade to drop off the knife and shatter at the man's feet. The man couldn't have looked more crestfallen if Verily had made a eunuch of him.

Debased men, but they all had something in common: They showed a keen regard for virtue, and tried to dress themselves in that costume. Hypocrisy, for all its bad reputation, at least showed a decent respect for goodness.

These Slave Finders, however, were not noble enough to be hypocrites. Not having risen above the level of reptiles and sharks, they showed no awareness of their own despicableness, and thus made no attempt to hide what they were. One was almost tempted to admire their brazenness, until one remembered what callous disregard for decency they must have in order to spend their lives, in exchange for mere money, chasing down the most helpless of their fellow-beings and returning them to lives of bondage, punishment, and despair.

Verily was pleased that Daniel Webster seemed to be almost as repulsed by these men as he was. Fastidiously the New England lawyer disdained to shake their hands, managing to be busy with his papers as each one arrived. Nor did he even bother to learn their names; having once ascertained that the entire group contracted for was properly assembled, he then addressed them only as a group, and without quite looking any of them in the eye. If they noticed his aloofness, they made no remark and showed no resentment. Perhaps this is how they were always treated. Perhaps those who hired them always did so with distaste, washing their hands after passing them the cachet of the slave they were to hunt down, washing again after giving them their Finder's fee. Didn't they understand that it is the murderer who is filthy, and not the knife?

It was ten-thirty in the morning before the Finders, seated at a single long table before the judge's bench, were satisfied that they had got the information they needed from the cachet belonging to a certain Cavil Planter of Oily Spring, Kenituck. The judge had the deposition, carefully taken by Mr. Webster at Mr. Planter's home in Carthage City, Wobbish. Planter had attempted to assert that the cachet was a collection of nail and hair clippings and a bit of dried skin taken from one Arthur Stuart of Hatrack River; but Webster insisted that he state the exact legal situation, which was that the items in the cachet were taken from an unnamed baby born on his farm in Appalachee to a slave woman belonging to Mr. Planter at the time, who had shortly afterward escaped—with, as Planter insisted on adding, the help of the devil, who gave her the power to fly, or so it was rumored among the ignorant and superstitious slaves.

The Finders were ready; the boys were led in, one at a time, and lined up in a row in front of them. All the boys were dressed in ordinary clothing, and all were more or less of a size. Their hands were covered, not with gloves, but with burlap bags tied above their elbows; a finer sacking material also covered their heads with loose-fitting hoods. No scrap of skin was visible; care had even been taken to make sure there was no gap between the buttons of their shirts. And just in case, a large placard with a number on it hung from each boy's neck, completely covering his shirtfront.

Verily watched carefully. Was there some difference between the Black sons of Mock Berry and the White boys? Something about their walk, their stance? Indeed, there were differences among the boys—this one's pose of insouciance, that one's nervous fidgeting—but Verily could not tell which were White and which were Black. Certainly he could not tell which one was Arthur Stuart, the boy who was not fully of either race. This did not mean, however, that the Finders did not know or could not guess.

Alvin assured him, though, that their knack would be useless to them, since Arthur Stuart was no longer a fair match for the cachet.

And Alvin was right. The Finders looked puzzled when the last boy was brought in and the judge said, "Well, which of them matches the cachet?" Clearly they had expected to know instantly which of them was their prey. Instead, they began to murmur.

"No conference," said the judge. "Each of you must reach his conclusion independently, write down the number of the boy you think matches the cachet, and have done with it."

"Are you sure someone hasn't held out the boy in question?" asked one Slave Finder.

"What you are asking me," said the judge, "is if I am either corrupt or a fool. Would you care to specify which accusation you are inquiring about?"

After that the Finders puzzled in silence.

"Gentlemen," said the judge—and was his tone somewhat dry when he called them that? "You have had three minutes. I was told your identification would be instant. Please write and have done."

They wrote. They signed their papers. They handed them to the judge.

"Please, return to your seats while I tabulate the results," said the judge.

Verily had to admire the way the judge showed no expression as he sorted through the papers. But it also frustrated him. Would there be *no* hint of the outcome?

"I'm disappointed," said the judge. "I had expected that the much-vaunted powers and the famous integrity of the Slave Finders would give me unanimous results. I had expected that you would either unanimously point the finger at one boy, or unanimously declare that the boy could not be one of this group. Instead, I find quite a range of answers. Three of you did declare under penalty of perjury that none of these boys matched the cachet. But four of you have named various boys—again, under penalty of perjury. Specifically, the four of you named three different boys. The only two who seemed to be in agreement both happened to be seated together, at my far right. Since you are the only two who agree in accusing one of the boys, I think we'll check your assertion first. Bailiff, please remove the hood from the head of boy number five."

The bailiff did as he was asked. The boy was Black, but he was not Arthur Stuart.

"You two—are you certain, do you swear before God, that this is the boy who matches the cachet? Remember please that it is your license to practice your profession in the state of Wobbish that hangs in the balance, for if you are found to be unreliable or dishonest, you will never be permitted to bring a slave back across the river again."

What they also knew, however, was that if they now backed down, they would be liable for charges of perjury. And the boy *was* Black.

"No sir, I am certain this is the boy," said one. The other nodded emphatically.

"Now, let's look at the other two boys that were named. Take the hoods from numbers one and two."

One of them was Black, the other White.

The Finder who named a White boy covered his face with his hands. "Again, knowing that your license is at stake, are you both prepared to swear that the boy you named is an exact match?"

The Finder who named the White boy began to stammer, "I don't know, I just don't, I was sure, I thought it was . . ."

"The answer is simple—do you continue to swear that this boy is an exact match, or did you lie under oath when you named him?"

The Finders who had sworn that the cachet matched no one were smiling now—they knew, obviously, that the others had lied, and were enjoying their torment.

"I did not lie," said the Finder who named the White boy.

"Neither did I," said the other defiantly. "And I *still* think I'm right. I don't know how these other boys could get it so wrong."

"But you—*you* don't think you're right, do you? You don't think some miracle turned that slave baby White, do you?"

"No, sir. I must be . . . mistaken."

"Give me your license. Right now."

The miserable Finder stood up and handed the judge a leather case. The judge took from the case a piece of paper with an official seal on it. He wrote in the margin and then on the back; then he signed it and crimped it with his own seal. "There you go," he said to the Finder. "You understand that if you're ever caught attempting to practice the profession of Slave Finding in the state of Hio, you will be arrested and tried and, when convicted, you will face at least ten years in prison?"

"I understand," said the humiliated man.

"And you are also aware that Hio maintains a reciprocity arrangement with the states of Huron, Suskwahenny, Irrakwa, Pennsylvania, and New Sweden? So that the same or similar penalties will apply to you there if you attempt to practice this profession?"

"I understand," he said again.

"Thank you for your help," said the judge. "You should only be grateful that you were incompetent, for if I had cause to suspect you of perjury, it would have been prison *and* the lash, I assure you, for if I thought that you had willfully named this boy falsely, I would have no mercy on you. You may go."

The others obviously got the message. As the unfortunate man fled the courtroom, the other three who had named one boy or another steeled themselves for what was to come.

"Sheriff Doggly," said the judge, "would you kindly inform us of the identity of these two boys who stand identified by three of our panel of Finders?"

"Sure, Your Honor," said Doggly. "These two is Mock Berry's boys, James and John. Peter's near growed and Andrew and Zebedee was too small."

"You're sure of their identity?"

"They've lived here in Hatrack all their lives."

"Any chance that either of them is, in fact, the child of a runaway slave?"

"No chance. For one thing, the dates are all wrong. They're

both way too old—the Berry boys is always short for their age, kind of late-blooming roses if you know what I mean, then they just shoot up like spring grass, cause Peter's about the tallest fellow around here. But these boys, they was already clever little tykes well known around town before ever the slave that cachet belongs to was born."

The judge turned to the Finders. "Well, now. I wonder how it happens that you appointed for slavery these two freeborn Black children."

One of them spoke up immediately. "Your Honor, I will protest this whole procedure. We were not brought here to be placed on trial ourselves, we were brought here to practice our profession and—"

The gavel slammed down on the desk. "You were brought here to practice your profession, that is true. Your profession requires that when you make an identification, it must be assumed by all courts of law to be both honest and accurate. Whenever you practice your profession, here or in the field, your license is on the line, and you know it. Now, tell me at once, did you lie when you identified these boys, or were you merely mistaken?"

"What if we was just guessing?" one of them asked. Verily almost laughed out loud.

"Guessing, in this context, would be lying, since you were swearing that the boy you named was a match for the cachet, and if you had to guess, then he was not a match. Did you guess?"

The man thought about it for a moment. "No sir, I didn't lie. I was just plain wrong I reckon."

Another man tried a different tack. "How do we know this sheriff isn't lying?"

"Because," said the judge, "I already met all these boys, and their parents, and saw their birth records in the county archive. Any more questions before you decide whether you'll lose your license or be bound over for trial as perjurers?"

The two remaining Finders quickly agreed that they had been

mistaken. Everyone waited while the judge signed and sealed the limitation on their licenses. "You gentlemen may also go."

They went.

Verily rose to his feet. "Your Honor, may I request that these young men who were not identified be allowed to remove their hoods? I fear that they may be growing quite uncomfortable."

"By all means. Bailiff, it's certainly time."

The hoods came off. The boys all looked relieved. Arthur Stuart was grinning.

To the three remaining Finders, the judge said, "You are under oath. Do you swear that none of these boys matches the cachet belonging to Mr. Cavil Planter?"

They all swore to it.

"I commend you for having the honesty to admit to not finding a match, when others were clearly tempted to find a match no matter what. I find your profession loathsome, but at least the three of you practice it honestly and with reasonable competence."

"Thank you, Your Honor," said one of them; the others, however, seemed to know they had just been insulted.

"Since this proceeding is a legal hearing under the Fugitive Slave Law, I don't have to have your signatures on anything, but I'd prefer it if you'd stay long enough to sign your names to an affirmation that specifically states that this young man, the mixup boy named Arthur Stuart, is definitely not a match with the cachet. Can you sign such a statement under oath before God?"

They could. They did. They were dismissed.

"Mr. Webster, I can't think what in the world you'd have to say, but since you represent Mr. Cavil Planter in this matter, I must ask you for any statement you'd like to make on this matter before I issue my finding."

Webster rose slowly to his feet. Verily wondered what the man could have the audacity to say, in the face of such evidence—what whining, sniveling complaint or protest he might utter.

"Your Honor," said Webster, "it is obvious to me that my client is the victim of fraud. Not today, your honor, for these proceedings have clearly been honest. No, the fraud was more than a year ago, when two Finders, hoping to collect a fee they had not earned, named this boy as Mr. Planter's property and proceeded to commit murder and get themselves killed in the effort to enslave a free boy. My client, believing them to be honest, naturally proceeded to secure the redress to which he would have been entitled by law; but now, I can assure you that as soon as my client learns that he was put upon most sorely by those Finders, he will be as horrified as I am by how close he came to enslaving a free child and, what is worse, extraditing for prosecution the young man named Alvin Smith, who it now seems was acting in proper self-defense when he killed the second of those malicious, lying, fraudulent men pretending to be Finders." Webster sat back down.

It was a pretty speech. Webster's voice was lovely to hear. The man should go into politics, Verily thought. His voice would be a noble addition to the halls of Congress in Philadelphia.

"You pretty much summed up my summing up," said the judge. "It is the finding of this court that Arthur Stuart is not the property of Mr. Cavil Planter, and therefore the Finders who were trying to take him back to Appalachee were not acting lawfully, and therefore the interference Margaret Guester and Alvin Smith offered them was legal and appropriate under the circumstances. I declare Alvin Smith to be absolved of all responsibility, criminal or civil, in the deaths of these Finders, and I declare Margaret Guester to be posthumously absolved in like manner. Under the terms of the Fugitive Slave Law, there may be no further attempt by anyone under any circumstances to bring Arthur Stuart into slavery regardless of any additional evidence—this action is final. Likewise there may be no further attempt to try Alvin Smith on any charges arising out of the illegal expedition undertaken by those fraudulent Finders, including their death. This action, likewise, is final."

Verily loved hearing those words, for all that language

insisting that such actions were final had been placed in the law for the purpose of blocking any effort on the part of anti-slavery forces to interfere with the recapture of a slave or the punishment of those who helped a runaway. This time, at least, that finality would work against the proponents of slavery. Hoist on their own petard.

The bailiff took the burlap bags off the boys' hands. The judge, the sheriff, Verily, and Marty Laws all shook the boys' hands and gave them—except Arthur, of course—the two bits they were entitled to for their service to the court. Arthur got something more precious. Arthur got a copy of the judge's decision making it illegal for him to be accosted by anyone searching for runaway slaves.

Webster shook Verily's hand, quite warmly. "I'm glad things worked out this way," he said. "As you know, in our profession we are sometimes called upon to represent clients in actions that we wish they would not pursue."

Verily held his silence—he supposed that for most lawyers this was probably true.

"I'm glad that my presence here will not result in anyone entering a life of slavery, or of your client being extradited under false charges."

Verily couldn't leave that statement alone. "And you would have been sad to see him extradited, if this hearing had turned out otherwise?"

"Oh, not at all," said Webster. "If the Finders had identified young Mr. Stuart, then justice would have demanded that your client be tried in Kenituck for murder."

"Justice?" Verily didn't try to keep the contempt from his voice.

"The law *is* justice, my friend," said Webster. "I know of no other measure available to us as mortal men. God has a better justice than ours, but until angels sit upon the bench, the justice of law is the best justice we can have, and I, for one, am glad we have it."

If Verily had been tempted to feel even a glimmer of guilt

over the fact that Arthur Stuart really was Cavil Planter's slave, by law, and that, again by law, Alvin Smith really should have been extradited, there was no chance of it now. Webster's narrow view of justice was just as truly satisfied by this outcome as Verily's much broader perspective. By God's justice, Arthur should be free and Alvin held to no penalty, and so the outcome had been just. But Webster's justice was as well served, for the letter of the law required the matching of the cachet to the slave, and if it so happened that Arthur Stuart had been changed somehow by a certain Maker so the cachet no longer matched—well, the law made no provision for exceptions, and so, as Webster had said, the law being satisfied, justice must also have been done.

"I'm grateful to know your mind upon the matter," said Verily. "I look forward to discovering, in my client's trial for larceny, precisely what your commitment to justice is."

"And so you shall," said Webster. "The gold belongs to Makepeace Smith, not his former apprentice. So when justice is done, Makepeace Smith will have his gold."

Verily smiled at him. "It shall be a contest, then, Mr. Webster."

"When two giants meet in battle," said Webster, "one giant will fall."

"And loud shall be the noise thereof," said Verily.

Webster took only a moment to realize that Verily was teasing him about his golden-voiced oratory; and when he did, instead of being insulted, he threw back his head and laughed, warmly, loudly, cheerfully. "I like you, Mr. Cooper! I shall enjoy all that lies ahead of us!"

Verily let him have the last word. But in his own mind, he answered, Not all, Mr. Webster. You shall not enjoy it all.

No one planned a meeting, but they arrived at Alvin's cell that evening almost at the same time, as if someone had summoned them. Verily Cooper had come to discuss what would happen during the selection of the jury and perhaps gloat a little over the easy victory in the hearing that morning; he was joined by Armor-of-God Weaver, who brought letters from family and wellwishers in Vigor Church; Arthur Stuart of course was there, as he was most evenings; Horace Guester had brought a bowl of roadhouse stew and a jug of the fresh cider—Alvin wouldn't take the cider that had turned, it dulled his mind; and no sooner were they all assembled in and around the open cell than the outer door opened and the deputy showed in Peggy Larner and a man that none but Alvin recognized.

"Mike Fink, as I live and breathe," said Alvin.

"And you're that smithy boy who bent my legs and broke my nose." Mike Fink smiled, but there was pain in the smile, and no one was sure but what there might not be a quarrel here.

"I see some scars and marks on you, Mr. Fink," said Alvin, "but I reckon from the fact you're standing here before us that those are marks of fights you won."

"Won fair and square, and hard fought," said Fink. "But I killed no man as didn't require me to, on account of trying to stick a knife in me and there being no other way to stop them."

"What brings you here, Mr. Fink?" asked Alvin.

"I owe you," said Fink.

"Not that I know of," said Alvin.

"I owe you and I mean to repay."

Still his words were ambiguous, and Arthur Stuart noticed how Papa Horace and Armor-of-God braced themselves to take on the powerful body of the riverman, if need arose.

It was Peggy Larner who made it clear. "Mr. Fink has come to give us information about a plot against Alvin's life. And to offer himself as a bodyguard, to make sure no harm comes to you."

"I'm glad to know you wanted to give me warning," said Alvin. "Come on in and sit down. You can share the floor with me, or sit on my cot—it's stronger than it looks."

"Don't have much to tell. I think Miss Larner already told you what I learned before, about a plot to kill you as they took you back for trial in Kenituck. Well, the men I know—if you can rightly call them men—haven't been fired from the plan. In fact what I heard this very afternoon was to pay no nevermind to how the extradition was squished—"

"Quashed," offered Verily Cooper helpfully.

"Mashed," said Fink. "Whatever. They got to pay no heed to it, because they'll still be needed. The plan is for you not to leave the town of Hatrack River alive."

"And what about Arthur Stuart?" asked Alvin.

"Not a word about no mixup boy," said Fink. "The way I see it, they don't give a damn about the boy, he's just an excuse for them to get you kilt."

"Please watch ..." Alvin began, mildly enough, but Mike Fink didn't need to hear him finish saying "your language with the lady."

"Beg your pardon, Miss Larner," he said.

"Don't that beat all," said Alvin admiringly. "He's already beginning to sound like one of your students." But was there a bite in his tone?

There was certainly a bite in Peggy's answer. "I'd rather hear him swear than hear you say 'don't' for 'doesn't.'"

Alvin leaned close to Mike Fink to explain, though he never took his eyes from Peggy's face. "You see, Miss Larner knows all the words, and she knows just where they ought to be."

Arthur Stuart could see the fury in her face, but she held her tongue. It was some kind of fight going on between the two of them; but what was it about? Miss Larner had *always* corrected their grammar, ever since she tutored Alvin and Arthur together when she was the schoolteacher in Hatrack River.

What puzzled Arthur Stuart all the more was the way the older men—not Verily, but Horace and Armor-of-God and even Mike Fink—sort of glanced around at each other and half-smiled like they all understood *exactly* what was going on between Alvin and Peggy, understood it better than those two did their own selves.

Mike Fink spoke up again. "Getting back to matters of life and death instead of grammar . . ."

At which point Horace murmured under his breath, "And lovers' spats."

"I'm sorry to say I can't learn no more of their plans than that," said Fink. "It's not like we're dear friends or nothing—more like they'd be as happy to stab me in the back as pee on my boots, depending on whether their knife or their . . . whatever . . . was in their hands." He glanced again at Peggy Larner and blushed. Blushed! That grizzled face, scarred and bent by battle, that missing ear, but still the blood rushed into his face like a schoolboy rebuked by his schoolmarm.

But before the blush could even fade, Alvin had his hand on Fink's arm and pulled him down to sit beside him on the floor, and Alvin threw an easy arm over his shoulder. "You and me, Mike, we just can't remember how to talk fine in front of some folks and plain in front of others. But I'll help you if you'll help me."

And there, in one easy moment, Alvin had put Mike Fink back to rights. There was just a kind of plain sincerity in Alvin's way of speaking that even when you knew he was trying to make you feel better, you didn't mind. You knew he cared about you, cared enough to try to make you feel better, and so you *did* feel better.

Thinking of Alvin making folks feel better made Arthur Stuart remember something that Alvin did to make *him* feel better. "Why don't you sing that song, Alvin?"

Now it was Alvin's turn to blush in embarrassment. "You know I ain't no singer, Arthur. Just because I sung it to you . . ."

"He made up a song," said Arthur Stuart. "About being locked up in here. We sung it together yesterday."

Mike Fink nodded. "Seems like a Maker got to keep making something."

"I got nothing to *do* but think and sing," said Alvin. "*You* sing it, Arthur Stuart, not me. You've got a good singing voice."

"I'll sing it if you want," said Arthur. "But it's your song. You made it up, words and tune."

"You sing it," said Alvin. "I don't even know if I'd remember all the words."

Arthur Stuart dutifully stood up and started to sing, in his piping voice:

> *I meant to be a journeyman,*
> *To wander on the earth.*
> *As quick as any fellow can*
> *I left the country of my birth—*
> *It's fair to say I ran.*

Arthur Stuart looked over at Alvin. "You got to sing the chorus with me, anyway."

So together they sang the rollicking refrain:

> *At daybreak I'll be risin',*
> *For never will my feet be still,*
> *I'm bound for the horizon—oh!*
> *I'm bound for the horizon.*

Then Arthur went back to the verse, but now Alvin joined him in a kind of tenor harmony, their voices blending sweetly to each other.

> *Till I was dragged from bed*
> *And locked inside a little cell.*
> *My journeys then were in my head*
> *On all the roads of hell.*

With the next verse, though, when Arthur began it, Alvin didn't join in, he just looked confused.

> *Alone with my imagining*
> *I dreamt the darkest dream—*

"Wait a minute, Arthur Stuart," said Alvin. "That verse isn't really part of this song."

"Well it fits, and you sung it to this tune your own self."

"But it's a nonsense dream, it don't mean a thing."

"I like it," said Arthur. "Can't I sing it?"

Alvin waved him to go ahead, but he still looked embarrassed.

> *Alone with my imagining*
> *I dreamt the darkest dream,*
> *Of tiny men, a spider's sting,*
> *And in a land of smoke and steam*
> *An evil golden ring.*

"What does that *mean?*" asked Armor-of-God.

"I don't know," said Alvin. "I wonder if sometimes I don't accidentally end up with somebody else's dream. Maybe that was a dream that belonged to somebody of ancient days, or maybe somebody who ain't even been born yet. Just a spare dream and I chanced to snag on it during my sleep."

Verily Cooper said, "When I was a boy, I wondered if the strange people in my dreams might not be just as real as me, and I was in *their* dreams sometimes too."

"Then let's just hope they don't wake up at a inconvenient moment," said Mike Fink dryly.

Arthur Stuart went on with the last verse.

> *The accusations all were lies*
> *And few believed the tale,*
> *So I was patient, calm and wise.*
> *But legs grow weak inside a jail*
> *And something in you dies.*

"This song may be the saddest one I ever heard," said Horace Guester. "Don't you *ever* have a cheerful thought in here?"

"The chorus is pretty sprightly," said Arthur Stuart.

"I had cheerful thoughts today," said Alvin, "thinking of four

Slave Finders losing their license to carry off free men and put them into bondage in the south. And now I'm cheerful again, knowing that the strongest man I ever fought is now going to be my bodyguard. Though the sheriff may not take kindly to it, Mr. Fink, since he thinks I'm safe enough as long as I'm in the care of him and his boys."

"And you are safe," said Peggy. "Even those deputies that don't like you would never raise a hand against you or allow you to be less than safe."

"There's no danger, then?" asked Horace Guester.

"Grave danger," said Peggy. "But not from the deputies, and most particularly not till the trail is over, and Alvin prepares to leave. That's when we'll need more than a bodyguard to die along with Alvin. We'll need subterfuge to get him out of town in one piece."

"Who says I'll die?" asked Fink.

Peggy smiled thinly. "Against any five men I think you two would do well."

"So there'll be more than five?" asked Alvin.

"There may be," said Peggy. "Nothing is clear right now. Things are in flux. The danger is real, though. The plot's in place and men have been paid. You know when money's involved, even assassins feel obliged to fulfill their contracts."

"But for the nonce," said Verily Cooper, "we're not to worry about our safety, or Alvin's?"

"Prudence is all that's needed," said Peggy.

"I don't know why we're putting our trust in knackery," said Armor-of-God. "Our Savior is guard enough for us all."

"Our Savior will resurrect us," said Peggy, "but I haven't noticed that Christians end up any less dead at the end of life than heathens."

"Well, one thing's sure," said Horace Guester. "If it wasn't for knackery Alvin wouldn't be in this blamed fix."

"Did you like the song?" asked Alvin. "I mean, I thought Arthur sung it real good. Real well. Very well." Each correction won a bit more of a smile from Miss Larner.

"*Sang* it very well," said Peggy. "But each version of the sentence was better than the one before!"

"I got another verse," said Alvin. "It's not really part of the song, on account of it isn't true yet, but do you want to hear it?"

"You got to sing it alone, I don't know another verse," said Arthur Stuart.

Alvin sang:

> *I trusted justice not to fail.*
> *The jury did me proud.*
> *Tomorrow I will hit the trail*
> *And sing my hiking song so loud*
> *It's like to start a gale!*

They all laughed, and allowed as how they hoped he could soon sing it for real. By the time the meeting ended, they'd decided that Armor-of-God, with Mike Fink to watch his back and keep him safe, would head for Carthage City and learn all he could about the men who were paying Daniel Webster's salary and see for sure if they were the same ones paying the river rats and other scoundrels to lie in wait to take Alvin's life. Other than that, everything was in Verily Cooper's hands. And to hear him tell it, it was up to the witnesses and the jury. Twelve good men and true.

There was a long line at the county clerk's office as Peggy came in for the first day of Alvin's trial. "Early voters," Marty Laws explained. "Folks that worry maybe the weather will keep them from casting their ballot election day. This Tippy-Canoe campaign has folks pretty riled up."

"Do you think they're voting for or against?"

"I'm not sure," said Marty. "You're the one who'd know, aren't you?"

Peggy didn't answer. Yes, she *would* know, if she cared to look. But she feared what she'd see.

"It's Po Doggly who knows about politics around here best. He says that if it was all up or down on the whole Red business, Tippy-Canoe wouldn't get him a vote. But he's also been playing on the western pride thing. How Tippy-Canoe is from our side of the Appalachee Mountains. Which don't make much sense to me, seeing as how Old Hickory—Andy Jackson—he's every bit as western as Harrison. I think folks worry about how Andy Jackson, being from Tennizy, he's probably too much for slavery. Folks around here don't want to vote in somebody who'll make the slavery thing any worse than it is."

Peggy smiled thinly. "I wish they knew Mr. Harrison's real position on slavery."

Marty cocked an eyebrow. "You know something I don't know?"

"I know that Harrison is the candidate that those who wish to expand slavery into the northern states will want to support."

"Ain't a soul here who wants to see that happen."

"Then they shouldn't vote for Harrison—if he becomes president, it *will* happen."

Marty stared long and hard at her. "Do you know this the way most folks know their political opinions, or do you know it as . . . as . . ."

"I know it," said Peggy. "I don't say that of mere opinions."

Marty nodded and looked off into space. "Well damn. Wouldn't you know it."

"You have a habit of betting on the wrong horse lately," said Peggy.

"You can say that again," said Marty. "I kept telling Makepeace for years that there wasn't a case against Alvin and I wasn't going to get him extradited from Wobbish. But then he showed up here, and what could I do? I had Makepeace, and he had him a witness besides himself. And you never know what juries are going to do. I think it's a bad business."

"Then why don't you move to dismiss the charges?" asked Peggy.

Marty glowered. "I can't do that, Miss Peggy, for the plain

good reason that there *is* a case to be made. I hope this English lawyer Alvin's folks found for him can win him free. But I'm not going to roll over and play dead. What you got to understand, Miss Peggy, is I like most of the people in this county, and most of the time the folks I got to prosecute, they're people that I like. I don't prosecute them because I don't like them. I prosecute them because they done wrong, and the people of Hatrack County elected me to set things right. So I hope Alvin gets off, but if he does, it won't be because I failed to fulfill my responsibilities."

"I was there on the night the plow was made. Why don't you call *me* as a witness?"

"Did you see it made?" asked Marty.

"No. It was already finished when I saw it."

"Then what exactly are you a witness *of?*"

Peggy didn't answer.

"You want to get on that stand because you're a torch, and the people of Hatrack know you're a torch, and if you say Makepeace is lying, they'll believe you. But here's the thing I worry about, Miss Peggy. I know you and Alvin was once sweet for each other, and maybe still are. So how do I know that if you get on the stand, you won't commit some grievous sin against the God of truth in order to win the freedom of this boy?"

Peggy flushed with anger. "You know because you know my oath is as good as anyone's and better than most."

"If you get on the stand, Miss Peggy, I will rebut you by bringing up witnesses to say you lived in Hatrack for many months in complete disguise, lying to everyone that whole time about who you were. Covered with hexes, pretending to be a middle-aged spinster schoolteacher when the whole time you were seeing the smith's prentice boy under the guise of tutoring him. I know you had your reasons for doing all those things. I know there was a reason why on the night the plow was supposedly made, the same night your mother was killed, you and Alvin were seen running from the smithy together, only Alvin was stark naked. Do you get my drift, Miss Peggy?"

"You're advising me not to testify."

"I'm telling you that while some folks will believe you, others will be sure you're just helping Alvin as his co-conspirator. My job is to make sure every possible doubt of your testimony is introduced."

"So you *are* Alvin's enemy, and the enemy of truth." Peggy hurled the words, meaning them to bite.

"Accuse me all you like," said Marty, "but my job is to make the case that Alvin stole that gold. I don't think your testimony, based entirely on your unverifiable claim as a torch that Makepeace is a liar, should be allowed to stand unchallenged. If it did stand that way, then every half-baked dreamspeaker and soothsayer in the country would be able to say whatever he pleased and juries would believe them, and then what would happen to justice in America?"

"Let me understand you," said Peggy. "You plan to discredit me, destroy my reputation, and convict Alvin, all for the sake of justice in America?"

"As I said," Marty repeated, "I hope your lawyer can do as good a job defending Alvin as I'm going to do prosecuting him. I hope he can find as much damning evidence against my witnesses as Mr. Webster and I have found concerning Alvin. Because, frankly, I don't *like* my witnesses much, and I think Makepeace is a greedy lying bastard who should go to jail himself for perjury but I can't prove it."

"How can you live with yourself, then, working in the service of evil when you know so clearly what is good?"

"It's also good for the public prosecutor to prosecute, instead of setting himself up as judge."

Peggy nodded gravely. "As so often is the case, there is no clear choice that has all the good on its side, opposed to one that is nothing but bad."

"That's the truth, Peggy. That's God's honest truth."

"You advise me not to testify."

"Nothing of the kind. I just warned you of the price you'd pay for testifying."

"It's unethical for us to have had this conversation, isn't it?"

"A little bit," said Marty. "But your pa and I go back a long way."

"He'd never forgive you if you discredited me."

"I know, Miss Peggy. And that would break my heart." He nodded his good-bye, touching his forehead as if to tip the hat he wasn't wearing indoors. "Good day to you."

Peggy followed him into the courtroom.

That first morning was spent questioning the eight witnesses who had been shown the golden plow. First was Merlin Wheeler, who rolled in on his wheelchair. Peggy knew that Alvin had offered once, years ago, to heal him so he could walk again. But Merlin just looked him in the eye and said, "I lost the use of my legs to the same men who killed my wife and child. If you can bring them back, then we'll see about my legs." Alvin didn't understand then, and truth to tell, Peggy didn't really understand now. How did it help his wife and children for Merlin to go around in a wheelchair all the time? But then, maybe it helped Merlin himself. Maybe it was like wearing widow's weeds. A public symbol of how he was crippled by the loss of those he loved best. Anyway, he made a sturdy witness, mostly because people knew he had a knack for seeing what was fair and right, making him a sort of informal judge, though it wasn't all that common for both parties in a dispute to agree to get him to arbitrate for him. One or the other of them, it seemed, always felt it somehow inconvenient to have the case decided by a man who was truly evenhanded and fair. Anyway, the jury was bound to listen when Wheeler said, "I ain't saying the plow's bewitched cause I don't know how it got to be the way it is. I'm just saying that it appears to be gold, it hefts like gold, and it moves without no hand touching it." ·

Wheeler set the tone for all the others. Albert Wimsey was a clockmaker with a knack for fine metalwork, who fled to

America when his business rivals accused him of using witchery in making his clocks—when *he* said the plow was gold, he spoke with authority, and the jury would entertain no further doubt about the metal it was made of. Jan Knickerbacker was a glassmaker who was said to have an eye to see things more clearly than most folks. Ma Bartlett was a frail old lady who once was a schoolteacher but now lived in the old cabin in the woods that Po Doggly built when he first settled in the area; she got a small pension from somewhere and mostly spent her days under an oak tree by Hatrack River, catching catfish and letting them go. People went to her to find out if they could trust other folks, and she was always right, which made it so many a budding romance got nipped in the bud, until folks sort of shied away from asking certain questions of her.

Billy Sweet made candy, a young and gullible young fellow that nobody took all that seriously, but you couldn't help but like him no matter how foolish the things he said and did. Naomi Lerner made a little money tutoring, but her knack was ignorance, not teaching—she could spot ignorance a mile away, but wasn't much good at alleviating it. Joreboam Hemelett was a gunsmith, and he must have had a touch of fire knackery because it was well known that no matter how damp a day it might be, the powder in a Hemelett gun always ignited. And Goody Trader—whose first name was rumored to be either Chastity or Charity, both names used ironically by those who didn't like her—kept a general store on the new end of Main Street, where she was well known to stock her shelves, not just with the things folks wanted, but also with the things they needed without knowing it.

All through their testimony, about hefting the plow, about how it moved, or hummed, or trembled, or warmed their hands, the jurors' eyes were drawn again and again to the burlap sack under Alvin's chair. He never touched it or did anything to call attention to it, but his body moved as if the plow inside the sack were the fulcrum of his balance. They wanted to see for themselves. But they knew, from Alvin's posture, that they would not see it. That these eight had seen for them. It would have to be enough.

The eight witnesses were well known to the people in town, all of them trusted (though Billy Sweet was only trusted *this* far, seeing as how he was so trusting himself that any liar could get him to believe any fool thing) and all of them well enough liked, apart from the normal quarrels of small-town life. Peggy knew them all, better than they knew each other, of course, but perhaps it was that very knowledge of them that blinded her to a thing that only Arthur Stuart seemed to notice.

Arthur was sitting beside her in the courtroom, watching the testimony, wide-eyed. It was only when all eight of the witnesses were done testifying that he leaned up to Peggy and whispered, "Sure are a lot of folks with sharp knacks here in Hatrack, aren't there?"

Peggy grew up around here, and for all that a lot of folks had moved in after she left, she always felt that she pretty much knew everybody. But was that so? She had run off the first time just before Alvin got to Hatrack to start his prenticeship with Makepeace Smith, and in the more than eight years since then, she had only spent that single year in Hatrack—less than a year, really—when she was in disguise. During those eight years a lot of people had moved in. More, in fact, by twice, than had lived here at the time she left. She had scanned their heartfires, routinely, because she wanted to get a sense of who lived in this place.

But she hadn't realized until Arthur's whispered remark that of the newcomers, an unusual number had quite remarkable knacks. It wasn't that the eight witnesses were different from the rest of the town. Knacks were thick on the ground here, much more so than any other place that Peggy had visited.

Why? What brought them here?

The answer was easy and obvious—so obvious that Peggy doubted it at once. Could they really have been drawn here because Alvin was here? It was in Hatrack that the prentice learned to hone his knack until it became an all-encompassing power of powers. It was here that Alvin made the living plow. Was there something about his Making that drew them? Something that kindled a fire inside them and set their feet to wandering until they came to rest in this place, where Making was in the air?

Or was it more than that? Was there Someone perhaps guiding them, so it wasn't just the makery in Hatrack that drew them, but rather the same One who had brought Alvin to this town? Did it mean there was purpose behind it all, some master plan? Oh, Peggy longed to believe *that*, for it would mean she was not responsible for making things turn out all right. If God is tending to things here, then I can put away my broom and set aside my needle and thread, I have neither cleaning nor stitchery to do. I can simply be about my business.

One way or the other, though, it was plain that Hatrack River was more than just the town where Alvin happened to be in jail right now. It was a place where people of hidden powers congregated in goodly numbers. Just as Verily Cooper had crossed the sea to meet Alvin, perhaps unwittingly all these others had also crossed sea or mountains or vast reaches of prairie and forest to find the place where the Maker Made his golden plow. And now these eight had handled the plow, had seen it move, knew it was alive. What did it mean to them?

For Peggy, to wonder was to find out: She looked at their heartfires and found something startling. On past examination, none of them had shown paths in their future that were closely tied to Alvin's. But now she found that their lives were bound up in his. All of them showed many paths into the future that led to a crystal city by the banks of a river.

For the first time, the Crystal City of Alvin's vision in the tornado was showing up in someone else's future.

She almost fainted from the relief of it. It wasn't just a formless dream in Alvin's heart, with no path guiding her as to how he would get there. It could be a reality, and if it was, all of these eight souls would be a part of it.

Why? Just because they had touched the living plow? Was

that what the thing was? A tool to turn people into citizens of the Crystal City?

No, not that. No, it would hardly be the free place Alvin dreamed of, if folks were forced to be citizens because of touching some powerful object. Rather the plow opened up a door in their lives so they could enter into the future they most longed for. A place, a time where their knacks could be brought to full fruition, where they could be part of something larger than any of them were capable of creating on their own.

She had to tell Alvin. Had to let him know that after all that trying in Vigor Church to teach those of feeble knack how to do what they could not really do, or not easily, here in his true birthplace his citizens were already assembling, those who had the natural gifts and inclinations that would make them co-Makers with him.

Another thought struck her, and she began to look into the heartfires of the jurors. Another group of citizens, randomly chosen—and again, while not all had spectacular knacks, they were all people whose knacks defined them, people who might well have been searching for what their gifts might mean, what they were *for*. People who, consciously or not, might well have found themselves gravitating toward the place where a Maker had been born. A place where iron was turned to gold, where a mixup boy had been changed so a cachet no longer named him as a slave. A place where people with knacks and talents and dreams might find purpose, might build something together, might become Makers.

Did they know how much they needed Alvin? How much their hopes and dreams depended on him? Of course not. They were jurors, trying to stay impartial. Trying to judge according to the law. And that was good. That was a kind of Making, too—keeping to the law even when it hurt your heart to do it. Maintaining good order in the community. If they showed favoritism to one person just because they admired him or needed him or liked him or even loved him, that would be the undoing of justice, and if justice were ever undone, were ever openly disdained, then that would be the end of good order. To corrupt justice was the Unmaker's trick. Verily Cooper would have to prove his case, or at least disprove Makepeace Smith's assertions; he would have to make it *possible* for the jury to acquit.

But if they did acquit, then the paths that opened in their heartfire were like the paths of the witnesses: They would be with Alvin one day, building great towers of shimmering crystal rising into the sky, catching light and turning it into truth the way it had happened when Tenskwa-Tawa took Alvin up into the waterspout.

Should I tell Alvin that his fellow-Makers are here around him in this courtroom? Would it help his work or make him overconfident to know?

To tell or not to tell, the endless question that Peggy wrestled with. Next to that one, Hamlet's little quandary was downright silly. Contemplations of suicide were always the Unmaker's work. But truth-telling and truth-hiding—it could go either way. The consequences were unpredictable.

Of course, for ordinary people consequences were *always* unpredictable. Only torches like Peggy were burdened by having such a clear idea of the possibilities. And there weren't many torches like Peggy.

Makepeace wasn't a very good witness in his own cause. Surly and nervous—not a winning combination, Verily knew. But that was why Laws and Webster had put him on first, so that his negative impression would be forgotten after the testimony of more likable—and believable—witnesses.

The best thing Verily could do, in this case, was to let Makepeace have his say—as memorably as possible, as negatively as possible. So he made no objection when Makepeace peppered his account with slurs on Alvin's character. "He was always the laziest prentice I ever had." "I never could get the boy to do nothing without standing over him and yelling in his ear." "He was a slow learner, everybody knowed that." "He ate like a pig even on days when he didn't lift a finger." The onslaught of slander was so relentless that everyone was getting uncomfortable with it—even Marty Laws, who was starting to glance at Verily to see why he wasn't raising any objections. But why should Verily object, when the jurors were shifting in their seats and looking away from Makepeace with every new attack on Alvin? They all knew these were lies. There probably wasn't a one of them that hadn't come to the smithy hoping that Alvin rather than his master would do the work. Alvin's skill was famous—Verily had learned that from overhearing casual conversation in the roadhouse at evening meals—so all Makepeace was doing was damaging his own credibility.

Poor Marty was trapped, however. He couldn't very well cut short Makepeace Smith's testimony, since it was the foundation of his whole case. So the questioning went on, and the answering, and the slander.

"He made a plow out of plain iron. I saw it, and so did Pauley Wiseman who was sheriff then, and Arthur Stuart, and the two dead Finders. It was setting on the workbench when they come by to get me to make manacles for the boy. But I wouldn't make no manacles, no sir! That's not decent work for a smith, to make the chains to take a free boy into slavery! So what do you know but Alvin himself, who *said* he was such a friend to Arthur Stuart, *he* up and says he'll make the manacles. That's the kind of boy he was and is today—no loyalty, no decency at all!"

Alvin leaned over to Verily and whispered in his ear. "I know it's wicked of me, Verily, but I want so bad to give old Makepeace a bad case of rectal itch."

Verily almost laughed out loud.

The judge shot him a glare, but it wasn't about his near laughter. "Mr. Cooper, aren't you going to object to any of these extraneous comments upon your client's character?"

Verily rose slowly to his feet. "Your Honor, I am sure the jury will know *exactly* how seriously to take all of Mr. Makepeace

Smith's testimony. I'm perfectly content for them to remember both his malice and his inaccuracy."

"Well, maybe that's how it's done in England, but I will instruct the jury to *ignore* Mr. Smith's malice, since there's no way to know whether his malice came as a result of the events he has recounted, or predated them. Furthermore, I will instruct Mr. Smith to make no more aspersions on the defendant's character, since those are matters of opinion and not of fact. Did you understand me, Makepeace?"

Makepeace looked confused. "I reckon so."

"Continue, Mr. Laws."

Marty sighed and went on. "So you saw the iron plow, and Alvin made the manacles. What then?"

"I told him to use the manacles as his journeyman piece. I thought it would be fitting for a traitorous scoundrel to go through his whole life knowing that the manacles he made for his friend were the—"

The judge interrupted, again glaring at Verily. "Makepeace, it's words like 'traitorous scoundrel' that's going to get you declared in contempt of court. Do you understand me now?"

"I been calling a spade a spade all my life, Your Honor!" Makepeace declared.

"At this moment you're digging a very deep hole with it," said the judge, "and I'm the man to bury you if you don't watch your tongue!"

Cowed, Makepeace put on a very solemn look and faced forward. "I apologize, Your Honor, for daring to live up to my oath to speak the truth, the whole truth, and nothing but the—"

The gavel came down.

"Nor will I allow sarcasm directed at this bench, Mr. Smith. Continue, Mr. Laws."

And so it went, till Makepeace had finished with his tale. It truly was a weak and whining little complaint. First there was an iron plow, made of the very iron Makepeace had provided for the journeyman piece. Then there was a plow made of solid gold. Makepeace could only think of two possibilities. First, that Alvin had somehow used some sort of hexery to change the iron into gold, in which case it was made from the iron Makepeace had given him and, according to time-honored tradition and the terms of Alvin's prentice papers, the plow belonged to Makepeace. Or it was a different plow, not made from Makepeace's iron, in which case where did Alvin get such gold? The only time Alvin had ever done enough digging to bring up buried treasure like that was when he was digging a well for Makepeace, which he dug in the wrong place. Makepeace was betting Alvin had dug in the right place first, found the gold, and then hid it by digging in another spot for the actual well. And if the gold was found on Makepeace's land, well, it was Makepeace's gold that way, too.

Verily's cross-examination was brief. It consisted of two questions.

"Did you see Alvin take gold or anything like gold out of the ground?"

Angry, Makepeace started to make excuses, but Verily waited until the judge had directed him to answer the question yes or no.

"No."

"Did you see the iron plow transformed into a golden plow?"

"Well so what if I didn't, the fact is there *ain't* no iron plow so where *is* it then?"

Again, the judge told him to answer the question yes or no.

"No," said Makepeace.

"No more questions for this witness," said Verily.

As Makepeace got up and left the witness box, Verily turned to the judge. "Your Honor, the defense moves for immediate dismissal of all charges, inasmuch as the testimony of this witness is not sufficient to establish probable cause."

The judge rolled his eyes. "I hope I'm not going to have to listen to motions like that after *every* witness."

"Just the pathetic ones. Your Honor," said Verily.

"Your point is made. Your motion is denied. Mr. Laws, your next witness?"

"I would like to have called Makepeace's wife, Gertie, but she passed away more than a year ago. Instead, with the court's permission, I will call the woman who was doing kitchen help for her the day the golden plow was first . . . evidenced. Anga Berry."

The judge looked at Verily. "This will make her testimony hearsay, after a fashion. Do you have any objection, Mr. Cooper?"

Alvin had already assured Verily that nothing Anga could say would do him any possible harm. "No objection, Your Honor."

Alvin listened as Anga Berry testified. She didn't really witness to anything except that Gertie told her about Makepeace's accusations the very next morning, so the charge wasn't one he dreamed up later. On cross-examination, Verily was kind to her, only asking her whether Gertie Smith had said anything to lead Anga to believe she thought Alvin was as bad a boy as Makepeace said.

Marty rose to his feet. "Hearsay, Your Honor."

Impatiently the judge replied, "Well, Marty, we *know* it's hearsay. It was for hearsay that *you* called her in the first place!"

Abashed, Marty Laws sat back down.

"She never said nothing about his smithery or nothing," said Anga. "But I know Gertie set quite a store by the boy. Always helped her out, toted water for her whenever she asked—that's the *worst* job—and he was good with the children and just . . . always helping. She never said a bad word about him, and I reckon she had a high opinion of his goodness."

"Did Gertie ever tell you he was a liar or deceiver?" asked Verily.

"Oh, no, unless you count hiding some job he was doing till it was done, so as to surprise her. If *that's* deception, then he done that a couple of times."

And that was it. Alvin was relieved to know that Gertie hadn't been unkind to him behind his back, that even after her death she was a friend to him. What surprised Alvin was how glum Verily was when he sat down at the table next to him. Marty was busy calling his next witness, a fellow named Hank Dowser whose tale Alvin could easily guess—this was a man who *did* have malice and it wouldn't be pleasant to hear him. Still, he hadn't seen anything either, and in fact the well-digging had nothing to do with the plow so what did it matter? Why did Verily look so unhappy?

Alvin asked him.

"Because there was no reason for Laws to call that woman. She worked against his case and he had to know that in advance."

"So why did he call her?"

"Because he wanted to lay the groundwork for something. And since she didn't say anything new during his examination of her, it must have been during the cross-examination that the new groundwork was laid."

"All you asked Anga was whether Gertie had the same low opinion of me that her husband had."

Verily thought for a moment. "No. I also asked her if you had ever deceived Gertie. Oh, I'm such a fool. If only I could recall those words from my lips!"

"What's wrong with that?" asked Alvin.

"He must have some witness that calls you a deceiver, a witness who is otherwise irrelevant to this case."

In the meantime, the dowser, in a state of high dudgeon, was speaking of how uppity Makepeace's prentice was, how he dared to tell a dowser how to dowse. "He's got no respect for any man's knack but his own!"

Verily spoke up. "Your Honor, I object. The witness is not competent to testify concerning my client's respect or lack of it toward other people's knacks in general."

The objection was sustained. Hank Dowser was a quicker learner than Makepeace; there was no more problem with him. He quickly established that the prentice had obviously dug the well in a different place from the place where Hank had declared water could be found.

Verily had only one question for him. "Was there water in the place where he dug the well?"

"That's not the question!" declared Hank Dowser.

"I'm sorry to have to tell you, Mr. Dowser, that I am the one authorized by this court to ask questions at this time, and I tell you that it *is* the question that I would like you to answer. At this time."

"What was the question?"

"Did my client's well reach water?"

"It reached a *kind* of water. But compared to the pure water *I* found, I'm sure that what he got was a sludgy, scummy, foul-tasting brew."

"Do I take it that your answer is yes?"

"Yes."

And that was that.

For his next witness, Marty called a name that sent a shiver down Alvin's spine. "Amy Sump."

A very attractive girl arose from the back of the courtroom and walked down the aisle.

"Who is *she?*" asked Verily.

"A girl from Vigor with a *very* active imagination."

"About what?"

"About how she and I did what a man has no business doing with a girl so young."

"Did you?"

Alvin was annoyed by the question. "Never. She just started telling stories and it grew from there."

"Grew?"

"That's why I took off from Vigor Church, to give her lies a chance to settle down and die out."

"So she started telling stories about you and you *fled?*"

"What does it have to do with the plow and Makepeace Smith?"

Verily grimaced. "A certain matter of whether you deceive people or not. Marty Laws roped me in."

Marty was explaining to the judge that, because he had had no chance to talk with this witness himself beforehand, his illustrious co-counsel would conduct the examination. "The girl is young and fragile, and they have established a rapport."

Verily thought that the idea of Webster and Amy having rapport wasn't very promising when it came to getting honest testimony from her, but he had to tread carefully. She was a child, and a girlchild at that. He couldn't seem to be hostile or fearful of her before she spoke, and in cross-examination he'd have to proceed delicately lest he seem to be a bully.

Unlike Makepeace Smith and Hank Dowser, who were obviously angry and malicious, Amy Sump was absolutely believable. She spoke shyly and reluctantly. "I don't want to get Alvin in no trouble, sir," she said.

"And why not?" asked Daniel Webster.

Her answer came in a whisper. "Because I still love him."

"You . . . you still love him?" Oh, Webster was a fine actor, worthy of the boards in Drury Lane. "But how can you—why do you still love him?"

"Because I am with child," she whispered.

A buzzing arose through the courtroom.

Again, Webster feigned grieved surprise. "You are with . . . Are you married, Miss Sump?"

She shook her head. Glistening tears flew from her eyes onto her lap.

"Yet you are with child. The child of some man who didn't even have the decency to make an honest woman of you. *Whose* child, Miss Sump?"

This was already out of control. Verily leapt to his feet. "Your Honor, I object on the grounds that this can have *no* conceivable connection with—"

"It goes to the issue of deception, Your Honor!" cried Daniel Webster. "It goes to the issue of a man who will say whatever it takes to get his way, and then absconds without so much as a farewell, having taken away that which is most precious from the very one who trusted him!"

The judge smacked down his gavel. "Mr. Webster, that was such a fine summing up that I'm inclined to charge the jury and end the trial. Unfortunately this is *not* the end of the trial and I'd appreciate it if you'd refrain from jumping up on a stump and making a speech when it ain't speechifying time."

"I was responding to my worthy opponent's objection."

"Well, you see, Daniel, that's where you made your mistake. Because his objection was addressed to me, me being the judge here, and I didn't really need your help at that moment. But I'm grateful to know that your help is right there, ready for me, if ever I *do* need it."

Webster answered the sarcasm with a cheerful smile. What did he care? His point was already made.

"The objection is overruled, Mr. Cooper," said the judge. "Who is the father of your child, Miss Sump?"

She burst into tears—still on cue, despite the interruption. "Alvin," she said, sobbing. Then she looked up and gazed soulfully across the court into Alvin's eyes. "Oh, Al, it ain't too late! Come back and make a wife of me! I love you so!"

◈ 15 ◈

Love

VERILY COOPER, DOING his best to hide his astonishment, turned languidly to look at Alvin. Then he raised an eyebrow.

Alvin looked vaguely sad. "It's true she's pregnant," he whispered. "But it ain't true I'm the father."

"Why didn't you tell me if you knew?" Verily whispered.

"I didn't know till she said it. Then I looked and yes, there's a baby growing in her womb. About the size of a nib. No more than three weeks along."

Verily nodded. Alvin had been in jail for the past month, and traveling far from Vigor Church for several months before that. The question was whether he could get the girl to admit under cross-examination that she was barely a month along in her pregnancy.

In the meantime, Daniel Webster had gone on, eliciting from Amy a lurid account of Alvin's seduction of her. No doubt about it, the girl told a convincing story, complete with all kinds of details that made it sound true. It seemed to Verily that the girl wasn't lying, or if she was, she believed her own lies. For a few moments he had doubts about Alvin. Could he have done this? The girl was pretty and desirable and from the way she talked, she was certainly willing. Just because Alvin was a Maker didn't mean he wasn't a man all the same.

He quickly shook off such thoughts. Alvin Smith was a man with self-control, that was the truth. And he had honor. If he really did such things with this child, he'd certainly marry her and not leave her to face the consequences alone.

It was a measure of how dangerous the girl's testimony was, if she could get Alvin's own attorney to doubt him.

"And then he left you," said Daniel Webster.

Verily thought of objecting, but figured there was no point.

"It was my own fault, I know," said Amy, breaking down—again—into pathetic tears. "I shouldn't have told my best friend Ramona about Alvin and me, because she mouthed it around to everybody and they didn't understand about our true love and so of course my Alvin had to leave because he has great works to do in the world, he can't be tied down to Vigor Church just now. I didn't want to come here and testify! I want him to be free to do whatever he needs to do! And if my baby grows up without a pa, at least I can tell my child that she comes of noble blood, with Makery as her heritage!"

Oh, that was a nice touch, making her the suffering saint who is content that "her" Alvin is a lying seducing deceiving abandoning bastard-making cradle-robber, because she loves him so.

It was time for cross-examination. This had to proceed delicately indeed. Verily couldn't give a single hint that he believed her; at the same time, he didn't dare to be seen to attack her, because the jury's sympathy was all with the girl right now. The seeds of doubt had to be planted gently.

"I'm sorry you had to come all the way down here. It must be a hard journey for a young lady in your delicate condition."

"Oh, I'm doing all right. I just puke once in the morning and then I'm fine for the rest of the day."

The jury laughed. A friendly, sympathetic, believing laugh. Heaven help me, thought Verily.

"How long have you known you were going to have a baby?"

"A long time," she said.

Verily raised an eyebrow. "Now, that's a pretty vague answer. But before you hear my next question, I just want you to remember that we can bring your mother and father down here if need be, to establish the exact time this pregnancy began."

"Well I didn't tell them till just a few days ago," said Amy. "But I've been pregnant for—"

Verily raised his hand to silence her, and shook his head. "Be careful, Miss Sump. If you think for just a minute, you'll realize that your mother certainly knows and your father probably knows that you couldn't possibly have been pregnant for more than a few weeks."

Amy looked at him in a puzzled way for a long moment. Then dawning realization came across her face. She finally realized: Her mother would know, from washing rags, when she last menstruated. And it wasn't months and months ago.

"Like I was going to say all along, I got pregnant in the last month. Sometime in the last month."

"And you're sure that Alvin is the father?"

She nodded. But she was no fool. Verily knew she was doing the math in her head. She obviously had counted on being able to lie and say she'd been pregnant for months, since before Alvin left Vigor; when the baby was born she could say it had taken so long because it was a Maker's child, or some such nonsense. But now she had to have a better lie.

Or else she'd been planning this lie all along. That, too, was possible.

"Of course he is," she said. "He comes to me in the night even now. He's really excited about the baby."

"What do you mean by 'even now'?" asked Verily. "You know that he's in jail."

"Oh, posh," said Amy. "What's a jail to a man like him?"

Once again, Verily realized that he'd been playing into Webster's hands. Everybody knew Alvin had hidden powers. They knew he worked in stone and iron. They knew he could get out of that jail whenever he wanted.

"Your Honor," said Verily, "I reserve the right to recall this witness for further cross-examination."

"I object," said Daniel Webster. "If he recalls Miss Sump then she's *his* witness, it won't be cross-examination, and she's not a hostile witness."

"I need to lay the groundwork for further questioning," said Verily.

"Lay all you want," said the judge. "You'll have some leeway, but it won't be cross. The witness may step down, but don't leave Hatrack River, please."

Webster stood again. "Your Honor, I have a few questions on redirect."

"Oh, of course. Miss Sump, I beg your pardon. Please remain seated and remember you're still under oath."

Webster leaned back in his chair. "Miss Sump, you say that Alvin comes to you in the night. How does he do that?"

"He slips out of his cell and right through the walls of the jail and then he runs like a Red man, all caught up in . . . in . . . Redsong, so he reaches Vigor Church in a single hour and he ain't even tired. No, he is *not* tired!" She giggled.

Redsong. Verily had had enough conversation with Alvin by now to know that it was greensong, and if he'd really had any intimacy with this girl she'd know that. She was remembering things she'd heard from his lessons months and months ago in Vigor Church, when she went to class with people trying to learn to be Makers. That's all this was—the imaginings of a young girl combined with scraps of things she learned about Alvin. But it might take the golden plow away from him, and perhaps more important, it might send him to jail and destroy his reputation forever. This was not an innocent fib, and for all her pretense at loving Alvin, she knew exactly what she was doing to him.

"Does he come to you every night?"

"Oh, he can't do that. Just a couple of times a week."

Webster was done with her, but now Verily had a couple more questions. "Miss Sump, *where* does Alvin visit you?"

"In Vigor Church."

"You're only a girl, Miss Sump, and you live with your parents. Presumably you are supervised by them. So my question is quite specific—where are you when Alvin visits you?"

She was momentarily flustered. "Different places."

"Your parents let you go about unchaperoned?"

"No, I mean—we always start out at home. Late at night. Everybody's asleep."

"Do you have a room of your own?"

"Well, no. My sisters sleep in the same room with me."

"So where do you meet Alvin?"

"In the woods."

"So you deceive your parents and sneak into the woods at night?"

The word *deceive* was a red flag to her. "I don't deceive nobody!" she said, with some heat.

"So they know you're going to the woods alone to meet Alvin."

"No. I mean—I know they'd stop me, and it's true love between us, so—I don't sneak out, because Papa bars the door and he'd hear me so I—at the county fair I was able to slip away and—"

"The county fair was in broad daylight, not at night," said Verily, hoping he was right.

"Argumentative!" shouted Webster. But his interruption served not to help the girl but fluster her more.

"If this happens a couple of times a week, Miss Sump, you surely don't depend on the county fair to provide you with opportunities, do you?" asked Verily.

"No, that was just the once, just the one time. The other times . . ."

Verily waited, refusing to ease her path by filling her long silence with words. Let the jury see her making things up as she went along.

"He comes into my room, all silent. Right through the walls. And then he takes me out the same way, silent, through the walls. And then we run with the Redsong to the place where he gives me his love by moonlight."

"It must be an amazing experience," said Verily. "To have your lover appear at your bedside and raise you up and carry you through the walls and take you silently across miles and miles in an instant to an idyllic spot where you have passionate embraces by moonlight. You're in your nightclothes. Doesn't it get cold?"

"Sometimes, but he can make the air warm around me."

"And what about moonless nights? How do you see?"

"He . . . makes it light. We can always see."

"A lover who can do the most miraculous things. It sounds quite romantic, wouldn't you say?"

"Yes, it is, very very romantic," said Amy.

"Like a dream," said Verily.

"Yes, like a dream."

"I object!" cried Webster. "The witness is a child and doesn't realize the way the defense attorney can misconstrue her innocent simile!"

Amy was quite confused now.

"What did I say?" she asked.

"Let me ask it very clearly," said Verily Cooper. "Miss Sump, isn't it possible that your memories of Alvin come from a dream? That you dreamed all this, being in love with a strong and fascinating young man who was too old even to notice you?"

Now she understood why Webster had objected, and she got a cold look in her eye. She knows, thought Verily. She knows she's lying, she's not deceived, she knows exactly what she's doing and hates me for tripping her up, even a little. "My baby ain't no dream, sir," she said. "I never heard of no dream as gives a girl a baby."

"No, I've never heard of such a dream, either," said Verily. "Oh, by the way, how long ago was the county fair?"

"Three weeks ago," she said.

"You went with your family?"

Webster interrupted, demanding to know the relevance.

"She gave the county fair as a specific instance of meeting Alvin," explained Verily, when the judge asked. The judge told him to proceed. "Miss Sump," said Verily, "tell me how you got off by yourself to meet Alvin at the fair. Had you already arranged to meet him there?"

"No, it was—he just showed up there."

"In broad daylight. And no one recognized him?"

"Nobody saw him but me. That's a fact. That's—it's a thing he can do."

"Yes, we're beginning to realize that when it comes to spending time with you, Alvin Smith can and will do the most amazing, miraculous things," said Verily.

Webster objected, Verily apologized, and they went on. But Verily suspected that he was on a good track here. The way Amy made her story so believable was by adding detail. When it came to the events that didn't happen, the details were all dreamy and beautiful—but she wasn't just making them up, it was clear she had really had such dreams, or at least daydreams. She was speaking from memory.

But there must be another memory in her mind—the memory of her time with the man who was the true father of the child she carried. And Verily's hunch was that her mention of the county fair, which didn't fit in at all with the pattern she had established for her nighttime assignations with Alvin, was tied in with that real encounter. If he could get her drawing on memory with this one . . .

"So only you could see him. I imagine that you went off with him? May I ask you where?"

"Under the flap of the freak show tent. Behind the fat lady."

"Behind the fat lady," said Verily. "A private place. But . . . why there? Why didn't Alvin whisk you away into the forest?

To some secluded meadow by a crystal stream? I can't imagine it was very comfortable for you—in the straw, perhaps, or on the hard ground, in the dark . . ."

"That's just the way Alvin wanted it," she said. "I don't know why."

"And how long did you spend there behind the fat lady?"

"About five minutes."

Verily raised an eyebrow. "Why so hasty?" Then, before Webster could object, he plunged into his next question. "So Alvin escaped from the Hatrack County jail in broad daylight, journeyed all the way to Vigor Church on the far side of the state of Wobbish from here, in order to spend five minutes with you behind the fat lady?"

Webster spoke up again. "How can this young girl be expected to know the defendant's motivations for whatever bizarre acts he performs?"

"Was that an objection?" asked the judge.

"It doesn't matter," said Verily. "I'm through with her for now." And this time he let a little contempt into his voice. Let the jury see that he no longer had any regard for this girl. He hadn't destroyed her testimony, but he had laid the groundwork for doubt.

It was three in the afternoon. The judge adjourned them for the day.

Alvin and Verily had supper in his cell that night, conferring over what was likely to happen the next day, and what had to happen in order to acquit him. "They actually haven't proved anything about Makepeace," said Verily. "All they're doing is proving you're a liar in general, and then hoping the jury will think this removes all reasonable doubt about you and the plow. The worst thing is that every step of the way, Webster and Laws have played me like a harp. They set me up, I introduced an idea they were hoping I'd bring up in my cross-examination, and presto! There's the groundwork for the next irrelevant, character-damaging witness."

"So they know the legal tricks in American courts better than you do," said Alvin. "You know the law. You know how things fit together."

"Don't you see, Alvin? Webster doesn't care whether you're convicted or not—what he loves is the stories the newspapers are writing about this trial. Besmirching your reputation. You'll never recover from that."

"I don't know about never," said Alvin.

"Stories like this don't disappear. Even if we manage to find the man who impregnated her—"

"Oh, I know who it was," said Alvin.

"What? How could you—"

"Matt Thatcher. He's a couple of years younger than me, but all us boys knew him in Vigor. He was always a rapscallion of the first stripe, and when I was back there this past year he was always full of brag about how no girl could resist him. Every now and then some fellow'd have to beat him up cause of something he said about the fellow's sister. But after last year's county fair, he was talking about how he drove his tent spike into five different girls in the freak show tent behind the fat lady."

"But that was more than a year ago."

"A boy like Matt Thatcher don't got much imagination, Verily. If he found himself a spot that worked once, he'll be back there. For what it's worth, though, he never did name any of the girls he supposedly got last year, so we all figured he just found the spot and *wished* he could get himself some girl to go with him there. I just figure that this year he finally succeeded."

Verily leaned back on his stool, sipping his mug of warm cider. "The thing that puzzles me is, Webster must have found Amy Sump when he visited in Vigor Church long before I got there. *Before* the county fair, too. She must not have been pregnant when he found her."

Alvin smiled and nodded. "I can just imagine him telling Amy's parents, 'Well it's a good thing she's not with child.

Though if she were, I dare say Alvin's wandering days would be over.' And she listens and goes and gets herself pregnant with the most willing but stupid boy in the county."

Verily laughed. "You imitate his voice quite well, sir!"

"Oh, I'm nothing at imitations. I wish you could have heard Arthur Stuart back in the old days. Before . . ."

"Before?"

"Before I changed him so the Finders couldn't identify him."

"So you didn't just subvert their cachet. You changed the boy himself."

"I made him just a little bit less Arthur and a little bit more Alvin. I'm not glad of it. I miss the way he could make hisself sound like anybody. Even a redbird. He used to sing right back to the redbird."

"Can't you change him back? Now that he has the official court decision, he can never be hauled into court again."

"Change him back? I don't know. It was hard enough changing him the first time. And I don't think I remember well enough how he used to be."

"The cachet has the way he used to be, doesn't it?"

"But I don't have the cachet."

"Interesting problem. Arthur doesn't seem to mind the change, though, does he?"

"Arthur's a sweet boy, but what he doesn't mind now he might well come to mind later, when he's old enough to know what I done to him." Alvin was drumming on his empty dish now. Clearly his mind kept going back to the trial. "I got to tell you, it's only going to get worse tomorrow, Verily."

"How so?"

"I didn't understand it till now, till what Amy said about me sneaking out of jail and all. But now I know what the plan is. Vilate Franker came in here covered with hexes, maneuvered me close enough to her that the same hex worked on me, too— an overlook-me, and a right good one. Then in comes Billy Hunter, one of the deputies, and when he looks in the cell, he doesn't see anybody at all. He runs off and gets the sheriff, and when he comes back, Vilate's gone but here *I* am, and I tell them I been nowhere, but Billy Hunter knows what he saw—or didn't see—and they're going to bring him into court, and Vilate too. Vilate too."

"So they'll have a witness to corroborate that you have indeed left your cell during your incarceration here."

"And Vilate's likely to say anything. She's a notorious gossip. Goody Trader plain hates her, and so does Horace Guester. She also thinks of herself as quite a beauty, though those particular hexes don't work on me no more. Anyway Arthur Stuart saw her . . ."

"I was here when Arthur told you about her. About the salamander."

"That ain't no regular salamander, Verily. That's the Unmaker. I've met it before. Used to come on me more directlike. A shimmering in the air, and there it was. Trying to take me over, rule me. But I wouldn't have it, I'd make something—a bug basket—and he'd go away. Nowadays I'd be more likely to make up some silly rhyme or song and commit it to memory to drive him back. But here's the thing—the Unmaker has a way of being different things to different people. There was a minister in Vigor Church, Reverend Philadelphia Thrower; he saw the Unmaker as an angel, only it was a kind of terrible angel, and one time—well, it doesn't matter. Armor-of-God saw it, not me. With Vilate the Unmaker's got that salamander doing some kind of hexery that makes Vilate see . . . somebody. Somebody who talks to her and tells her things. Only that somebody is really speaking the words of the Unmaker. You know what Arthur Stuart saw. Old Peg Guester, the woman who was the only mother he knew. The Unmaker appears as somebody you can trust, somebody who fulfills your most heartfelt dream, but in the process he perverts everything so that without quite realizing it, you start destroying everything and everybody around you. This whole thing, you don't have to look toward Webster to find the conspiracy. The Unmaker is all the connection they need. Putting together Amy Sump and Vilate Franker and Makepeace Smith and Daniel Webster and . . . not one of them thinks he's doing something all that awful. Amy probably thinks she really loves me. Maybe so does Vilate. Makepeace has probably talked himself into believing the plow really belongs to him. Daniel Webster probably believes I really am a scoundrel. But . . ."

"But the Unmaker makes everything work together to undo you."

Alvin nodded.

"Alvin, that makes no sense," said Verily. "If the Unmaker's really out to Unmake everything, then how can he put together such an elaborate plan? That's a kind of Making, too, isn't it?"

Alvin lay back on the cot and whistled for a moment. "That's right," he said.

"The Unmaker sometimes Makes things, then?"

"No," said Alvin. "No, the Unmaker can't Make nothing. Can't. He just takes what's already there in twists and bends and breaks it. So I was wrong. The Unmaker's working on all these people, but if it's all fitting together into a plan, then somebody's planning it. Some person."

Verily chuckled. "I think we already have the answer," he said. "Your speculation about Daniel Webster. He discovers Amy Sump as he searches in Vigor Church for any kind of dirt about you. She wasn't part of any plan, just a girl who started pretending that her daydreams were true. But then he puts into her head the idea of getting pregnant and the idea of testifying against you to clip your wings and force you to come home. She works out the rest herself, her own plan—the Unmaker doesn't have to teach her anything. Then Daniel Webster comes here to Hatrack and of course he meets the town gossip as he searches for dirt about you here. Vilate Franker barely knows you, but she *does* know everybody else's story, and they converse many times. He happens to let slip how Amy Sump's story will just sound like the imaginings of a dreamy but randy young girl unless they can get some kind of evidence that you actually do leave your cell. And then Vilate comes up with her *own* plan and the Unmaker just sits back and encourages her."

"So the plan is all coming from Daniel Webster, only he doesn't even know it," said Alvin. "He wishes for something, and then it just happens to come true."

"Don't give him too much credit for integrity," said Verily. "I suspect this is a method he's been using for a long time, wishing for some key piece of evidence, and then trusting in his client or one of his client's friends to come up with the testimony that he needs. He never quite soils his hands, but the effect is the same. Yet nothing can ever be proven—"

The outer door opened, and Po Doggly came in with Peggy Larner. "Sorry to interrupt your supper and confabulation, gentlemen," said the sheriff, "but something's come up. You got you a visitor with special circumstances, he's come a long way but he can only come in and see you after dark and I'm the only guard as can let him in, on account of he already sat me down and told me a tale."

Alvin turned to Verily. "That means it's someone from home. Someone besides Armor-of-God. Someone who's under the curse."

"He shouldn't be under it," said Peggy. "If it weren't for his grand gesture of including himself in a curse he didn't personally deserve."

"Measure," said Alvin. To Verily he explained, "My older brother."

"He's coming," said the sheriff. "Arthur Stuart's leading him in with his hat low and his eyes down so he won't see anybody who doesn't already know the story. Doesn't want to spend all night telling folks about the massacre at Tippy-Canoe. So the doors will be open here, but I'll still be outside, watching. Not that I think you'd try to escape, Alvin."

"You mean you don't think I've been making twice-a-week trips to Vigor Church?"

"For *that* girl? I don't think so." With that, Doggly walked out, leaving the outer door open.

Peggy came on in and joined Alvin and Verily inside Alvin's cell. Verily stood up to offer her his stool, but with a gesture she declined to sit.

"Howdy, Peggy," said Alvin.

"I'm fine, Alvin. And you?"

"You know I never did any of those things she said," he told her.

"Alvin," she said, "I know that you *did* find her attractive. She saw that you paid her a little special attention. She began to dream and wish."

"So you're saying it's my fault after all?"

"It's her fault that dreams turned into lies. It's your fault that she had hopeless dreams like that in the first place."

"Well why don't I just shoot myself before I ever look at a woman with desire? It always seems to turn out pretty lousy when I do."

She looked as if he slapped her. As usual, Verily felt a keen sense of being left out of half of what went on in Alvin's life. Why should it bother him so much? He wasn't here, and they were under no obligation to explain. Still, it was embarrassing. He got up. "Please, I'll step outside so you can have this conversation alone."

"No need," said Peggy. "I'm sure Arthur is almost here with Measure by now."

"She doesn't want to talk to me," said Alvin to Verily. "She'll try to get me acquitted because she wants to see the Crystal City get built, only she can't offer me a lick of help in trying to figure out how to build it, seeing as how I don't know and she seems to know everything. But just cause she wants me acquitted doesn't mean she actually likes me or thinks I'm worth spending time with."

"I don't like being in the middle of this," said Verily.

"You're not," said Peggy. "There's no 'this' to be in the middle of."

"There never *was* no 'this,' either, was there?" asked Alvin.

Verily was quite sure he had never heard a man sound so miserable.

Peggy took a moment to answer. "I'm not—there was and is a—it hasn't a thing to do with you, Alvin."

"What doesn't have a thing to do with me? My still being crazy in love with you after a whole year with only one letter from you, and that one as cold as you please, like I was some kind of scoundrel you still had to do business with or something? Is that the thing that doesn't have anything to do with me? I asked you to marry me once. I understand that things have been pretty bleak since then, your mother getting killed and all, that was terrible, and I didn't press you, but I did write to you, I did think about you all the time, and—"

"And I thought of you, Alvin."

"Yes, well, *you're* a torch, so you *know* I'm thinking about you, or you do if you care to look, but what do *I* know when there's no sign from you? What do I know except what you tell me? Except what I see in your face? I know I looked in your face that night in the smithy, I looked in your eyes and I thought I saw love there, I thought I saw you saying yes to me. Did I make that up? Is that the 'this' that there isn't one of?"

Verily was thoroughly miserable, being forced to be a witness of this scene. He had tried to make his escape before; now it was clear they didn't want him to go. If only he knew how to disappear. How to sink through the floor.

It was Arthur who saved him. Arthur, with Measure in tow; and, just as the sheriff had said, Measure had his hat so low and his head bent so far down that he really did need Arthur Stuart to lead him by the hand. "We're here," said Arthur. "You can look up now."

Measure looked up. "Al," he said.

"Measure!" Alvin cried. It took about one stride each, with those two long-legged men, for them to be in each other's embrace. "I've missed you like my own soul," said Alvin.

"I've missed you too, you ugly scrawny jailbird," said Measure. And in that moment, Verily felt such a pang of jealousy that he thought his heart would break. He was ashamed of the feeling as soon as he was aware of it, but there it was: He was jealous of that closeness between brothers. Jealous because he knew that he would never be that close to Alvin Smith. He would always be shut out, and it hurt so deeply that for a moment he thought he couldn't breathe.

And then he did breathe, and blocked that feeling away in another part of himself where he didn't have to stare it in the face.

In a few minutes the greetings were over, and they were down to business. "We found out Amy was gone and it didn't take no genius to figure out where she went. Oh, at first the rumor was she got pregnant at the county fair and was sent off to have the baby somewhere, but we all remembered the tales she told about Alvin and Father and I went to her pa and got it out of him right quick, that she was off to testify in Hatrack. He didn't like it much, but they're paying them and he needs the money and his daughter swears it's true but you could tell looking at him that he don't believe her lies either. And in fact as we were leaving he says, When I find out who it was got my daughter pregnant I'm going to kill him. And Pa says, No you ain't. And Mr. Sump he says, I am so because I'm a merciful man, and killing him's kinder than making him marry Amy."

They all laughed at that, but in the end they knew it wasn't exactly funny.

"Anyhow, Eleanor says, Amy's best friend is that mouse of a girl Ramona and I'm going to get the truth out of her."

Alvin turned to Verily. "Eleanor's our sister, Armor-of-God's wife."

Another reminder that he wasn't inside this circle. But also a reminder that Alvin thought of him and wanted to include him.

"So Eleanor gets Ramona and sets her down inside that hex you made for her in the shop, Alvin, the one that makes liars get so nervous, only I don't know as how it was really needed. Eleanor says to her, Who's the father of Amy's baby, and Ramona says, How should I know? only it's a plain lie, and finally when Eleanor won't let up, Ramona says, Last time I told the truth it only caused Alvin Maker to have to run away cause of Amy's lies, but she *swore* it was true, she *swore* it and so I believed her but now she's saying it was Alvin got her pregnant and I know that's not true cause she got into the freak show tent with—"

Alvin held up his hand. "Matt Thatcher?"

"Of course," said Measure. "Why we didn't just castrate him along with the pigs I don't know."

"She *saw* them or is it hearsay?" asked Verily.

"Saw them and stood guard where they went under the tent and heard Amy cry out once and heard Matt panting and then it was done and she asked Amy what it was like and Amy looked positively stricken and says to her, It's awful and it hurts. Ramona's got no doubt Amy was a virgin up till then, so all the other stories is lies."

"She's not competent to testify about Amy's virginity," said Verily, "but she'd still be a help. It would take care of the pregnancy and make it plain that Amy is something of a liar. Reasonable doubt. How long will it take to get her down here?"

"She's here," said Peggy. "I got her to the roadhouse and Horace Guester's feeding her."

"I'll want to talk to her tonight," said Verily. "This is good. This is something. And until now, we had nothing."

"*They* have nothing," said Peggy. "And yet . . ."

"And yet they'd convict me if they voted right now, wouldn't they?" Alvin asked.

Peggy nodded. "I thought they knew you better."

"This is all so extraneous to Makepeace's assertions," said Verily. "None of this would have been permitted in an English court."

"Next time somebody tries to get me arrested for larceny

and a crazy girl claims to be pregnant by me, I'll arrange to have it tried in London," said Alvin, grinning.

"Good idea," said Verily. "Besides, we have a much higher grade of crazy girls in England."

"I'm going to testify," said Peggy.

"I don't think so," said Alvin.

"You aren't a witness of anything," said Verily.

"You saw how the rules go in this court," said Peggy. "You can work me in."

"It won't help," said Verily. "They'll chalk it up to your being in love with Alvin."

Alvin sighed and lay back on his cot.

"No they won't," said Peggy. "They know me."

"They know Alvin, too," said Verily.

"Don't mean to contradict you, sir," said Arthur Stuart, "but everybody knows Miss Larner here is a torch, and everybody knows that before she tells a lie, you can boil an egg in a pan of snow."

"If I testify, he won't be convicted," said Peggy.

"No," said Alvin. "They'll drag you through the mud. Webster doesn't care about convicting me, you know that. He only wants to destroy me and everybody near me, because that's what the people who hired him want."

"We don't even know who they are," said Verily.

"I don't know their names, but I know who they are and what they want. To you it looks as though Amy's testimony is a sidetrack, but it's Amy's testimony they wanted. And if they could get testimony about me and Peggy in the smithy on the night the plow was made—"

"I'm not afraid of their calumnies," said Peggy.

"It ain't calumnies I'm talking about, it's the plain truth," said Alvin. "I was naked, we was alone in the smithy. Can't help what conclusions folks draw from that, and so I won't have you getting on the stand and all that story coming out in the papers in Carthage and Dekane and heaven knows where else. We'll do it another way."

"Ramona will be a help," said Verily.

"Not Ramona either," said Alvin. "It does no good to have one friend betray another for my sake."

The others were flabbergasted.

"You got to be joking!" cried Measure. "After I brought her all the way here? And she wants to testify."

"I'm sure she does," said Alvin. "But after the papers are through hacking at Amy, how will Ramona feel *then*? She'll always remember that she betrayed a friend. That's a hard one. It'll hurt her. Won't it, Peggy?"

"Oh, you actually want my advice about something?"

"I want the truth. I've been telling the truth, and so have you, so just say it."

"Yes," said Peggy. "It would hurt Ramona greatly to testify against Amy."

"So we won't do it," said Alvin. "Nor do I want to see Vilate humiliated by having her hexes removed. She sets a store by being taken for beautiful."

"Alvin," said Verily, "I know you're a good man and wiser than me, but surely you can see that you can't let courtesy to a few individuals destroy all that you were put here on this earth to do!"

The others agreed.

Alvin looked as miserable as Verily had ever seen a man look, and Verily had seen men condemned to hang or burn. "Then you *don't* understand," he said. "It's true that sometimes people have to suffer to make something good come to be. But when I have it in my power to save them from suffering it, and bear it myself, well then that's part of what I do. That's part of Making. If I have it in my power, then I bear it. Don't you see?"

"No," said Peggy. "You *don't* have it in your power."

"Is that the honest torch talking? Or my friend?"

She hesitated only a moment. "Your friend. This passage in your heartfire is dark to me."

"I figured it was. And I think the reason is because I got to do some Making. I got to do something that's never been done before, to Make something new. If I do it, then I can go on. If I don't, then I go to jail and my path through life takes another course."

"*Would* you go to jail?" asked Arthur Stuart. "Would you really stay in prison for years and years?"

Alvin shrugged. "There are hexes I can't undo. I think if I was convicted, they'd see to it that I was bound about like that. But even if I could get away, what would it matter? I couldn't do my work here in America. And I don't know that my work could be done anywhere else. If there's any reason to my life at all, then there's a reason I was born here and not in England or Russia or China or something. Here's where my work's to be done."

"So you're saying that I can't use the two best witnesses to defend you?" asked Verily.

"My best witness is the truth. Somebody's going to speak it, that's for sure. But it won't be Miss Larner, and it won't be Ramona."

Peggy leaned down and looked Alvin in the eye, their faces not six inches apart. "Alvin Smith, you wretched boy, I gave my childhood to you, to keep you safe from the Unmaker, and now you tell me I have to stand by and watch you throw all that sacrifice away?"

"I already asked you for the whole rest of your life," said Alvin. "What do I want with your ruin? You lost your childhood for me. You lost your mother for me. Don't lose any more. I would have taken everything, yes, and given you everything too, but I won't take less because I can't give less. You'll take nothing from me, so I'll take nothing from you. If that don't make sense to you then you ain't as smart as you let on, Miss Larner."

"Why don't those two just get married and make babies?" said Arthur Stuart. "Pa said that."

Her face stony, Peggy turned away from them. "It has to be on *your* terms, doesn't it, Alvin. Everything on your terms."

"*My* terms?" said Alvin. "It wasn't my terms to say these things to you in front of others, though at least it's my friends and not strangers who have to hear them. I love you, Miss Larner. I love you, Margaret. I don't want you in that courtroom, I want you in my arms, in my life, in all my dreams and works for all time to come."

Peggy clung to the bars of the jail, her face averted from the others.

Arthur Stuart walked around to the outside of the cell and looked guilelessly up into her face. "Why don't you just marry him instead of crying like that? Don't you love him? You're real pretty and he's a good-looking man. You'd have damn cute babies. Pa said that."

"Hush, Arthur Stuart," said Measure.

Peggy slid down until she was kneeling, and then she reached through the bars and took Arthur Stuart's hands. "I can't, Arthur Stuart," she said. "My mother died because I loved Alvin, don't you see? Whenever I think of being with him, it just makes me feel sick and . . . guilty . . . and angry and . . ."

"My mama's dead too, you know," said Arthur Stuart. "My Black mama and my White mama both. They both died to save me from slavery. I think about that all the time, how if I'd never been born they'd both still be alive."

Peggy shook her head. "I know you think of that, Arthur, but you mustn't. They want you to be happy."

"I know," said Arthur Stuart. "I ain't as smart as you, but I know *that*. So I do my best to be happy. I'm happy most of the time, too. Why can't you do that?"

Alvin whispered an echo to his words. "Why can't you do that, Margaret?"

Peggy raised her chin, looked around her. "What am I doing here on the floor like this?" She got to her feet. "Since you won't take my help, Alvin Smith, then I've got work to do. There's a war in the future, a war over slavery, and a million boys will die, in America and the Crown Colonies and even New England before it's done. My work is to make sure those boys don't die in vain, to make sure that when it's over the slaves are free. That's what my mother died for, to free one slave. I'm not going to pick just one, I'm going to save them all if I can." She looked fiercely at the men who watched her, wide-eyed. "I've made my last sacrifice for Alvin Smith—he doesn't need my help anymore."

With those words she strode to the outer door.

"I do so," murmured Alvin, but she didn't hear him, and then she was gone.

"If that don't beat all," said Measure. "I ask you, Alvin, why didn't you just fall in love with a thunderstorm? Why don't you just go propose to a blizzard?"

"I already did," said Alvin.

Verily walked to the door of the cell. "I'm going to interview Ramona tonight in case you change your mind, Alvin," he said.

"I won't," said Alvin.

"I'm quite sure, but other than that there's nothing else I *can* do." He debated saying the next words, but decided that he might as well. What did he have to lose? Alvin was going to go to prison and Verily's journey to America was going to turn out to have been in vain. "I must say that I think you and Miss Larner are a perfect match. The two of you together must have more than seventy percent of the world's entire store of stupid bullheadedness."

It was Verily's turn to head for the outer door. Behind him as he left, he heard Alvin say to Measure and Arthur: "That's my lawyer." He wasn't sure if Alvin spoke in pride or mockery. Either way, it only added to his despair.

Billy Hunter's testimony was pretty damaging. It was plain that he liked Alvin well enough and had no desire to make him look bad. But he couldn't change what he saw and had to tell the truth—he'd looked into the jail and there was nowhere Alvin and Vilate could have hidden.

Verily's cross-examination consisted merely of ascertaining that when Vilate entered the cell, Alvin was definitely there, and that the pie she left behind tasted right good. "Alvin didn't want it?" asked Verily.

"No sir. He said . . . he said he sort of promised it to an ant." Some laughter.

"But he let you have it anyway," said Verily.

"I guess so, yes."

"Well, I think that shows that Alvin is unreliable indeed, if he can't keep his word to an ant!"

There were some chuckles at Verily's attempt at humor, but that did nothing to ameliorate the fact that the prosecution had cut into Alvin's credibility, and rather deeply at that.

It was Vilate's turn then. Marty Laws laid the groundwork, and then came to the key point. "When Mr. Hunter looked into the jail and failed to see you and Alvin, where were you?"

Vilate made a great show of being reluctant to tell. He was relieved to see, however, that she was quite the actress Amy Sump had been, perhaps because Amy half-believed her own fantasies, while Vilate . . . well, this was no schoolgirl, and these were no fantasies of love. "I should never have let him talk me into it, but . . . I've been alone too long."

"Just answer the question, please," asked Laws.

"He took me through the wall of the jail. We passed through the wall. I held his hand."

"And where did you go?"

"Fast as the wind we went—I felt as though we were flying. For a time I ran beside him, taking strength from his hand as he held mine and led me along; but then it became too much for me, and I, fainting, could not go on. He sensed this in that way of his and gathered me into his arms. I was quite swept away."

"Where did you go?"

"To a place where I've never been."

There were some titters at that, which seemed to fluster her a little. Apparently she was not aware of her own double entendre—or perhaps she was a better actress than Verily thought.

"By a lake. Not a large one, I suppose—I could see the far shore. Waterbirds were skimming the lake, but on the grassy bank where we . . . reclined . . . we were the only living things. This beautiful young man and I. He was so full of promises and talk of love and . . ."

"Can we say he took advantage of you?" asked Marty.

"Your Honor, he's leading the witness."

"He did *not* take advantage of me," Vilate said. "I was a willing participant in all that happened. The fact that I regret it now does not change the fact that he did *not* force me in any way. Of course, if I had known then how he had said the same things, done the same things with that girl from Vigor Church . . ."

"Your Honor, she has no personal knowledge of—"

"Sustained," said the judge. "Please limit your responses to the questions asked."

Verily had to admire her skill. She managed to sound as if she were defending Alvin rather than trying to destroy him. As if she loved him.

❧ 16 ❧

Truth

WHEN IT CAME Verily's turn to question Vilate, he sat for a moment contemplating her. She was the picture of complacent confidence, with her head just slightly cocked to the left, as if she were somewhat—but not very—curious to hear what he would ask of her.

"Miss Franker, I wonder if you can tell me—when you passed through the wall from the jail, how did you get up to ground level?"

She looked momentarily confused. "Oh, is the jail below ground? Well, I suppose when we went through the wall, we—no, of course we didn't. The jail is on the second floor of the courthouse, and it's about a ten-foot drop to the ground. That was mean of you, to try to trick me."

"My question still stands," said Verily. "That must have been quite a drop, coming through the wall into nothing."

"We handled it gently. We . . . floated to the ground. It was part of the remarkable experience. If I had known you wanted so much detail, I'd have said so from the start."

"So Alvin . . . floats."

"He *is* a remarkable young man."

"I imagine so," said Verily. "In fact, one of his extraordinary talents is the ability to see through hexes of illusion. Did you know that?"

"No, I . . . no." She looked puzzled.

"For instance, he sees through the hex you use to keep people from seeing that little trick you play with your false teeth. Did you know that?"

"Trick!" She was mortified. "False teeth! What a terrible thing to say!"

"Do you or do you not have false teeth?"

Marty Laws was on his feet. "Your Honor, I can't see what relevancy false teeth have to the case at hand."

"Mr. Cooper, it does seem a little extraneous," said the judge.

"Your Honor has allowed the prosecution to cast far afield in trying to impugn the veracity of my client. I think the defense is entitled to the same latitude in impugning the veracity of those who claim my client is a deceiver."

"False teeth is a bit personal, don't you think?" asked the judge.

"And accusing my client of seducing her *isn't*?" asked Verily.

The judge smiled. "Objection overruled. I think the prosecution opened the door wide enough for such questions."

Verily turned back to Vilate. "Do you have false teeth, Miss Franker?"

"I do not!" she said.

"You're under oath," said Verily. "For instance, didn't you waggle your upper plate at Alvin when you said that he was a beautiful young man?"

"How can I waggle an upper plate that I do not have?" she said.

"Since that is your testimony, Miss Franker, would you be willing to appear in court without those four amulets you're wearing, and without the shawl with the hexes sewn in?"

"I don't have to sit here and . . ."

Alvin leaned over and tugged at Verily's coattail. Verily wanted to ignore him, because he knew that Alvin was going to forbid him to pursue this line any further. But there was no way he could pretend that he didn't notice a movement so broad that the whole court saw it. He turned back to Alvin, ignoring Vilate's remonstrances, and let Alvin whisper in his ear.

"Verily, you know I didn't want—"

"My duty is to defend you as best I—"

"Verily, ask her about the salamander in her handbag. Get it out in the open if you can."

Verily was surprised. "A salamander? But what good will that do?"

"Just get it out in the open," said Alvin. "On a table in the open. It won't run away. Even with the Unmaker possessing it, salamanders are still stupid. You'll see."

Verily turned back to face the witness. "Miss Franker, will you kindly show us the lizard in your handbag?"

Alvin tugged on his coat again. Mouth to ear, he whispered, "Salamanders ain't lizards. They're amphibians, not reptiles."

"Your pardon, Miss Franker. Not a lizard. An amphibian. A salamander."

"I have no such—"

"Your Honor, please warn the witness about the consequences of lying under—"

"If there's such a creature in my handbag, I don't have any idea who put it there or how it got there," said Vilate.

"Then you won't object if the bailiff looks in your bag and removes any amphibious creatures he might find?"

Overcoming her uncertainty, Vilate replied, "No, not at all."

"Your Honor, who is on trial here?" asked Marty Laws.

"I believe the issue is truthfulness," said the judge, "and I find this exercise fascinating. We've watched you come up with scandal. Now I'll be interested to see an amphibian."

The bailiff rummaged through the handbag, then suddenly hooted and jumped back. "Excuse me, Your Honor, it's up my sleeve!" he said, trying to maintain his composure as he wriggled and danced around.

With a flamboyant gesture, Verily swept his papers off the defense table and pulled it out into the middle of the courtroom. "When you retrieve the little fellow," he said, "set him here, please."

Alvin leaned back on his chair, his legs extended, his ankles crossed, looking for all the world like a politician who just won an election. Under his chair, the plow lay still inside its sack.

Alone of all the people in the court, Vilate paid no attention whatever to the salamander. She simply sat as if in a trance; but no, that wasn't it. No, she sat as if she were at a soiree where something slightly rude was being said, and she was pretending to take no notice of it.

Verily had no idea what would come of this business with the salamander, but since Alvin wouldn't let him try any other avenue to discredit Vilate or Amy, he'd have to make it do.

Alvin had been watching Vilate during her testimony—watching close, not just with his eyes, but with his inner sight, seeing the way the material world worked together. One of the first things he marked was the way Vilate cocked her head just a little before answering. As if she were listening. So he sent out his doodlebug and let it rest in the air, feeling for any tremors of sound. Sure enough, there *were* some, but in a pattern Alvin had never seen before. Usually, sound spread out from its source like waves from a rock cast into a pond, in every direction, bouncing and reverberating, but also fading and growing weaker with distance. This sound, however, was channeled. How was it done?

For a while he was in danger of becoming so engrossed in the scientific question that he might well forget that he was on trial here and this was the most dangerous but possibly the weakest witness against him. Fortunately, he caught on to what was happening very quickly. The sound was coming from two sources, very close together, moving in parallel. As the sound waves crossed each other, they interfered with each other, turning the sound into mere turbulence in the air. When Alvin listened closely, he could hear the faint hiss of the chaotic noise. But in the direction where the sound waves were perfectly parallel, they not only didn't interfere with each other, but rather seemed to increase the power of the sound. The result was that for someone sitting exactly in Vilate's position, even the faintest whisper would be audible; but for anyone anywhere else in the courtroom, there would be no sound at all.

Alvin found this curious indeed. He hadn't known that the Unmaker actually used sound to talk to his minions. He had supposed that somehow the Unmaker spoke directly into their minds. Instead, the Unmaker spoke from two sound sources, close together. Then Alvin had to smile. The old saying was true: The liar spoke out of both sides of his mouth.

Looking with his doodlebug into Vilate's handbag, Alvin soon found the source of the sound. The salamander was perched on the top of her belongings, and the sound was coming from its mouth—though salamanders had no mechanism for producing a human voice. If only he could hear what the salamander was saying.

Well, if he wasn't mistaken, that could be arranged. But first he needed to get the salamander out into the open, where the whole court could see where its speech was coming from. That was when he began to pay attention to the proceedings again— only to discover, to his alarm, that Verily was about to defy him and try to take away Vilate's beautiful disguise. He reached out and tugged on Verily's coat, and whispered a rebuke that was as mild as he could make it. Then he told him to get the salamander out of the bag.

Now, with the salamander in a panic, trapped in the bailiff's dark sleeve, it took Alvin a few moments to get his doodlebug inside the creature and start to help it calm down—to slow the heartbeat, to speak peace to it. Of course he could feel no resistance from the Unmaker. That was no surprise to Alvin.

The Unmaker was always driven back by his Making. But he could sense the Unmaker, lurking, shimmering in the background, in the corners of the court, waiting to come back into the salamander so it could speak to Vilate again.

It was a good sign, the fact that the Unmaker needed the help of a creature in order to speak to Vilate. It suggested that she was not wholly consumed by the lust for power or Unmaking, so that the Unmaker could not speak to her directly.

Alvin didn't really know that much about the Unmaker, but with years in which to speculate and reason about it, he had come to a few conclusions. He didn't really think of the Unmaker as a person anymore, though sometimes he still called it "him" in his own thoughts. Alvin had always seen the Unmaker as a shimmering of air, as something that retreated toward his peripheral vision; he believed now that this was the true nature of the Unmaker. As long as a person was engaged in Making, the Unmaker was held at bay; and, in fact, most people weren't particularly attractive to it. It was drawn only to the most extraordinary of Makers—and the most prideful destroyers (or destructively proud; Alvin wasn't sure if it made a difference). It was drawn to Alvin in the effort to undo him and all his works. It was drawn to others, though, like Philadelphia Thrower and, apparently, Vilate Franker, because they provided the hands, the lips, the eyes that would allow the Unmaker to do its work.

What Alvin guessed, but could not know, was that the people to whom the Unmaker appeared most clearly had a kind of power over it. That the Unmaker, having been drawn into relations with them, could not suddenly free itself. Instead, it acted out the role that its human ally had prepared for it. Reverend Thrower needed an angelic visitor that was ripe with wrath—so that was what the Unmaker became for him. Vilate needed something else. But the Unmaker could not withhold itself from her. It could not sense that there was danger in being exposed, unless Vilate sensed that danger herself. And since Vilate was unable to be rational enough to know there even *was* a salamander—something Alvin had learned from Arthur Stuart's report—there was a good chance that the Unmaker could be led to expose itself to the whole courtroom, as long as Alvin worked carefully and took Vilate by surprise.

So he watched as the bailiff finally took the calm—well, calmer, anyway—salamander from the collar of his shirt, whither it had fled, and set it gently on the table. Gradually Alvin withdrew his doodlebug from the creature, so that the Unmaker could come back into possession of it. Would it come? Would it speak again to Vilate, as Alvin hoped?

It did. It would.

The column of sound arose again.

Everyone could see the salamander's mouth opening and closing, but of course they heard nothing and so it looked like the random movements of an animal.

"Do you see the salamander?" asked Verily.

Vilate looked quizzical. "I don't understand the question."

"On this table in front of you. Do you see the salamander?"

Vilate smiled wanly. "I think you're trying to play with me now, Mr. Cooper."

A whisper arose in the courtroom.

"What I'm trying to do," said Verily, "is determine just how reliable an observer you are."

Daniel Webster spoke up. "Your Honor, how do we know there isn't some trick going on that the defense is playing? We already know that the defendant has remarkable hidden powers."

"Have patience, Mr. Webster," said the judge. "Time enough for rebuttal on redirect."

In the meantime, Alvin had been playing with the double column of sound coming from the salamander and leading straight to Vilate. He tried to find some way to bend it, but of course could not, since sound must travel in a straight line— or at least to bend it was beyond Alvin's power and knowledge.

What he could do, though, was set up a counterturbulence right at the source of one of the columns of sound, leaving the other to be perfectly audible, since there would be no interference from the column Alvin had blocked. The sound would still be faint, however; Alvin had no way of knowing whether it could be heard well enough for people to understand it. Only one way to find out.

Besides, this might be the new thing he had to Make in order to get past the dark place in his heartfire where Peggy couldn't see.

He blocked one of the columns of sound.

Verily was saying, "Miss Franker, since everyone in the court but you is able to see this salamander—"

Suddenly, a voice from an unexpected source became audible, apparently in midsentence. Verily fell silent and listened.

It was a woman's voice, cheery and encouraging. "You just sit tight, Vilate, this English buffoon is no match for you. You don't have to tell him a single thing unless you want to. That Alvin Smith had his chance to be your friend, and he turned you down, so now you'll show him a thing or two about a woman scorned. He had no idea of your cleverness, you sly thing."

"Who is that!" demanded the judge.

Vilate looked at him, registering nothing more than faint puzzlement. "Are you asking me?" she said.

"I am!" the judge replied.

"But I don't understand. Who is what?"

The woman's voice said, "Something's wrong but you just stay calm, don't admit a thing. Blame it on Alvin, whatever it is."

Vilate took a deep breath. "Is Alvin casting some kind of spell that affects everyone but me?" she asked.

The judge answered sharply. "Someone just said, 'Blame it on Alvin, whatever it is.' Who was it that said that?"

"Ah! Ah! Ah!" cried the woman's voice—which was obviously coming from the salamander's mouth. "Ah! How could he hear me? I talk only to you! I'm *your* best friend, Vilate, nobody else's! They're trying to trick you! Don't admit a thing!"

"I ... don't know what you mean," said Vilate. "I don't know what you're hearing."

"The woman who just said, 'Don't admit a thing,' " said Verily. "Who is that? Who is this woman who says she's your best friend and no one else's?"

"Ah! Ah! Ah! Ah!" cried the salamander.

"My best friend?" asked Vilate. Suddenly her face was a mask of terror—except for her mouth, which still wore a pretty grin. Sweat beaded on her forehead.

On impulse, Verily strode to her and took hold of her shawl. "Please, Miss Franker, you seem overwarm. Let me hold your shawl for you."

Vilate was so confused she didn't realize what he was doing until it was done. The moment the shawl came from her shoulders, the smile on her mouth disappeared. In fact, the face that everyone knew so well was gone, replaced by the face of a middle-aged woman, somewhat wrinkled and sunburnt; and most remarkable of all, her mouth was wide open and inside it, the upper plate of her false teeth were clicking up and down, as if she were raising and lowering it with her tongue.

The buzz in the courtroom became a roar.

"Verily, dammit," said Alvin. "I told you not to—"

"Sorry," said Verily. "I see you need that shawl, Miss Franker." Quickly he replaced it.

Aware now of what he had done to her, she snatched the shawl close to her. The clicking false teeth were immediately replaced by the same lovely smile she had worn before, and her face was again thin and young.

"I believe we have some idea of the reliability of this witness," said Verily.

The salamander cried out, "They're winning, you foolish ninny! They trapped you! They tricked you, you silly twit!"

Vilate's face lost its composure. She looked frightened. "How can you talk like that to me," she whispered.

Vilate wasn't the only one who looked frightened. The judge himself had shrunk back into the far corner of his space behind the bench. Marty Laws was sitting on the back of his chair, his shoes on the seat.

"To whom are you speaking?" asked the judge.

Vilate turned her face away from judge and salamander both. "My friend," she said. "My best friend, I thought." Then she turned to the judge. "All these years, no one else has ever heard her voice. But you hear her now, don't you?"

"I do," said the judge.

"You're telling them too much!" cried the salamander. Was its voice changing?

"Can you see her?" asked Vilate, her voice thin and quavering. "Do you see how beautiful she is? She taught me how to be beautiful, too."

"Shut up!" cried the salamander. "Tell them nothing, you bitch!"

Yes, the voice was definitely lower in pitch now, thick in the throat, rasping.

"I can't see her, no," said the judge.

"She's not my friend, though, is she," said Vilate. "Not really."

"I'll rip your throat out, you . . ." The salamander let fly with a string of expletives that made them all gasp.

Vilate pointed at the salamander. "She made me do it! She told me to tell those lies about Alvin! But now I see she's really hateful! And not beautiful at all! She's not beautiful, she's ugly as a . . . as a newt!"

"Salamander," said the judge helpfully.

"I hate you!" Vilate cried at the salamander. "Get away from me! I don't want to see you ever again!"

The salamander seemed poised to move—but not away from her. It looked more as if it meant to spring from the table, leap the distance between it and Vilate, and attack her as its hideous voice had threatened.

* * *

Alvin was searching carefully through the salamander's body, trying to find where and how the Unmaker had control of it. But however it was done, it left no physical evidence that Alvin could see.

He realized, though, that it didn't matter. There were ways to get a person free of another person's control—an off-my-back hex. Couldn't it work for the salamander, if it was perfectly done? Alvin marked out in his mind the exact spots on the table where the hex would need to be marked, the order of the markings, the number of loops that would have to be run linking point to point.

Then he sent his doodlebug into that part of the salamander's brain where such sense as it had resided. Freedom, he whispered there, in the way he had that animals could understand. Not words, but feelings. Images. The salamander seeking after food, mating, scampering over mud, through leaves and grass, into cool mossy stone crevices. Free to do that instead of living in a dry handbag. The salamander longed for it.

Just do this, said Alvin silently into the salamander's mind. And he showed it the loops to make to get to the first mark.

The salamander had been poised to leap from the table. But instead it ran the looping pattern, touched one toe on the exact point; Alvin made it so the toe penetrated the wood just enough to make a mark, though no human eye could have seen it, the mark was so subtle. Scamper, loop, mark, and mark again. Six tiny prickings of the table's surface, and then a bound into the middle of the hex.

And the Unmaker was gone.

The salamander raced in a mad pattern, too fast to follow clearly; ran, then stopped stockstill in the middle of the table.

And then, suddenly, the intelligence seemed to go out of its movements. It no longer looked at Vilate. No longer looked at anyone in particular. It nosed across the table. Not certain yet whether the spell that bound the creature was done or not, no one moved toward it. It ran down the table leg, then scurried straight toward Alvin. It nosed the sack under his chair that contained the plow. It ran inside the sack.

Consternation broke out in the courtroom. "What's happening!" cried Marty Laws. "Why did it go in that sack!"

"Because it was spawned in that sack!" cried Webster. "You can see now that Alvin Smith was the source of all this mischief! I have seen the face of the devil and he sits cocky as you please in yonder chair!"

The judge banged with his gavel.

"He's not the devil," said Vilate. "The devil wears a much more lovely face than that." Then she burst into tears.

"Your honor," said Webster, "the defendant and his lawyer have turned this court into a circus!"

"Not until after you turned it into a cesspool of scandalous lies and filthy innuendoes!" Verily roared back at him.

And as he roared, the spectators burst into applause.

The judge banged the gavel again. "Silence! Come to order, or I'll have the bailiff clear the court! Do you hear me?"

And, after a time, silence again reigned.

Alvin bent over and reached into the sack. He took out the limp body of the salamander.

"Is it dead?" asked the judge.

"No, sir," said Alvin. "She's just asleep. She's very, very tired. She's been rode hard, so to speak. Rode hard and given nothing to eat. It ain't evidence of nothing now, Your Honor. Can I give her to my friend Arthur Stuart to take care of till she has her strength back?"

"Does the prosecution have any objection?"

"No, Your Honor," said Marty Laws.

At the same time, Daniel Webster rose to his feet. "This salamander never *was* evidence of anything. It's obvious that it was introduced by the defendant and his lawyer and was always under their command. Now they've taken possession of an honest woman and broken her! Look at her!"

And there sat beautiful Vilate Franker, tears streaming down her smooth and beautiful cheeks.

"An honest woman?" she said softly. "You know as well as I do how you hinted to me about how you needed corroboration for that Amy Sump girl, how if you just had some way of proving that Alvin did *indeed* leave the jail, then she would be believed and no one would believe Alvin. Oh, you sighed and pretended that you weren't suggesting anything to me, but I knew and you knew, and so I learned the hexes from my friend and we did it, and now there you sit, lying again."

"Your Honor," said Webster, "the witness is clearly distraught. I can assure you she has misconstrued the brief conversation we had at supper in the roadhouse."

"I'm sure she has, Mr. Webster," said the judge.

"I have not misconstrued it," said Vilate, furious, whirling on the judge.

"And I'm sure you have not," said the judge. "I'm sure you're both completely correct."

"Your Honor," said Daniel Webster, "with all due respect, I don't see—"

"No, you don't see!" cried Vilate, standing up in the witness box. "You claim to see an honest woman here? I'll show you an honest woman!"

She peeled her shawl off her shoulders. At once the illusion of beauty about her face disappeared. Then she reached down and pulled the amulets out of her bodice and lifted their chains from around her neck. Her body changed before their eyes: Now she was not svelte and tall, but of middle height and a somewhat thickened middle-aged body. There was a stoop to her shoulders, and her hair was more white than gold. "*This* is an honest woman," she said. Then she sank down into her seat and wept into her hands.

"Your Honor," said Verily, "I believe I have no more questions for this witness."

"Neither does the prosecution," said Marty Laws.

"That's not so!" cried Webster.

"Mr. Webster," said Marty Laws quietly, "you are discharged from your position as co-counsel. The testimony of the witnesses you brought me now seems inappropriate to use in court, and I think it would be prudent of you to retire from this courtroom without delay."

A few people clapped, but a glare from the judge quieted them.

Webster began stuffing papers into his briefcase. "If you are alleging that I behaved unethically to any degree—"

"Nobody's alleging anything, Mr. Webster," said the judge, "except that you have no further relationship with the county attorney of Hatrack County, and therefore it's appropriate for you to step to the other side of the railing and, in my humble opinion, to the other side of the courtroom door."

Webster rose to his full height, tucked his bag under his arm, and without another word strode down the aisle and out of the courtroom.

On his way out, he passed a middle-aged woman with brown-and-grey hair who was moving with some serious intent toward the judge's bench. No, toward the witness stand, where she stepped into the box, put her arm around Vilate Franker's shoulders, and helped the weeping woman rise to her feet. "Come now, Vilate, you did very bravely, you did fine, we're right proud of you."

"Goody Trader," Vilate murmured, "I'm so ashamed."

"Nonsense," said Goody Trader. "We all want to be beautiful, and truth to tell, I think you still are. Just—mature, that's all."

The spectators watched in silence as Goody Trader led her erstwhile rival from the courtroom.

"Your Honor," said Verily Cooper, "I think it should be clear to everyone that it is time to return to the real issue before the court. We have been distracted by extraneous witnesses, but the fact of the matter is that it all comes down to Makepeace Smith and Hank Dowser on one side, and Alvin Smith on the other. Their word against his. Unless the prosecution has more witnesses to call, I'd like to begin my defense by letting Alvin give his word, so the jury can judge between them at last."

"Well said, Mr. Cooper," said Marty Laws. "That's the real issue, and I'm sorry I ever moved away from it. The prosecution rests, and I think we'd all like to hear from the defendant. I'm glad he's going to speak for himself, even though the constitution of the United States allows him to decline to testify without prejudice."

"A fine sentiment," said the judge. "Mr. Smith, please rise and take the oath."

Alvin bent over, scooped up the sack with the plow in it, and hoisted it over his shoulder as easy as if it was a loaf of bread or a bag of feathers. He walked to the bailiff, put one hand on the Bible and raised the other, sack and all. "I do solemnly swear to tell the truth, the whole truth, and nothing but the truth so help me God," he said.

"Alvin," said Verily, "just tell us all how this plow came to be."

Alvin nodded. "I took the iron my master gave me—that's Makepeace, he was my master in those days—and I melted it to the right hotness. I'd already made my plow mold, so I poured it in and let it cool enough to strike off the mold, and then I shaped and hammered and scraped all the imperfections out of it, till near as I could tell it had the shape of a plow as perfect as I could do it."

"Did you use any of your knack for Making as you did it?" asked Verily.

"No sir," said Alvin. "That wouldn't be fair. I wanted to earn the right to be a journeyman smith. I did use my doodlebug to inspect the plow, but I made no changes except with my tools and my two hands."

Many of the spectators nodded. They knew something of this matter, of wanting to do something with their hands, without the use of the extraordinary knacks that were so common in this town these days.

"And when it was done, what did you have?"

"A plow," said Alvin. "Pure iron, well shaped and well tempered. A good journeyman piece."

"Whose property was that plow?" asked Verily. "I ask you not as an expert on law, but rather as the apprentice you were at the time you finished it. Was it your plow?"

"It was mine because I made it, and his because it was his iron. It's custom to let the journeyman keep his piece, but I knew it was Makepeace's right to keep it if he wanted."

"And then you apparently decided to change the iron."

Alvin nodded.

"Can you explain to the court your reasoning on the matter?"

"I don't know that it could be called reasoning, rightly. It wasn't rational, as Miss Larner would have defined it. I just knew what I wanted it to be, really. This had nothing to do with going from prentice to journeyman smith. More like going from prentice to journeyman Maker, and I had no master to judge my work, or if I do, he's not yet made hisself known to me."

"So you determined to turn the plow into gold."

Alvin waved off the idea with one hand. "Oh, now, that wouldn't be hard. I've known how to change one metal to another for a long time—it's easier with metals, the way the bits line up and all. Hard to change air, but easy to change metal."

"You're saying you could have turned iron to gold at any time?" asked Verily. "Why didn't you?"

"I reckon there's about the right amount of gold in the world, and the right amount of iron. A man doesn't need to make hammers and saws, axes and plowshares out of gold—he needs iron for that. Gold is for things that need a soft metal."

"But gold would have made you rich," said Verily.

Alvin shook his head. "Gold would have made me famous. Gold would have surrounded me with thieves. And it wouldn't have got me one step closer to learning how to be a proper Maker."

"You expect us to believe that you have no interest in gold?"

"No sir. I need money as much as the next fellow. At that time I was hoping to get married, and I hardly had a penny to my name, which isn't much in the way of prospects. But for most folks gold stands for their hard labor, and I don't see how I should have gold that didn't come from *my* hard labor, too. It wouldn't be fair, and if it's out of balance like that, then it ain't good Making, if you see my point."

"And yet you *did* transform the plow into gold, didn't you?"

"Only as a step along the way," said Alvin.

"Along the way to what?"

"Well, you know. To what the witnesses all said they seen. This plow ain't common gold. It moves. It acts. It's alive."

"And that's what you intended?"

"The fire of life. Not just the fire of the forge."

"How did you do it?"

"It's hard to explain to them as don't have the sight of a doodlebug to get inside things. I didn't create life inside it— that was already there. The bits of gold *wanted* to hold the shape I'd given them, that plow shape, so they fought against the melting of the fire, but they didn't have the strength. They didn't know their *own* strength. And I couldn't teach them, either. And then all of a sudden I thought to put my own hands into the fire and *show* the gold how to be alive, the way I was alive."

"Put your hands into the fire?" asked Verily.

Alvin nodded. "It hurt something fierce, I'll tell you—"

"But you're unscarred," said Verily.

"It was hot, but don't you see, it was a Maker's fire, and finally I understood what I must have known all along, that a Maker is part of what he Makes. I had to be in the fire along with the gold, to show it how to live, to help it find its own heartfire. If I knew exactly how it works I could do a better job of teaching folks. Heaven knows I've tried but ain't nobody learned it aright yet, though a couple or so is getting there, step by step. Anyway, the plow came to life in the fire."

"So now the plow was as we have seen it—or rather, as we have heard it described here."

"Yes," said Alvin. "Living gold."

"And in your opinion, whom does that gold belong to?"

Alvin looked around at Makepeace, then at Marty Laws, then at the judge. "It belongs to itself. It ain't no slave."

Marty Laws rose to his feet. "Surely the witness isn't asserting the equal citizenship of golden plows."

"No sir," said Alvin. "I am not. It has its own purpose in being, but I don't think jury duty or voting for president has much to do with it."

"But you're saying it doesn't belong to Makepeace Smith and it doesn't belong to you either," said Verily.

"Neither one of us."

"Then why are you so reluctant to yield possession of it to your former master?" asked Verily.

"Because he means to melt it down. He said as much that very next morning. Of course, when I told him he couldn't do that, he called me thief and insisted that the plow belonged to him. He said a journeyman piece belongs to the master unless he gives it to the journeyman and, I think he said, 'I sure as hell don't!' Then he called me thief."

"And wasn't he right? Weren't you a thief?"

"No sir," said Alvin. "I admit that the iron he gave me was gone, and I'd be glad to give that iron back to him, fivefold or tenfold, if that's what the law requires of me. Not that I stole it from him, mind you, but because it no longer existed. At the time, of course, I was angry at him because I was ready to be a journeyman years before, but he held me to all the years of the contract anyway, pretending all the time that he didn't know I was already the better smith—"

Among the spectators, Makepeace leapt to his feet and shouted, "A contract is a contract!"

The judge banged the gavel.

"I kept the contract, too," said Alvin. "I worked the full term, even though I was kept as a servant, there wasn't a thing he could teach me after the first year or so. So I figured at the time that I had more than earned the price of the iron that was lost. Now, though, I reckon that was just an angry boy talking. I can see that Makepeace was within his rights, and I'll be glad to give him the price of the iron, or even make him another iron plow in place of the one that's gone."

"But you won't give him the actual plow you made."

"If he gave me gold to make a plow, I'd give him back as much gold as he gave me. But he gave me iron. And even if he had a right to that amount of gold, he doesn't have the right to *this* gold, because if it fell into his hands, he'd destroy it, and such a thing as this shouldn't be destroyed, specially not by them as has no power to make it again. Besides, all his talk of thief was before he saw the plow move."

"He saw it move?" asked Verily.

"Yes sir. And then he said to me, 'Get on out of here. Take that thing and go away. I never want to see your face around here again.' As near as I can recall them, those were his exact words, and if he says otherwise then God will witness against him at the last day, and he knows it."

Verily nodded. "So we have your view on it," he said. "Now, as to Hank Dowser, what about the matter of digging somewhere other than the place he said?"

"I knew it wasn't a good place," said Alvin. "But I dug where he said, right down till I reached solid stone."

"Without hitting water?" asked Verily.

"That's right. So then I went to where I knew I should have dug in the first place, and I put the well there, and it's drawing pure water even today, I hear tell."

"So Mr. Dowser was simply wrong."

"He wasn't wrong that there was water there," said Alvin. "He just didn't know that there was a shelf of rock and the water flowed under it. Bone dry above. That's why it was a natural meadow—no trees grew there, then or now, except some scrubby ones with shallow roots."

"Thank you very much," said Verily. Then, to Marty Laws: "Your witness."

Marty Laws leaned forward on his table and rested his chin on his hands. "Well, I can't say as how I have much to ask. We've got Makepeace's version of things, and we've got your version. I might as well ask you, is there any chance that you didn't actually turn iron into gold? Any chance that you *found* the gold in that first hole you dug, and then shaped it into a plow?"

"No chance of that, sir," said Alvin.

"So you didn't hide that old iron plow away in order to enhance your reputation as a Maker?"

"I never looked for no reputation as a Maker, sir," said Alvin. "And as for the iron, it ain't iron anymore."

Makepeace nodded. "That's all the questions I've got."

The judge looked back at Verily. "Anything more from you?"

"Just one question," said Verily. "Alvin, you heard the things Amy Sump said about you and her and the baby she's carrying. Any truth to that?"

Alvin shook his head. "I never left the jail cell. It's true that I left Vigor Church at least partly because of the stories she was putting out about me. They were false stories, but I needed to leave anyway, and I hoped that with me gone, she'd forget about dreaming me into her life and fall in love with some fellow her own age. I never laid a hand on her. I'm under oath and I swear it before God. I'm sorry she's having trouble, and I hope the baby she's carrying turns out fine and strong and makes a good son for her."

"It's a boy?" asked Verily.

"Oh yes," said Alvin. "A boy. But not my son."

"Now we're finished," said Verily.

It was time for final statements, but the judge didn't give the word to begin. He leaned back in his chair and closed his eyes for a long moment. "Folks, this has been a strange trial, and it's taken some sorry turns along the way. But right now there's only a few points at issue. If Makepeace Smith and

Hank Dowser are right, and the gold was found not made, then I think it's fair to say the plow is flat out Makepeace's property."

"Damn straight!" cried Makepeace.

"Bailiff, take Makepeace Smith into custody please," said the judge. "He's spending the night in jail for contempt of court, and before he can say another word I'll inform him that every word he says will add another night to his sentence."

Makepeace nearly burst, but he didn't say another word as the bailiff led him from the courtroom.

"The other possibility is that Alvin made the gold out of iron, as he says, and that the gold is something called 'living gold,' and therefore the plow belongs to itself. Well, I can't say the law allows any room for farm implements to be self-owning entities, but I will say that since Makepeace gave Alvin a certain weight of iron, then if Alvin made that iron disappear, he owes Makepeace the same weight of iron back again, or the monetary equivalent in legal tender. This is how it seems to me at this moment, though I know the jury may see other possibilities that escape me. The trouble is that right now I don't know how the jury can possibly make a fair decision. How can they forget all the business about Alvin maybe or maybe not having scandalous liaisons? A part of me says I ought to declare a mistrial, but then another part of me says, that wouldn't be right, to make this town go through yet another round of this trial. So here's what I propose to do. There's one fact in all of this that we can actually test. We can go out to the smithy and have Hank Dowser show us the spot where he called for the well to be dug. Then we can dig down and see if we find either the remnants of some treasure chest—and water—or a shelf of stone, the way Alvin said, and not a drop of water. It seems to me then we'll at least know something, whereas at the present moment we don't know much at all, except that Vilate Franker, God bless her, has false teeth."

Neither the defense nor the prosecution had any objections.

"Then let's convene this court at Makepeace's smithy at ten in the morning. No, not tomorrow—that's Friday, election day.

I see no way around it, we'll have to do it Monday morning. Another weekend in jail, I'm afraid, Alvin."

"Your Honor," said Verily Cooper. "There's only the one jail in this town, and with Makepeace Smith forced to share a cell in the same room with my client—"

"All right," said the judge. "Sheriff, you can release Makepeace when you get Alvin back over there."

"Thank you, Your Honor," said Verily.

"We're adjourned till ten on Monday." The gavel struck and the spectacle ended for the day.

✶ 17 ✶

Decisions

BECAUSE CALVIN USED to keep to himself so much in Vigor Church, he always thought of himself as a solitary sort of fellow. Everybody in Vigor who wasn't besotted with Alvin turned out to be pretty much of an idiot, when it came down to it. What did Calvin want with pranks like luring skunks under porches or pushing over outhouses? Alvin had him cut out of anything that mattered, and any other friends he might have had didn't amount to much.

In New Amsterdam and London, Calvin was even more alone, being concentrated as he was on the single-minded goal of getting to Napoleon. It was the same on the streets of Paris, when he was going around trying to get a reputation as a healer. And once he got the Emperor's attention, it was all study and work.

For a while. Because after a few weeks it became pretty clear that Napoleon was going to stretch out his teaching as long and slow as possible. Why should he do otherwise? As soon as Calvin was satisfied that he had learned enough, he'd

leave and then Napoleon would be the victim of gout. Calvin
toyed with the idea of putting on some pressure by increasing
Napoleon's pain, and with that in mind he went and found the
place in the Emperor's brain where pain was registered. He
had some idea of using his doodling bug to poke directly
into that place of pure agony, and then see if Napoleon didn't
suddenly remember to teach Calvin a few things that he'd
overlooked till now.

That was fine for daydreaming, but Calvin wasn't no fool.
He could do that agony trick once, and get one day's worth of
teaching, but then before he next fell asleep, he'd better be
long gone from Paris, from France, and from anywhere on
God's green Earth where Napoleon's agents might find him.
No, he couldn't force Napoleon. He had to stay and put up
with the excruciatingly slow pace of the lessons, the sheer
repetitiveness. In the meantime, he observed carefully, trying
to see what it was Napoleon was doing that Calvin didn't
understand. He never saw a thing that made sense.

What was left for him, then, but to try out the things Napoleon
had taught him about manipulating other people, and see if he
could figure out more by pure experimentation? That was what
finally brought him into contact with other people—the desire
to learn how to control them.

Trouble was, the only people around were the staff, and they
were all busy. What's worse, they were also under Napoleon's
direct control, and it wouldn't do to let the Emperor see that
somebody else was trying to win control of his toadies. He
might get the wrong idea. He might think Calvin was trying
to undermine his power, which wasn't true—Calvin didn't care
a hoot about taking Napoleon's place. What was a mere Emperor
when there was a Maker in the world?

Two Makers, that is. Two.

Who could Calvin try out his new-learned powers on? After
a little wandering around the palace and the government buildings, he began to realize that there was another class of person

altogether. Idle and frustrated, they were Calvin's natural subjects: the sons of Napoleon's clerks and courtiers.

They all had roughly the same biography: As their fathers
rose to positions of influence, they got sent away to steadily
better boarding schools, then emerged at sixteen or seventeen
with education, ambition, and no social prestige whatsoever,
which meant that most doors were closed to them except to
follow in their fathers' footsteps and become completely dependent upon the Emperor. For some of them, this was perfectly
all right; Calvin left those hardworking, contented souls alone.

The ones he found interesting were the desultory law students, the enthusiastically untalented poets and dramatists, the
gossiping seducers looking around for women rich enough to
be desirable and stupid enough to be taken in by such pretenders.
Calvin's French improved greatly the more he conversed with
them, and even as he followed Napoleon's lessons and learned
to find what vices drove these young men, so he could flatter
and exploit and control them, he also discovered that he enjoyed
their company. Even the fools among them were entertaining,
with their lassitude and cynicism, and now and then he found
some truly clever and fascinating companions.

Those were the most difficult to win control of, and Calvin
told himself that it was the challenge rather than the pleasure
of their company that kept him coming back to them again and
again. One of them most of all: Honoré. A skinny, short man
with prematurely rotten teeth, he was a year older than Calvin's
brother Alvin. Honoré was without manners; Calvin soon
learned that it wasn't because he didn't know how to behave,
but rather because he wished to shock people, to show his
contempt for their stale forms, and most of all because he
wished to command their attention, and being faintly repulsive
all the time had the desired effect. He might start with their
contempt or disgust, but within fifteen minutes he always had
them laughing at his wit, nodding at his insights, their eyes
shining with the dazzlement of his conversation.

Calvin even allowed himself to think that Honoré had some

of the same gift Napoleon had been born with, that by studying him Calvin might learn a few of the secrets the Emperor still withheld.

At first Honoré ignored Calvin, not in particular but in the general way that he ignored everyone who had nothing to offer him. Then he must have heard from someone that Calvin saw the Emperor every day, that in fact the Emperor used him as his personal healer. At once Calvin became acceptable, so much so that Honoré began inviting him along on his nighttime jaunts.

"I am studying Paris," said Honoré. "No, let me correct myself—I am studying humankind, and Paris has a large enough sampling of that species to keep me occupied for many years. I study all people who depart from the norm, for their very abnormalities teach me about human nature: If the actions of this man surprise me, it is because I must have learned, over the years, to expect men to behave in a different way. Thus I learn not only the oddity of the one, but also the normality of the many."

"And how am I odd?" asked Calvin.

"You are odd because you actually listen to my ideas instead of my wit. You are an eager student of genius, and I half suspect that you may have genius yourself."

"Genius?" asked Calvin.

"The extraordinary spirit that makes great men great. It is perfect piety that turns men into saints or angels, but what about men who are indifferently pious but perfectly intelligent or wise or perceptive? What do they become? Geniuses. Patron saints of the mind, of the eye, of the mind's eye! I intend, when I die, to have my name invoked by those who pray for wisdom. Let the saints have the prayers of those who need miracles." He cocked his head and looked up at Calvin. "You're too tall to be honest. Tall men always tell lies, since they assume short men like me will never see clearly enough to contradict them."

"Can't help being tall," said Calvin.

"Such a lie," said Honoré. "You wanted to be tall when you were young, just as I wanted to be closer to the earth, where my eye could see the details large men miss. Though I do hope to be fat someday, since fatness would mean I had more than enough to eat, and that, my dear Yankee, would be a delicious change. It's a commonplace idea that geniuses are never understood and therefore never become popular or make money from their brilliance. I think this is pure foolishness. A true genius will not only be smarter than everyone else, but will be *so* clever that he'll know how to appeal to the masses without compromising his brilliance. Hence: I write novels."

Calvin almost laughed. "Those silly stories women read?"

"The very ones. Fainting heiresses. Dullard husbands. Dangerous lovers. Earthquakes, revolutions, fires, and interfering aunts. I write under several *noms de plume*, but my secret is that even as I master the art of being popular and therefore rich, I am also using the novel to explore the true state of humankind in this vast experimental tank known as Paris, this hive with an imperial queen who surrounds himself with drones like my poor stingless unflying father, the seventh secretary of the morning rotation—you gave him a hotfoot once, you miserable prankster, he wept that night at the humiliation of it and I vowed to kill you someday, though I think I probably won't—I have never kept a promise yet."

"When do you write? You're here all the time." Calvin gestured to include the environs of the government buildings.

"How would you know, when you *aren't* here all the time? By night I pass back and forth between the grand salons of the cream of society and the finest brothels ever created by the scum of the earth. And in the mornings, when you're taking emperor lessons from M. Bonaparte, I hole up in my miserable poet's garret—where my mother's housekeeper brings me fresh bread every day, so don't weep for me yet, not until I get syphilis or tuberculosis—and I write furiously, filling page after page with scintillating prose. I tried my hand at poetry once, a long play, but I discovered that by imitating Racine, one learns primarily to become as tedious as Racine, and by studying

Molière, one learns that Molière was a lofty genius not to be trifled with by pathetic young imitators."

"I haven't read either of them," said Calvin. In truth he had never heard of either one and only deduced that they were dramatists from the context.

"Nor have you read my work, because in fact it is not yet genius, it is merely journeyman work. In fact I fear sometimes that I have the ambition of a genius, the eye and ear of a genius, and the talent of a chimneysweep. I go down into the filthy world, I come up black, I scatter the ashes and cinders of my research onto white papers, but what have I got? Paper with black marks all over it." Suddenly he gripped Calvin's shirtfront and pulled him down until they were eye to eye. "I would cut off my leg to have a talent like yours. To be able to see *inside* the body and heal or harm, give pain or relieve it. I would cut off both legs." Then he let go of Calvin's shirt. "Of course, I wouldn't give up my more fragile parts, for that would be too great a disappointment to my dear Lady de Berny. You will be discreet, of course, and when you gossip about my affair with her you will never admit you heard about it from me."

"Are you really jealous of me?" asked Calvin.

"Only when I am in my right mind," said Honoré, "which is rare enough that you don't yet interfere with my happiness. You are not yet one of the major irritations of my life. My mother, now—I spent my early childhood pining for some show of love from her, some gentle touch of affection, and instead was always greeted with coldness and reproof. Nothing I did pleased her. I thought, for many years, that it was because I was a bad son. Then, suddenly, I realized that it was because she was a bad mother! It wasn't me she hated, it was my father. So one year when I was away at school, she took a lover— and she chose well, he is a very fine man whom I respect greatly—and got herself impregnated and gave birth to a monster."

"Deformed?" asked Calvin, curious.

"Only morally. Otherwise he is quite attractive, and my

mother dotes on him. Every time I see her fawning on him, praising him, laughing at his clever little antics, I long to do as Joseph's brothers did and put him in a pit, only *I* would never be softhearted enough to pull him out and sell him into mere slavery. He will also probably be tall and she will see to it he has full access to her fortune, unlike myself, who am forced to live on the pittance my father can give me, the advances I can extort from my publishers, and the generous impulses of the women for whom I am the god of love. After careful contemplation, I have come to the conclusion that Cain, like Prometheus, was one of the great benefactors of humankind, for which of course he must be endlessly tortured by God, or at least given a very ugly pimple in his forehead. For it was Cain who taught us that some brothers simply cannot be endured, and the only solution is to kill them or have them killed. Being a man of lazy disposition, I lean toward the latter course. Also one cannot wear fine clothes in prison, and after one is guillotined for murder, one's collars never stay on properly; they're always sliding off to one side or the other. So I'll either hire it done or see to it he gets employed in some miserable clerical post in a faroff colony. I have in mind Reunion in the Indian Ocean; my only objection is that its dot on the globe is large enough that Henry may not be able to see the entire circumference of his island home at once. I want him to feel himself in prison every waking moment. I suppose that is uncharitable of me."

Uncharitable? Calvin laughed in delight, and regaled Honoré in turn with tales of his own horrible brother. "Well, then," said Honoré, "you must destroy him, of course. What are you doing here in Paris, with a great project like that in hand!"

"I'm learning from Napoleon how to rule over men. So that when my brother builds his Crystal City, I can take it away from him."

"Take it away! Such shallow aims," said Honoré. "What good is taking it away?"

"Because he built it," said Calvin, "or he *will* build it, and then he'll have to see me rule over all that he built."

"You think this because you are a nasty person by nature, Calvin, and you don't understand nice people. To you, the end of existence is to control things, and so you will never build anything, but rather will try to take control of what is already in existence. Your brother, though, is by nature a Maker, as you explain it; therefore he cares nothing about who rules, but only about what exists. So if you take away the rule of the Crystal City—when he builds it—you have accomplished nothing, for he will still rejoice that the thing exists at all, regardless of who rules it. No, there is nothing else for you to do but let the city rise to its peak—and then tear it down into such a useless heap of rubble that it can never rise again."

Calvin was troubled. He had never thought this way, and it didn't feel good to him. "Honoré, you're joking, I'm sure. *You* make things—your novels, at least."

"And if you hated me, you wouldn't just take away my royalties—my creditors do that already, thank you very much. No, you would take my very books, steal the copyright, and then revise them and revise them until nothing of truth or beauty or, more to the point, my genius remained in them, and then you would continue to publish them under my name, causing me to be shamed with every copy sold. People would read and say, 'Honoré de Balzac, such a fool!' That is how you would destroy me."

"I'm not a character in one of your novels."

"More's the pity. You would speak more interesting dialogue if you were."

"So you think I'm wasting my time here?"

"I think you're *about* to waste your time. Napoleon is no fool. He's never going to give you tools powerful enough to challenge his own. So leave!"

"How can I leave, when he depends on me to keep his gout from hurting? I'd never make it to the border."

"Then heal the gout the way you used to heal those poor

beggars—that was a cruel thing for you to do, by the way, a miserable selfish thing, for how did you think they were going to feed their children without some suppurating wound to excite pity in passersby and eke out a few sous from them? Those of us who were aware of your one-man messianic mission had to go about after you, cutting off the legs of your victims so they'd be able to continue to earn their livelihood."

Calvin was appalled. "How could you do such a thing!"

Honoré roared with laughter. "I'm joking, you poor literal-minded American simpleton!"

"I can't heal the gout," said Calvin, coming back to the subject that interested him: his own future.

"Why not?"

"I've been trying to figure out how diseases are caused. Injuries are easy. Infections are, too. If you concentrate, anyway. Diseases have taken me weeks. They seem to be caused by tiny creatures, so small I can't see them individually, only *en masse*. Those I can destroy easily enough, and cure the disease, or at least knock it back a little and give the body a chance to defeat it on its own. But not all diseases are caused by those tiny beasts. Gout baffles me completely. I have no idea what causes it, and therefore I can't cure it."

Honoré shook his oversized head. "Calvin, you have such native talents, but they have been bestowed unworthily upon you. When I say you must heal Napoleon, of course I don't care whether you actually cure the gout. It isn't the gout that bothers him. It's the *pain* of the gout. And you already cure that every day! So cure it once and for all, thank Napoleon kindly for his lessons, and get out of France as quickly as possible! Have done with it! Get back about your life's work! I'll tell you what—I'll even pay your passage to America. No, I'll do more. I'll come with you to America, and add the study of that astonishingly crude and vigorous people to my vast store of knowledge about humankind. With your talent and my genius, what is there we couldn't accomplish?"

"Nothing," said Calvin happily.

He was especially happy because not five minutes before, Calvin had decided that he wanted Honoré to accompany him to America, and so by the tiniest of gestures, by certain looks and signs that Honoré was never aware of, he caused the young novelist to like him, to be excited by the work that Calvin had to do, and to want so much to be a part of it that he would come home to America with him. Best of all, Calvin had brought it off so skillfully that Honoré obviously had no idea that he had been manipulated into it.

In the meantime, Honoré's idea of curing Napoleon's pain once and for all appealed to him. That place in the brain where pain resided still waited for him. Only instead of stimulating it, all he had to do was cauterize it. It would not only cure Napoleon's gout, but would also cure all other pains he might feel in the future.

So, having thought of it, having decided to do it, that night Calvin acted. And in the morning, when he presented himself to the Emperor, he saw at once that the Emperor knew what he had done.

"I cut myself this morning, sharpening a pen," said Napoleon. "I only knew it when I saw the blood. I felt no pain at all."

"Excellent," said Calvin. "I finally found the way to end your pain from gout once and for all. It involved cutting off *all* pain for the rest of your life, but it's hard to imagine you'd mind."

Napoleon looked away. "It was hard for Midas to imagine that he would not want *everything* he touched to turn to gold. I might have bled to death because I felt no pain."

"Are you rebuking me?" said Calvin. "I give you a gift that millions of people pray for—to live a life without pain—and you're rebuking me? You're the Emperor—assign a servant to watch you day and night in order to make sure you don't unwittingly bleed to death."

"This is permanent?" asked Napoleon.

"I can't cure the gout—the disease is too subtle for me. I never pretended to be perfect. But the pain I could cure, and so I did. I cured it now and forever. If I did wrong, I'll restore the pain to you as best I can. It won't be a pleasant operation, but I think I can get the balance back to about what it was before. Intermittent, wasn't it? A month of gout, and then a week without it, and then another month?"

"You've grown saucy."

"No sir, I merely speak French better, so my native sauciness can emerge more clearly."

"What's to stop me from throwing you out, then? Or having you killed, now that I don't need you anymore?"

"Nothing has ever stopped you from doing those things," said Calvin. "But you don't needlessly kill people, and as for throwing me out—well, why go to the trouble? I'm ready to leave. I'm homesick for America. My family is there."

Napoleon nodded. "I see. You decided to leave, and then finally cured my pain."

"My beloved Emperor, you wrong me," said Calvin. "I found I could cure you, and then decided to leave."

"I still have much to teach you."

"And I have much to learn. But I fear I'm not clever enough to learn from you—the last several weeks you have taught me and taught me, and yet I keep feeling as if I have learned nothing new. I'm simply not a clever enough pupil to master your lessons. Why should I stay?"

Napoleon smiled. "Well done. Very well done. If I weren't Napoleon, you would have won me over completely. In fact, I would probably be paying your passage to America."

"I was hoping you would, anyway, in gratitude for a painfree life."

"Emperors can't afford to have petty emotions like gratitude. If I pay your passage it's not because I'm grateful to you, it's because I think my purpose will be better served with you gone and alive than with you, say, here and alive or, perhaps, here and dead, or the most difficult possibility, gone and dead." Napoleon smiled.

Calvin smiled back. They understood each other, the Emperor

and the young Maker. They had used each other and now were done with each other and would cast each other aside—but with style.

"I'll take the train to the coast this very day, begging your consent, sir."

"My consent! You have more than my consent! My servants have already packed your bags and they are doubtless at the station as we speak." Napoleon grinned, touched his forelock in an imaginary salute, and then watched as Calvin rushed from the room.

Calvin the American Maker and Honoré Balzac the annoyingly ambitious young writer, both gone from the country in the same day. And the pain of the gout now gone from him.

I'll have to be careful getting into the bath. I might scald myself to death without knowing it. I'll have to get someone else to climb into the water before me. I think I know just the young servant girl who should do it. I'll have to have her scrubbed first, so she doesn't foul the water for me. It will be interesting to see how much of the pleasure of the bath came from the slight pain of hot water. And was pain a part of sexual pleasure? It would be infuriating if the boy had interfered with *that*. Napoleon would have to have him hunted down and killed, if the boy had ruined that sport for him.

It didn't take long for the ballots to be counted in Hatrack River—by nine P.M. Friday, the elections clerk announced a decisive victory countywide for Tippy-Canoe, old Red Hand Harrison. Some had been drinking all through the election day; now the likker began to flow in earnest. Being a county seat, Hatrack drew plenty of farmers from the hinterland and smaller villages, for whom Hatrack was the nearest metropolis, having near a thousand people now; it was swollen to twice that number by ten in the evening. As word came in from each of the neighboring counties and from some across river that Tippy-Canoe was winning there, too, guns were shot off and so were mouths, which led to fisticuffs and a lot of traffic into and out of the jail.

Po Doggly came in about ten-thirty and asked Alvin if he'd mind too much being put on his own parole to go spend the night in the roadhouse—Horace Guester was standing bail for him, and did he give his solemn oath etcetera etcetera because the jail was needed to hold drunken brawlers ten to a cell. Alvin took the oath and Horace and Verily escorted him through back lots to the roadhouse. There was plenty of drinking and dancing downstairs in the common room of the roadhouse, but not the kind of rowdiness that prevailed at rougher places and out in the open, where wagons filled with likker were doing quite a business. Horace's party, as always, was for locals of the more civilized variety. Still, it wouldn't do no good for Alvin to show his face there and get rumors going, especially since there was bound to be some in the crowds infesting Hatrack River as wasn't particular friends of Alvin's—and a few that *was* particular friends of Makepeace's. Not to mention them as was always a particular friend of any amount of gold that might be obtained by stealth or violence. It was up the back stairs for Alvin, and even then he stooped and had his face covered and said nary a word the whole jaunt.

Up in Horace's own bedroom, where Arthur Stuart and Measure already had cots, Alvin paced the room, touching the walls, the soft bed, the window as if he had never seen such things before. "Even cooped up in here," said Alvin, "it's better than a cell. I hope never to be back in such a place again."

"Don't know how you've stood it this far," said Horace. "I'd go plain bonkers in a week."

"Who's to say he didn't?" said Measure.

Alvin laughed and agreed with him. "I was crazy not to let Verily go with his plans, I know that," said Alvin.

"No, no," said Verily. "You were right, you came through in your own defense."

"But what if I hadn't figured out how to let the salamander's voice be heard? I've been thinking about that ever since yesterday. What if I hadn't done it? They was all talking like I could do anything, like I could fly or do miracles on the moon just by thinking about it. I wish I could. Sometimes I wish I could. It's still nip and tuck with the jury, ain't it, Verily?"

Verily agreed that it was. But they all knew that he wasn't likely to get convicted of anything now—assuming, of course, that the shelf of rock was still there in the spot Hank Dowser marked for a well. The real damage was to his good name. The real damage was to the Crystal City, which now would be harder to build because of all them stories going around about how Alvin Smith seduced young girls and old women and walked through walls to get to them. Never mind that the story had turned out to be lies and foolishness—there was always folks stupid enough to say, "Where there's smoke there's fire," when the saying should have been, "Where there's scandalous lies there's always malicious believers and spreaders-around, regardless of evidence."

The whooping and hollering in the street, with youngsters or drunken oldsters riding their horses at a breakneck speed up and down until Sheriff Doggly or some deputy could either stop the horse or shoot it, that guaranteed no sleep for anyone, not early, anyway. So they were all still awake, even Arthur Stuart, when two more men came into the common room of the roadhouse, looking wore out and dirty from hard travel. They waited at the counter, nursing a mug of cider each, till Horace came downstairs to check on things and recognized them at once. "Come on up, he's here, he's upstairs," whispered Horace, and the three of them was up the stairs in a trice.

"Armor," said Alvin, greeting him with a brotherly hug. "Mike." And Mike Fink got him a hug as well. "You picked a good night to return."

"We picked a *damn* good night," said Fink. "We was afraid we might be too late. The plan was to take you out of the jail and hang you as part of the election night festivities. Glad the sheriff thought ahead."

"He just needed the space for drunk and disorderly," said Alvin. "I don't think he had any inkling about no plot."

"There's twenty boys here," said Fink. "Twenty at least, all of them well paid and likkered up. I hope well enough paid that they're *really* likkered up so they'll just fall down, puke, and go to sleep, and then slink off home to Carthage in the morning."

"I doubt it," said Measure. "I been caught up in plots against Alvin before. Somebody once pretty much took me apart."

Fink looked at him again. "You wasn't so tall then," he said. "I was plain ashamed of what I done to you," he said. "It was the worst thing I ever done."

"I didn't die," said Measure.

"Not for lack of trying on my part," said Fink.

Verily was baffled. "You mean this man tried to kill you, Measure?"

"Governor Harrison ordered it," said Measure. "And it was years ago. Before I was married. Before Alvin came here to Hatrack River as a prentice boy. And if I recall aright, Mike Fink was a little prettier in those days."

"Not in my heart," said Frank. "But I bore you no malice, Measure. And after Harrison had me do that to you, I left him, I wanted no truck with him. It don't make up for nothing, but it's the truth, that I'm not a man who'd let such as him boss me around, not anymore. If I thought you was the type of man to get even, I wouldn't run, I'd let you do it. But you ain't that kind of man."

"Like I said," Measure answered, "no harm done. I learned some things that day, and so did you. Let's have done with that now. You're Alvin's friend now, and that makes you my friend as long as you're loyal and true."

There were tears in Mike Fink's eyes. "Jesus himself couldn't be more kind to me, and me less deserving."

Measure held out his hand. Mike took and held it. Just for a second. Then it was done, and they set it behind them and went on.

"Found out a few things," said Armor-of-God. "But I'm glad Mike was with me. Not that he had to do any violence, but there was a couple of times that some fellows didn't take kindly to the questions I was asking."

"I did throw a fellow into a horsetrough," said Fink, "but I didn't hold him under or nothing so I don't think that counts."

Alvin laughed. "No, I reckon that was just playing around."

"It's some old friends of yours behind all this, Alvin," said Armor-of-God. "The Property Rights Crusade is mostly Reverend Philadelphia Thrower and a couple of clerks opening letters and mailing out letters. But there's some money people behind him, and he's behind other people who need money."

"Like?" asked Horace.

"Like one of his first and longest and loyalest contributors is a fellow name of Cavil Planter, who once owned him a farm in Appalachee and still clings to a certain cachet like it was gold bullion," said Armor-of-God, with a glance at Arthur Stuart.

Arthur nodded. "You're saying that's the white man as raped my mama to make me."

"Most likely," said Armor-of-God.

Alvin stared at Arthur Stuart. "How do you know about such things?"

"I hear everything," said Arthur Stuart. "I don't forget none of it. People said things about that stuff when I was too young to understand it, but I remembered the words and said them to myself when I was older and *could* understand them."

"Damn," said Horace. "How was Old Peg and me supposed to know he'd be able to figure it out later?"

"You did nothing wrong," said Verily. "You can't help the knacks your children have. My parents couldn't predict what I'd do, either, though heaven knows they tried. If Arthur Stuart's knack let him learn things that were painful to know, then I'd also have to say his inward character was strong enough to deal with it and let him grow up untroubled by it."

"I ain't troubled by it, that's true," said Arthur Stuart. "But I'll never call him my pa. He hurt my mama and he wanted to make a slave of me, and that's no pa." He looked at Horace Guester. "My own Black mama died trying to get me here, to a real pa and to a ma who'd take her place when she died."

Horace reached out and patted the boy's hand. Alvin knew how Horace had never liked having the boy call him his father, but it was plain Horace had reconciled himself to it. Maybe it was because of what Arthur just said, or maybe it was because Alvin had taken the boy away for a year and Horace was realizing now that his life was emptier without this half-Black mixup boy as his son.

"So this Cavil Planter is one of the money men behind Thrower's little group," said Verily. "Who else?"

"A lot of names, we didn't get but a few of them but it's prominent people in Carthage, and all of them from the pro-slavery faction, either openly or clandestine," said Armor. "And I'm pretty sure about where most of the money's going *to*."

"We know some of it went to pay Daniel Webster," said Alvin.

"But a lot more of it went to help with White Murderer Harrison's campaign for president," said Armor.

They fell silent, and in the silence more gunshots went off, more cheering, more galloping of horses and whooping and hollering. "Tippy-Canoe just carried him another county," said Horace.

"Maybe he won't do so well back east," said Alvin.

"Who knows?" said Measure. "I can guarantee you he didn't get a single vote in Vigor Church. But that ain't enough to turn the tide."

"It's out of our hands for now," said Alvin. "Presidents ain't forever."

"I think what's important here," said Verily, "is that the same people whose candidate for president just won the election are also out to get you killed, Alvin."

"I'd think about lying low for a while," said Measure.

"I *been* lying low," said Alvin. "I had about all the low-lying I can stand."

"Being in jail so's they know right where you be ain't lying low," said Mike Fink. "You got to be where they don't think to look for you, or where if they do find you they can't do nothing to hurt you."

"The first place I can think of that fills those requirements is the grave," said Alvin, "but I reckon I don't want to go there yet."

There was a soft rap on the door. Horace went to it, whispered, "Who's there?"

"Peggy," came the answer.

He opened the door and she came in. She looked around at the assembled men and chuckled. "Planning the fate of the world here?"

Too many of them remembered what happened the last time they met together for her casual tone to be easily accepted. Only Armor and Fink, who weren't there in Alvin's cell that night, greeted her with good cheer. They filled her in on all that had happened, including the fact that Harrison's election was taken for a sure thing all along the route from Carthage City to Hatrack.

"You know what I don't think is fair?" said Arthur Stuart. "That old Red Hand Harrison is walking around with blood dripping off'n him and they made him president, while Measure here has to stay half-hid and all them other good folks daresn't leave Vigor Church cause of that curse. It seems to me like the good folks is still punished and the worsest one got off scot-free."

"Seems the same to me," said Alvin. "But it ain't my call."

"Maybe it ain't and maybe it is," said Arthur Stuart.

They all looked at him like he was a mess on the floor. "How is it Alvin's call?" asked Verily.

"That Red chief ain't dead, is he?" said Arthur Stuart. "That Red prophet what put the curse on, right? Well, him as puts on a curse can take it off, can't he?"

"Nobody can talk to them wild Reds no more," said Mike Fink. "They fogged up the river and nobody can get across.

There ain't even no trade with New Orleans no more, damn near broke my heart."

"Maybe nobody can get across the river," said Arthur Stuart. "But Alvin can."

Alvin shook his head. "I don't know," he said. "I don't think so. Besides, I don't know if Tenskwa-Tawa's going to see things the same way as us, Arthur. He might say, The White people of America are bringing destruction on themselves by choosing White Murderer Harrison to be their leader. But the people of Vigor Church will be saved from that destruction because they respected the curse I gave them. So he'll say the curse is really a blessing."

"If he says that," said Measure, "then he ain't as good a man as I thought."

"He sees things a different way, that's all," said Alvin. "I'm just saying you can't be sure what he'll say."

"Then *you* can't be sure either," said Armor-of-God.

"I'm thinking something, Alvin," said Measure. "Miss Larner here told me somewhat about how she and Arthur figured out there's a lot of people with sharp knacks in this place. Maybe drawn here cause you was born here, or cause you made the plow here. And there's all them people you've been teaching up in Vigor, folks who maybe don't got so sharp a knack but they know the things you taught them, they know the way to live. And I also have my own idea that maybe the curse forced us all to live together there, so we had to get along no matter what, we had to learn to make peace among ourselves. If the curse was lifted from the folks of Vigor Church, them as wanted to could come here and teach them as has the knacks. And teach them meantime how to live together in harmony."

"Or folks from here could go there," said Alvin. "Even if the curse ain't lifted."

Measure shook his head. "There's like a hundred people or more in Vigor Church who's already trying to follow the Maker way. Nobody here even knows about it, really. So if you said to the folks in Vigor, please come to Hatrack, they'd come;

but if you said to the folks in Hatrack, please come to Vigor, they'd laugh."

"But the river's still fogged up," said Mike Fink, "and the curse is still on."

"If it comes to that," said Miss Larner, "there might be another way to talk to Tenskwa-Tawa without crossing the river."

"You got a pigeon knows the way to the Red Prophet's wigwam?" asked Horace, scoffing.

"I know a weaver," said Miss Larner, "who has a door that opens into the west, and I know of a man named Isaac who uses that door." She looked at Alvin, and he nodded.

"I don't know what you're talking about," said Measure, "but if you think you can talk to Tenskwa-Tawa, then I hope you'll do it. I hope you will."

"I will for you," said Alvin. "For your sake and the sake of my family and friends in Vigor Church, I'll ask even though I fear the answer will be worse than no."

"What could be worse than no?" asked Arthur Stuart.

"I could lose a friend," said Alvin. "But when I weigh that friend against the people of Vigor and the hope that they might help teach other folks to be Makers and help build the Crystal City—then I don't see as how I've got no choice. I was a child when I went there, though, to that weaver's house." He was silent for a moment. "Miss Larner knows the way, if she'll guide me there." It was his turn to look at her, waiting. After a moment's hesitation, she nodded.

"One way or another, though," said Verily Cooper, "you *will* leave this place as soon as the trial's over."

"Win or lose," said Alvin. "Win or lose."

"And if anybody tries to stop him or harm him, they'll have to deal with me first," said Mike Fink. "I'm going with you, Alvin, wherever you go. If these people have the president in their pocket, they're going to be all the more dangerous and you ain't going nowhere without me to watch your back."

"I wish I was younger," said Armor-of-God. "I wish I was younger."

"I don't want to travel alone," said Alvin. "But there's work to be done here, especially if the curse is lifted. And you have responsibilities, too, you married men. It's only the single ones, really, who are free to wander as I'll have to wander. Whatever I find out at the weaver's house, whatever happens when and if I talk to Tenskwa-Tawa, I still have to learn how to build the Crystal City."

"Maybe Tenskwa-Tawa can tell you," said Measure.

"If he knows, then he could have told me back when you and I was boys and in his company," said Alvin.

"I'm unmarried," said Arthur Stuart. "I'm coming with you."

"I reckon so," said Alvin. "And Mike Fink, I'll be glad of your company, too."

"I'm not married either," said Verily Cooper.

Alvin looked at him oddly. "Verily, you're already a dear friend, but you're a lawyer, not a woodsman or a wandering tradesman or a river rat or whatever the rest of us are."

"All the more reason you need me," said Verily. "There'll be laws and courts, sheriffs and jails and writs wherever you go. Sometimes you'll need what Mike Fink has to offer. And sometimes you'll need me. You can't deny me, Alvin Smith. I came all this way to learn from you."

"Measure knows all I know by now. He can teach you as well as I can, and you can help him."

Verily looked at his feet for a moment. "Measure's learned from you, and you from him, since you're brothers and have been for a long time. May it not be taken as an offense, I beg you, if I say that I'd be glad of a chance to learn from you directly for a while, Alvin. I mean to belittle no one else by saying that."

"No offense taken," said Measure. "If you hadn't said it, I would have."

"These three then to go with me on the long road," said

Alvin. "And Miss Larner to go with me as far as Becca Weaver's house."

"I'll go too," said Armor-of-God. "Not the whole road, but as far as the weavers. So I can bring back word about what Tenskwa-Tawa says. I hope you'll forgive my presumption, but I crave the chance to be the one as brings the good news to Vigor Church, if they're set free."

"And if they're not?"

"Then they need to learn that too, and from me."

"Then our plans are laid, such as they are," said Alvin.

"All except how to get out of Hatrack River alive, with all these thugs and ruffians about," said Verily Cooper.

"Oh, me and Armor already got that figured out," said Mike Fink with a grin. "And we pretty much won't have to beat nobody to a pulp to do it, neither, if we're lucky."

There was such glee in Mike Fink's face when he said it, though, that more than one of the others wondered whether Mike really thought it would be *good* luck not to have to pulverize somebody. Nor were a few of them altogether sure that they didn't wish to do a little pulp-beating themselves, if push came to shove.

Fink and Armor-of-God were about to head downstairs with Horace then, to freshen up from their journey before he put them to bed in his attic, a good clean space but one he never rented out, just in case of late-night sudden visitors like these, when Measure called out, "Mike Fink."

Fink turned around.

"There's a story I got to tell you before I go to sleep tonight," he said.

Fink looked puzzled for a moment.

"Measure's under the curse," said Armor-of-God. "He's got to tell you or he'll go to bed with bloody hands."

"I came this close to being under the curse myself," said Fink. "But you? How did you get under it?"

"He took it on himself," said Miss Larner. "But that doesn't mean the same rules don't apply."

"But I already know the story."

"That'll make the telling of it easier," said Measure. "But I got to do it."

"I'll come back up when I've peed and et," said Fink. "Begging your pardon, ma'am."

There they were, then, looking at each other, Alvin and Peggy—but once again with Verily Cooper, Arthur Stuart, and Measure looking on.

"Don't the two of you get tired of playing out your scenes in front of an audience?"

"There's no scene to play," said Miss Larner.

"Too bad," said Alvin. "I thought this was the part of the play where I says to you, 'I'm sorry,' and you says to me—"

"I say to you, There is nothing to be sorry for."

"And I say to you, Is so. And you say, Is not. Is so, Is not, Is so, back and forth till we bust out laughing."

At which she burst out laughing.

"I was right, you didn't need to testify," Alvin said.

Her face went stern at once.

"Hear me out, for pete's sake, cause you were right too, if it came right down to it, it wasn't my place to tell you whether or not you could testify. It's not my decision whether you get to make this sacrifice or that one, or whether it's worth it. You decide your own sacrifices, and I decide mine. Instead of me bossing you about it, I should have just asked you to hold off and see if I could manage without. And you would have said yes. Wouldn't you."

She looked him in the eye. "Probably not," she said. "But I *should* have."

"So maybe we ain't so bullheaded after all."

"The day after—no, two days later—that's when we're not so bullheaded."

"That'll do, if we just stay friends till we soften up a little."

"You're not ready for married life, Alvin," said Miss Larner. "You still have many leagues to travel, and until you're ready to build the Crystal City, you have no need of me. I'm not going to sit home and pine for you, and I'm not going to try to tag along with you when the companions you need are men like these. Speak to me when your journey's done. See if we still need each other then."

"So you admit we need each other now."

"I'm not debating with you now, Alvin. I concede no points to you, and petty contradictions will not be explained or reconciled."

"These men are my witnesses, Margaret. I will love you forever. The family we make together, that will be our best Making, better than the plow, better than the Crystal City."

She shook her head. "Be honest with yourself, Alvin. The Crystal City will stand forever, if you build it right. But our family will be gone in a few lifetimes."

"So you admit we'll have a family."

She grinned. "You should run for office, Alvin. You'd lose, but the debates would be entertaining." She was turning toward the door when it opened without a knock. It was Po Doggly, his eyes wide. He scanned the room till he saw Alvin. "What are you doing sitting there like that, and not a gun in the room!"

"I wasn't robbing any of them, and they wasn't robbing me," said Alvin. "We didn't think to bring guns along."

"There was a break-in at the jail. A man claiming to be Amy Sump's father riled up the crowd and about thirty men broke into the courthouse and overpowered Billy Hunter and took away his keys. They hauled every damn prisoner out of there and started beating on them till they told which one of them was you. I got there before they killed anybody and I run them off all right, but they can't get far from town in one night and I don't know but what somebody's going to tell them where you are so I want you to sleep with guns tonight."

"Don't worry about it," said Miss Larner. "They won't come here tonight."

Po looked at her, then at Alvin. "You sure?"

"Don't even post a guard, Po," said Miss Larner. "It will only draw attention to the roadhouse. The men hired to kill

Alvin are all cowards, really, so they had to get drunk in order to make the attempt. They'll sleep it off tonight."

"And go away after that?"

"Make sure the trial is well guarded, and after that if Alvin is acquitted he'll leave Hatrack and your nightmares will be over."

"They broke into my jail," said Doggly. "I don't know who your enemies are, boy, but if I was you I'd get rid of that golden plow."

"It ain't the plow," said Alvin. "Though some of them probably thinks it is. But plow or no plow, the ones as want me dead would be sending boys like those after me."

"And you really don't want my protection?" asked Doggly.

Both Alvin and Miss Larner agreed that they did not.

When Po made his good-byes and was ready to leave, Miss Larner slipped her arm through his. "Take me downstairs, please, and on to the room I'm sharing with my new friend Ramona." She gave not so much as a backward glance at Alvin.

Measure hooted once—after the door was closed. "Alvin, is she testing you? Just to make sure that you'll *never* turn wife-beater, no matter what the provocation?"

"I got a feeling I ain't seen provocation yet." But Alvin was smiling when he said it, and the others got the idea he didn't mind the idea of sparring with Miss Larner now and then—sparring with words, that is, words and looks and winks and nasty grins.

After the candles were doused and the room was dark and still, with all of them in bed and wishing to sleep, Alvin murmured: "I wonder what they meant to do to me."

Nobody asked who he meant; Measure didn't have to. "They meant to kill you, Alvin. Does it matter what method they used? Hanging. Burning alive. A dozen musket balls. Do you really care which way you die?"

"I'd like to have a corpse decent-looking enough that the coffin can be open and my children can bear to look at me and say good-bye to me."

"You're dreaming then," said Measure. "Cause even right now I don't know how no wife and children could bear to look at you, though I daresay they'll say good-bye readily enough."

"I expect they were going to hang me," said Alvin. "If you ever see folks about to hang me, don't waste your time or risk your life trying to save me. Just come along after they've given up on me so you can get me on home."

"So you got no fear of the rope," said Measure.

"Nor fear of drowning or suffocation," said Alvin. "Nor falling—I can fix up breaks and make the rocks soft under me. But fire, now. Fire and beheading and too many bullets, those can take me right off. I could use some help if you see them going at me like that."

"I'll try to remember that," said Measure.

Monday morning behind the smithy, everyone was gathered by ten o'clock; but from dawn onward, heavily armed deputies were on guard all around the site. The judge arranged things so the whole jury could see, as well as Marty Laws, Verily Cooper, Alvin Smith, Makepeace Smith, and Hank Dowser. "This court is now in session," said the judge loudly. "Now, Hank Dowser, you show us the exact place you marked."

Verily Cooper spoke up. "How do we know he'll mark the same place?"

"Cause I'll dowse it again," said Hank Dowser, "and the same spot will still be best."

Alvin spoke up then. "There's water everywhere here. There's not a place you can pick where there won't be water if you just go far enough down."

Hank Dowser whirled on him and glared. "There it is! He's got no respect for any man's knack except his own! You think I don't know there's water most everywhere? The question is, is the water pure? Is it close to the surface? That's what I find— the easy dig, the clean water. And I'll tell you, by the use of hickory and willow wands, that the water is purest here, and closest to the surface here, and so I mark this spot, as I would have more'n a year ago! Tell me, Alvin Journeyman, if you're so clever, is this or is it not the same spot I marked, exactly?"

"It is," said Alvin, sounding a little abashed. "And I didn't mean to imply that you weren't a real dowser, sir."

"You didn't exactly mean *not* to imply it either, though, did you!"

"I'm sorry," said Alvin. "The water is purest here, and closest to the surface, and you truly found it twice the same, the exact spot."

The judge intervened. "So after this unconventional courtroom exchange, which seems appropriate to this unconventional courtroom, you both agree that this is the spot where Alvin says he dug the first well and found nothing but solid impenetrable stone, and where it is Makepeace's contention that there was no such stone, but rather a buried treasure which Alvin stole and converted to his own use while telling a tale of turning iron into gold."

"For all we know he hid my iron underground here!" cried Makepeace.

The judge sighed. "Makepeace, please, don't make me send you to jail again."

"Sorry," muttered Makepeace.

The judge beckoned to the team of workingmen he'd arranged to come do the digging. Paying them would come out of the county budget, but with four diggers it couldn't take long to prove one or the other right.

They dug and dug, the dirt flying. But it was a dryish dirt, a little moist from the last rain which was only a week ago, but no hint of a watery layer. And then: *chink.*

"The treasure box!" cried Makepeace.

A few moments later, after scraping and prying, the foreman of the diggers called out, "Solid stone, your honor! Far as we can reach. Not no boulder, neither—feels like bedrock if'n I ever saw it."

Hank Dowser's face went scarlet. He muscled his way to the hole and slid down the steep side. With his own handkerchief he brushed away the soil from the stone. After a few minutes of examination, he stood up. "Your Honor, I apologize to Mr. Smith, as graciously, I hope, as he just apologized to me a moment ago. Not only is this bedrock—which I did not see, for I have never found such a sheet of water *under* solid stone like this—but also I can see old scrape marks against the stone, proving to me that the prentice boy *did* dig in this spot, just as he said he did, and reached stone, just as he said he did."

"That don't prove he didn't find gold along the way!" cried Makepeace.

"Summations to the jury!" the judge called out.

"In every particular that we could test," said Verily Cooper, "Alvin Smith has proven himself to be truthful and reliable. And all the county has to assail him is the unproven and unprovable speculations of a man whose primary motive seems to be to get his hands upon gold. There are no witnesses but Alvin himself of how the gold came to be shaped like a plow, or the plow came to be made of gold. But we have eight witnesses, not to mention His Honor, myself, and my respected colleague, not to mention Alvin himself, all swearing to you that this plow is not just gold, but also alive. What possible property interest can Makepeace Smith have in an object which clearly belongs to itself and only keeps company with Alvin Smith for its own protection? You have more than a reasonable doubt—you have a certainty that my client is an honest man who has committed no crime, and that the plow should stay with him."

It was Marty Laws' turn then. He looked like he'd had sour milk for breakfast. "You've heard the witnesses, you've seen the evidence, you're all wise men and you can figure this out just fine without my help," said Laws. "May God bless your deliberations."

"Is that your summing up?" demanded Makepeace. "Is that how you administer justice in this county? I'll support your opponent in the next local election, Marty Laws! I swear you haven't heard the end of this!"

"Sheriff, kindly arrest Mr. Makepeace Smith again, three

days this time, contempt of court and I'll consider a charge of attempted interference with the course of justice by offering a threat to a sitting judge in order to influence the outcome of a case."

"You're all ganging up against me! All of you are in this together! What did he do, Your *Honor*, bribe you? Offer to share some of that gold with you?"

"Quickly, Sheriff Doggly," said the judge, "before I get angry with the man."

When Makepeace's shouting had died down enough to proceed, the judge asked the jury, "Do we need to traipse on back to the courtroom for hours of deliberation? Or should we just stand back and let you work things out right here?"

The foreman whispered to his fellow jurors; they whispered back. "We have a unanimous verdict, Your Honor."

"What say you, etcetera etcetera?"

"Not guilty of all charges," said the foreman.

"We're done. I commend both attorneys for fine work in a difficult case. And to the jury, my commendation for cutting through the horse pucky and seeing the truth. Good citizens all. This court stands adjourned until the next time somebody brings a blame fool charge against an innocent man, at least that's what I'm betting on." The judge looked around at the people, who were still standing there. "Alvin, you're free to go," he said. "Let's all go home."

Of course they didn't all go; nor, strictly speaking, was Alvin free. Right now, surrounded by a crowd and with a dozen deputies on guard, he was safe enough. But as he gripped the sack with the plow inside, he could almost feel the covetings of other men directed toward that plow, that warm and trembling gold.

He wasn't thinking of that, however. He was looking over at Margaret Larner, whose arm was around young Ramona's waist. Someone was speaking to Alvin—it was Verily Cooper, he realized, congratulating him or something, but Verily would understand. Alvin put a hand on Verily's shoulder, to let him know that he was a good friend even though Alvin was about to walk away from him. And Alvin headed on over to Miss Larner and Ramona.

At the last moment he got shy, and though he had his eyes on Margaret all the way through the crowd, it was Ramona he spoke to when he got there. "Miss Ramona, it was brave of you to come forward, and honest too." He shook her hand.

Ramona beamed, but she was also a little upset and nervous. "That whole thing with Amy was my fault I think. She was telling *me* those tales about you, and I was doubting her, which only made her insist more and more. And she stuck to it so much that for a while I believed maybe it *was* true and that's when I told my folks and that's what started all the rumors going, but then when she went with Thatch under the freak show tent and she comes out pregnant but babbling about how it was you got her that way, well, I had my chance then to set things straight, didn't I? And then I didn't get to testify!"

"But you told my friends," said Alvin, "so the people who matter most to me know the truth, and in the meantime you didn't have to hurt your friend Amy." In the back of his mind, though, Alvin couldn't shake the bitter certainty that there would always be some who believed her charges, just as he was sure that she would never recant. She would go on telling those lies about him, and some folks at least would go on believing them, and so he would be known for a cad or worse no matter how clean he lived his life. But that was spilled milk.

Ramona was shaking her head. "I don't reckon she'll be my friend no more."

"But you're *her* friend whether she likes it or not. So much of a friend that you'd even hurt her rather than let her hurt someone else. That's something, in my book."

At that moment, Mike Fink and Armor-of-God came up to him. "Sing us that song you thought up in jail, Alvin!"

At once several others clamored for the song—it was that kind of festive occasion.

"If Alvin won't sing it, Arthur Stuart knows it!" somebody said, and then there was Arthur tugging at his arm and Alvin joined in singing with him. Most of the jury was still there to hear the last verse:

> *I trusted justice not to fail.*
> *The jury did me proud.*
> *Tomorrow I will hit the trail*
> *And sing my hiking song so loud*
> *It's like to start a gale!*

Everybody laughed and clapped. Even Miss Larner smiled, and as Alvin looked at her he knew that this was the moment, now or never. "I got another verse that I never sung to anybody before, but I want to sing it now," he said. They all hushed up again to hear:

> *Now swiftly from this place I'll fly,*
> *And underneath my boots*
> *A thousand lands will pass me by,*
> *Until we choose to put down roots,*
> *My lady love and I.*

He looked at Margaret with all the meaning he could put in his face, and everybody hooted and clapped. "I love you, Margaret Larner," he said. "I asked you before, but I'll say it again now. We're about to journey together for a ways, and I can't think of a good reason why it can't be our honeymoon journey. Let me be your husband, Margaret. Everything good that's in me belongs to you, if you'll have me."

She looked flustered. "You're embarrassing me, Alvin," she murmured.

Alvin leaned close and spoke into her ear. "I know we got separate work to do, once we leave the weavers' house. I know we got long journeys apart."

She held his face between her hands. "You don't know what

you might meet on that road. What woman you might meet and love better than me."

Alvin felt a stab of dread. Was this something she had seen with her torchy knack? Or merely the worry any woman might feel? Well, it was *his* future, wasn't it? And even if she saw the possibility of him loving somebody else, that didn't mean he had to let it come true.

He wrapped his long arms around her waist and drew her close, and spoke softly. "You see things in the future that I can't see. Let me ask you like an ordinary man, and you answer me like a woman that knows only the past and the present. Let my promise to you now keep watch over the future."

She was about to raise another objection, when he kissed her lightly on the lips. "If you're my wife, then whatever there is in the future, I can bear it, and I'll do my best to help you bear it too. The judge is right here. Let me begin my life of new freedom with you."

For a moment, her eyes looked heavy and sad, as if she saw some awful pain and suffering in his future. Or was it in her own?

Then she shook it off as if it was just the shadow of a cloud passing over her and now the sun was back. Or as if she had decided to live a certain life, no matter what the cost of it, and now would no longer dread what couldn't be helped. She smiled, and tears ran down her cheeks. "You don't know what you're doing, Alvin, but I'm proud and glad to have your love, and I'll be your wife."

Alvin turned to face the others, and in a loud voice he cried, "She said yes! Judge! Somebody stop the judge from leaving! He's got him one more job to do!" While Peggy went off to find her father and drag him back so he could give her away properly, Verily Cooper fetched the judge.

On the way over to where Alvin waited, the judge put a kindly arm across Verily's back. "My lad, you have a keen mind, a lawyer's mind, and I approve of that. But there's something about you that sets a fellow's teeth on edge."

"If I knew what it was, sir, you may be sure that I'd stop."

"Took me a while to figure it out. And I don't know what you can do about it. What makes folks mad at you right from the start is you sound so damnably English and educated and fine."

Verily grinned, then answered in the vernacular accent he had grown up with, the one he had spent so many years trying to lose. "You mean, sir, that if I talks like a common feller, I'll be more likable?"

The judge whooped with laughter. "That's what I mean, lad, though I don't know as how *that* accent is much better!"

And with that they reached the spot where the wedding party was assembled. Horace stood beside his daughter, and Arthur Stuart was there as Alvin's best man.

The judge turned to Sheriff Doggly. "Do the banns, my good sir."

Po Doggly at once cried out, "Is there a body here so foolish as to claim there's any impediment to the marriage of this pair of good and godly citizens?" He turned to the judge. "Not a soul as I can see, Judge."

So Alvin and Peggy were married, Horace Guester on one side, Arthur Stuart on the other, all standing there in the open on the grounds of the smithy where Alvin had served his prenticehood. Just up the hill was the springhouse where Peggy had lived in disguise as a schoolteacher; the very springhouse where twenty-two years before, as a five-year-old girl, she had seen the heartfires of a family struggling across the Hatrack River in flood, and in the womb of the mother of that family there was a baby with a heartfire so bright it dazzled her, the like of which she'd never seen before or since. She ran, then, ran down this hill, ran to this smithy, got Makepeace Smith and the other men gathered there to race to the river and save the family. All of it began here, within sight of this place. And now she was married to him. Married to the boy whose heartfire shone like the brightest star in her memory, and in all her life since then.

There was dancing that night at Horace's roadhouse, you

can bet, and Alvin had to sing his song five more times, and the last verse thrice each time through. And that night he carried his Margaret—his now, and he was hers—in those strong blacksmith's arms up the stairs to the room where Margaret herself had been conceived twenty-eight years before. He was awkward and they both were shy and it didn't help that half the town was charivareeing outside the roadhouse halfway till dawn, but they were man and wife, made one flesh as they had so long been one heart even though she had tried to deny it and he had tried to live without her. Never mind that she had seen his grave in her mind, and herself and their children standing by it, weeping. That scene was possible in every wedding night; and at least there would be children; at least there would be a loving widow to grieve him; at least there would be memory of this night, instead of regretful loneliness. And in the morning, when they awoke, they were not quite so shy, not quite so awkward, and he said such things to her as made her feel more beautiful than anyone who had ever lived before, and more beloved, and I don't know who would dare to say that in that moment it wasn't the pure truth.

✦ 18 ✦

Journeys

Two DAYS LATER they were ready to light out. They made no secret about the carriage Armor-of-God hired in Wheelwright, ready to take them off the ferry as soon as they crossed the Hio. That would be enough to decoy the stupid ones. As for the clever ones, well, Mike Fink had his own plan, and even Margaret allowed as how it might well work.

Friends came to the roadhouse all that evening to bid good-bye. Alvin and Peggy and Arthur were well known to them all; Armor-of-God had a few friends here, from business traveling; and Verily had made some new friends, having been the spokesman for the winning side in a highly emotional trial. If Mike Fink had local friends, they weren't the sort to show up in Horace Guester's roadhouse; as Mike confided to Verily Cooper, his friends were most of them the very men Alvin's enemies had hired to kill him and take the plow once he got out on the road tomorrow.

When the last soul had left, Horace embraced his daughter and his new son-in-law and the adopted son he had helped to raise, shook hands with Verily, Armor, and Mike, and then went about as he always did, dousing the candles, putting the night log on the fire, checking to make sure all was secure. As he did, Measure helped the travelers make their way, lightly burdened, quietly down the stairs and out the back, finding the path with only the faintest sliver of moon. Even at that, they walked at first toward the privy, so that anyone casually glancing wouldn't think a thing amiss, unless they noticed the satchel or bag each one carried. Meantime, Measure kept watch, in case someone else was thinking to snatch Alvin that night while he was relieving himself. He kept watch even though Peggy Larner—or was it Goody Smith now?—assured him that not a soul was watching the back of the house.

"All my teaching is in your hands now, Measure," Alvin whispered as he was about to step off the back porch into the night. "I leave you behind this time again, but you know that we set out on the real journey together as true companions, and always will be to the end."

Measure heard him, and wondered if Peggy maybe whispered to him something she had seen in his heartfire, that Measure worried lest Alvin forget how much Measure loved him and wanted to be on this journey by his side. But no, Alvin didn't need Peggy to tell him he had a brother who was more loyal than life and more sure than death. Alvin kissed his brother's cheek and was gone, the last to go.

They met up again in the woods behind the privy. Alvin went about among them, calming them with soft words, touching them, and each time he touched them they could hear it just a little clearer, a kind of soft humming, or was it the soughing of the wind, or the call of a far-off bird too faint to hear, or perhaps a distant coyote mumbling in its sleep, or the soft scurry of squirrel feet on a tree on the next rise? It was a kind of music, and finally it didn't matter what it was that produced the sound, they fell into the rhythm of it, all holding each other's hands, and at the head of the line, Alvin. They moved swift and sure, keeping step to the music, sliding easily among the trees, making few sounds, saying nothing, marveling at how they could have walked past these woods before and never guessed that such a clear and well-marked path was here; except when they looked back, there was no path, only the underbrush closed off again, for the path was made by Alvin's progress in the midst of the greensong, and behind his party the forest relaxed back into its ordinary shape.

They came to the river, where Po Doggly waited, watching over two boats. "Mind you," he whispered, "I'm not sheriff tonight. I'm only doing what Horace and I done so many times in the past, long before I had me a badge—helping folks as ought to be free get safe across the river." Po and Alvin rowed one of them and Mike and Verily the other, for though he was unaccustomed to such labor, no wooden oar would ever leave a blister on Verily's hands. Silently they moved out across the Hio. Only when they got to the middle did anyone speak. Peggy, controlling the tiller, whispered to Alvin, "Can we talk a little now?"

"Soft and low," said Alvin. "And no laughing."

How had he known she was about to laugh? "We passed a dozen of them as we walked through the woods, all of them asleep, waiting for first light. But there's none on the opposite shore, except the heartfire we're looking for."

Alvin nodded, and gave a thumbs up to the men in the other boat.

They skirted the shore on the Appalachee side for about a quarter mile before coming to the landing site they looked for. Once it had been a putting-in place for flatboats, before the Red fog on the Mizzipy and the new railroad lines slowed and then stopped most of the flatboat traffic. Now an elderly couple lived there mostly from fishing and an orchard that still produced, poorly, but enough for their needs.

Dr. Whitley Physicker was waiting in the front yard of that house with his carriage and four saddled horses; he had insisted on buying or lending them himself, and refused any thought of reimbursement. He also paid the old folks who lived there for the annoyance of having visitors arrive so late at night.

He had a man with him—Arthur Stuart recognized him at once and called him by name. John Binder smiled shyly and shook hands all around, as did Whitley Physicker. "I'm not much for rowing, at my age," Dr. Physicker explained. "So John, being as trustworthy a man as ever there was, agreed to come along, asking no questions. I suppose all the questions he *didn't* ask are answered now."

Binder smiled and chuckled. "Reckon so, all but one. I heard about how you was teaching folks about Makery away out there in Vigor Church, and I hoped you might teach some of it here. Now you're going."

Alvin reassured him. "My brother is holed up in the roadhouse. Nobody's to know he's there, but if you go to Horace Guester and tell him I sent you, he'll let you go up and talk to Measure. There's a hard tale he'll have to tell you—"

"I know about the curse."

"Well good," said Alvin. "Cause once that's done, he can teach you just what I was teaching in Vigor Church."

Po Doggly and John Binder pushed the boats off the shore before the others were even mounted on their horses or properly seated in the carriage; Whitley Physicker waved from Binder's boat. Alvin shook hands with the old couple, who had got up from their beds to see them off. Then he climbed up into the front seat of the carriage with Margaret; Verily and Arthur sat behind. Armor and Mike rode two of the horses; Verily's horse and the horse that Alvin and Arthur would ride together were tied to the back of the carriage.

As they were about to leave, Mike brought his horse—stamping and fuming, since Mike was a sturdy load and not much of a horseman—beside the carriage and said to Alvin, "Well this plan worked too well! I was looking forward to scaring some poor thug half to death before the night was through!"

Peggy leaned over from the other side of the front seat and

said, "You'll get your wish about a mile up the road. There's two fellows there who saw Dr. Physicker's carriage come here this afternoon and wondered what he was doing with four horses tied behind. They're just keeping watch on the road, but even if they don't stop us, they'll give the alarm and then we'll be chased instead of getting away clean."

"Don't kill them, Mike," said Alvin.

"I won't unless they make me," said Mike. "Don't worry, I ain't loose with other folks' lives no more." He rode to Armor, gave him the reins, and said, "Here, bring this girl along with you. I do better on my feet for this kind of work." Then he dismounted and took off running.

Near as I can gather from Mike Fink's tale of the event—and you got to understand that a fellow who wants his story to be truthful has to allow for a lot of brag before deciding what's true in a tale of Mike Fink's heroic exploits—those two smarter-than-normal thugs was dozing while sitting with their backs to opposite sides of the same stump when all of a sudden they both felt their arms pretty near wrenched right out of their sockets and then they were dragged around, grabbed by the collars, and smacked together so hard their noses bled and they saw stars.

"You're lucky I took me a vow of nonviolence," said Mike Fink, "or you'd be suffering some pain right now."

Since they were already suffering something pretty excruciating, they didn't want to find out what this night-wandering fellow thought of as pain. Instead, they obeyed him and held very still as he tied their hands to a couple of lengths of rope, so that the one man's right hand was tied on one end of a rope that held the other man's left, with about two feet of rope between them; and the same with their other two hands. Then Fink made them kneel, picked up a huge log, and laid it down across the two lengths of rope that joined them. What he could lift alone they couldn't lift together. They just knelt there as if they were praying to the log, their hands too far apart even to dream of untying their bonds.

"Next time you want gold," said Fink, "you ought to get yourself a pick and shovel and dig for it, stead of lying in wait in the night for some innocent fellow to come by and get himself robbed and killed."

"We wasn't going to rob nobody," burbled one of the men.

"It's a sure thing you wasn't," said Fink, "cause any man ever wants to get at Alvin Smith has to go through me, and I make a better wall than window, I'll tell you that right now."

Then he jogged back to the road, waved to the others, and waited for them to come alongside so he could mount his horse. In a couple of minutes it was done, and they rode briskly south along a lacework of roads that would completely bypass Wheelwright—including the fancy carriage waiting all day empty by the river, until Horace Guester crossed over, got in the carriage, and used it to shop for groceries in the big-city market that was Wheelwright's pride and joy. That's when the ruffians knew they had been fooled. Oh, some of them lit out in search of Alvin's group, but they had a whole day's head start, or nearly so, and not a one of them found anything except a couple of men kneeling before a log with their butts in the air.

All the way to the coast, Calvin expected to be accosted by Napoleon's troops, the carriage blown to bits with grapeshot or set afire or some other grisly end. Why he expected Napoleon to be ungrateful he didn't know. Perhaps it was simply a feeling of general unease. Here he was, not yet twenty years old, and already he had moved through the salons of London and Paris, had spent hours alone discussing a thousand different things with the most powerful man in the world, had learned as many of the secrets of that powerful man as he was likely ever to tell, spoke French if not fluently then competently, and through it all had remained aloof, untouched, his life's dream unchanged. He was a Maker, far more so than Alvin, who remained at the rough frontier of a crude upstart country that couldn't properly call itself a nation; who had Alvin known, except other homespun types like himself? Yet Calvin felt vaguely afraid at the thought of going back to America. Something was trying to stop him. Something didn't want him to go.

"It is nerves," said Honoré. "You will face your brother. You know now that he is a provincial clown, but still he remains your nemesis, the stick against which you must measure yourself. Also you are traveling with me, and you are constantly aware of the need to make a good impression."

"And why would I need to impress *you*, Honoré?"

"Because I am going to write you into a story someday, my friend. Remember that the ultimate power is mine. You may decide what you will do in this life, up to the point. But I will decide what others think of you, and not just now but long after you're dead."

"If anyone still reads your novels," said Calvin.

"You don't understand, my dear bumpkin. Whether they read my novels or not, my judgment of your life will stand. These things take on a life of their own. No one remembers the original source, or cares either."

"So people will only remember what you say about me— and you they won't remember at all."

Honoré chuckled. "Oh, I don't know about that, Calvin. I intend to be memorable. But then, do I care whether I'm remembered? I think not. I have lived without the affection of my own mother; why should I crave the affection of strangers not yet born?"

"It's not whether you're remembered," said Calvin. "It's whether you changed the world."

"And the first change I will make is: They must remember me!" Honoré's voice was so loud that the coachman slid open the panel and inquired whether they wanted something from him. "More speed," cried Honoré, "and softer bumps. Oh, and when the horses relieve themselves: Less odor."

The coachman growled and closed the panel shut.

"Don't you intend to change the world?" asked Calvin.

"Change it? A paltry project, smacking of weak ambition and much self-contempt. Your brother wants to build a city. You want to tear it down before his eyes. *I* am the one with vision, Calvin. I intend to *create* a world. A world more fascinating, engrossing, spellbinding, intricate, beautiful, and real than this world."

"You're going to outdo God?"

"He spent far too much time on geology and botany. For him, Adam was an afterthought—oh, by the way, is man found upon the Earth? I shall not make that mistake. I will concentrate on people, and slip the science into the cracks."

"The difference is that your people will all be confined to tiny black marks on paper," said Calvin.

"My people will be more real than these shallow creatures God has made! I, too, will make them in my own image—only taller—and mine will have more palpable reality, more inner life, more connection to the living world around them than these mud-covered peasants or the calculating courtiers of the palace or the swaggering soldiers and bragging businessmen who keep Paris under their thumbs."

"Instead of worrying about the emperor stopping us, perhaps I should worry about lightning striking us," said Calvin.

It was meant as a joke, but Honoré did not smile. "Calvin, if God was going to strike you dead for anything, you'd already be dead by now. I don't pretend to know whether God exists, but I'll tell you this—the old man is doddering now! The old fellow talks rough but it's all a memory. He hasn't the stuff anymore! He can't stop us! Oh, maybe he can write us out of his will, but we'll make our own fortune and let the old boy stand back lest he be splashed when we hurtle by!"

"Do you ever have even a moment of self-doubt?"

"None," said Honoré. "I live in the constant certainty of failure, and the constant certainty of genius. It is a species of madness, but greatness is not possible without it. Your problem, Calvin, is that you never really question yourself about anything. However you feel, that's the right way to feel, and so you feel that way and everything else better get out of your way. Whereas I endeavor to change my feelings because my feelings are always wrong. For instance, when approaching a woman you lust after, the foolish man acts out his feelings and clutches at an inviting breast or makes some fell invitation that gets him slapped and keeps him from the best parties for the rest of the year. But the wise man looks the woman in the eye and serenades her about her astonishing beauty and her great wisdom and his own inadequacy to explain to her how much she deserves her place in the exact center of the universe. No woman can resist this, Calvin, or if she can, she's not worth having."

The carriage came to a stop.

Honoré flung open the door. "Smell the air!"

"Rotting fish," said Calvin.

"The coast! I wonder if I shall throw up, and if I do, whether the sea air will have affected the color and consistency of my vomitus."

Calvin ignored his deliberately crude banter as he reached up for their bags. He well know that Honoré was only crude when he didn't much respect his company; when with aristocrats, Honoré never uttered anything but bon mots and epigrams. For the young novelist to speak that way to Calvin was a sign, not so much of intimacy, but of disrespect.

When they found an appropriate ship bound for Canada, Calvin showed the captain the letter Napoleon had given him. Contrary to his worst fears, after seeing a production of a newly revised and prettied-up script of *Hamlet* in London, the letter did not instruct the captain to kill Calvin and Honoré at once—though there was no guarantee that the fellow didn't have orders to strangle them and pitch them into the sea when they were out of sight of land.

Why am I so afraid?

"So the Emperor's treasurer will reimburse me for all expenses out of the treasury when I come back?"

"That's the plan," said Honoré. "But here, my friend, I know how ungenerous these imperial officials can be. Take this."

He handed the captain a sheaf of franc notes. Calvin was astonished. "All these weeks you've pretended to be poor and up to your ears in debt."

"I *am* poor! I *am* in debt. If I didn't owe money, why would I ever steel myself to write? No, I simply borrowed the price of my passage from my mother *and* my father—they never talk, so they'll never find out—and from two of my publishers, promising each of them a completely exclusive book about my travels in America."

"You borrowed to pay our passage, knowing all along that the Emperor would pay it?"

"A man has to have spending money, or he's not a man," said Honoré. "I have a wad of it, with which I have every intention of being generous with you, so I hope you won't condemn my methods."

"You're not terribly honest, are you?" said Calvin, half appalled, half admiring.

"You shock me, you hurt me, you offend me, I challenge you to a duel and then take sick with pneumonia so that I can't meet you, but I urge you to go ahead without me. Keep in mind that *because* I had that money, the captain will now invite us into his cabin for dinner every night of the voyage. And in answer to your question, I am perfectly honest when I am creating something, but otherwise words are mere tools designed to extract what I need from the pockets or bank accounts of those who currently but temporarily possess it. Calvin, you've been too long among the Puritans. And I have been too long among the Hypocrites."

It was Peggy who found the turnoff to Chapman Valley, found it easily though there was no sign and she was coming this time from the other direction. She and Alvin left the others with the carriage under the now-leafless oak out in front of the weavers' house. For Peggy, coming to this place now was both thrilling and embarrassing. What would they think of the way things had turned out since they set her on this present road?

Then, just as she raised her hand to knock on the door, she remembered something.

"Alvin," she said. "It slipped my mind, but something Becca said when I was here a few months ago—"

"If it slipped your mind, then it was supposed to slip your mind."

"You and Calvin. You need to reclaim Calvin, find him and reclaim him before he turns completely against the work you're doing."

Alvin shook his head. "Becca doesn't know everything."

"And what does that mean?"

"What makes you think Calvin wasn't already the enemy of our work before he was born?"

"That's not possible," said Peggy. "Babies are born innocent and pure."

"Or steeped in original sin? Those are the choices? I can't believe that you of all people believe either idea, you who put your hands on the womb and see the futures in the baby's heartfire. The child is already himself then, the good and bad, ready to step into the world and make of himself whatever he wants most to be."

She squinted at him. "Why is it that when we're alone, talking of something serious, you don't sound so much the country bumpkin?"

"Because maybe I learned everything you taught me, only I also learned that I don't want to lose touch with the common people," said Alvin. "They're the ones who are going to build the city with me. Their language is my native language—why should I forget it, just because I learned another? How many educated folks do you think are going to come away from their fine homes and educated friends and roll up their sleeves to make something with their own hands?"

"I don't want to knock on this door," said Peggy. "My life changes when I come into this place."

"You don't have to knock," said Alvin. He reached out and turned the knob. The door opened.

When he made as if to step inside, Peggy took his arm. "Alvin, you can't just walk in here!"

"If the door wasn't locked, then I can walk in," said Alvin. "Don't you understand what this place is? This is the place where things are as they must be. Not like the world out there, the world you see in the heartfires, the world of things that can be. And not like the world inside my head, the world as it might be. And not like the world as it was first conceived in the mind of God, which is the world as it should be."

She watched him step over the threshold. There was no alarum in the house, nor even a sound of life. She followed him. Young as he was, this man she had watched over from his infancy, this man whose heart she knew more intimately than her own, he could still surprise her by what he did of a sudden without thought, because he simply knew it was right and had to be this way.

The endless cloth still lay folded in piles, linked each to each, winding over furniture, through halls, up and down stairs. They stepped over the spans and reaches of it. "No dust," said Peggy. "I didn't notice that the first time. There's no dust on the cloth."

"Good housekeepers here?" asked Alvin.

"They dust all this cloth?"

"Or maybe there's simply no passage of time within the cloth. Always and forever it exists in that one present moment in which the shuttlecock flew from side to side."

As he said these words, they began to hear the shuttlecock. Someone must have opened a door.

"Becca?" called Peggy.

They followed the sound through the house to the ancient cabin at the house's heart, where an open door led into the room with the loom. But to Peggy's surprise, it wasn't Becca seated there. It was the boy. Her nephew, the one who had dreamed of this. With practiced skill he drove the shuttlecock back and forth.

"Is Becca . . ." Peggy couldn't bring herself to ask about the weaver's death.

"Naw," said the boy. "We changed the rules a little here. No more pointless sacrifice. You done that, you know. Came here as a judge—well, your judgment was heeded. I take my shift for a while, and she can go out a little."

"So is it you we talk to now?" asked Alvin.

"Depends on what you want. I don't know nothing about nothing, so if you want answers, I don't think I'm it."

"I want to use the door that leads to Ta-Kumsaw."

"Who?" the boy asked.

"Your uncle Isaac," said Peggy.

"Oh, sure." He nodded with his head. "It's that one."

Alvin strode toward it.

"You ever used one of these doors before?" asked the boy.

"No," said Alvin.

"Well then ain't you the stupid one, heading right for it like it was some ordinary door."

"What's different? I know it leads to the Red lands. I know it leads to the house where Ta-Kumsaw's daughter weaves the lives of the Reds of the west."

"Here's the tricky part. When you pass through the door, you can't have no part of yourself touching anything here but air. You can't brush up against the doorjamb. You can't let a foot linger on the floor. It's not a step through the door, it's a leap."

"And what happens if some part of me *does* touch?"

"Then that part of this place drags you down just a little, slows you, lowers you, and so instead of you passing through the door in one smooth motion, you go through in a couple of pieces. Ain't nobody can put you together after that, Mr. Maker."

Peggy was appalled. "I never realized it was so dangerous."

"Breathing's dangerous too," said the boy, "if'n you breathe in something to make you sick." He grinned. "I saw you two get all twined up together here. Congratulations."

"Thanks," said Alvin.

"So what do they call you now, judge woman?" the boy asked Peggy. "Goody Smith?"

"Most still call me Peggy Larner. Only they say Miz Larner now, and not Miss."

"I call her Margaret," said Alvin.

"I reckon you'll really be married when she starts to think of herself by the name you call her, instead of the name her parents called her by." He winked at Peggy. "Thanks for getting me my job. My sisters are glad, too, they had nightmares, I'll tell you. There ain't no love of the loom in them." He turned back to Alvin. "So are you going or what?"

At that moment the door flew open and a tied-up bundle flew through it.

"Uh-oh," said the boy. "Best turn your back. Becca's coming through, and she travels stark nekkid, seeing as how women's clothing can't fit through that door without touching."

Alvin turned his back, and so did Peggy, though unlike Alvin she cheated and allowed herself to watch anyway. It was not Becca who came through the door first, however. It was Ta-Kumsaw, a man Peggy had never met, though she had seen him often enough in Alvin's heartfire. He was not naked, but rather clothed in buckskins that clung tightly to his body. He saw them standing there and grunted. "Boy Renegado comes back to see the most dangerous Red man who ever lived."

"Howdy, Ta-Kumsaw," said Alvin.

"Hi, Isaac," said the boy. "I warned him about the door like you said."

"Good boy," said Ta-Kumsaw. He turned his back on them then, just in time for Becca to leap through the door wearing only thin and clinging underwear. He gathered her at once into his arms. Then together they untied the bundle and unfolded it into a dress, which she drew down over her head. "All right," said Ta-Kumsaw. "She's dressed enough for a White woman now."

Alvin turned around and greeted her. There were handshakes, and even a hug between women. They talked about what had happened in Hatrack River over the past few months, and then Alvin explained his errand.

Ta-Kumsaw showed no emotion. "I don't know what my brother will say. He keeps his own counsel."

"Does he rule there in the west?" asked Alvin.

"Rule? That's not how we do things. There are many tribes, and in each tribe many wise men. My brother is one of the greatest of them, everyone agrees to that. But he doesn't make law just by deciding what it should be. We don't do anything as foolish as you do, electing one president and concentrating too much power in his hands. It was good enough when good men held the office, but always when you create an office that a man can lay hands on, an evil man will someday lay hands on it."

"Which is going to happen on New Year's day when Harrison—"

Ta-Kumsaw glowered. "Never say that name, that unbearable name."

"Not saying it won't make him go away."

"It will keep his evil out of this house," said Ta-Kumsaw. "Away from the people I love."

In the meantime, Becca had finished dressing. She came to the boy and bumped him with her hip. "Move over, stubby-fingers. That's my loom you're tangling."

"Tightest weave ever," the boy retorted. "People will always know which spots I wove."

Becca settled onto the chair and then began to make the shuttlecock dance. The whole music of the loom changed, the rhythm of it, the song. "You came for a purpose, Maker? The door's still open for you. Do what you came to do."

For the first time Peggy really looked at the door, trying to see what lay beyond it; and what lay beyond was nothing. Not blackness, but not daylight either. Just ... nothing. Her eyes couldn't look at it; her gaze kept shifting away.

"Alvin," she said. "Are you sure you want to—"

He kissed her. "I love it when you worry about me."

She smiled and kissed him back. As he took off his cap and his boots, and his long coat that might flap against the doorjamb, he couldn't see how she reached into the small box she kept in a pocket of her skirt; how she held the last scrap of his birth caul between her fingers and then watched his heartfire, ready to spring into action the moment he needed her, to use his power to heal him even if he, in some dire extremity, could not or dared not or would not use it himself.

He ran for the door, leapt toward it left-foot-first, his right foot leaving the ground before any part of him broke the plane of the door. He sailed through with his head ducked down; he missed the top of the door by an inch.

"I don't like it when people leap through all spread out like that," said Ta-Kumsaw. "Better to spring from both feet at once, and curl up into a ball as you go."

"You athletic men can do that," said Becca. "But I can't see myself hitting the floor like that and rolling. Besides, you leap half the time yourself."

"I'm not as tall as Alvin," said Ta-Kumsaw. He turned to Peggy. "He grew to be very tall."

But Peggy didn't answer him.

"She's watching his heartfire," said Becca. "Best leave her alone till he comes back."

Alvin tumbled and fell when he hit the floor on the other side; he sprawled into a pile of cloth and heard the sound of laughter. He got up and looked around. Another cabin, but a newish one, and the girl at the loom was scarcely older than he was. She was a mixup like Arthur, only half-Red instead of half-Black, and the combination of Ta-Kumsaw and Becca was becoming in her.

"Howdy, Alvin," she said. He had expected her voice to

sound like Ta-Kumsaw's and Tenskwa-Tawa's, accented when she spoke in English, but she spoke like Becca, a bit old-fashioned sounding but like a native speaker of the tongue.

"Howdy," he said.

"You sure came through like a ton of bricks," she said.

"Made a mess of the piles of cloth here."

"Don't fret," she said. "That's why they're there. Papa always smacks into them when he comes through like a cannonball."

With that he ran out of conversation, and so did she, so he stood there watching as she ran her loom.

"Go find Tenskwa-Tawa. He's waiting for you."

Alvin had heard so much about the fog on the Mizzipy that he had halfway got it into his head that the whole of the western lands was covered with fog. When he opened the cabin and stepped outside, though, he found that far from being foggy, the sky was so clear it felt like he could see clear into heaven in broad daylight. There were high mountains looming to the east, and he could see them so crisp and clear that he felt as though he could trace the crevices in the bare granite near the top, or count the leaves on the oak trees halfway up their craggy flanks. The cabin stood at the brow of a hill separating two valleys, both of which contained lakes. The one to the north was huge, the far reaches of it invisible because of the curve of the Earth, not because of any haze or thickness of the air; the lake to the south was smaller, but it was even more beautiful, shining like a blue jewel in the cold sunlight of late autumn.

"The snow is late," said a voice behind him.

Alvin turned. "Shining Man," he said, the name slipping from his lips before he could think.

"And you are the man who learned how to be a man when he was a boy," said Tenskwa-Tawa.

They embraced. The wind whistled around them. When they parted, Alvin glanced around again. "This is a pretty exposed place to build a cabin," he said.

"Had to be here," said Tenskwa-Tawa. "The valley to the south is Timpa-Nogos. Holy ground, where there can be no houses and no wars. The valley to the north is grazing land, where the deer can be hunted by families that run out of food in the winter. No houses either. Don't worry. Inside a weaver's house is always warm." He smiled. "I'm glad to see you."

Alvin wasn't sure if he could remember Tenskwa-Tawa ever smiling before. "You're happy here?"

"Happy?" Tenskwa-Tawa's face went placid again. "I feel as though I stand with one foot on this earth and the other foot in the place where my people wait for me."

"Not all died that day at Tippy-Canoe," said Alvin. "You still have people here."

"They also stand with one foot in one place, one foot in the other." He glanced toward a canyon that led up into a gap between the impossibly high mountains. "They live in a high mountain valley. The snow is late this year, and they're glad of that, unless it means poor water for next year, and a poor crop. That's our life now, Alvin Maker. We used to live in a place where water leapt out of the ground wherever you struck it with a stick."

"But the air is clear. You can see forever."

Tenskwa-Tawa put his fingers to Alvin's lips. "No man sees forever. But some men see farther. Last winter I rode a tower of water into the sky over the holy lake Timpa-Nogos. I saw many things. I saw you come here. I heard the news you told me and the question you asked me."

"And did you hear your answer?"

"First you must make my vision come true," said Tenskwa-Tawa.

So Alvin told him about Harrison being elected president by bragging about his bloody hands, and how they wondered if Tenskwa-Tawa might release the people of Vigor Church from their curse, so they could leave their homes, those as wanted to, and become part of the Crystal City when Alvin started to build it. "Was that what you heard me ask you?"

"Yes," said Tenskwa-Tawa.

"And what was your answer?"

"I didn't see my answer," said Tenskwa-Tawa. "So I have had all these months to think of what it was. In all these months, my people who died on that grassy slope have walked before my eyes in my sleep. I have seen their blood again and again flow down the grass and turn the Tippy-Canoe Creek red. I have seen the faces of the children and babies. I knew them all by name, and I still remember all the names and all the faces. Each one I see in the dream, I ask them, Do you forgive these White murderers? Do you understand their rage and will you let me take your blood from their hands?"

Tenskwa-Tawa paused. Alvin waited, too. One did not rush a shaman as he told of his dreams.

"Every night I have had this dream until finally last night the last of them came before me and I asked my question."

Again, a silence. Again, Alvin waited patiently. Not patiently the way a White man waits, showing his patience by looking around or moving his fingers or doing something else to mark the passage of time. Alvin waited with a Red man's patience, as if this moment were to be savored in itself, as if the suspense of waiting was in itself an experience to be marked and remembered.

"If even one of them had said, I do not forgive them, do not lift the curse, then I would not lift the curse," said Tenskwa-Tawa. "If even one baby had said, I do not forgive them for taking away my days of running like a deer through the meadows, I would not lift the curse. If even one mother had said, I do not forgive them for the baby that was in my womb when I died, who never saw the light of day with its beautiful eyes, I would not lift the curse. If even one father had said, The anger still runs hot in my heart, and if you lift the curse I will still have some hatred left unavenged, then I would not lift the curse."

Tears flowed down Alvin's face, for he knew the answer now, and he could not imagine himself ever being so good that even in death he could forgive those who had done such a terrible thing to him and his family.

"I also asked the living," said Tenskwa-Tawa. "Those who lost father and mother, brother and sister, uncle and aunt, child and friend, teacher and helper, hunting companion, and wife, and husband. If even one of these living ones had said, I cannot forgive them yet, Tenskwa-Tawa, I would not lift the curse."

Then he fell silent one last time. This time the silence lasted and lasted. The sun had been at noon when Alvin arrived; it was touching the tops of the mountains to the west when at last Tenskwa-Tawa moved again, nodding his head. Like Alvin, he, too, had wept, and then had waited long enough for the tears to dry, and then had wept again, all without changing the expression on his face, all without moving a muscle of his body as the two of them sat facing each other in the tall dry autumn grass, in the cold dry autumn wind. Now he opened his mouth and spoke again. "I have lifted the curse," he said.

Alvin embraced his old teacher. It was not what a Red man would have done, but Alvin had acted Red all afternoon, and so Tenskwa-Tawa accepted the gesture and even returned it. Touched by the Red Prophet's hands, his cheek against the old man's hair, the old man's face against his shoulder, Alvin remembered that once he had thought of asking Tenskwa-Tawa to strengthen the curse on Harrison, to stop him from misusing his bloody hands. It made him ashamed. If the dead could forgive, should not the living? Harrison would find his own way through life, and his own path to death. Judgment would have to come, if it came at all, from someone wiser than Alvin.

When they arose from the grass, Tenskwa-Tawa looked north toward the larger lake. "Look, a man is coming."

Alvin saw where he was looking. Not far off, a man was jogging lightly along a path through the head-high grass. Not running in the Red man's way, but like a White man, and not a young one. His hatless bald head glinted momentarily in the sunset.

"That ain't Taleswapper, is it?" asked Alvin.

"The Sho-sho-nay invited him to come and trade stories with them," said Tenskwa-Tawa.

Instead of asking more questions, Alvin waited with Tenskwa-Tawa until Taleswapper came up the long steep path. He was out of breath when he arrived, as might have been expected. But as Alvin sent his doodlebug through Taleswapper's body, he was surprised at the old man's excellent health. They greeted each other warmly, and Alvin told him the news. Taleswapper smiled at Tenskwa-Tawa. "Your people are better than you thought they were," he said.

"Or more forgetful," said Tenskwa-Tawa ruefully.

"I'm glad I happened to be here, to hear this news," said Taleswapper. "If you're going back through the weaver's house, I'd like to go with you."

When Alvin and Taleswapper returned to Becca's cabin within the heart of the weaver's house, it had been dark for two hours. Ta-Kumsaw had gone outside and invited Peggy's and Alvin's friends to come in and eat with his family. Becca's sister and her daughters and her son joined them; they ate a stew of bison meat, Red man's food cooked the White man's way, a compromise like so much else in this house. Ta-Kumsaw had introduced himself by the name of Isaac Weaver, and Peggy was careful to call him by no other name.

Alvin and Taleswapper found them all lying on their bedrolls on the floor of the parlor, except for Peggy, who was sitting on a chair, listening as Verily Cooper told them tales of his life in England, and all the subterfuges he had gone through in order to conceal his knack from everyone. She turned to face the door before her husband and their old friend came through it; the others also turned, so all eyes were on them. They knew at once from the joy on Alvin's face what Tenskwa-Tawa's answer had been.

"I want to ride out tonight and tell them," said Armor-of-God. "I want them to know the good news right *now*."

"Too dark," said Ta-Kumsaw, who came in from the kitchen where he had been helping his sister-in-law wash the dishes from supper.

"There's no more rules, now, the curse is lifted free and clear," said Alvin. "But he asks that we do something all the same. That everyone who used to be under the curse gather their family together once a year, on the anniversary of the massacre at Tippy-Canoe, and on that day eat no food, but instead tell the story as it used to be told to all strangers who came through Vigor Church. Once a year, our children and our children's children, forever. He asks that we do that, but there'll be no punishment if we don't. No punishment except that our children will forget, and when they forget, there's always the chance that it might happen again."

"I'll tell them that too," said Armor. "They'll all take a vow to do that, you can be sure, Alvin." He turned to Ta-Kumsaw. "You can tell your brother that for me when next you see him, that they'll all take that vow."

Ta-Kumsaw grunted. "So much for calling myself Isaac in order to conceal from you who I really am."

"We've met before," said Armor, "and even if we hadn't, I know a great leader when I see one, and I knew who it was Alvin came to see."

"You talk too much, Armor-of-God, like all White men," said Ta-Kumsaw. "But at least what you say isn't always stupid."

Armor nodded and smiled to acknowledge the compliment.

Alvin and Peggy were given a bedroom and a fine bed, which Peggy suspected was Ta-Kumsaw's and Becca's own. The others slept on the floor in the parlor—slept as best they could, which wasn't well, what with all the excitement and the way Mike Fink snored so loud and the way Armor had to get up to pee about three times an hour it seemed like, till Peggy heard the activity, woke Alvin up, and Alvin *did* something with his doodlebug inside Armor's body so he didn't feel like his bladder was about to bust all the time. When morning came the men in the parlor slept a little late, and woke to the smell of a country breakfast, with biscuits and gravy and slabs of salted ham fried with potatoes.

Then it was time for parting. Armor-of-God was like an

eager horse himself, stamping and snorting till they finally told him to go *on*. He mounted and rode out of Chapman Valley, waving his hat and whooping like those damn fools on election night the week before.

Alvin's and Peggy's parting was harder. She and Taleswapper would take Whitley Physicker's carriage and drive it to the next town of any size, where she'd hire another carriage and Taleswapper would drive this one north to Hatrack River to return it to the good doctor. From there Peggy intended to go to Philadelphia for a while. "I hope that I might turn some hearts against Harrison's plans, if I'm there where Congress meets. He's only going to be president, not king, not emperor—he has to win the consent of Congress to do anything, and perhaps there's still hope." But Alvin knew from her voice that she had little hope, that she knew already along what dark roads Harrison would lead the country.

Alvin felt nearly as bleak about his own prospects. "Tenskwa-Tawa couldn't tell me a thing about how to make the Crystal City, except to say a thing I already knew: The Maker is a part of what he Makes."

"So . . . you will search," said Peggy, "and I will search."

What neither of them said, because both of them knew that they both knew, was that there was a child growing already in Margaret's womb; a girl. Each of them could calculate nine months as well as the other.

"Where will you be next August?" asked Alvin.

"Wherever I am, I'll make quite sure you know about it."

"And wherever you are, I'll make quite sure I'm there."

"I think the name should be Becca," said Peggy.

"I was thinking to call her after you. Call her Little Peggy."

Peggy smiled. "Becca Margaret, then?"

Alvin smiled back, and kissed her. "People talk about fools counting chickens before they hatch. That's nothing. We name them."

He helped her up into the carriage, beside Taleswapper, who

already had the reins in hand. Arthur Stuart led Alvin's horse to him, and as he mounted, the boy said, "We made up a song about us last night, while you two was upstairs!"

"A song?" said Alvin. "Let's hear it then."

"We made it up like as if it was you singing it," said Arthur Stuart. "Come on, you all got to sing! And at the end I made up a chorus all by myself, I made up the last part *alone* without *no help* from *nobody*."

Alvin reached down and hauled the boy up behind him. Arthur Stuart's arms went around his middle. "Come on," the boy shouted. "Let's all sing."

As they began the song, Alvin reached down and took hold of the harness of the carriage's lead horse, starting the parade up the road leading out of Chapman Valley.

> *A young man startin' on his own*
> *Must leave his home so fair.*
> *Better not go wand'rin' all alone*
> *Or you might get eaten by a bear!*
>
> *I'm wise enough to heed that song,*
> *But who'll make up my pair?*
> *If I choose my boon companion wrong*
> *Then I might get eaten by a bear!*
>
> *I'll take a certain mixup lad—*
> *He's small, but does his share—*
> *And I'll watch him close, cause I'd be sad*
> *If the boy got eaten by a bear!*
>
> *I'll take along this barrister*
> *With lofty learned air,*
> *And I'll make of him a forester*
> *So he won't get eaten by a bear!*
>
> *Behold this noble river rat*

With brag so fine and rare!
He's as dangerous as a mountain cat—
He will not get eaten by a bear!

Now off we go, where'er we please.
We're heroes, so we dare
To defy mosquitoes, wasps, and fleas,
And we won't get eaten by a bear!

They reached the main road and Peggy turned right, heading north, while the men took their horses south. She waved from the driver's seat, but did not look back. Alvin stopped to watch her, just for a moment, just for a lingering moment, as Arthur Stuart behind him shouted, "Now I get to sing the last part that I made up all by myself! I get to!"

"So sing it," said Alvin.

So Arthur Stuart sang.

Grizzly bear, grizzly bear,
Run and hide, you sizzly bear!
We'll take away your coat of hair
And roast you in your underwear!

Alvin laughed till tears streamed down his face.

⊁ 19 ⊱

Philadelphia

WHEN CALVIN'S AND Honoré's ship arrived in New Amsterdam, the newspapers were full of chat about the inauguration, which was only a week away in Philadelphia. Calvin remembered Harrison's name at once—how many times had he listened to the tale of the massacre at Tippy-Canoe? He remembered meeting the bloody-handed bum on the streets of New Amsterdam, and told the tale to Honoré.

"So you created him."

"I helped him make the best of his limited possibilities," said Calvin.

"No, no," said Honoré. "You are too modest. This man created himself as a monster who killed people for political gain. Then this Red prophet destroyed him with a curse. Then, from the hopeless ruin of his life, you turned his path upward again. Calvin, you finally impress me. You have achieved, in life, that infinite power which is usually reserved to the novelist."

"The power to use up enormous amounts of paper and ink to no avail?"

"The power to make people's lives take the most illogical turns. Parents, for instance, have no such power. They can help their children along, or, more likely, shatter their lives as someone's mother once did with her casual adultery even as she abandoned her child to the tender mercies of the boarding school. But such parents have no power then to heal the child they have injured. Having brought the child low, they cannot raise the child up. But *I* can bring a man low, then raise him up, then bring him low again, all with a stroke of the pen."

"And so can I," said Calvin thoughtfully.

"Well, to a degree," said Honoré. "To be honest, however, you did not bring him low, and now, having raised him up, I doubt you can bring him low again. The man has been elected president, even if his domain consists primarily of trees and tree-dwelling beasts."

"There's several million people in the United States," said Calvin.

"It was to them that I referred," said Honoré.

The challenge was too much for Calvin to resist. Could he bring down the president of the United States? How would he do it? This time there could be no scornful words that would provoke him into self-destruction, as Calvin's words had helped the man resurrect himself from shameful oblivion. But then, Calvin had learned to do much more subtle things than mere talk in the many months since then. It would be a challenge. It was almost a dare.

"Let's go to Philadelphia," said Calvin. "For the inauguration."

Honoré was perfectly happy to board the train and go along. He was amused by the size and newness of the tiny towns that Americans referred to as "cities," and Calvin constantly had to watch out for him as he practiced his feeble English with the kind of rough American who was likely to pick up the little Frenchman and toss him into a river. Honoré, armed only with an ornate cane he had purchased from a fellow-voyager, had fearlessly walked through the most wretched immigrant districts of New Amsterdam and now of Philadelphia. "These men aren't characters in novels," said Calvin, more than once. "If they break your neck, it'll really be broken!"

"Then you'll have to fix me, my talented knackish friend." He said the word *knackish* in English, though truth to tell no one would have understood the word but Calvin himself.

"There's no such word as *knackish* in the English language," Calvin said.

"There is now," said Honoré, "because I put it there."

As Calvin awaited the inauguration, he considered many possible plans. Nothing with mere words would do the job. Harrison's election had been so openly based on lies that it was hard to imagine how anything could now be revealed about Harrison that would shock or disappoint anyone. When the people elected a president like this one, who ran a campaign like the one he ran, it was hard to imagine what kind of scandal might bring him down.

Besides, Calvin's knack was now way beyond words. He wanted to get inside Harrison's body and do some mischief. He remembered Napoleon and how he suffered from the gout; he toyed with the idea of giving Harrison some debilitating condition. Regretfully he concluded that this was beyond his power, to fine-tune such a thing so that it would cause pain without killing. No doubt Calvin would have to wait around to watch, to make sure that whatever he did wasn't cured. And besides, pain wouldn't bring Harrison low any more than gout had stopped Napoleon from fulfilling all his ambitions.

Pain without killing. Why had he put such a ridiculous limitation on himself? There was no reason not to kill Harrison. Hadn't the man ordered the death of Calvin's own brother Measure? Hadn't he slaughtered all those Reds and caused all of Calvin's family and neighbors to be under a curse for most of Calvin's life? Nothing brought a man lower than dying. Six feet under the ground, that was as low as a body ever got.

The day of the inauguration, the first day of the new year, was bitterly cold, and as Harrison walked through the streets of Philadelphia to the temporary stand where he would take the oath in front of several thousand spectators, it began to snow. Proudly he refused even to put on a hat—what was cold weather to a man from the west?—and when he reached the platform to give his speech, Calvin was delighted to see that the new president's throat was already sore, his chest already somewhat congested. It was really a simple matter of Calvin to send his doodling bug inside the chest of White Murderer Harrison and encourage the little animals inside his lungs to grow, to multiply, to spread throughout his body. Harrison, you're going to be one very, very sick man.

The speech lasted an hour, and Harrison didn't cut out a single word, though by the end he was coughing thickly into his handkerchief after every sentence. "Philadelphia is colder to hell," Honoré said in his feeble English as they finally left the square. "And your President he is one dammit long talker." Then, in French, Honoré asked, "Did I say it right? Did I swear properly?"

"Like a stevedore," said Calvin. "Like a river rat. I was proud of you."

"I was proud of you too," said Honoré. "You looked so serious, I thought maybe you were paying attention to his speech. Then I thought, No, the lad is using his powers. So I hoped you might sever his head as he stood there and make it roll down splat on his speech. Let him put his hands on *that* to take his oath of office."

"That would have been a memorable inauguration," said Calvin.

"But it wouldn't be good for you to take another man's life," said Honoré. "All joking aside, my friend, it isn't good for a man to get a taste for blood."

"My brother Alvin killed a man," said Calvin. "He killed a man who needed killing, and nobody said boo to him about it."

"Dangerous for him, but perhaps more dangerous for you," said Honoré. "Because you are already filled with hate—I say this not as criticism, it's one of the things I find most attractive about you—you are filled with hate, and so it is dangerous for you to open the faucet of murder. That is a stream you may not be able to damp."

"Not to worry," said Calvin.

They lingered in Philadelphia for several more weeks, as Harrison's bad cold turned into pneumonia. He struggled on, being something of a tough old nut, but in the end he died, scarcely a month after his inauguration, having never been healthy enough even to name a cabinet.

This being the first time a president of the United States had died in office, there was some unresolved ambiguity in the Constitution about whether the vice-president merely acted as president or actually took the office. Andrew Jackson neatly resolved the issue by walking into Congress and placing his hand on the Bible they kept there as a reminder of all the virtues they worked so hard to get the voters to believe they possessed. In a loud voice he took the oath of office in front of all of them, daring them to deny him the right to do so. There were jokes about "His Accidency the President" for a while, but Jackson wasn't a man to be trifled with. All of Harrison's cronies found themselves with sore backsides from bouncing down the steps of the George Washington Building where the executive branch of the government had its offices. Whatever Harrison had planned for America would never happen now, or at least not in the way that he had planned it. Jackson was in nobody's pocket but his own.

Calvin and Honoré agreed that they had done a great service for the nation. "Though my part of it was very small," said Honoré. "A mere word. A suggestion." Calvin knew, however, that in his own heart Honoré undoubtedly took credit for the whole thing, or at least for everything beneficial that resulted from it. That knowledge scarcely bothered Calvin, though. Nothing really bothered him now, for his power had been confirmed in his own heart. *I brought down a president and no one knew that I did it. Nothing messy or awkward like Alvin's* killing of that Finder with his own bare hands. I learned more than the honing of my knack on the continent. I acquired finesse. Alvin will never have that, crude frontiersman that he is and always will be.

How easy it had been. Easy and free of risk. There was a man who needed to die, and all it took was a little maneuvering in his lungs and it was done. Well, that plus a few adjustments as the man lay in his sickbed in the presidential mansion. It wouldn't do to have his body fight off the infection and recover, would it? But I never had to touch him. Never even had to speak to him. Didn't even have to get ink on my fingers, like poor Honoré, whose characters never really breathe despite all his skill, and so never really die.

Calvin allowed himself, on the last night he and Honoré spent in Philadelphia, to lie in bed imagining Alvin's death. A slow agonizing death from some miserable disease like lockjaw. I could do that, thought Calvin.

Then he thought, No I couldn't, and went to sleep.

TOR

Award-winning authors
Compelling stories

Please join us at the website
below for more information
about this author and other great
Tor selections, and to sign up for
our monthly newsletter!

www.tor-forge.com